ALIX RICKLOFF is a sensation!

EARL OF DARKNESS

"A tangled tale of good and evil, magic and mystery, passion and desire—one that won't be easily forgotten."

—*Romantic Times* (Top Pick)

"This book is magic personified."

—Night Owl Reviews

"A sexy and intense tale packed with dark passions and even darker magic."

—*USA Today* bestselling author Caridad Pineiro

DANGEROUS AS SIN

"A heady blend of historical romance, deadly mystery, and deep betrayals. Add to that a dash of the paranormal and you have one heck of a book."

—Fallen Angel Reviews

"A magical novel."

—Joyfully Reviewed

LOST IN YOU

"A fascinating debut filled with sensory details and a deep sense of lore."

—*Booklist*

"A riveting tale full of magic, danger, and sensuality."

—*New York Times* bestselling author Hannah Howell

Lord of Shadows is also availabl

Also by Alix Rickloff

Earl of Darkness

Lord of Shadows

BOOK TWO

ALIX RICKLOFF

Pocket Books
New York London Toronto Sydney

Pocket Books
A Division of Simon & Schuster, Inc.
1230 Avenue of the Americas
New York, NY 10020

First Pocket Books paperback edition July 2011

POCKET and colophon are registered trademarks of Simon & Schuster, Inc.

For information about special discounts for bulk purchases, please contact Simon & Schuster Special Sales at 1-866-506-1949 or business@simonandschuster.com.

The Simon & Schuster Speakers Bureau can bring authors to your live event. For more information or to book an event contact the Simon & Schuster Speakers Bureau at 1-866-248-3049 or visit our website at www.simonspeakers.com.

Cover illustration by Gene Mollica.

Manufactured in the United States of America

10 9 8 7 6 5 4 3 2

ISBN 978-1-4391-7037-3
ISBN 978-1-4391-7059-5 (ebook)

For John

Acknowledgments

My heartfelt gratitude goes out as always to those who have brought this book from blank page to "The End."

My fellow desperate writers, Maggie and Do. The best friends and critics a writer could have. They question, answer, inspire, and prod in equal measures. Thanks for the popcorn, the Martini Bianco, and the laughter. Without you, this book would have been a whole lot harder to write.

Kevan Lyon and Megan McKeever for their editing polish.

Bethan Davies for helping Daigh find his Welsh.

The Beau Monde and their infinite knowledge of the Regency.

And, as always, my wonderful family, who know when the door closes, they're on their own.

One

Off the southwest coast of Ireland
November 1815

He'd prayed the storm would kill him. One solid lightning strike to splinter his body into so many pieces no amount of mage energy could fit him back together.

A vain prayer. He'd moved far beyond the reach of any god's aid.

The ocean had calmed from the froth of hurricane swells to a slick of black, rolling water. Good for inducing nausea, but not death. Clouds passed eastward, taking their lightning with them, leaving a sky shimmering with frozen stars, full moon hanging low on the horizon. Picturesque, yet his mood longed for a cyclone's destruction to match the chaotic madness infecting his mind.

The storm had pushed them off course. He'd heard the sailors mutter and witnessed the captain's frown as he prowled the quarterdeck. Behind schedule. Battered and in need of repairs. And Cobh harbor another day and a half away if the winds held.

So if the gods had deserted him, it fell to his own devices to find oblivion.

He'd been denied a split second's painless annihilation. But there were other paths to *Annwn*. Trackless dark ways that led just as surely to the land of the dead.

He only needed to discover them.

Leaning against the rail, he scanned the sea, his answer written upon every wave. But could he go through with it? Would the wards that kept him alive and untouchable unravel within the sea god Lir's cold fathoms, bringing the solace he craved? Or would the attempt result in endless suffering of a different kind within the clawing pull of the ocean tides?

The stars above rippled gold and silver upon the surface of the sea. Curled and eddied as if a hand drew shapes with light and water. Turned moonlight to a woman's pale face. The ocean's foam drifting across her features like a spill of dark hair, she breathed her love across the separating veil. Shone luminous in a world blanketed by shadows.

Had she been conjured from his tattered memories or was she mere dream? Impossible to distinguish. Names and faces drifted through his consciousness like ghosts. Sometimes as vivid as the existence he found himself trapped within. At other times, only emptiness met his probing efforts to remember. And he was left alone to fight the demonic rage that burned through him like acid. The fury of the damned.

He expected her to dissolve back into the waves any second, but she remained. Her eyes gleamed blue as cornflowers. Her smile brightening for a moment the hopelessness pressing against his heart, and he knew he must take the course offered. Now. Here. Before she vanished. Before she was beaten back by the howling viciousness, and he was once again left bereft of memories or even the comfort of memories. At least this way he wouldn't face the uncertainty of death alone.

Slinging a leg over the gunwale, he glanced to be sure none watched. But no, the deck remained quiet. He'd not get a better chance.

With a hard shove to propel him out of the ship's shadow, he plunged into the water. Arrowed far down below the waves.

The water jolted him alert. A stomach-punch of icy pain, stabbing needles of agony through every nerve. Releasing his breath on a cloud of bubbles, he dropped deeper. Lungs burning and muscles cramping as he fought the instinctual need to breathe. To live.

He struggled against the claustrophobic crush of water, but the seeping drugged cold of the sea made every movement excruciating. And then impossible.

The woman's smile urged him deeper.

Water filled his lungs. His body surrendered. Death came like a lover.

He answered her smile. And stepping through the curtain between them, embraced her at last.

"Sabrina! Where have you gotten yourself? Answer, or so help me . . ."

Normally such a threat would have shot Lady Sabrina Douglas from her hiding place like a bullet from a gun. Not so today. Today was different. It was the sixteenth of the month. Seven years ago on this date, her world had been turned upside down, and nothing had ever been quite the same since.

It wasn't like her to spend time reminiscing on the past.

The head of the Sisters of High *Danu* said it was useless spinning what-ifs in your head. One could lose oneself in the infinite possibilities of action and consequence until reality grew dangerously frayed. Madness lay in second-guessing.

But today, Sabrina courted madness. She'd forced herself to remember all that had occurred that long-ago November day from beginning to end. Let it flow from her brain to her journal in a mad scrawl. And at Sister Brigh's first shout was only as far along as noontime.

"You ungrateful, undisciplined hoyden, come out this moment."

When Sister Brigh scolded, Sabrina felt more like a disobedient ten-year-old than the woman of twenty-two she was. But then, Sister Brigh considered anyone younger than herself a recalcitrant child, which included almost the entire *bandraoi* community. The woman was a hundred if she was a day. Only Sister Ainnir rivaled her in age. The two like mossy twin holdovers from centuries past.

"Sabrina Douglas! I know you can hear me!"

Sister Brigh by far the mossier. And the louder.

Sabrina sighed, closing her journal on the pen marking her place.

November 16, 1808, would have to wait.

November 16, 1815, was calling.

The priestess's clamoring faded as she left the barn. Turned her search to the nearby outbuildings—creamery, laundry, gardener's sheds. The convent was large. It would take the head of novices ages to check everywhere.

Rising from her hiding place behind the stacked straw bales and grain bins, Sabrina dusted the grime from her skirts. Straightened her apron and the kerchief covering her hair before slipping back into the bustle of the order's life. And right into Sister Brigh's ambush.

"Gotcha!" Her talons sank through the heavy wool of Sabrina's sleeve. Squeezed with enough force to bring hot tears to her eyes. "Ard-siúr's had me searching for you this hour and more. And here you are, hiding as if there wasn't honest work to be done." She snatched the journal away. "Are you scribbling in that silly book again? You've been warned more than once about frittering away your time unwisely."

Sabrina stiffened, giving Sister Brigh her best quelling look. "I wasn't frittering. And I wasn't hiding."

It passed unnoticed. "Hmph. Come along. You've kept Ard-siúr waiting long enough."

As they passed through the sheltered cloister, a group gathered at the front gates. Voices raised in surprise and confusion, drawing even the determined Sister Brigh's eye from her purpose.

Sabrina craned her neck to peer over the crowd. "What's happening?"

Sister Brigh responded with a scornful huff. "No doubt a lot of stuff and nonsense. Wouldn't have happened in my day, you can be sure of that."

Her day being sometime during the last ice age. Sister Brigh dressed in furs and sporting a club, no doubt.

She tightened her hold on Sabrina. Doubled her pace. Up the steps. Throwing the door wide with barely a word. Slamming it closed with a whisper equally as effective.

The old priestess's sanity might be in doubt, but her magic was irrefutable.

The temperature plummeted once inside and out of the bleak afternoon sun. Frost hung in the passage leading to

Ard-siúr's office, causing Sabrina's nervous breath to cloud the chilly air. The cold seeped through her heavy stockings and the double layer of petticoats she'd donned beneath her gown.

It wasn't even winter yet and already she longed for spring. Spring and a release from scratchy underclothes and chilblains and runny noses and afternoon dusk and drafty passages. At this moment, she'd sell her soul for warmth and light and, well . . . something different.

So little varied within the order that any change, even the gradual shifting of seasons, seemed an adventure. But perhaps that was only because the genuine change she longed for still eluded her and would continue to do so if Sister Brigh had her grumpy way.

As they were shown through the antechamber to Ard-siúr's office, Sister Anne waved a cheery hello. Received a bulldog scowl from Sister Brigh. A wan smile from Sabrina.

Compared to the chilly atmosphere of the outside corridor, Ard-siúr's office seemed an absolute tropical paradise. A small stove put out heat enough to keep the tiny room comfortably cozy, and the thick rugs on the floor and bright wall hangings cheered the stark, color-draining stone. Add to that Ard-siúr's cluttered desk complete with purring cat and the slow tick of a tall case clock in a far corner and Sabrina's taut nerves began to relax.

The atmosphere seemed to have the opposite reaction for Sister Brigh. Her eyes darted around the room with fuming disapproval as she drew up in a quivering pose of long sufferance, only now releasing her death grip on Sabrina's arm.

Ard-siúr put up a restraining hand while she finished her thought, her pen scribbling across the page, her lip caught girlishly between her teeth as she worked.

The head of the Sisters of High *Danu* seemed as eternal as the ancient standing stones guarding a nearby cliff-top meadow. Tall. Broad. A face weathered by years, yet eyes that remained clear and bright and full of humor. Her powers as a *bandraoi* and sorceress seemed to rival those of the *Fey*, as did her air of regal self-containment. But Sabrina knew it took every ounce of her gifts both innate and learned to preside over an order of *Other* while concealing their true nature from a distrustful *Duinedon* world.

To all beyond the walls of the order's demesne, they were merely a reclusive house of contemplative religious women. It fell to Ard-siúr to see that it remained that way. An unenviable task. Though, come to think on it, there was one who envied it very much.

Sister Brigh breathed heavily though her nose like a kettle letting off steam.

Finally, Ard-siúr placed her pen in its tray. Scattered sand across the page. Shook it clean. Folded it. And cast her penetrating gaze upon the pair standing silently before her.

"Thank you, Sister Brigh, for locating Sabrina."

Her acknowledgment clearly meant as a signal for the head of novices to depart.

Instead Sister Brigh barged ahead with a list of grievances. They rolled off her tongue as if she'd prepared them ahead of time. "Three times in three days, Ard-siúr. Three times I've caught her with her head in the clouds when she should be working. That or she's scribbling in that diary of hers. You can't keep brushing it under the rug. It only encourages her to feel she's above the rules. The lord's daughter she once was rather than the aspiring *bandraoi* priestess she's supposed to be."

The sarcastic emphasis Sister Brigh placed on "aspiring"

had Sabrina bristling, but one look from Ard-siúr and she subsided without argument.

"Is this true, Sabrina? Do you feel above the rules? That your family's station in life entitles you to special consideration?"

"No, of course not, but—"

Sister Brigh slammed the journal on Ard-siúr's desk, sending the cat leaping for cover with a hiss. "Sabrina's lack of devotion and her failure to abide by our way of living undermine her candidacy. And I, for one, believe she would be better off leaving the order and returning to her family."

Ard-siúr turned her gaze upon Sabrina at last. "Sister Brigh brings up serious charges. Could it be that you aren't as committed to a life among us as you think? That you begin to yearn for the future you might have led but for tragic circumstance?"

Sabrina blinked. Had Ard-siúr brought that up on purpose? Did she know what Sabrina had been writing in her diary? Or had the mention been mere coincidence? Always difficult to know with the head of their order. She seemed to have a canny knack for discerning all manner of things. Especially the bits you didn't want known.

Perhaps forcing her mind back to that long-ago November day hadn't been such a good idea after all. She'd dredged up memories long buried. Forgotten how much they hurt.

"I'm more than ready to take up my full duties as *ban-draoi*." She shot an offended glance Sister Brigh's way. "And I didn't mean to make you wait, Ard-siúr. I was trying . . . you see, I needed . . . it happened today seven years ago, Ard-siúr. And I felt as if I needed to remember it clearly before it slipped away."

Ard-siúr gave a slow nod. "Ah yes, your father's death."

"His murder," she clarified. "It was seven years ago today the *Ambas-draoi* attacked and killed my father."

"And for good reason, if half the rumors are true," Sister Brigh mumbled. "Ard-siúr, even if it's not enough for you that Sabrina shirks her duties and carries on as if she were queen of the manor, you must see that her presence brings the order unwanted attention. Never in our history was one of our priestesses interrogated by the *Ambas-draoi*."

"It wasn't my fault they wanted to speak with me. I didn't tell them anything."

"Keeping secrets from the very brotherhood sworn to protect us? Worse and worse."

"That's not what I meant. You're twisting my words."

"Enough." Ard-siúr lifted a hand.

Momentum behind her, Sister Brigh barreled on. "A father working the demon arts. A fugitive brother running from the *Ambas-draoi*. The family of Douglas is cursed. And the sooner you're gone from here, the better for the order."

Sabrina turned a hot gaze on the elderly nun.

"I said enough." The whip crack of Ard-siúr's voice finally silenced Sister Brigh, though she remained red-faced and glaring with suppressed fury. "This is neither the time nor place. If you have valid arguments to make, bring them to me at another meeting and we can discuss it further."

Turning her attention to Sabrina, Ard-siúr smiled. "My dear, I requested your presence merely to deliver a letter that's come for you by messenger."

How did one simple sentence drop the bottom out of her stomach and create an immediate need to draw nonexistent covers over her head? In her experience, letters never boded well. Like holding an unexploded bomb in your hand.

The door burst open on the flustered face of Sister Anne. "Ard-siúr, Sabrina's needed in the infirmary right away. A man's been brought in. Found half drowned on the beach below the village."

"May I go?" Sabrina cast beseeching eyes in Ard-siúr's direction.

Sister Brigh looked as though she chewed nails, but the head of the order dismissed Sabrina with an imperious wave of her hand. "Go. Sister Ainnir needs your skills. The letter will await your return."

Plucking up her skirts, Sabrina dashed from the room in Sister Anne's wake. She could kiss the unlucky fisherman who'd rescued her. Saved in the nick of time.

It was only fair to return the favor.

"Guide the mage energy as you would a surgical instrument. Precise. Focused," Sister Ainnir advised quietly over the still form of the man lying between them.

Sabrina fought to check the magic simmering in her blood, humming along her bones. Less the accuracy of a stiletto than the bluntness of a battle-axe. Release the power now, she'd char the poor unfortunate man to cinders.

"Pay attention, Sabrina. Your mind is not on your work."

No, it was still seething with resentment at Sister Brigh's accusations. Lack of dedication. Above the rules. Frittering. If Sabrina wasn't careful, the head of novices would have her on a coach to Belfoyle before the year was out. Nasty cow.

"Sabrina! Careful."

The mage energy surged in a dramatic arc of red and gold and coral and the palest green. Lit up her insides until she felt the buzzing in her ears, the zing of it lifting the hairs on her arms, squeezing her chest like a pair of whalebone stays.

The man spasmed, gasping for a breath he could not catch. Animal rage boiled off him in waves. Desperation. Terror. Panic.

The emotions raked the inside of Sabrina's skull like caged animals. She staggered against the instant throbbing behind her eyes. Spots and pinwheels bursting across her vision like Guy Fawkes fireworks.

His throat constricted as he vomited a trickle of seawater from lungs full and useless. He flung out a fist, sending Sabrina leaping backward.

Frustration. Disappointment. Fury.

Stark and immediate and enough to make Sabrina dizzy. She threw up every mental barricade, yet still the echoes of his pain battled through to sink razored claws into her brain.

"Don't stop," Sister Ainnir urged. "Don't break your concentration. It's too soon."

The *Fey* threads of Sabrina's magic danced along her skin like an increasing storm charge. A shimmering will-o'-the-wisp at the corners of her sight. Whispering in her head like a breeze or an echo or a rush of water over rocks.

She wrapped herself in the sensations, the empathic crush of overpowering emotion lessening to a bearable degree. No longer in danger of passing out, at any rate.

Gathering the healing fire, she renewed her lost focus. Used her lingering anger to hone her determination to scalpel brilliance. Returned to his bedside, bringing her powers to the assistance of Sister Ainnir, whose strength waned after hours of fighting the underworld for possession of this lost sailor's soul.

"That's it. Feel the way it bends to your will. Careful. Don't force it." The infirmarian took Sabrina's hand, moving it to a spot just above his right lung. His flesh was icy cold, the palest milky blue but for the crisscross web of silver scars. "There now. See? Do you feel the way the life wavers just there?"

Sabrina let the rise and fall of his faltering breaths bear her along. In and out and in and out, winding her healing magic into the pattern. Steady. Unerring. But wait . . . something not quite right. Not as it should be. Instead, unfamiliar strands tangled and knotted and bound themselves without her aid or her powers. A new pattern. A strange weaving of life and mage energy, unfaltering darkness at its core. A rippling, slithering brush against her mind as she worked.

Then nothing. The unidentified magic vanishing as subtly as it appeared.

She delved deeper, but a jerk of the man's head and unconsciousness became sleep. Death receded.

"Sister Ainnir, did you feel that?" she asked, stealing a long, frowning look at the patient.

He breathed. Already his color returned, a dusky golden bronze where he'd recently been fish-belly white. But had it been their healing that had done it? For the merest fraction of a moment, she'd almost thought . . .

"That is life, Sabrina." Sister Ainnir sagged into a chair, her face as waxen as the dripping tapers behind them. "*Annwn* will have to wait for this one."

Sabrina's feeling of not-quite-rightness disappeared in the afterglow that always followed a success. This man had arrived at the convent unresponsive, given up for dead. And through her efforts he held to life. Her skills had saved him. This was something she, Sabrina, was good at. A prowess no lack of wealth or beauty or elegant Society airs could diminish.

She pulled the blanket up over the stranger. Let her eyes loiter for a moment over the harsh angles and grim lines of his face. Even asleep he looked prepared to do murder. Lips pressed in a thin slash of anger. Jaw clamped.

What misfortunes had landed him on a rocky beach, lungs full of ocean?

His emotions spoke of violence and combat. His body bore this out. The hardened muscles, the web of scarring, the frightening intensity of expression.

She pushed against his mind, barely connecting. A mere glancing caress. Hoping to transmit peace, safety, the warmth of a soft bed, the security of a quiet room. Yet even that lightest of touches brought back a ricochet pound of emotions. No more the cyclone's angry devastation. Instead there was grief and torment and a crushing anguish that stung her eyes with hot, unbidden tears.

She gasped, falling back into herself with a swipe of her sleeve over her burning cheeks. Forced her gaze and mind away from him, though she felt his knifing presence at her back, the looming silence of him like an approaching line of thunderheads in a yellow sky.

And yes, she read far too many novels if she was spinning such melodramatic notions from a half-drowned pirate.

She shook off her fancy to focus on Sister Ainnir, who returned her gaze with one of dazed exhaustion. Good heavens. Here she was dream-spinning when she should have been concerning herself with Sister Ainnir.

They'd been here for hours, dinner come and gone. Afternoon's heavy dusk deepening to night. Had it been too much for the aged priestess? Had she offered more of her strength than she could easily give?

"Let me help you back to your quarters." Sabrina offered the old woman an arm to lean against as she struggled to her feet.

"And the gentleman?" Sister Ainnir sighed. "Perhaps one of us should remain."

"It's my night to stay," Sabrina said, glancing back at the stranger with an unconscious shudder and, no, it was not excitement. "Sister Noreen is here now. I can have you settled and be back before she goes off duty."

"Then I accept your assistance with gratitude. This old body isn't as spry as it once was. And I've found I enjoy my bed far more than I used to."

The two of them made their painfully slow way through the passage into the main ward. "You've a great gift, my child," Sister Ainnir said. "Don't let anyone tell you otherwise."

The earlier bitterness resurfaced now that the emergency had passed. "Sister Brigh doesn't think so. I'm a grown woman, yet she treats me like a child."

Sister Ainnir paused, turning to face Sabrina. "Sister Brigh fears anything that would topple the delicate balance of the world we *Other* have created for ourselves. She believes our survival lies in remaining apart from the *Duinedon*. Not bringing attention to ourselves. Your family—your father—believed just the opposite. Rightly or wrongly, in her mind, that makes you a threat."

"If that's the case, how will I ever get her to see past my father's sins? She'll never agree to my taking final rites."

Sister Ainnir started walking, drawing Sabrina after. "Brigh is not the only one who matters in such things.

You've many allies within the community who recognize your potential." She chuckled. "Look around you. Don't think I don't know who it is who keeps this place running. I'm too old for wrestling death."

"You're not old, Sister," Sabrina countered diplomatically.

"And you're a horrid liar, young lady. I know exactly how old I am. I feel every year, especially on nights like this. No, it's up to you to take over here."

Up to her? Was Sister Ainnir saying what Sabrina thought she was saying? "I'm not a full priestess yet."

"Not yet, but who could deny your readiness after tonight's work?"

She was saying what she thought she was saying. Joy bubbled up through Sabrina's chest. She clamped on the whoop that threatened to spill out of her. A whoop was not an appropriate reaction for a dignified *bandraoi* priestess. Besides, she could heal the sick, raise the dead, and cure the common cold and Sister Brigh would still find a reason to hold up the final rites. Probably accuse Sabrina of showing off on top of all her other crimes.

Leaving the ward, they crossed through the hall and out into the night, the wind tugging at their skirts, clouds scudding silver-edged across the sky. A moon shining high and pale above, reflected in the scummy puddles of the courtyard.

"You possess an innate talent and have learned to use it as well as any fully promoted infirmarian." Sister Ainnir's words trembled thin and strained in the damp cold. "What can Ard-siúr say to that?"

"She can say, 'Thank you very much, but don't count on it.' I'm a Douglas, remember?"

"Aye, I do. And that in itself should seal your destiny as

bandraoi. For the Douglases have all been known to bear a *Fey* strength above the ordinary."

"And my family's accursedness?" She tried and failed to keep the resentment from her voice.

"Bah! Accursedness! Talk like that makes us sound like a gaggle of old superstitious crones."

Their bodies bent close, Sabrina noted Sister Ainnir's infirmity, the bony, liver-spotted hand, the weakness of her grip. Had this day's work been too much? Or had she always been this frail and Sabrina refused to notice?

"We make our own fate, child."

She sounded so certain. So confident. And why shouldn't she? Sister Ainnir had probably been here when they'd laid the first stone, or at least she gave that impression. Unfathomable wisdom. Indefatigable strength. She'd always been. Would always be. Like everything here. The buildings. The gray-robed sisters. The chapel. The toll of slow, sonorous bells.

It was what Sabrina loved about the order. The sense of forever in every mortared stone. The unaltering eternity as if time stopped within its walls. As if nothing could penetrate the sanctity and protection of this place. It was that very permanence that had attracted her to a life as a *bandraoi* priestess.

When change had battered Sabrina's well-ordered world like a hurricane tide and all she'd known and everyone she'd loved had vanished in a fury of blood and tears, the sisters of High *Danu* had become a harbor from the storm. Serene. Steady. Safe.

Only recently had she occasionally found monotony in the steady tread of passing time. Frustration in the rigid order. But these moments were rare and stamped out as soon as they surfaced. She knew where she belonged. And it was here.

They climbed the stairs to Sister Ainnir's chambers. Opened the door to a breath of perfumed air and the warmth of a fire recently stirred to cheerful life.

"I can manage from here. You go back now. Try to get some rest. There's naught more we can do for him tonight, but watch," Sister Ainnir said.

Sabrina smiled. "Thank you. For everything."

The priestess covered Sabrina's hand with her own. The clarity in her clear gray eyes revealing nothing of her body's weakness. Instead they bore a steady unflagging strength that seeped through Sabrina's skin into her bones, her tendons, her muscles. A gift of renewal when all her body craved was sleep.

"Your reasons for coming to us may have originated in a need to escape a painful past, but have you not found a home here?" Sister Ainnir asked. "A sisterhood in all but title?"

"I have. This life is all I've ever wanted. I've always been more comfortable here than among the airs and graces of Society's elite. I can be myself. I don't need to try to fit into someone's else's mold."

"Then the Sister Brighs of this world be damned."

Sabrina laughed. "You make it sound so easy."

The old woman chucked Sabrina's chin as she might a child's. "If it were easy, we'd have young women beating down our doors to get in. It's the difficulty keeps the riff-raff out."

Where was Lazarus? A missed meeting. No follow-up letters. Not one telltale clue.

Máelodor reached with his mind as far as he dared, yet no answering touch met his seeking fingers of thought. Only an empty echoing silence, a frozen, endless abyss spiraling always downward until his very skull flexed against the pressure. He surrendered to his body's frailty. He would eat. Rest. Begin the search for his mage-born *Domnuathi* again in the morning. He might feel death at the other end of their tenuous connection, but that was misleading. As long as Máelodor lived, Lazarus lived.

And Máelodor would find him. It was only a matter of time.

Which was all on his side.

He heaved himself from his chair to hobble painfully to the window. His prosthesis ground against the stumped remains of his leg, and the cold gnawed at bones grown brittle and twisted, but he refused to remain in his chair another moment.

Dusk fell early in the mountains, but the moon's reflection against the snow shone ghostly across the forested hillside. Furnished light enough to see by. To measure the man about to appear before him for instructions.

Across the valley, lights flickered from a few scattered homesteads. Strung out across the Cambrian Mountains like glimmering jewels set against the primitive isolation of the Welsh highlands.

The ancestors of these people had fought with a ferocity and a cleverness that kept them free for ages. Romans. Vikings. Saxons. Normans. They'd all tried to tame the wild Celtic nature. All had broken upon their shore and been turned aside.

But in all the eons of kings and warlords and princes who'd passed into and out of history, only one was remembered with the passion of the devoted. One stood higher. Burned brighter. Gathered followers long after there was naught left of their hero but bones.

Arthur.

Those who held the full knowledge hadn't let his demise hinder their dreams. The Nine and those devoted to them understood that death was temporary. Power was forever. And if Arthur returned, there would always be men and women who chose to follow his banner. With Máelodor to guide him and his own charismatic aura, the High King would march at the head of an army, and a world once again dominated by *Other* would be in reach. No longer the ignominy for the *Fey*-born of the cart's tail or a pitch-soaked scaffold. Instead, control. Command. Supremacy.

A new golden age.

Arthur was the key to success.

And Arthur was one step closer to being reborn.

Behind Máelodor, on the desk, lay his first victory. The Kilronan diary was in his possession. Its mysteries revealed after months of patient decoding. The only failure among so much success lay in the survival of Kilronan's pathetic whelp of an heir, Aidan Douglas.

Lazarus had paid dearly for allowing the man to live.

The *Domnuathi* wouldn't allow such scruples to surface again. Not now that he'd been reminded just who held the whip hand.

Not that it mattered overmuch. Máelodor had managed to defuse the threat posed by Douglas. He'd been deemed unhinged and as discredited as his executed father. His claims of Máelodor's existence as the head of a reconstituted network of disaffected *Other* termed the ravings of a man desperate to clear his power-mad younger brother.

Brendan Douglas remained at large seven years after the rest of the Nine had been exterminated. But not for long. The *Amhas-draoi,* guardians of the divide between mortal and *Fey,* tracked him with unceasing determination. And they weren't the only ones hunting the rogue *Other.* When Máelodor finally captured the youngest heir to Kilronan, he'd beg for death before the end.

A knock broke him from his more violent fantasies.

"Come."

A man bowed himself in. Slick. Smiling. Dark as a villain. "You summoned me?"

Máelodor straightened, throwing his crooked shoulders back. "Lazarus is missing. He was to contact a man in Cork. Their meeting never took place."

The man lounged against a table. Insolently picked through a bowl of fruit as if he were in the company of his mates and not his superior. "Mayhap he found himself a bit of something. Decided to dally a bit."

Máelodor's walking stick splintered beneath his increasing stranglehold. "A soldier of Domnu, a creature born of my magic and bound to my will, does not dally. He does as I order. Without question. Without thought."

The man straightened. "So what's the job? You want me to track your wayward slave down? Tell him Mummy's worried?"

Máelodor let his curse fly with a flick of his fingers. Felt a rush of satisfaction at the instant graying of the man's face. The widening of his terrified eyes as the air was squeezed from his throat. The lurching stumble against the table before he dropped to his knees, the pilfered apple rolling across the floor.

Máelodor shuffled to stand over this paltry excuse for a human. "You are new among us, so I shall make it simple. You will assume Lazarus's mission. Retrieve the Rywlkoth Tapestry. Bring it to me."

The man nodded, blue lips blubbering as he clawed at his throat.

Máelodor dissolved the curse with a second flick of his fingers. Allowed the man a moment of silent weeping before hooking one bony finger in his cravat and drawing him up. "You don't ask where you're being sent?"

The man's frightened eyes slid away, but Máelodor thrilled to the result of his dark powers. "You learn fast. Well, since you're such a quick study, I'll answer the question you dare not ask." He glanced back at the diary's burned binding. The pages blistered and cracked, but protected by the same spells keeping it indecipherable to any but the Nine. "You leave for Ireland, and the order of the Sisters of High *Danu*."

Crushing darkness. Muscles screaming. A mind in flames. And always the fanged jaws. The reptilian eye. A coiled presence at the very edges of his consciousness.

Dropping deeper and deeper into the black abyss, he reached for the woman, his hands coming away with naught but ocean, the glancing dart and glint of fish. He'd been fooled into believing she would be here waiting. Instead, he found only the pain of distant shredded memory. Useless against his current suffering.

Light speared the ocean's murk, descending even to the

drowning depths where he drifted frozen and blind. The slithering presence retreated. Turned its searching slitted gaze elsewhere.

He was alone.

For the first time in longer than he could remember, he was completely alone.

two

Tremors shuddered through him, chattering his teeth, turning fingers numb and jittery. Even his skull ached as if his brain had rattled itself loose. He tried swallowing, but his throat felt scraped raw, his tongue swollen and useless. He tried opening his eyes. Squinted against a piercing glare as if he stood within the sun. Golden yellow. Blinding. Sending new shocks of pain through his sloshy, scattered mind.

Slowly his sight acclimated. His surroundings coalescing into a cell-like room lined with cupboards, a low shelf running the perimeter. A sink with a pump. His pallet jammed into one corner. Beside him sat a small bench holding a ewer and basin and three stoppered bottles. A cane-backed chair drawn up close. Sunlight streamed in from a high window, and a three-legged brazier had been placed in the middle of the room, giving off a thin stream of smoke and just enough heat to keep him from freezing.

He burrowed deeper into the blankets in a vain attempt to get warm. A vainer attempt to figure out where he was. How he'd come to be here.

He remembered endless black. Crushing pressure. Cold so intense it tore him apart one frozen inch at a time. But when he sought the reasons for these sensations, he came against a barrier. A wall beyond which lay a vast emptiness.

He pushed harder, but the barrenness extended outward in all directions. Any attempt to concentrate only made his head hurt worse. Still he struggled, panic quickly replacing confusion until the shudders wracking his body had less to do with cold and more to do with sheer terror. The only memory he managed to squeeze from a brain scrambled as an egg was a woman's face, though her identity eluded him.

If he rose. Walked around. Perhaps that would help. He fought to stand. Lasted only moments. The room dipped and whirled like a ship caught in a storm, his stomach rebelling with a gut-knifing retch that left him doubled over and heaving.

Collapsing back onto the lumpy mattress, he stared up at the crumbling plaster ceiling, gripping the thin wool of his blankets. Clenching his teeth against a moan of pure animal fear.

Someone would come. They would tell him what had happened. Why he was here.

Who he was.

The latch lifted, the door swinging open on a figure shrouded by the dim light of the corridor beyond. Stepping into the room, she paused.

And he caught his breath on a startled oath.

Here stood the woman. His one and only memory.

She was called . . . he blanked.

"Please. What's your name?" he croaked, praying she wouldn't be insulted he couldn't remember.

Instead she smiled, turning her solemn face into something iridescent, and, crossing to sit beside him, placed the tray she carried on the bench. "I'm Sabrina. But, actually, I was rather hoping you could tell me your name."

Oh gods, she didn't know him. She couldn't fill in the holes. The truth kicked his last hopes out from under him. He was alone. On his own. And he hadn't a damned idea who he was.

She stared, head tilted, expectant, eager.

He shook his head, hating to disappoint. Hating the sick, horrible dread pressing him with a weight as crushing as the oblivion that preceded it. "I don't remember."

In the weak glow of the moon, he studied himself as he might a stranger. Beginning with details such as his heavy, calloused hands, a mole just below his collarbone, the tip of his left ring finger missing.

When no feature stoked a memory, he moved outward in ever more general circles. The strength of his body, his lean, powerful build. Long legs. Strong arms. Was he soldier? Sailor? Irish peasant? What life would result in such work-hardened toughness?

He came last to what most intrigued and most disgusted—the web of scars lacing his body. What horrible accident had caused these? Or had they been the result of an accident at all? Perhaps the disfigurement had been deliberate. What battles had he waged to earn such wounds? Or what crimes had he committed to bring about such punishment? Was it something he hadn't done? And did the architect of these injuries still hunt him?

He squeezed his eyes shut, pounding a fist against his forehead in frustration. Trying to knock even the slimmest of images from a mind blank as sand washed clean upon a beach.

Nothing.

So if pushing to remember brought naught but a headache, begin with the only image that did remain.

The woman.

Long after she'd left him, he still pictured her—slender as a willow withy, she moved with a lithesome grace no amount of modest garb could disguise. Her dark hair parted demurely and tucked beneath a snowy kerchief, vibrant blue eyes, upturned pert little nose, mouth a tad wide for her face, and the soft, rounded chin complete with a dimple that appeared when she laughed.

He knew this face. He'd seen it in his dreams. And yet, she looked upon him as a stranger.

Why? Why lie about knowing him? Or was he simply imagining things? Was he so starved for a past he'd grasp at any straw no matter how feeble?

The questions spun endlessly, but brought no answers. Only more questions. His hot, dry gaze traveled over the tangled scars of his arms. The long, angry slashes marring his torso. Repulsed, he closed his eyes.

No, the woman Sabrina was the key to unlocking his forgotten past. Among all his uncertainties, he knew that much with rare conviction. But what door would she open? And did he really want to know what lay behind it?

"Powea raga korgh. Krea raga brya."

Reaching out with her mind, Sabrina projected calm. Tranquillity. Health. Muscles relaxing. Chest clearing. It took only a few moments before the spell eased the consumptive coughs tearing at the frail priestess. Slowed her breathing to a peaceful, steady rhythm.

Satisfied, Sabrina broke the gossamer connection. Drew the blanket up to Sister Moira's chin. It would be hours before the old woman's congested lungs began to labor again. Until then, she would sleep.

She was the last on Sabrina's list. Sister Netta slept, her spiked fever slowly cooling. And Sister Clea needed only to be pointed back to bed should she rise disoriented, asking for her brother, Paul. A fisherman lost at sea some fifty years ago. Yet in her delirium Clea remained twelve years old, the decades since nothing more than a dream to her clouded mind.

Would it be the same for the man they'd pulled from the ocean? They'd given him back his life. But not his memories. Those remained lost. For days? Weeks? Forever? It was impossible to predict and so she'd explained to him, his face graying with her every word, a bleak desperation crowding the corners of his black eyes.

He'd fought to remain calm in her presence, but his tension had crackled the air like a storm, his fear thrumming the space between them. It made her ache for him as the helplessness of others always made her hurt. She loathed being in a position where nothing could be done. She needed to be doing. Fixing. Making it better. And this man's sickness was something she could not mend. Not even with all her *Other* gifts.

Her thoughts brought her back to his door. Or rightly the door to one of the stillrooms. Out of the way of the aged sisters. Separate from the few patients recovering in the main hospital.

She pressed her ear to the heavy wood, but no sound emanated from the room beyond. Did he sleep quietly? Or did he lie tossing and wakeful, fighting his fragile brain's betrayal? Undoing all her good work by worrying when he should be resting?

Turning the key, she cracked open the door.

A sliver of gray light from the high window bathed his cot. Created stark contrast in the rawboned angles of his face and the hollows of his eyes. Glinted blue amid his black hair, and silvered the crisscross slash of innumerable scars.

Old and new. Ancient, faded lines and angry, puckered blemishes. It was as if someone had acted out every cruel and vicious impulse upon his body. His chest had borne the worst of it—a web of violence marring the broad, hard-packed muscles—but no part of him had been spared.

Once upon a time he had been a target of a brutal killing intent. So why hadn't he died? Surely that many injuries should have proved fatal. One more question she could ask, but he couldn't answer.

He shifted, his hand coming up as if warding off a blow. His face grimaced in pain, his jaw hardening, his chest rising and falling as he gasped for breath. *"Mae gormod ohonynt. Tynnwch nol. Gwarchoda Tywysog Hywel. Amddiffyna'r tywysog."*

Odd. Not English. Nor Gaelic. A language unknown to her. She inched closer, unable to leave. Relock the door. Pretend she hadn't let curiosity draw her to his bedside. If she stayed, she might hear more. Hints of his past. Perhaps in sleep, he would remember. And she could relate all she learned in the morning. Jar a single memory loose, allowing the rest to spill forth. As a healer she'd been taught that all creatures deserved assistance. She would only be fulfilling her calling.

Not even Sister Brigh could quibble with that.

Fully justified, she sat down. Clasped her hands. Patience personified.

She was good at being silent. Waiting. Becoming invisible. It had always been thus, even when she was a child. As the baby of the family, she'd used that talent to her advantage. Her brothers would forget her presence in their private games or personal conversations. Her parents would forget she hadn't been sent to bed, but remained curled in a hidden corner with a book. Nurse would forget she even existed, too taken up with the nursery maid's gossip to worry overmuch about a silent child who demanded little attention. Especially in comparison to her harum-scarum older brothers.

He rolled over, arm over his face, neck taut and working. *"Dwi'n dy garu di."*

She mentally snapped her fingers. Welsh. She recognized the word for "love." She'd had a governess who'd come from Cardiff. Eres Jones-Abercrombie had been a sour stick of a woman with a sharp tongue and a quick hand. Sabrina had never been happier than when the woman had departed Belfoyle for a posting with Lord Markham's household.

So he was Welsh. And he loved someone. Somewhere out there someone missed him. Grieved for him. All the more reason to stay and learn as much as she could.

He jerked, his hand fisting on air. Deep lines biting into his cheeks. The muscles of his arms strained against an invisible foe. "The diary. Now."

English this time. Clipped in speech, almost a growl, but with a lilt held over from the Welsh of earlier. Authority rested in that uncompromising demand. This was a man who expected people to obey him. A ship's captain washed overboard? A victim of military mutiny? But a diary? A spy after enemy secrets? A wronged husband? That might fit with the word for love. Perhaps he had suffered a betrayal. The evidence written in his wife's diary.

Her imagination spun scenarios. Each one more lurid. More exiting. She wished for a pen and her journal before the varied conjectures escaped her.

"As you will." Sorrow edged those words, spoken so softly she barely heard them except she'd inched closer and had almost bent her ear to his mouth.

She held her breath. Waited, but nothing more.

Suddenly, he flailed, catching her chin with the back of his hand. Sent stars reeling across her vision. Came awake with eyes bleary and distracted. "Don't leave. Come back." His voice held such longing she wished with all her heart she were this woman he wanted so desperately.

"It's all right," she answered, wiggling her jaw, "you're safe now. Just a dream."

He focused, coming more awake. Sat up with a grimace. "I thought . . . but . . ."

"You called to someone. A lover? A wife?" she urged, thinking she'd jolt him into a recollection while his mind still held the ghost of her memory.

He shook his head as if trying to clear it. "But it's you. Yours is the face I dreamt."

"But I'm not. I'm—"

"Sabrina." His black eyes devoured her. "You are called Sabrina. I remember you."

This time the longing prickled along her own skin, and—healer's oath be damned—she caught up her skirts and fled.

three

"Rise and shine, slugabed. The sisters are calling us to breakfast."

Sabrina cracked open her eyes on a dawn filtered through a misty drizzle that added dampness to an already miserable, chilly morning.

"Go way. Tired." Rolling over, she stuffed her head under her pillow. Pretended she hadn't heard her friend's overly cheerful summons. Jane enjoyed annoying Sabrina far too much and had done so ever since they'd met.

Her pillow was yanked away. "Sister Brigh will be in here with the ice water if you're not quick."

Sabrina shivered, but even that threat didn't pull her out of bed. She'd worked in the infirmary until two in the morning. Used the following hours to complete her unfinished journal entry. By the time she'd closed the book, she'd a fierce headache and a heart heavy as lead.

So much of what she'd forgotten about those days returned beneath her pen. Her initial shock and terror. The screaming and cursing that followed. Her mother's wretched, furious weeping and the servants' quiet treachery as they slunk like rats abandoning a sinking ship from a house and a family labeled cursed. Sabrina hadn't known it could get worse until it did.

Her mother's grief quickly gave way to a vacant, staring sorrow that ended in a grave beside her husband. Sabrina's brother Aidan—the new Earl of Kilronan—retreated into surly silence behind the closed doors of her father's study. And, Brendan, the brother she'd loved with slavish devotion, simply vanished without a word of explanation. No one knew where, though everyone hinted at why.

After that, the Sisters of High *Danu* became a place of safety. A refuge.

A home.

She'd been content. Never contemplated a life beyond the community of *bandraoi*. Not until this last endless season when change flourished everywhere but here. Aidan's unexpected marriage. Her childhood friend and neighbor Elisabeth Fitzgerald's letter announcing her recent betrothal. Even Jane would be leaving Sabrina behind when she was elevated to full priestess at the next festival. Only Sabrina remained in frustrating limbo.

Dissatisfaction crept beneath her guard and set up shop. Unshakable. Uncomfortable.

"Are you even listening to me?" Jane scolded.

Sabrina pulled the blankets over her head. "Tell them I'm sick."

"You're not sick."

"Then tell them I'm dead. I don't care. I need sleep."

"You've slept for hours."

"And I'd like to continue doing so if you'd be so kind," she grumbled.

She disliked Jane in her perky, mothery mode. Especially since she could survive on a few snatched catnaps and didn't understand why Sabrina couldn't do the same.

"Can I borrow a clean pair of stockings? Mine have a great hole in the toe." Jane had given up on Sabrina and directed her conversation to the third occupant of their chamber, privacy not being high on the sisters' list of must-haves.

"Only if I can borrow an extra petticoat," Teresa bargained. "I almost froze in the library yesterday. Sister Ursula refuses to light a fire until icicles are hanging from my nose."

"Try the kitchens. It's hot as a bloody oven in there."

"Jane! Your language."

"Well it is. I almost fainted the day before yesterday."

What Sabrina wouldn't give for her lost bedchamber at Belfoyle. Sweet privacy. Space to toss her things about. Quiet when she needed it.

She clamped her pillow back over her head to drown out the others' morning chatter; banging drawers, requests for assistance in buttoning or unbuttoning; the clink of pitchers and basins, the thump of sturdy boots across the floor. And always the relentless conversation. It seeped around the edges of her pillow, muffled but intelligible.

Jane's excited voice penetrated like a cannon salvo. "Did you ever find out who the man is they brought in yesterday?"

The final reason for her exhaustion dragged at Sabrina like an anchor—the man.

She'd wished for change—any change—and been rewarded with a mysterious, glowering stranger who watched her as though he could pull the very thoughts from her head. No more wishes for her.

Unable to erase his intense, endless black gaze, she'd tossed and turned for hours.

"I heard he can't remember anything," Jane continued with relish.

Sabrina began to suffocate under her blankets. And a few escaping feathers made her nose itch.

"I think he's here to murder us all in our beds," Teresa speculated. "I slept with a kitchen knife under my pillow, just in case."

Sabrina flung back the covers. Gulped in a chilly breath of air just as Jane shot back, "You would."

She was right. Teresa thought every outsider held sinister intentions.

"Have you seen him?" Jane plopped on the end of Sabrina's bed with a friendly bounce. Already dressed, she talked while shoving her hair up under her prim white kerchief. A crime. Sabrina's own brown tangle was only improved by concealment, but Jane's floating mass of auburn waves deserved to be admired.

Surrendering to Jane's buoyant cheerfulness, Sabrina stretched. Two hours of sleep would have to do. "I have. And spoken with him."

No need to reveal her schoolgirl flight. Even now she writhed with mortification. What had frightened her into running away in such a ridiculous fashion? Teresa, yes. She was barely seventeen. Wet behind the ears and still in that giggly, graceless stage. But Sabrina had left that awkward childhood self-consciousness behind long ago. Hadn't she?

"Is he handsome as they say?" Jane leaned forward eagerly.

"Who says?" Teresa chimed in.

Thankfully, Jane's attention drifted back to Teresa,

relieving Sabrina of the need to explain the man's primal, yet sensual appeal. Not that she could. Even to herself.

"Two of the sisters. They said he was delicious as sin and wished they could—"

"Jane!"

She sniffed. "I'm only relating the comments of others."

People would be surprised at the earthiness found within the confines of an all-female community. With no men to hinder tongues or curb actions, normally taboo subjects could be openly discussed, joked about, or explained in depth. Sabrina only wished this particular discussion would end before the heat flooding her cheeks was noticed.

"So is he?" Jane prodded Sabrina. "Handsome, I mean."

A prickly tingle cruised her skin like static. "You could call him that," she murmured.

Somewhere a bell was ringing. Or was that the roaring of blood in her ears?

A pillow caught her square in the face.

"Blast! We're late! There's last call." Jane and Teresa dashed from the room, leaving Sabrina alone and wishing for a good dousing of Sister Brigh's ice water.

He tried not to squirm beneath the unblinking stare of the old woman, but it was difficult in his present position—flat on his back and naked—a few thin blankets the only shield between him and the hefty mountain towering over him.

"Sister Ainnir says you have no recollection of how you came to be washed up on our beach with enough seawater in you to float an armada."

"No, mistress. I remember nothing before waking in this chamber yesterday."

A flicker of her eyes. A slight shifting in her pose. But what she reacted to, he couldn't tell. Something he'd said? Hadn't said? Did she know who he was? Did they all know, but chose not to tell him?

"Not even your name?" she asked.

Anger flared along nerves like a lit fuse.

"I told you. Nothing."

Again came the infinitesimal glimmer of knowledge in the woman's eyes, causing his hands to fist at his sides as he struggled to quell a mounting rage he didn't comprehend.

"And that brand on your forearm?" she continued, smooth and cool as glass. "It's an unusual symbol."

His hand rose to touch the brand burned into his left forearm, a broken arrow and crescent.

"Can you recall what it signifies?" she prodded. "Why you would mark yourself in such a grisly fashion?"

Did she think he lied? That he was feigning memory loss for some hidden purpose? He only wished it were that simple. His anger swelled, twitching muscles. Bringing him to an edgy awareness of his surroundings—the inches separating them, the rain hissing against the window, the thick, humid air. His awareness expanded to the blood moving through arteries and veins, the quickening beat of his heart, the breath filling his lungs. And something more. Something that was and wasn't a part of him. A sliding, slithering presence lurking in the hidden recesses of his mind. Seeking access. Seeking control.

"I don't know," he snarled. "I can't remember."

He pushed back. Harder. Defied the questing sensation. Damped the fury to manageable levels, though it cost him in a burst of pain across his temples. Gut-gripping nausea.

A satisfied smile creased the wrinkles of her face, and

she nodded as if making up her mind of something. "Very well. We can't simply keep calling you the man in the still-room. Until you recall your own name, we'll choose one for you. How about"—she tapped a thoughtful finger to her lips—"how about Daigh?"

He cocked a questioning brow, caught off balance by her sudden change of topic.

Again one of those wise, all-knowing smiles, this time with a hint of humor. "I had a younger brother named Daigh. He had a bit of your dark looks." The seams of her face resettled into properly stern lines. "We can only hope you don't end as he did. Anyhow, let's see. Daigh"—the finger kept tapping—"Daigh . . . Daigh MacLir."

It was his turn to favor her with a smile, though it felt feeble and unnatural on his face. "Son of the sea. How poetic of you, mistress."

She straightened, shoulders back. Head up. "I am Ard-siúr and head of this community."

"Where am I? What is this place?"

Her brows disappeared into her kerchief. "You've washed ashore in Glenlorgan among the Sisters of High *Danu*. An order of *bandraoi* priestesses devoted to a spiritual life. One where we may remain true to our *Other* heritage away from the mistrust of our *Duinedon* neighbors."

He knew those terms. *Other*—*Fey*-tainted human half bloods. *Duinedon*—mortals without the powers that signified their mage-touched human neighbors. Why did he know this? What did *Other* and *Duinedon* mean to him? What part did they play in his life?

"You risk much to tell me this. Suppose I betray you all?"

"That is a possibility. But my bones tell me you will not do so."

"Your bones?"

"I sense great pride in you. Some might see it as arrogance even. But there is also much honor."

"If you know all that about me, why the questions?" That flash of anger sparked anew. His hand closed around an invisible weapon. Felt the lack with a strange twinge of regret.

The priestess had raised inscrutability to an art form. She leveled him with a quiet stare that seemed to penetrate blankets, flesh, bone, and a few layers of soul to his very core. But her gaze drew away, confusion disturbing a woman who, he suspected, was used to certainty.

"Because of what I do not sense, Mr. MacLir. That is what worries me."

"Time to eat." Juggling a tray while maneuvering open a door with her elbow, Sabrina backed her way into the stillroom. Luncheon was late today. A product of too many *bandraoi* spoiling the broth. Household magic was well and good, but an excess of mage energy in an enclosed space could make for chaos—as those assigned to the kitchens found when the stove began belching black smoke and the scullery sinks sent rivers of dirty dishwater spilling over the floors. "I apologize for the delay, but—"

Turning, she gasped, jiggling her tray ominously. Her patient was abed no longer. Nor was he comfortingly obscured by mountains of blankets. Instead he loomed above her like some titan from myth, his head scraping the low ceiling, his body seeming to fill every spare inch of room. Even air was at a premium. She couldn't get enough to catch her breath.

She blinked, her gaze traveling over a bare muscled torso chiseled as granite, the accumulation of scars like some strange warrior's language written upon his body in blood. But instead of wielding a battle-notched blade or an infantryman's musket, he held only a shirt.

"Up here," came an amused growl.

Heat rushed to her face as she lifted her gaze to his, the view only staggering her anew. Not handsome in the classical sense. No, his visage held too much toughness to be considered good-looking. All rugged angles and strong lines, a clenched jaw hewn from stone. Straight, firm mouth. Hair cropped unfashionably short and close to the head. And always that devouring black stare stripping her down to an awkward girl.

"Oh, excuse me," she stammered. "I didn't know . . . no one told me . . ." With a few shuddery gulps, she fought to recover her lost aplomb. "That is, I'm surprised to see you up and dressed."

"Dress-*ing*. As you see." He spread his hands, the shirt clasped on one great fist.

"Yes, well . . ." She tried looking anywhere but at him. "At least you're wearing breeches."

Again came gruff amusement. "At least."

Had she really said that? Had she really looked . . . Oh, if only the floor would open and swallow her whole. Her entire body flamed with humiliation. A *bandraoi* did not go about ogling men. Not even if the man in question was exquisite ogling material.

He eased the tray from her before she dropped it. Placed it on the bench. Drew the shirt over his head, snapping her out of her daze.

She wiped her damp hands down her apron. Shifted under his enigmatic stare. "I best be getting back. Sister Ainnir will—"

"Stay." A request that sounded very much like a command.

"Excuse me?"

"Stay with me. Please." His eyes pleaded with her as if he were drowning and she held his only lifeline. "Sabrina."

With his fluid lilting voice, her name on his tongue rolled and rippled like water. Sent a shivery rush straight to her center.

"Your Sister Ainnir doesn't talk, she glowers. Ard-siúr asks questions but provides no answers." He plowed a hand through his dark hair. Exhaled a heavy sigh. "I need to learn what brought me here. Who I am. That's impossible closeted in this monk's cell."

He held his fear close, but flashes of it speared her consciousness. Punched through her strongest defenses until she sensed his dread. Understood his panic. Her mind reeled with untamed emotion. It hammered behind her eyes. Kinked the muscles at the base of her neck. Never had anyone affected her in such a dramatic fashion. Bursting into her consciousness like a tidal wave.

Did he know what effect he caused? Or was his invasion unintentional?

She forced herself to relax. Clasping her hands in a posture of patience, she focused on locking her mind more firmly against his intrusion. It worked. Somewhat. At least she could breathe again. But the sensation of being caught and buffeted in the rip curl of his thoughts and feelings lingered.

"I'll help if I can, but there's not much to tell. One of the village children discovered you washed up in the shallows." There. She'd managed two complete sentences without stammering like a child. "It's an odd sort of cove.

The current brings all sorts of things into the rocks there. Old timbers, broken barrels washed off ships. Bodies or what's left of them." Catching her gaffe, she stuttered to a halt. Just when she found herself easing into normalcy, she stepped right in her own words.

His gaze flickered and went still. A hand fisted at his side.

"I can take you there if you'd like." She heard the words. Looked around in surprise as if someone else had just suggested a lonely trek to the cove. Was she mad? The last thing she needed was to be alone with this man who made her feel as if she'd been turned inside out, upside down, and back to front.

He didn't answer until she wondered if he'd even heard her. Perhaps she hadn't spoken aloud after all. Perhaps she was saved from her own foolish impulses. Uncomfortable with his continuing brooding silence, she filled it with the first thought that popped into her head. "You speak Welsh."

"I do?" An excited glimmer brightened his dark gaze.

Her pulse sped up, but she met his eyes with a sheepish smile. "You did last night in your sleep. Just a few words. Nothing that made sense."

"You kept this from me." The accusation implicit. "What else have you learned?"

Tipping her chin in a determined show of reserve, she ignored the drumming of her heart. "You mentioned a diary."

His brows drew together in a scowl of concentration. "A diary? What did I say?"

"You were asking for it. Demanding it. Does that mean anything to you?"

He closed his eyes, breathing deeply. His effort to make sense of the riddle she'd presented almost tangible. When he opened them again, tension shivered off him. Stirred the air like a storm charge. "I have sensations. Impressions. But no memories. Not about a diary. Not about anything. My mind's empty of the past."

"Except for the woman," she reminded him, "The one in your dream."

His gaze narrowed on her with renewed determination. "It was your face. I must know you. I just can't remember from where. But it's you. Of that, I'm certain."

Impossible. She'd know if she'd met this devastating giant of a man whose mage energy radiated like an electrical storm. Men like him didn't visit the *bandraoi*. And she'd not traveled farther from Glenlorgan than Cork in the last three years.

"People imagine funny things when they're ill," she suggested.

"Do they imagine women they've never met? I don't believe it could be so, Sabrina." Her name like a caress.

Butterflies threatened to explode out her stomach. Smoothing her apron, she cleared her throat with nursely efficiency. "I should be getting back to my duties." Patted his shoulder like she might a child, though the masculine frame beneath her fingers was decidedly un-childlike, and she was certain he felt her trembling. "You were more dead than alive when the villagers brought you to us. It will take time for you to recover your memory, but I'm sure it will happen."

He gazed down on his calloused palm, the slash of old cuts evident even there. Closing his fist, he shrugged. "You've seen my scars," he replied, hunching his shoulders as if warding off a blow. "Perhaps it's best if I don't."

"I've made up my mind." Ard-siúr held up a hand before Sister Brigh could argue—again. "And that's final."

From her inconspicuous seat behind Sister Ainnir, Sabrina clamped her lips together, smothering a smile. She couldn't help it. She loved seeing the cranky old priestess stymied every once in a while.

Sister Ainnir's low-pitched voice responded to Ard-siúr's resolve. "We can't make him remain if he chooses to go."

"No, we can't force him to stay, Sister Ainnir," Ard-siúr agreed. "But we can make it clear that his injuries still impair his mind. And while he may feel he's fully healed, his body can weaken without warning. Dizziness. Fatigue. Headaches. Until he recovers his memory, it would be better for him to remain."

"But his continued presence disrupts our routine," Sister Anne chirped. "Already rumors circulate among us. He's a wanted brigand. A smuggler. A murderer. Each story more hair-raising than the last."

"Wouldn't be surprised," Sister Brigh sniffed. "You just have to look at him to see he's a dangerous rogue likely to slit your throat. No respectable gentleman carries scarring like that."

It was true. The man's body spoke of untold violence and a sinister past as dark as his eyes. But Sabrina had seen no signs of murderous intent. Felt no fear in his presence other than the fear that she was making a fool of herself.

Sister Brigh's assumptions were taken up with worried agreement by the others. Argument ensued, voices competing for dominance as each brought their views before Ard-siúr.

Sabrina burrowed deeper into her chair. Why she'd been included in this afternoon's meeting had not been made clear—possibly because Sister Ainnir's work in the hospital fell more and more to Sabrina as the elderly priestess's health waned—but she didn't want anyone to suddenly question her right to be included. That "anyone" most likely to be Sister Brigh, who questioned every decision and took every opportunity to challenge Ard-siúr's authority.

Ard-siúr's quiet control cut through the squabbling. "All your concerns are understandable and duly noted, but my decision is made." Ard-siúr's pointed stare directed squarely at Sister Brigh. There followed the rustle of skirts, the babble of conversation. "You may go, my sisters."

Sabrina eased out of her chair. Took up her place at the end of the line of chattering women.

"Hold a moment, Sabrina," Ard-siúr said with a hand upon her arm. Waiting until the flock of women withdrew before ushering her back to her seat. Leaning against her desk, arms folded, lips tipped in amusement. "Do you agree with my decision? Or, like Sister Brigh and the others, do you think I should have sent the poor man on his way?"

The head of the order asked her opinion? This was a first. And a hopeful portent. Perhaps her elevation to full priestess drew close. She hesitated, weighing her words. It wouldn't do to queer things now with some rash, unthinking response. "I believe, Ard-siúr, you acted in the only way you could. That is to say, all sorts of dangers lay beyond our boundaries. Worse for someone who'd have no idea from where the danger might come." Her words came faster, her thoughts racing ahead of her tongue. "No, he must stay. At least until he recovers his health. And I discover . . . I mean, we discover who he is and what happened to him." Now she babbled, plain and simple.

Ard-siúr's wrinkles stretched in a half smile. "You've taken quite an interest in Daigh MacLir's fate."

Heat crept up Sabrina's throat to stain her cheeks.

Ard-siúr nodded her dismissal, moving past Sabrina toward the door. Turning in a swish of skirts. "I nearly forgot. The letter." Returning to her desk, she pulled a folded and sealed page from a drawer. Handed it over. "I believe it's from your brother."

"Kilronan?" Sabrina asked stupidly, the smooth, expensive foolscap slippery beneath her fingers.

Ard-siúr caught her in a sharp, appraising look. "Would you be expecting word from another brother?"

A dull lump swelled in her chest. Oh, why had she felt it necessary to put the whole horrible episode down on paper? She'd not dwelled on her family's fractured separation for years. Now she knew why. It hurt too much. "No, ma'am. No letter. Nothing."

"Very well. You may go."

Sabrina slid the letter into her apron pocket. Moved with stinging eyes toward the door. Wiped them with the back of her sleeve. She'd tried putting her family behind her. But reliving that tragic day had brought all her hurt and abandonment to the surface like oil upon water.

"And Sabrina?"

"Ma'am?"

Ard-siúr's solemn, weighty stare pinned her to the floor. "Should Brendan Douglas ever attempt to contact you, you will let me know, won't you?"

Sabrina escaped without answering. Jostled her blind way through a crowd of women in the passage. Disregarded

Jane's shouted halloo across the cloister. Ignored Sister Brigh's outraged mutter as she bumped into her upon the dormitory stairs.

Only stopped to catch her breath in the blessed momentary privacy of her bedchamber. Shuddering. Her back pressed against the door panels. Stupid tears burning her eyes.

For seven years she'd assumed Brendan was dead. How else to account for his lack of letters or visits or any word at all. But could the *Amhas-draoi* be telling the truth? Could Brendan still live? Could he be the blackhearted villain they claimed he was?

Ard-siúr certainly seemed to believe it.

So, what if he did contact her?

Where did her true loyalty reside?

If asked to make a choice between her old family and her new, whom would she betray?

four

Daigh scanned the room he'd been brought to with a searching eye. Desk. Case clock. A pairing of old cane-backed chairs. A long, low table upon which stood decanters, a scattering of various stones, shards of quartz, a bowl of dried petals. Thick Turkey carpets covered the flagged floor. Wall tapestries moved in the incessant breeze through poorly chinked mortar. He found himself transfixed by stags and hounds in regal red and gold. Stylized sea creatures amid a woolen sea of blues and greens. Flowers and leaves needled in exquisite detail so that one's eye couldn't help but follow the woven floral design across the cloth. A rendering of gray-veiled attendants following a curtained litter toward an open tomb. He scowled, focusing on a lone attendant standing with outstretched hands and eyes cast up toward a single star.

"You've recovered far faster than we expected, considering the shape you were in upon your arrival."

He drew his attention back from the puzzled tangle

of his own impenetrable thoughts. Stood body braced and shoulders back. Met the triple spear-point stares of the trio of gray-gowned *bandraoi* with a sharp, assenting jerk of his head.

"After discussing your health with Sister Ainnir, we've decided a busy mind and body may bring about your full recovery. Therefore, as you no longer require medical attention, I am putting you in Sister Liotha's charge." Ard-siúr motioned toward the tallest of the women. Flat nosed. Wind-burned cheeks. Hands broad and tough as leather. And a no-nonsense manner reminding him of Griffid. That skeptical, show-me air . . .

He staggered against the snatch of an image. His knees weak as water as he clutched at the slippery pieces of memory sliding through his mind.

Griffid?

The grizzled soldier returned to him, gap-toothed and grinning. His face as clear as the cluster of women in front of him. His temples thundered, a snarling pressure knotting his spine as he fought to concentrate. To battle his way through the shimmering stained-glass wash of color bursting across his vision.

"Are you unwell?" A touch upon his forehead. A hand upon his sleeve. And Griffid vanished. Lost in the endless well where Daigh's past swam but rarely surfaced.

He steadied himself, shaking off the proffered aid. Refusing to let these women see his weakness. His anguish. They saw too much as it was. Picked him apart like a flock of vultures. Yet despite all their probing, soul-searing stares, they could offer him no hint about his lost past. Of that, they were as uncertain as he. Time, they assured. Time and freedom would restore him.

But as he followed Sister Liotha to his new duties, a vague, unsettling notion clawed at his consciousness. He could count on neither time nor freedom. Both waned with every passing day. And why that was, like all else, he could not remember.

Sabrina crumpled the letter, flinging it away with a satisfying toss. She'd have to pick it up later—before Jane found and read it—but for now, it felt good to take out her frustrations on a scrap of paper that couldn't fight back.

Aidan requested her immediate presence in Dublin. Again. This was the fifth such letter she'd received in the space of two months. He couched his command in conciliating language, but the essence remained the same. While he understood her desire to withdraw from Society following the tumultuous aftermath of their father's death, he could no longer allow her to hide herself away from the world.

He talked of unity. Purpose. The Douglases against the world. Like they were a family. But you needed more than shared blood to be a family. And their father's murder had shattered those familial ties. Aidan couldn't just glue them back together with sticking plaster and false optimism. Pretend the last years hadn't happened.

The Sisters of High *Danu* were her only family now.

Even Sister Brigh, though Sabrina hated to admit it.

That was the conclusion she'd come to after hours of soul-searching. She was sticking with it.

She wouldn't go to Dublin. Period. She didn't care how many letters Aidan penned.

Her eldest brother had never understood her devotion to the cloistered *bandraoi* life. He'd always been far more comfortable among the bustle and confusion of the city. Could slide into the skin of a *Duinedon* without difficulty. And had rarely, if ever, showed any interest in his *Other* inheritance besides the most basic of household magics.

Not Sabrina. She'd always sensed her *Other* blood was written upon her face, clear as day. Always felt like a fish on dry land when called upon to pretend otherwise. She recalled with discomfort the stilted conversations of afternoon social calls and the wallflower shyness of parties. The fluttering, simpering young women with nothing on their minds besides making advantageous marriages. As the proper wife of a proper peer, when would she ever get the chance to use her powers? She'd be relegated to a life half lived. The best parts of her left behind, unwanted and forgotten.

Her endeavors to become a *bandraoi* might not be progressing as she'd envisioned. But it was a life she understood. Her previous existence seemed, with every passing year, a dream belonging to some other Lady Sabrina Douglas. Certainly not to her.

The tower bells rang the hour. Time to report to Sister Ainnir and her duties.

Lately, the daily routine of the infirmary and hospital had become, well . . . routine. Assisting those suffering from accidents and illness. Short forays to the neighboring farmsteads and villages when a healer or midwife was needed.

The stranger's disturbing arrival had shaken her from the rut for a few days, but with Daigh's removal to new quarters, she'd lost even that frisson of anticipation when her stomach went jittery and her breathing quickened.

It was just as well.

She'd become far too aware of him waiting at the end

of the long, low-ceilinged passage. The impatient way he prowled his quarters. His aura of command, shaken by circumstance yet there in the arrogant set of his jaw. The ruthless intensity chained in the depths of his forever gaze.

Daigh MacLir. The name Ard-siúr had chosen for him. Like pulling an identity from a hat. But it suited him. Hard. Sharp.

She rolled the name on her tongue. "Daigh. Daigh MacLir."

Shaking off the quiver that skittered up her spine, she rose to retrieve the balled letter. No, Sabrina. No. Daigh was off-limits. Out of bounds. A treacherous obstacle placed upon her path. She offered a prayer to the gods for strength.

Sister Brigh called him dangerous. Sabrina wouldn't go that far. But power did ripple off him like smoke. She'd felt it immediately. She might not know who he was. But she knew what he was.

Other.

Like her.

Tossing Aidan's summons on the fire, she watched the edges blacken and curl to ash.

A merging of *Fey* and human. A product of both worlds.

And like her, belonging to neither.

She moved with clever nimbleness like a shy forest creature who perceived predators in every shadow. Not timid. No. More as if each dawn were a gift that couldn't be taken for granted. Each twilight a lucky success. But beneath that quick furtiveness, he sensed a courage untested. A strength belied by the willowy grace of her stance.

Her dark hair, struggling to remain confined beneath her kerchief. The inquisitive tilt of her head as she hastened down the path, the way her body leaned toward him as if he held all her attention. Her blue eyes alight with gemstone brilliance.

He'd asked about her in the days since he'd been released to Sister Liotha. Subtle inquiries. Leading conversations. There were always those who enjoyed relaying information no matter who posed the questions.

Lady Sabrina Douglas.

Daughter and sister to the earls of Kilronan

A member of the order since coming to the sisters seven years ago at the age of fifteen.

An *Other* with a rare empathic gift for healing and an aspiring priestess to High *Danu*.

With each piece added to the puzzle, he sought to understand the strange, unshakeable connection between them. The sense that Sabrina Douglas had been part of his past. Remained important to his future.

"Here we are." She lifted her head to the cold, salty air. Inhaled with a lung-filling breath. Cast her eyes out across the cove's narrow beach to the choppy pewter sea beyond, a wistfulness to her features.

He'd been surprised when she'd actually sought him out that morning. Volunteered to lead him to the spot where he'd been found. He'd accepted. Not only hoping a sight of the place might jog his memory. But because it had been a perfect chance to glean more about her in innocent conversation. More difficult to do than he'd imagined, as his every gambit had been met by her clever turn of topic. By the time they'd reached the well-worn path down to the beach, he felt he knew less about this woman than he did when they'd started out.

Purposeful evasion or simply a woman unfamiliar with attention's center?

She pushed the kerchief back off her head, hair spilling free from its pins in a riot of mahogany curls. "There were awful storms a week ago. Could your ship have foundered? Could you have been washed overboard?"

He clamped down on the sudden desire her unconscious gesture released. "Could have been, but no memory of it comes to me." He shrugged, unable to look away as she repaired the damage. Pinned her hair and hid it away.

"I have dreams of drowning," he said. "Water closing over my head. Fighting for air." Speaking it aloud sent icy panic knifing through him.

"Dreams are sometimes helpful. Any others?"

He hesitated. Ran a hand across his forehead, his gaze turned inward on the stark images burning up through him. "Destruction. Heartbreak. A man's hatred. A woman's weeping."

"And, well, uh . . . sometimes dreams are merely dreams," she stammered, her distress clear in the tremble of her voice and her horrified expression.

His absorption broken, he knelt, plucking a barnacle-encrusted stave from between two rocks. One of at least half a dozen scattered across the pebbly shoreline. "So I was just one piece of a steady stream of flotsam." Chucked the rotten wood far out into the water.

"This cove provides a livelihood for the villagers. They search it daily. Broken lumber for their houses and barns. Barrels of cargo lost to storms they can use or sell."

Lifting her skirts, she stepped out onto a flat shelf of stone, waves lapping against the crumbing edge. "What they find here can sometimes spell the difference between survival or starvation."

"And the bodies?" His question came sharper than intended as he strove to ignore the wind pressing her skirts close against her legs, outlining long, sleek limbs. The enticing junction between. "What is their fate?"

"We send them on to *Annwn* with the proper rites and prayers," she answered simply, bending to catch up a few pebbles. Tossed them one by one into the foam.

"No doubt after they've been robbed of anything valuable." He cast his own long gaze out across the water to billowing sails hull-up on the horizon. "And what of those not willing to part with their possessions?"

A guilty light darkened her eyes. "Desperation can make a savage of any man."

Shadows blotting out the sun. Angry conversation. Crude laughter. The cold press of a knife slashing his skin. Blood, hot and flowing over his chest. Leaking onto the pebbled beach.

Rage burst against his skull. Flared along his limbs. "Had I strength to resist, they would have murdered me, wouldn't they?"

She winced, her face going pale. She stumbled, one foot coming down hard in the surf. She righted herself with a muttered oath. Dragged her sopping hem clear of the water before meeting his gaze again, though a frown now marred the brightness of her eyes. "We prevent what violence we can, but sometimes we're too late."

Clamping down on the flare of brain-seething emotion, he strode the length of the cove. Pushed aside bare overhanging branches. Splashed the frozen shallows. Scattered feeding terns that scurried out of his way.

He'd remembered. A flare of a moment. But where lurked one memory, others must remain.

The knife. The blood. If his mind didn't play him false, the scavengers had sought to kill him. He rubbed absently at a spot above his heart. A tingle answering his touch.

Wheeling around, he caught Sabrina's frightened look before it vanished behind a calm mask.

"So what kept them from murdering me?" he asked, his voice bleak against his tongue.

She chewed the edge of one fingernail. Raked him with an appraising eye, her brows scrunched in thought. "Honestly? I don't know."

He watched her. She felt his gaze in a pricking between her shoulder blades. His presence like the churn of heavy air before a storm. She crossed the courtyard on her way from the dormitory to the library. Steps quick as she threaded puddles. Skirts pulled up to keep them from dragging through the mud. Yet she sensed him lurking in the stable's shadows, pausing only as she passed.

She slanted her gaze in his direction. Coat discarded. Sleeves rolled back, revealing the slash of scarring. Harsh midnight visage like some ancient effigy. The shovel in his hands gripped with grim executioner familiarity.

Anguish. Grief. And heartbreaking loneliness. The surge of his emotions hit her like a series of crushing body blows. And as happened at the seashore, the air seemed to shimmer around Daigh, and in place of his coarse homespun, she could have sworn she caught the glint of armor, the luxury of a fur-lined cloak, and a scabbard hanging low upon his hip.

She blinked, and the image vanished as suddenly as it

had come. Only a queer fluttering in her stomach remained, accompanied by a sweep of heat that flushed her skin. Made November's damp chill resemble sultry June.

He caught her eyes on him. Offered her a nod of acknowledgment.

"Did you only attend to your duties with as much eagerness," Sister Brigh snipped, passing Sabrina like an agitated crow. All beady eyes and ruffled black skirts.

She cast an embarrassed smile in Daigh's direction, but he'd resumed his work and did not look her way again.

Still, long after she'd left him, the strange, swooping plunge of her insides troubled her. His haunted stare lingered in her mind's eye. His desperation wrenched her soul.

She was his last hope. She alone could save him. She knew this as strongly as if someone had etched it upon her heart.

But how? And from what?

The kitchen's low banked fire cast a warm glow over the stone floor and up the whitewashed walls. Rain pattered against the high windows, and a smell of baking hung sweet and doughy in the air.

Up to her elbows in dishwater, Jane pushed a bedraggled strand of hair from her face with an elbow. "Why do you suppose Kilronan wants you to join him? I would have hardly called him a doting brother."

Sabrina forked a piece of cold ham onto a plate. Added some boiled potatoes. "He's not. Or he hasn't been until now. I place the blame squarely at the feet of that woman he married. She's probably decided she wants an unpaid companion and thinks I'm the perfect candidate."

"Would Kilronan allow his only sister to be bullied about by his wife?" Jane asked.

"Would he marry a penniless nobody with a murky past and doubtful morals? Had you asked me that last year, I'd have said never. But then here we are, so I can't say I know what my brother is capable of."

Some pickles. A roll. Sabrina had missed lunch and dinner today. Sister Ainnir had finally forced her to leave the infirmary to grab a late meal.

"Naught will change in ten minutes, Sabrina," she'd said as she pushed her out of the ward.

A dollop of mustard. A bit of leftover tart. Sabrina nibbled a corner. Apple. Her favorite. Make that two tarts. She turned her attention back to Jane. "Which is why I refuse to go to Dublin. The next thing I know Aidan will have me locked in a room until I marry some horrid, smelly man with a fortune obtained in the sheep bladder industry."

"Can't imagine there'd be much money to be had in sheep's bladders," Jane commented, "though I did know a gentleman in Belfast who'd made all his money from kippered herring. Smelled perpetually of dead fish." She placed the saucepan in the drying rack. Began scrubbing an enormous blackened pot. By the looks of the pile still soaking in the sink, she'd be here all night.

"What did you do that has you chained to the scullery so late? Aren't there usually more of you to do the washing up?"

Sabrina didn't envy her friend her duties in the Glenlorgan kitchens even if Sister Evangeline was by far the jolliest of the *bandraoi,* with a rosy, cherubic face and an enormous round belly. In fact, she bore a marked resemblance to the Prince Regent in a dress. Frightening thought.

"Usually there are more to help," Jane explained, "but Sister Miriam is sick with a head cold, Prudence is suffering her monthlies, and Charlotte is visiting her sister in Cork who's just had a baby, so I volunteered. I don't mind. I like the time alone to think."

No more needed to be said. Solitude was a precious commodity in Glenlorgan. Sabrina had the quiet hours of night duty in the infirmary. Jane had her after dinner washing-up. One lived here long enough, one learned to carve out a small oasis of quiet. That, or one followed Sister Bertha's dubious example and went stone deaf. Drastic, but effective.

"I saw you with Mr. MacLir this afternoon." Jane flashed her a wicked grin, fanning herself with a sudsy hand. "Now I'd marry him if he smelled like dead hippopotamus."

"Jane!"

"Don't tell me you haven't thought the very same thing, Sabrina Douglas. I see the way you look at him when you think no one's watching."

Sabrina sniffed. "He's a former patient. That's all."

"Mm-hmm. So was One-Eyed Toby from the village who got that fishhook in his lip, but I never saw you gawk at him like that."

"Oh my, look at the time. I have to get back. Sister Moira's taken a turn. I need to be there in case she wakes." Sabrina motioned toward the sink. "Best get to it. That pot won't scrub itself."

At which point wet suds caught her square in the face.

Laughing, she grabbed up her tray. "See you back at our chamber later?"

"I'll believe it when I see it. If I know you, Sister Ainnir will have to force you to get some sleep." Jane scoured the pot with vigor enough to put a hole right through the bottom.

Tray in hand, Sabrina crossed the refectory. Up the stairs. Opened the door on a downpour, wind whipping the rain across the courtyard in sheets. Well, that was just perfect. She'd be soaked to the bone if she risked that mess. Nothing left of her dinner but mush.

Turning back, she retraced her steps. If she took the upper corridor that ran past the offices she could come down the east stairwell. That would leave only a quick dash across to the main ward. She'd still get wet, but not sopping. And her dinner might even survive.

The passage up here lay deep in shadow, broken periodically by tall rain-smeared windows casting wavery pools of gray over the floor. As usual, an eternal draft swept along, fluttering her kerchief, gooseflesh rising on her arms. Up ahead a door creaked back and forth in perfect spooky gothic fashion. Where were the ghostly moans? Rattling chains? A spectral lady in white?

As she passed Ard-siúr's office, a horrible, low, rumbly growl lifted the hairs at the back of her neck. The wind chose that moment to kick up, throwing rain like pebbles against the windows even as the growl rose in pitch to a whining, snarling hiss.

She'd had to ask.

The growl culminated in a frenzy of hissing and yowling, the sound of glass breaking, and a definite non-ghoulish, "What the hell—you bit me."

Ard-siúr's cat zipped past her, tearing up the corridor followed by an enormous, looming body, black against the gray and silver shadows behind him.

"Daigh?"

He drew to a startled halt. "Sabrina? Is that you?"

"What are you doing here?" Unease slithered up her

spine. Could he be stealing? There was little in Ard-siúr's office to tempt a thief. The treasures kept there personal, not profitable. Still, there might be enough to tempt a determined thief. And Daigh MacLir was nothing if not determined.

"It's naught to worry you." He sucked the skin between his thumb and forefinger. "In your Ard-siúr's office earlier, I had a flash of memory. A feeling I'd been there before. Something I knew. It sounds like madness, but I had to come back . . ."

"That's wonderful. What was it that triggered the memory?" She stood on tiptoe, peering over his shoulder into the dark room.

He shrugged. "It doesn't matter. When I try to force it, I just come up against a damned hole. No recall. No memories." Pain bit into the angles of his face, straining the muscles in his neck. "It's driving me mad."

"Come. Let's go in together." Before she could think of the wisdom of her actions, she grabbed him by the hand, leading him into the dark office. Lit the nearest taper, the wick sputtering to life with a few whispered words.

Nothing seemed out of place in the cluttered chamber. No obvious signs of disruption or theft. They stood together in the middle of the room, Daigh rigid with tension beside her.

Hopelessness. Misery. Desolation. Confusion.

His feelings hammered Sabrina in a relentless mental assault, a blinding headache shooting down her spine all the way to her toes. She fought to clear a space in her mind amid the cacophony of foreign emotion. Room enough to think of something beyond the slosh of her brain and the spots dancing before her eyes.

"Are you all right?" His black gaze swung to her, the meager light flickering over his stubbled chin, aquiline nose, broad warrior's brow.

Her reply caught in her throat. She sought to tear herself free from his riveting stare, but found herself trapped. Unable to move. Barely able to breathe. For a fraction of a second, she felt a sense of falling. Wind rushing past her ears. Darkness closing in on her, and Daigh's face filling her vision, though not Daigh's face. He was different. But how? She'd no time to decide before he lurched away from her, breaking the dangerous connection between them.

"Sabrina?" he asked. "What's wrong? Answer me."

She recovered, suddenly as tired as if she'd been working in the infirmary for a week on no sleep. Eyes scratchy and stinging, muscles aching, the headache of before dulled to a continuous pounding throb at her temples. She still gripped her dinner tray, the everyday smells of ham and potatoes oddly comforting against the backdrop of darkness and mystery and magic that surrounded this man like an aura. "I don't know. For a moment, I felt as if I might faint. And you were . . . but"—he frowned, his eyes like chips of obsidian in a grim face—". . . never mind. I'm tired and I haven't eaten. That must be it."

Without a word, he took the tray from her. Offered his elbow for support. "Come. It's no use. I remember nothing."

She nodded, allowing him to guide her limp body. Leaning against him was like leaning against a tree. Solid. Unwavering. Though no tree she'd encountered had ever sent a tingly pleasantness buzzing up through her center. Or a warm blush touching her cheeks.

At the door, he paused, leaving her to reenter the office.

Bent to blow out the candle. For a long moment, he stood in the dark, staring round him, shoulders braced.

"Daigh? We should go. You don't belong here."

"You're right, Sabrina," he muttered. "I don't belong here. That's the only thing I *do* know for certain."

Pinching out the tiny flame of her candle, Sabrina closed her diary, having answered none of the questions scurrying through her brain like mice in a cluttered attic. Instead, putting her thoughts to paper only added to the bewildering array of puzzles. Daigh at the heart of every one like the center of some great black storm cloud. Who was he? What event in his past had caused the brutal scarring of his body? Why did he insist he knew her? Why was she suddenly experiencing flashes of another, armored Daigh? What was he doing in Ard-siúr's office? Had he told her the truth about the memory? What was he hiding? And why did she have the eerie premonition that events closed in around them? Dragging her into his orbit whether she willed it or not?

"Jane?" Sabrina whispered. "Are you awake?"

A grumpy mumble floated up out of the dark. "I am now."

"May I ask you a question?"

"You've already asked two. Three's my limit for the middle of the night."

"Have you noticed anything unusual about Daigh MacLir?"

"Everything about the man is unusual. Can I go back to sleep now?"

"No. Listen. Ever since he arrived, I feel as if he holds some importance to me. And I to him."

Jane heaved a sigh. The mattress creaking as she rolled over. "He's got the devil's own looks and watches you with that possessive midnight stare of his. Have you never sensed desire before?"

Sabrina squirmed beneath her blankets, her body awake to sensations she couldn't put a name to. "It's more than that. He breaches all my barriers. No matter what I do, I can't keep him out. And twice now, there's been more. I caught a glimpse of something. A vision. But it vanished so quickly I couldn't tell you what I saw or if I even really saw it. It was Daigh, but it wasn't. He was dressed oddly. From another time. Another age. And then tonight—"

"So you woke me up to tell me you may or may not have seen something or nothing."

"Well, when you put it like that . . ."

"You're tired, Sabrina. You work too much and sleep too little. It's no wonder you're hallucinating. Sleep. You'll feel better in the morning."

Practical, sensible Jane, the gods love her. "And his insistence in thinking he knows me? That he's met me before?"

A grumble that had nothing complimentary about it and then another heavy sigh. "He was pulled from the ocean full of seawater and with no pulse. I'd not trust anything he contends."

"So you think he's mistaken?"

"Have you met him before?"

"No."

"Ever laid eyes on him at all?"

"I don't think so."

"There. Now sleep. You and I have to be up at dawn. Good night, Sabrina."

She lay back, hands behind her head. Stared up into the ceiling, a nagging annoyance tickling the edge of her consciousness before snapping into place. "Of course," she exclaimed. "His eyes. That was the difference. His eyes were green, not black."

"Green, black, or polka dots, go to sleep already," Jane moaned.

Teresa's grouchy voice interrupted from the last bed in the row. "I'll just be happy when Daigh MacLir leaves, and we can all go back to normal."

Sabrina shut her mouth, forcing herself to lie still. Even absent, Daigh played havoc on her senses. What was happening to her? Why was she feeling this way? And why did a return to normal now seem like the last thing she wanted?

five

Sabrina hitched up her skirts. Hiked her bag higher on her shoulder. Placed one booted foot upon the fallen log. Wobbled, arms swinging out to balance herself.

Beneath her, the stream churned against its banks, sending a muddy spill of water racing under the log. Upstream, broken tree limbs piled against an exposed root, caught in a growing dam of branches.

"Aren't we past these juvenile games?" Jane asked.

"Enough out of you, Sister Brigh. Being a grown woman does not necessarily equal being a moldy old bore."

"Very well. But your grown self is going to end up soaked to the skin if you aren't careful," Jane warned.

"But I'm being careful. And so will you." She glanced back over her shoulder where Jane stood, arms folded, disapproval stamped upon her freckled features. "Come. You're not a full sister yet."

Tapping her foot, Jane rendered a skeptical grimace.

"Just." With surefooted agility, Sabrina picked her way

across the slick, knobby log. "Like." Dropped back to the path, sweeping her friend a deep bow. "That."

Heaving a long-suffering sigh, Jane stepped onto the log. "You're completely incorrigible."

Sabrina shot her a grin. "That's the nicest thing anyone's ever said to me."

Rolling her eyes as she bobbled her unsteady way across the log, Jane joined her friend on the path. "It's getting late." She darted a nervous glance at the encroaching wood. "I wish you hadn't taken so long with Mrs. O'Brian. We should have been home by now."

Dusk filtered gray and purple through the trees. Drew long shadows in the spaces between. Branches scraped in the rising wind, clouds flattening low and angry across the sky. Rain and the damp, moldy pungency of earth scenting the air.

"Babies don't exactly wear watches," Sabrina replied. "As it was, it was a very short labor so be happy for small favors. We might have been there all night."

"At least then we'd have been traveling in the morning. It's awfully dark through here."

"Come along. If we hurry we might still be in time for supper." Sabrina grabbed Jane's hand, and the pair hurried along the narrow winding track. Never noticed the strangers until they'd stepped into the path. Others drawing up behind them like specters.

"Sabrina?" Jane's fear trembled her voice.

"It's all right." Sabrina's gaze moved over the filthy, matted features of wild, landless men. "They wouldn't dare harm us."

She lifted her head. Let their greasy, hollow gazes slide over the snow-white kerchief covering her hair. The somber habit. Let them conclude they'd not grown desperate enough to molest a pair of holy women.

A bone-thin man in torn trousers and a shirt that looked as if it had been made for a much stouter figure stepped forward. Sabrina's throat closed at the flash of knife glinting in his fist.

The countryside crawled with gangs of destitute peasants turned off their land. Rumors of the crimes committed by these bandits were a common staple of daily gossip. Ard-siúr warned all to take care upon the roads and travel together when leaving the protection of the demesne. But she and Jane traveled upon *bandraoi* land. The village only a half mile beyond the last field's border. They should have been safe. Should have been out of harm's way.

Her heart thrashed against her ribs, her mouth dry and sticky. Should-have-beens were useless. What she needed were steady nerves and a plan. Any plan. But all her whirling, panicked mind did was curl into a ball and pretend to be dead. Hardly helpful.

"Hand over the bag. And aught else of value," Bone-Thin Man demanded.

From behind, a dirty hand slid around her waist. Drew her close, a hiss of sour breath against her cheek. A barrel's dig against her ribs. "Do as you're told. Isn't that what them women teach ya? Obedience?"

She dragged her bag from her shoulder to the ground. She might be brave, but she wasn't foolish. They could have it, though they'd find little of use among the medicines it contained. "That's all we have."

Jane whimpered, her freckles standing out in splotches against her white face.

A second man closed in. Tipped her quivering chin to

the light, a leering gleam in his eye. With a wrench, he tore the kerchief from her head, hair spilling in a copper wave down her back. "I say we take more than a few measly coins and a trinket or two. Probably starved for a man, they is. Like a good ride? Eh, pet?"

Jane's eyes darted wildly, her body visibly shuddering.

The sight of her friend's panicked terror ignited a spark of defiance in Sabrina. A spark that caught. Flared and sizzled in her like a sputtering candle. She glared. If only the flames heating her blood could shoot straight from her eyes. "Take your hands off her."

The man's slimy attention swung her direction. "Jealous, are ya, pet?" His crude braying laughter touched off the others, who snorted and stamped their approval of his wit. "You'll have yer turn soon enough. There's plenty of us to go round."

"Take care. You address a lady."

The familiar, menacing growl punctured Sabrina's swelling terror. Sent her peering into the dimming gray light for signs of her savior.

It couldn't be. She'd last seen him under the watchful eye of Sister Liotha, raking down straw for the cows. She must be mistaken. But oh, how she hoped she wasn't.

A shadow glided among the trees. Huge. Dark. Silent as a wraith. Never emerging from the overgrowth, but always there. Watching. Waiting.

"Show yourself, friend," Bone-Thin Man shouted, his knife steady, his eyes narrow and searching.

"Let the women go. Take yourselves off." Clipped, battle-edged tones. A quiet confidence, so different from the nervy bravado of the men.

The bandit scoffed. Spat in the dirt. "I'll not be takin'

orders from a coward what hides in the bushes like vermin. And if you won't reveal yourself, I'll have my men flush you out. Then we'll see what's what. And who's givin' the orders."

He motioned at his comrades, who fanned out into the shrubbery. Two dropping back. One beating aside the undergrowth with the barrel of a rusty blunderbuss. Jane's tormentor twitched his reluctance, but released her to crash into the bracken alongside his compatriots.

Slimy kept a firm warning hold on Sabrina, though his attention was all for the woods.

Dusk deepened, the heavy gray fading into night. Trees black and clawing against the sky. Cold rain spattering through the branches. Calls from man to man all that broke the unnatural stillness of the scene.

Suddenly, a flock of chattering starlings rose in a whirr of wings as a scream ripped the silence. Ended just as abruptly.

"Abe?" Bone-Thin Man jerked one way then another, hunting the wood. His knife whipping the air. "Kelly!"

A crash of branches. A grunt and whoof of spent breath. No answer.

The remaining men crowded closer together like a herd sensing danger.

Slimy wrenched Sabrina close. His pistol's barrel chilling her neck. "Come out or the sister gets hers! Call him, Sister. Tell him I'm meaning business."

She opened her mouth. Squeaked. Swallowed and tried again. "Come . . . come out. Please, Daigh."

"Yes, come out, Daigh," he mocked in a sneer that turned her stomach. "Please."

"As you will." An enormous, looming shadow detached

itself from the darkness like some creature from the deepest *Unseelie* abyss. Eyes, hellish pits in a grim face. A body rippling with raw magic. This wasn't Daigh. This was some horrible, distorted version of him. He bestrode the roadway not like a bewildered shipwreck victim, but like a warrior who knew his business. Knew it and enjoyed it.

"Let them go." His quiet command holding more violence than any shouting threat could. And even unarmed, danger simmered in the air around him. "Or join your friends."

The men's focus was all on Daigh for the moment. She'd not get a better chance. "Run, Jane," Sabrina hissed. "Run for help."

Jane moaned her terror but did as instructed. Darting beneath the cursing reach of Slimy. Swerving past Daigh as if he were the devil himself. None stopped her. All eyes riveted to the monstrous, grim-featured goliath blocking the path.

The remaining ruffians closed ranks to meet this intruder, only Slimy staying back. Holding Sabrina in front of him like a shield.

Daigh's gaze swung over the group. Settled on her, the flicker of some lost emotion surfacing in the empty hollows of his eyes.

The world wavered and spun, the path dropping from under her, the trees bleeding into a haze of spring white and green. As she watched, the flick of a fur-lined cloak and a sword's silver edge overlapped Daigh's coarse linen and leather. She blinked, the vision vanishing as Daigh's rage slammed at the base of her skull. Hot. Terrible.

She grimaced at the headache now clamping her brain. And though he seemed in complete control of the situation, she got the sense Daigh held to sanity by the thinnest of threads. And that—unlikely as it sounded—he looked to her for rescue.

The alien, probing presence pounded against his brain. Some undefined evil slithered along his nerves. His vision filled with a crackling, pulsing light. A wash of frozen fire behind which everything hovered in shades of nightmare.

Through the haze of his own madness, he felt the men shift, a grumble like distant thunder as they took his measure. Adjusted their attack. He allowed them their fill. It would avail them nothing, though how he knew this was lost to him like so much else.

At some invisible signal, a man struck from the trees. A knife thrust at his side. Scoring his ribs.

Cursing, he caught his attacker's wrist. Bones grinding under his fingers. The man's scream ripping through the last barrier between conscious thought and animal instinct.

A turbulent, endless void warped him like a sword upon the smithy's anvil. Heart beating with the hammer's clang. Reshaping him into something unnatural. Unstoppable. Unheeding of pain or fear or loss. Knowing only killing. Only hate. Only death.

The man's groaning agony seemed to break the standoff. The rest flung themselves forward like a pack of snarling, snapping dogs scenting rabid prey.

He reacted without thought. Without reason. Muscles stretched and rippled beneath his skin. Blood ran like acid through narrowed veins. Hazed his vision in scarlet hellfire.

The assault faltered as the dead and dying sprawled in tumbled broken heaps. At one point, he found himself clutching a rusty, pitted dagger, hot and dripping with his own blood. He flipped it in his hand. Gripped the handle. Embedded it in the stomach of a man charging him in a screaming bull-rush.

Shouts filtered through the roar in his ears, but he ignored them. They shouted a name that meant nothing to him. His true identity ground to dust among the scattered fragments of his injured mind.

He wasn't Daigh. He wasn't a man.

He was death undone.

Sabrina watched in growing horror. Held her breath for the moment when Daigh hesitated. Faltered. Weakened. And the remaining men would close in for the kill.

But it never came. Every moment seemed to strengthen his killer cunning, the unearthly sixth sense that kept him alert and alive beneath the onslaught. Until those remaining fled the chaos. Faded into the shielding twilight. Were replaced by the whispering shush of skirts upon the ground. The murmur of worried fearful voices as the sisters approached.

Slimy gripped her in an ever-increasing stranglehold, his elbow clamped around her throat. Cutting her air until pinpricks spotted her vision and her lungs cramped with effort. He jerked at each loss, his curses loud and increasingly panicked. Clutching Sabrina as the last buffer between Daigh and imminent death.

"I'll kill her."

Harsh words pierced the fog of his madness. A blood-freezing sight met Daigh's hazy vision.

Sabrina caught around the neck, a pistol jammed beneath her breast.

He paused, blood-soaked. Chest heaving as his lungs fought for air. Met the man's stare, each seeing murder in the other's eyes.

Actions slowed to infinity. A weapon leveled at his chest. The explosion of sound and flame. Followed immediately by a punch to the chest. Blood hot and streaming from the wound. The sudden weight of drugged limbs.

Lurching to his knees, he concentrated his aim. Let his dagger fly. Watched with ruthless satisfaction as it found its intended target.

The brigand dragged at Sabrina's skirts as he fell. Dead as he hit the ground.

She screamed.

And oblivion swallowed him.

"What was he doing out here?"

"Lambing time. Sent him to check on the ewes."

"Have you ever seen the like?"

"Mad. He's mad. Dangerous. Summon the authorities."

"Saved Jane. Sabrina. A hero."

The clucking worried babble of the *bandraoi*. The hum of nervous confusion. The shush of heavy skirts and cloaks as they moved among the carnage.

Sabrina knelt beside Daigh, rifling among her bag as if the potions and cures she carried could stanch the blood or halt the ebbing life beneath her hand. Pain bit deep lines into the gray pallor of his face. Blue tinted his lips. No human medicines would avail him now. But if she delved within the magic of her race, she might buy him time if not survival.

She tore the remnants of his shirt open. Laid bare the shredded and bloody flesh. Swallowed the bile clawing its way up her throat. Focused instead on the mage energy rising like a tide within her. The texture and quality and weight of the power. Using what she'd learned from Sister Ainnir to shape its flow. Hone it. Sharpen it to scalpel brilliance.

"Sabrina?"

She met his pain-clouded gaze with a smile of false reassurance.

"It's not needed," he explained through clenched teeth.

"Don't talk," she comforted. "You'll be all right. I can . . ."

A shadow loomed over her. The rustle of skirts. Breathing heavy and frantic.

Daigh's gaze moved beyond her. "Tell her. You understand."

Sabrina threw a confused look over her shoulder. Ard-siúr. Sister Ainnir. Both frowning. Both frightened.

"He's right, Sabrina," Ard-siúr intoned. "Your gifts are not necessary."

"But . . ." She clamped down on her fear. Focused instead on the blood. The gore. Sticky. Black. A stench of murder and vicious death rising in fetid waves.

Daigh shuddered, his muscles leaping in spasms. His breath quick and sharp and painful. Pupils dilated and unseeing.

But no wounds.

Nothing but puckered pink flesh marring the hard-packed ridges of his stomach. The broad expanse of his chest.

"He's . . ." Her hands curled to claws, the nails digging into her palms. Unable to shake the image of a man reveling in the battle. Drunk on mayhem. Lost to everything but killing. "It makes no sense. He was shot. I saw it." She searched the faces of the *bandraoi*. "Why? How?"

"That would be a question for Mr. MacLir." Ard-siúr's attention never left the man lying upon the ground in his own spilled blood.

He shook his head. Spoke through chattering teeth. As horrified as any of them. "I don't know. I can't remember."

Six

"Rapid healing from lesser injuries, I've seen. But never from a killing wound. Never to such an extent and so quickly." Sister Ainnir shook her head as she paced the room with slow, arthritic steps, hands clasped behind her back. "I'd say it was impossible did I not see it with my own eyes."

"It's unfortunate you were not the only one among us to witness it. Already the order's abuzz with lurid stories of our mysterious guest." Ard-siúr followed Sister Ainnir's painful perambulations from her desk, face a study of thoughtful worry as she stroked the fat, purring tabby.

Sabrina huddled in her corner seat, mind swirling with questions and possibilities. None of them sensible. All of them the stuff of wild, outrageous fantasies.

Was Daigh true *Fey*? That would explain his apparent invincibility. The crushing, impenetrability of his stare. The strength contained within a titan's frame. But a tiny voice persisted in denying that explanation. Pushed her to look elsewhere for answers. It was the same irritating voice whispering to her in the bleak hours of night, warning her Daigh's arrival was not coincidence. He'd been brought here for a purpose. And if she could only puzzle out the bizarre bond they shared, all the other answers would follow like tumbling dominoes.

"So do we follow Sister Brigh's stern counsel and send him on his way?"

"It would seem the most prudent course."

Ard-siúr and Sister Ainnir's back-and-forth sounded as a dull bass line to her own noisy thoughts.

If not *Fey*, what? No normal human could survive a pistol shot square to the chest. Or the myriad dagger cuts spilling a river of blood she relived in nauseating crimson detail every time she closed her eyes. But if he wasn't *Fey* and wasn't human, what did that leave?

"Or would it be wiser to keep him close while we seek to unravel what nature of man he is?" Ard-siúr continued with her slow deliberation.

Sabrina picked at the dried blood remaining beneath her nails despite a hasty scrubbing. Skin still crawling with the feel of the bandit's hand at her throat. The stench of his unwashed body souring her nose. Daigh had saved her. He'd been her knight-errant. Her champion. Could she remain silent while others argued out his fate? Or should she risk speaking out?

She lifted her head. Searched out Ard-siúr's cool, appraising eyes. "You can't send him away," she decreed.

Sister Ainnir regarded her with shock, as if she were a piece of furniture sprung to life. Or a normally submissive apprentice gaining will and voice.

Ard-siúr's pale brows rose to be lost in her kerchief. "You have something to say, Sabrina?"

Now that she'd become their focus, she lost the certainty of her own conviction. Who was she to tell Ard-siúr what to do? What did she know? It was her larking about that had resulted in her and Jane being caught in the ambush.

"I . . . that is, he . . . we can't just . . . that is after . . ." Her words trailed off as she deflated beneath their level, questing stares, returning to the childhood comfort of silence.

Sister Ainnir shook her off like a bothersome fly. Resumed her worried pacing. But Ard-siúr's gaze never faltered. She caught Sabrina in a disconcerting look that seemed to see right through her to the wall behind. "Go on. If you have something to add to the discussion, voice it now."

Courage surfaced through an icy layer of nervousness. Now that the urge to speak her opinion had come, it slid over her like a glove on a hand. "No matter who or what he is, he didn't abandon me. I can't abandon him." Hurried to amend. "We can't abandon him."

Ard-siúr's smile felt like sun through clouds. She nodded. "Well spoken, Sabrina. And though Mr. MacLir's body remains inviolate, I am as unclear about his mind. His is an odd tangle of impossibilities that makes me question my scrying's accuracy. As a result, I believe keeping him within our care would be best."

As if only waiting on Ard-siúr's official word, Sister Ainnir immediately shifted focus. "Perhaps a consult of the texts that deal with this type of magic," she agreed eagerly. "Sister Ursula would know where best to search."

"A good thought. And I have my own sources who may be able to guide us in our understanding."

Absorbed with their own planning, they turned their attention from Sabrina.

Each passing moment spiraled her deeper into an unknown, unnamed fear shredding her insides. Tugging her to her feet. This was wrong. All wrong. Daigh needed her. He looked to her for help. Not them. Her. She sensed the call more strongly each moment. As if the gods guided her thoughts.

She scrambled out of her chair, an immediate need to escape pressing against her heart. Fresh air. Rain upon her face. A scrubbing of his blood off her skin. If only she could cleanse the endless well of his horrified gaze from her mind. His pounding dread from her soul.

"Sabrina." Ard-siúr's sharp voice, catching Sabrina short.

"Ma'am?"

"Remember. A wounded animal can be unpredictable. Trapped, he can become deadly." Her stare drew inward on some scene invisible to Sabrina, her face falling into care-worn lines. "Daigh MacLir is both."

He collapsed on his pallet, head in hands. Body braced against a flash of pain that struck him like the slam of an axe between the eyes.

A man's face. Rage burning like hellfire in his gold-brown eyes. His mouth open on a scream of hate.

The image filled every corner of Daigh's mind until his brain threatened to spill out his ears and sickness churned his gut. Twisted him into so many knots it left him retching his supper into the slops jar.

Instantly the coiling nightmare awareness he'd experienced in the woods slid up out of the darkest parts of his consciousness. He sensed it waiting upon the far side of that vast empty chasm of memory. Seeking entry. Enjoying his anguish.

Anger touched him like spark from a flint. Burned up through him in a funeral pyre conflagration. Muscles constricted on a destructive emotional whirlpool, his vision clouding as the man's enraged features receded to a crimson fog blanketing and thick as the rain clouds outside.

A hand upon his shoulder threw Daigh to his feet in an instinctual defensive move that swung him around, one arm dragging the intruder close. Another locking around their neck, windpipe crushed in the crook of his elbow.

A gurgling plea chased the red from his eyes. Pulled him back from the brink. The enemy beneath his hold dissolved into a gray-gowned woman, kerchief dangling, hair falling in a cascade of lost pins over thin, trembling shoulders.

He released her with a broken oath. Stumbled back to fall heavy on his pallet. "Gods, forgive me."

Sabrina stood shaking in the far corner of the stillroom, her face white as the kerchief she threaded through unsteady fingers. "I startled you. I . . . you didn't mean to hurt me."

He flexed his hands. The scars incised into his palms, a sickening reminder that what he didn't know about himself might kill. "Are you sure of that?"

He looked up to see her straighten, certainty asserting itself. Bright steel entering a gaze that until now had always remained petal soft. "You didn't mean to harm me," she said again.

Whom did she seek to convince?

Exhaustion rushed in to replace the earlier maelstrom as

if he carried the weight of centuries upon his back. "You were in the woods. You saw what happened, Sabrina. By rights I should be dead."

The men on the beach. The knife. The tearing, clutching hands. It became clearer.

"This isn't the first time it's happened."

"There's an explanation. You'll see." She knelt to gather up pieces of broken crockery; less fortunate victims of his attack, giving him a perfect view of the sleek spill of gilded brown hair, the arch of her neck where the fragile bones moved beneath skin flushed pink.

Heat that had nothing of anger about it sparked down leaden limbs. Flashed across a gulf between past and present. Between a dim vision of this woman laughing up at him amid a wrinkled heap of blankets and another more tactile impression of a body sweet and taut molded to his chest. Breathing quick and fast. Her fragrance clean and fresh and holding none of the grave about it; important to him though he'd no idea why.

She sucked in a sharp breath, her hand closing on a broken shard, a stinging between her fingers. Her body swayed as if she might faint.

"Sabrina?" he spoke roughly through a throat scratchy and hoarse with his own hesitation. Took her under the arm to steady her.

She flinched before allowing him to assist her. But even then, she seemed off-balance and confused.

"Your hand," he said, turning her palm up to examine the narrow cut in the flesh between thumb and finger.

"It's nothing." She sucked away the thin line of blood before shoving her hand into her apron pocket.

"Are you unwell?" he asked.

She gave a shrug and a confused smile. "A little light-headed. No supper. I wasn't hungry."

She studied him as if she searched for something in his face, and he met her clear gaze head-on. Stars glowed in the blue depths of her eyes. Points of light holding at bay a midnight void that seemed to suck him always downward. He held her gaze as if he gripped a cliff edge. Drew himself up to stand above her, her face tilted to meet him.

She barely reached as high as his collarbone, and his hands could span her tiny waist, but she never once regarded him with fear or hesitation. As if she read beyond the menacing strength of his body and the violence lurking in his mind.

"So much for the pitcher of water I brought you."

He tipped her chin. Swam in that star-shot sea of blue. Sensed her curious excitement in the hesitant parting of her lips, the slight sway of her body toward him. If he kissed her, she'd respond. It wouldn't take more than moments to have her answering his need with her own.

Caressing the line of her jaw, the column of her throat, he felt her mounting anticipation. A passion bound but not broken by the order's constraints.

He bent to brush his lips against hers. She closed her eyes, fluttering black lashes shadowing the rose of her cheeks. One shy hand touched his chest. Fingers spread against the jump of muscles beneath his skin.

And with an earth-rocking explosion that tore through him with the force of a gunshot, present exploded into past.

The coiled serpent freed itself. Shattered his control, bringing with it a bowel-knifing ferocity. The man's face returned. Pitiless. Twisted in frenzied, ruthless hate. A sword cut the air. Its downward thrust punching through Daigh's flesh with screaming agony. And again. The blade sending ice cascading along his veins. And an answering ferocity that singed his heart.

He shoved her away, falling onto the pallet, head on fire. Body numb. Struggling against the memory while battling the menacing presence that seemed bent on its own dark purpose. It wanted him. But for what?

"Oh gods, let me help you." She knelt at his side, taking hold of his hand, but he shook her off. Unable to endure the transformation of her touch from desire to sympathy.

"Leave me."

Hurt clouded her clear blue gaze.

"If you know what's good for you, you'll get out." He hardened his heart. Not difficult while his body remained caught in this malignant storm. Retching, he drew himself into a fetal ball, shuddering against the paroxysms raking him like a fusillade.

"I'll get Sister Ainnir."

He scrubbed the back of his hand across his mouth. "You'll get no one. You'll tell no one. Do you hear me?"

Despite his humiliation and fear, his tone still carried the bite of command.

She nodded slowly as she groped for the door handle. "You won't harm me, Daigh. I know that for truth. No matter what Ard-siúr says."

So, she'd been warned away from him? Sorrow touched the frozen place in him, and he almost wished he never remembered. That his past could be shed like an outgrown skin. He could become someone new. Someone honorable. Someone worthy of Sabrina's trust.

Sabrina stumbled into night's damp, bone-chilling fog. Steadied herself against a column as she inhaled long, dragging gulps, letting the cold air settle thoughts ricocheting from heart-thundering desire to jagged alarm, hitting every emotion in between.

Her head swam, making her woozy and sick. Just as it had done moments earlier when she'd bent to the water pitcher and experienced diamond-clear images of her and Daigh together—she squirmed—doing things she had never done. Not with Daigh. Not with any man. It had been so real. An instant in time but she'd reveled in his hands upon her skin, welcomed the light of desire in his eyes, heard the gasp of her own breath as he entered her.

Had he hypnotized her? Cast some spell of seduction? Did that explain the strange flashes and queer feelings he generated? Or was she merely fishing for excuses to justify her own hoydenish behavior? She'd almost let him kiss her. Wanted him to kiss her. Badly.

Thoughts whirled and spun in an endless tangled loop. Her stomach lurched as her vision clouded and burst with odd spearing lights and colors. Black. Gold. Red. Purple.

The fog thickened, muffling sound, erasing everything around her, including the column she leaned against. She clung to it, trying not to faint, hoping the air would clear her head, but the sweet tang of wet leaves and wood smoke filled her nose.

As the fog dissipated, she stood in a clearing, arms wrapped about a huge moss-covered tree trunk, branches lifting away into the sky to mix with branches from hundreds and thousands of other trees as massive as this oak. A path wound off to her left, and she heard water passing over stones, the jingle of harness from a tethered horse. A man emerged into the dappled light. Daigh. Though he carried himself with an easy stride, unlike his usual tension-filled prowling.

She stepped forward into his embrace, his arms encircling her. His breath warm against her cheek. And it happened. The kiss she'd been waiting for. Her stomach leapt into her throat. He bent and . . .

A blast of air stung her face. An icy rain chilled her skin. She stood alone. In the dark. The courtyard, rather than the primeval forest, rising around her. The fog had thinned to streamers of heavy mist, leaving her shivering and afraid, yet aching with a unexpected yearning to return to that forest glen.

Was Daigh conjuring these visions? Was she?

She looked to the lighted windows of Ard-siúr's office. Nearly called out for help. She needed Sister Ainnir. Ard-siúr. Someone older and wiser and more experienced. But Daigh had begged her silence. Done more than beg. He'd demanded it. And no wonder. They already questioned his continued stay among them. Any more bizarre behavior and he'd be sent away.

She should heed Ard-siúr's warning. That was the sensible thing to do. The safe thing to do.

She frowned, decision hardening to cool purpose.

But it was not the right thing to do.

Her body stiffened as if meeting an invisible challenge. She wouldn't betray Daigh. Not yet. Not now. Not until she understood what the devil was happening.

A blanket drawn up over his shuddering shoulders. Words washing over his consciousness like a soothing draught. Clear. Melodious. Octaves purring up and down in a mantra, easing the tight bands across his back, the aching bowels where not even water rested easily.

He'd not scared her away. She'd returned. Gazed upon him with an incandescent smile that warmed a heart long frosted over. Challenged the darkness invading his soul to sit beside him. Whisper to him. Used her magic to lull him into a sleep untroubled by nightmares.

A glimpse of thick, unbroken forest speared by shafts of golden light. Gilding her hair. Sparkling in her blue eyes. Light hands cooling the raging fever heat of his body. He used these to fight the presence balanced startled and uncertain at the edge of his awareness.

"Sabrina." He threaded his fingers with hers. Gripped her hand as if she might vanish with his other dreams.

She answered, but his name upon her lips tangled in the meeting rush of sleep. He heard nothing more.

Seven

"Come, Sister Clea. It's long past the time when you should be asleep."

Sabrina took the frail woman's shoulders. Tried guiding her back to the bed at the end of the row while projecting the warmth of a soft bed. The snuggly security of heavy quilts. The delight at being safe and protected while outside the weather howled.

"I've got to find Paul," Sister Clea whined. "Where's Paul? Mother said he'd be home by the end of the summer." She dug in her heels. Tried twisting out of Sabrina's grasp. "I want Paul. He promised to be back by my birthday."

"Shhh. You'll wake the others." Shuttered lamps at each end of the room sent long shafts of wavery light across the floor. Picked out the few filled beds. Blankets heaped against damp from the rain tapping at the windows.

Sister Clea kept up her insistence. "But he said he'd be back. Said to meet him at the wharf, and he'd bring me a gift."

An unbidden image of Brendan, grim-faced and pale, assuring Sabrina he'd return in a month at the latest pushed its way into her sleep-deprived mind. He'd ridden out that same afternoon. The pain of his departure swallowed all too soon in the monumental agony of her father's murder. Her mother's death. If only she'd known it would be the last time she'd see her brother, she would have parted with him differently. No sulking. No cold shoulder. No standing like a statue in the circle of his farewell embrace. Those last horrible moments still haunted her.

"I'm sure Paul will be home soon," Sabrina comforted.

But he wouldn't.

Her brother would never return to the sister who still mourned him.

"I want Paul. He said he'd come. It's my birthday, and he promised me." Sister Clea writhed in Sabrina's arms, her voice growing frantic, her actions frenzied. Not even the strength in Sabrina's empathic link enough to calm the confused old woman.

"I'm home, lass. Just as I promised."

A shadow stretched over Sabrina's shoulder. Flickered in the uneven light like a risen spirit.

Her heart slammed into her throat, and she wheeled around to find herself face to chest with Daigh. Untucked shirt. Bare feet. A day's growth of stubble darking his chin. Disconcerting in the extreme, but not, thankfully, the seaweed-soaked corpse she'd half expected.

"Paul?" Sister Clea's reedy voice piped with sudden excitement, her wild gyrations subsiding as she peered with rheumy eyes at his shadow-hidden features. "Is that you?" One birdlike hand reached up. Her lips curved in a toothless smile. "It is you. I knew you'd come." She sighed, leaning into his arm. Letting him guide her back to bed. "I've been waiting so, so long, Paul. It was naughty of you to stay away."

"I tried coming home to you, lass, but . . ." His gaze passed over the hunched old woman to settle on Sabrina. "In the end, it was impossible."

A prickly buzz shimmied up her spine like the perfect struck note of a tuning fork. The air shifting and shimmering with a million darting lights.

"But now I'm back . . ." Daigh's voice came deep and echoing as if spoken through water. "For you."

"You'll stay this time?" Sister Clea asked, her girlish joy infectious. "For good?"

He offered a slow, solemn nod, though whether directed at Clea or Sabrina she couldn't be certain.

The air turned hot and thick and humid despite the November rain outside. Sabrina tried catching her breath, but her lungs felt squashy. Vertigo had the room tipping and falling, dinner rising into her throat. Lamplight shivered and streaked. Before she could call out, the room fell away, and she stood within the circle of Daigh's embrace. Tears hot upon her cheeks. His heart beating steady beneath her ear.

He stepped out of her arms. Gave her an awkward grin. One last kiss. "I'll be back, *cariad.* I promise. Your worries are for nothing."

Her skin prickled over muscles that suddenly seemed made of water. A familiar voice called to her. And the room collapsed into a pair of mesmerizing, forever eyes.

"Better?"

From flat on her back, Sabrina blinked up into Daigh's worried face. Presented an embarrassed smile as answer.

"I'll take that as yes."

She struggled to sit, though it took a great deal more effort than she'd imagined it would. She cradled her wobbly head in her hands. "How long?"

"A minute or two. Your face went blank just before you collapsed."

Taking the cup he held out to her, she swung her legs over the side of the bed. Swished the water around in her mouth, hoping to alleviate the fuzziness of her tongue as if she'd swallowed a ball of yarn. Her head throbbed all the way down to her toes, her vision splashed with color and light, and an ache in her heart as if she'd been stabbed.

"Sister Clea?" She peered through the blinding starbursts, the room still rolling uncomfortably.

"Asleep. Put to bed with a drink of water and a peck on the forehead like a good brother ought." He took back the cup. Refilled it. Set it on a nearby table. Such homey actions seemed at odds from a man who'd scythed his way through a gang of thieves like death himself.

"It was kind of you to pretend for her."

"I didn't do it for her."

"Oh," she breathed, a trembling beginning low in her stomach that had nothing of sickness about it.

Massaging her temples, she closed her eyes. Reclaimed a tenuous grip. When she reopened them, her sight at least seemed less volatile. The rest of her remained frustratingly unstable as if the quivery, fluttery butterflies had overtaken every part of her body.

What had she seen in those last seconds? Another unexplained imagining? Had it been a piece of Daigh's life superimposed on her mind? Had she somehow tapped more than emotion? Called forth an actual memory? Perhaps these visions weren't purposeful at all on Daigh's part. No spell, but merely her mind's momentary faltering. A breach through which Daigh's past rushed in.

She nervously gnawed the edge of one fingernail. Rubbed at her forehead as if she might bring back the already fading vision. Her stomach danced a queasy jig that had her reaching again for the water. She let the cool tang ease her parched throat. "I don't usually faint like that. It must have been something I ate or perhaps the late hour—"

He shrugged deeper into the shadows. "You don't have to explain, Sabrina."

"I just didn't want you to think that—"

"You might be less than strong? I don't. You've a streak in you that would put many a battle-hardened warrior to shame."

"A warrior like you?"

A muscle jumped in that iron jaw of his, his body drawing into itself until barely a breath stirred him. "I can't deny it. Not after . . ." He gave a queer shrug as if trying to shake free of this newfound knowledge of himself. An apologetic dip of his head.

A mannerism she recognized. She'd seen it only moments earlier.

In her mind.

The two of them. A tearful parting. And that same sheepish awkwardness.

"I lied to you, Daigh."

He cocked a brow in question.

"I didn't swoon because of what I ate. It was because of what I saw. A vision, but with more substance. More like a memory. Your memory. But I was there with you. How could that be?"

"I know no more than you." He folded his arms across his chest with studied composure, but his eagerness knifed the air. Prickled against her brain like static electricity. "Go on."

"The vision—it was you I saw," she blurted, the ache in her heart returned and spreading. Her throat sore and scratchy. Eyes hot with unshed tears. "You promised me you'd be back."

Stark misery stamped his features. As if every word she spoke bore the agony of a hammer blow. He took her by the elbows. Dragged her roughly to her feet so they stood inches apart. His gaze boring a hole through her. "Back from where? What did you see? Tell me everything."

"You told me I worried over nothing. You promised you'd return."

His pupils dilated as his grip crushed. Chest heaving. Voice ragged. "I didn't return. Couldn't."

"Why not?" The air felt charged with invisible eavesdroppers. The room's meager light holding them in a circle of solitude. A time out of time. "Why didn't you keep your promise?"

His eyes seemed to reflect back at her with a bonfire glow as he struggled to answer. "I tried. But on the road"—he took a deep shaky breath—"there was an ambush. Too many of them." He shuddered, his face a sickly gray. "I remember blood. And the mud as I fell."

The long stare shrank to the space separating them as if he suddenly realized he held her. The questions she'd asked. The answers he'd given.

She tipped her head back, heart racing, shivers jolting along her nerves. The fireworks returned. Flares of light and heat arcing between them. Mage energy dancing across the surface of her skin. Raw. Wild. Nothing like the gentle, meditative flow emitted by the priestesses. This held a snarling, rabid rage. Chained, but always hunting. Always seeking escape.

She drowned in the untamed energy. Felt herself swamped within Daigh's powers.

"You," he murmured. "I was right. You were there. I remember."

"No," she countered, hands splayed against his immovable chest as if to push him away. But pushing him away was the last thing she wanted. She wanted him closer. Like a moth drawn to a flame, she felt an inescapable pull. A deadly attraction.

Crushing his mouth to hers, he backed against the wall, his body solid against hers. Only his heart's wild beating an indication he felt the same tumult of emotion.

She reached under his shirt. Skimmed the line of his torso. The ridges of scars rough beneath her fingers.

He groaned, his tongue teasing her lips apart. Sliding within. Dropping the bottom out of her world with the way it probed and retreated. A soldier seeking an enemy's weakness.

She opened to him. Couldn't help it. Her mind had divorced itself from her body. Thought seemed irrelevant. She was all about the senses. His skin's blazing heat. The warm wine taste on his tongue. A clean soap and man scent tickling her nose. His harsh, quick inhalations in response to her every caress.

He pulled free her kerchief. Loosed her hair from its confining combs so that it spilled across her shoulders. Threaded his hands through it, sending a shiver racing through her as he backed her toward the bed.

She dropped heavily onto the mattress, and he knelt at her feet like a knight from a tale, his eyes locked with hers, his intentions burning in the darkest reaches of his sin-black gaze. Turning her to jelly.

A door opened at the far end of the room, sending a chilly draft whistling through the room. The candle guttered and went out. The moment broken.

Daigh rose from his knees, scrubbing the heels of his hands against his eyes. Lines bit into the corners of his mouth. The lamplight creating frightening ghostly hollows in his face.

"It *was* you in my dream. I'm not mistaken," he hissed accusingly. "Why do you pretend as if you don't know who I am?"

She glanced toward the door, but whoever had interrupted them had turned left toward the stairs.

"Answer me, Sabrina." He stepped menacingly forward, his brows drawn into a scowl, his jaw set.

How did one go from blazing hot to arctic cold within a heartbeat? She hugged her body, drawing her knees up. "I'm not pretending. I swear. I don't know why you remember me. I don't know you. I never saw you before two weeks ago. Honestly."

He flexed his hands. Stiff-legged and shoulders set as if meeting his fate head-on. "But you and I . . . and the promise. That was real. How can I remember something that didn't happen?"

"I don't know. But we'll only figure out the answer together. Of that, I'm sure."

He seemed to consider this, his face losing some of its horrible ferocity. "Why take such a risk for a man you don't know?"

"It has as much to do with me as you." She rubbed a

hand over her forehead as if wiping away the heartbreaking image of their final parting. "I'm the one having visions of the two of us that never happened."

Daigh speared her with a grim stare. "Oh, they're real, Sabrina. I remember."

She swallowed back a whimper of panic. Because she knew he told the truth. Because she remembered too.

Daigh opened his eyes on a whisper of breeze through his room. A shift in air pressure. A sound that should be silence. Rising, he dragged a shirt over his head. Pulled his boots on. Lifted the latch on his door, cracking it slowly.

The passage was empty, but for the tangle of overlapping shadows. Silent but for a steady drip of water.

Not Sabrina.

She'd fled him hours earlier. The anguish in her eyes cutting into the icy fist of his heart. He'd let her go despite his questions. And his need. But he refused to ignore either for long. Not when she traversed the mysterious junction of past and present. His key to understanding both.

The same instinct that pulled him alert and out of bed had him padding silently down the passage and into the main ward of the hospital. Sister Clea remained asleep. Nothing and no one out of place.

Outside, rain pricked his exposed skin like claws. Peering into the night, he scanned the courtyard. The locked gate. Shuttered barns and storehouses. Dark windows of the buildings opposite.

Somewhere a door slammed in the wind. A gutter rattled. Animals shifted upon their bedding. All normal night sounds. Nothing that should have touched off his wary soldier sense.

A sister unable to sleep. A servant rising to stoke a fire. No more than that, surely.

Still he kept watch. Waited for the telltale slipup that would reveal the intruder.

There. A latch falling. A furtive step. A light glinting then dying in a doorway. He hadn't imagined it. Across the way in the main building.

The plaguing sense of an unseen force pushing against his brain sank through him. He accepted its seeking, slithering presence. Let it glide between the walls of his mind. Easier than struggling and less painful. It also allowed him to hold onto the shreds of a fast diminishing illusion of control.

Hunching his shoulders, he stepped out of the shelter of the cloister. Picked his way through the concealing gloom. The order's rectory stood imposing and grim. Narrow, arched, staring windows. A shallow set of steps to a double door.

He bypassed the main entrance. The sounds he'd heard had come from the side. A less conspicuous entrance.

As he slid inside, he felt the stir of air from an upper corridor. A muffled breath. Whoever he followed held a knowledge of stealth. Yet it gained him little. Daigh was better. Quiet and inescapable as a tomb.

At the top of the steps, he followed the weak light of a shielded taper down a wide corridor.

Ard-siúr's office lay in this direction.

Anger writhed and curled with needle-sharpness along his nerves. Burned black and wicked with his blood. Buried itself so deep within him, he could no longer be sure where he ended and the presence began. The strength of one augmenting the other until they became one.

Stalking the last few yards to the door to Ard-siúr's office, he slid into the antechamber, alive to any waiting danger. Bookshelves. A glass-fronted highboy. A desk holding an open ledger. A stack of books. A set of chairs lined like sentinels against the far wall. An inner door, standing cracked. A sliver of pale light pointing like a dagger at his feet.

Tapping the inner door wider, he stepped into the narrow breach. Barely dodged the downward plunge of a heavy vessel aimed at his head. Took the makeshift weapon on his shoulder, numbing pins and needles shooting down his arm. He swung into the room, escaping a second attempt to brain him.

The figure remained impossible to distinguish from the thick cluster of shadows. A twisting slick of ghostly movement that had Daigh sucking wind from a punch to the gut. Brought him to his knees with a chop to the neck.

He shook his head in an attempt to clear it. Let the vicious lick of flame torching his body ignite the predator in him. His vision contracted onto a man. Dark. Lean. Dressed in unrelieved black, but for the silver flash of a knife. It swept at Daigh's throat. Sliced a deep wound across the palm of the hand he threw up to deflect the blow.

Unfolding from the floor with slow deliberation, he speared the attacker with a furious glare. The dagger arced a second time. Stung Daigh across the ribs. And again—this time aimed at his stomach.

He threw himself to the side but not in time.

The dagger pierced his flesh with a hot agony. Tore through muscles. Tendons. Ended buried hilt-deep and quivering against a rib. Daigh opened his mouth on a scream. Choked it back until his cry became only a muffled, anguished moan.

This was his hunt. The intruder his quarry. He'd not alert the *bandraoi*. Not until he understood the danger.

The man smiled, his eyes wide with triumph. Turning from Daigh's still crumpled body, he relit his candle stub. Worked in a methodical inch-by-inch search, starting at the shelves to the right of the door.

Ignoring Daigh.

Bad idea.

Wounds would slow but not stop the relentless hammer of his battle prowess. Death would be turned aside.

He wrapped a hand around the blood-slicked dagger. Yanked it free, almost passing out from the pain. His whole body tremored until he grit his teeth against the spasms ripping through him. Squeezing his eyes shut, he counted to one hundred slowly. Opened them to another freshly healed scar crisscrossing his torso. A road map through hell and back.

He traced the puckered ridge of skin with the tip of one finger. Experienced a tingly icy numbness, but beyond that no lasting effects from a wound that should have killed him.

The man paused at the tapestry hanging behind Ardsiúr's desk—figures bearing a litter toward an open tomb. Fingered the heavy cloth for a moment before wrenching it from the wall with a shrug and a grunt of success. Shoved it into a waiting satchel.

This was Daigh's cue. He rose like the walking dead, the blood-sticky dagger gripped in one trembling fist. His body stretched taut as a bowstring, every nerve screaming. "You should make certain of your kills."

The man froze in a pose of astonishment mixed with terror. "How?" he breathed. "I saw"—his eyes flicked to the dagger—"no one should have survived such a thrust. No man alive could . . ." He straightened, comprehension dawning in a grim smirk. "But you're not a man, are you?" he mocked in a cruel jest. "Nor alive in the strictest sense."

The presence strained to be released. The beast uncoiling with serpent strength. Sinking its fangs into his bloodstream.

Daigh contained it through sheer will. Twitched against the jags trembling his hands. Shallowing his breathing to an animal pant. This black-jacketed villain knew him. Who he was. What he was.

Daigh couldn't kill him until the thief spilled what he knew. Then he would do as he wished.

Buckling the satchel, the man slung it over his shoulder. "My apologies. Máelodor gave you up for dead."

Daigh's lips curled in an empty smile. "As you see, harder than it looks."

"Poor phrasing on my part. Not dead then, but absent from your meeting in Cork. Máelodor's anxious to recover the tapestry. He sent me in your stead."

"Did he?"

Máelodor? The tapestry? None of it stirred any answering memory within. He focused on his first and loudest thought.

"You say I'm not a man. What would you term me?"

Black Jacket stiffened with wary apprehension. Eyed Daigh like a disease as he drew the satchel up onto his shoulder. "I meant no offense."

"Then what did you mean?" Daigh asked through gritted teeth, patience waning.

"It's obvious isn't it? Look at you. Looming up out of the dark like a demon from a nightmare. I'd not really believed Máelodor's claims of resurrecting a *Domnuathi*. Too far-fetched, like something out of a faery story." He shifted slightly, his gaze flicking to the open office door. "The name suits you though. Lazarus rising from the dead, eh?"

Daigh flinched, his vision hazing as the final door was flung open.

Not Lazarus. Never Lazarus.

He had another name. Another life.

The creature exploded through his skull. Daigh heard it laughing as it crushed him in its coils.

He flung himself at the man, reason lost amid the howl of killing ecstasy. Heard the bark of a pistol through the pounding in his ears. Stumbled to his knees at the slash of sizzling heat gouging a path through his chest.

The man never paused. Instead he leapt for the door, footsteps slapping across the flagstones. Any pretense at secrecy over.

Daigh could do nothing but watch as the man vanished, satchel in hand.

Máelodor. A tapestry. *Domnuathi.*

Not a man. Not alive.

Lazarus rising from the dead.

He clutched his bloody chest, but it was the whirlwind in his skull that held him immobile.

Oh gods, what nightmare had he stumbled into? And how could he hope to battle his way back out?

Eight

How had she slept through it all? Had she really been so tired she'd been unaware of a commotion that turned the convent into a seething mass of raised voices, hostile interrogations, and in one or two cases, womanly vapors bordering on hysteria?

Apparently she could.

And did.

Now, standing in the stillroom doorway, she breathed deeply through her nose. Pulled her pathetic self together as she scanned the empty room. Every trace of its recent occupant had been erased. Even the scent of Daigh destroyed beneath a new layer of soapy clean. All as if he'd never been. As if he'd only been a very involved and lifelike hallucination.

She tried swallowing past the lump in her throat. Breathing around the tightness in her chest. Rubbing her arms in an attempt to ward off the gooseflesh pebbling her skin. No hallucination—no matter how convincing—would leave her flushed with passion's afterglow. His embrace had been real. His kiss had been very real.

It was only the snatched glimpses of herself as part of Daigh's past that held the stuff of delirium. And those, in the reassuring light of day, she chalked up to the overflow of his tumultuous emotions seeping into her mind. *Other* empathy gone awry. Nothing more.

Trailing back up the passage, she pictured an empty ribbon of long days stretching before her. A lifetime of dawns and dusks where every day was like every other day. Safe. Quiet. Serene.

Devoid of meaning.

Sister Ainnir bent over Sister Moira, listening to her chest.

"How could you simply let him go?" Sabrina demanded.

The elderly priestess faced her with a wrinkled lowering of her brows. Straightened, ushering Sabrina before her back down the row of beds to her tiny office. Closing the door firmly behind her.

"We didn't let him go. He absconded in the middle of the night," she answered curtly once they were alone. "After ransacking Ard-siúr's office. Making off with sacred valuables, and stealing a horse."

Ard-siúr's office? Sabrina's chest collapsed on a swift exhalation. The night she found him there—had he lied to her? Had this been his purpose all along? "I don't believe it."

"You don't have to believe it. The evidence is indisputable. The man was a common thief who played us all for fools. No doubt his intention all along was to gain freedom enough to move about unwatched. Once our guard was down, he opened the gates to his accomplices in crime."

"He must not have known what he was doing. Or they forced him. Threatened him somehow."

Sister Ainnir heaved a derisive snort. "And pigs can fly. No one could force that man to do anything he didn't want to."

"I heard there was blood in Ard-siúr's office. Lots of it. How do you explain that?"

Sister Ainnir's lips pursed, unmoved by Sabrina's fervent defense. "A quarrel among thieves. We've seen already MacLir's inexplicable ability to heal from wounds that would kill a normal human—even the most powerful of *Other*. That alone should have given us more pause than it did."

"We couldn't have misjudged him so horribly. Ard-siúr would have seen his intentions. Known him for what he was."

Sabrina should have.

His tenderness with Sister Clea. The stolen kiss in the night. It couldn't have been merely a con man's sly conniving. The polished art of the deceiver. What of his grief? His pain? She'd sensed them both. But if she were being completely honest, she'd also felt an underlying rage that frightened her with its feral intensity.

Had those stolen glimpses hinted at something darker? A corrupt purpose he'd hidden even from the skilled scrying of the *bandraoi*? Had her childish fantasies blinded her to the warning signs?

"Argue as you will, Sabrina. Even if it's as you say and Daigh MacLir is wholly innocent, his departure was past due. As sisters of High *Danu*, we walk a careful line. No hint of our order's true nature must escape these walls. No suspicions must taint the careful construct we've made of our lives. Mr. MacLir threatened that. You know it as well as I. He was a danger, and he brought danger with him. It's good he left. Now perhaps we can return to normal." Her pointed stare included Sabrina's return to normal in that statement.

It was clear she deemed the conversation at an end. Even before she'd finished speaking, she'd begun tidying away the remnants of her work. Returning bottles to their shelves. Checking supplies, marking her tally against an inventory.

"But what about—" Sabrina swallowed her words.

What about me? Her newly emerged, defiant self wanted to shout. Thought better of it.

Already Sister Ainnir watched her with increasing concern. Jane cast her fleeting, worried glances when she thought Sabrina wasn't looking, and Sister Brigh searched for more reasons to postpone her elevation to priestess. If she exposed her foolish fascination with a man she'd known for scant days, revealed the inner tangle of captured memories and swamping emotions, or told anyone that Daigh's disappearance pushed against her heart with an ancient and remembered ache, they'd call her mad. And rightly so. All she wanted would be jeopardized. Best to keep quiet. After all, Daigh had left. Slithered away in the night without even a good-bye to mark his leaving. Her life would go back to the way it was before Daigh MacLir had washed up upon their beach.

And that was a good thing.

What she wanted.

Wasn't it?

"What about what?" Sister Ainnir's canny eye focused on Sabrina's forehead like a giant magnifying glass.

Had she been speaking? Sabrina scrambled to clutch the threads of lost conversation. "The . . . um . . . the still-room," she blurted. "Does it need to be cleaned?" As if she hadn't smelled the biting stench of lye already. Hadn't seen for herself the sparse sterility of the tiny space.

Sister Ainnir sighed. "It's done already. You're free until your duties this afternoon."

She spoke this like a reward when it only meant Sabrina would have hours to roll events in her head. Tumble them into new shapes. Sort through every shared look and exchanged word that passed between her and Daigh for clues to his duplicity. End brooding over her complete and utter gullibility.

Perhaps if she wrote it all down in her journal. Seeing it on the page in black and white might help her to place Daigh and her naive infatuation in its proper place. Make her see it all for what it really was. A momentary diversion when she most needed one. Not the life-altering passion her overactive imagination had turned it into.

Suddenly she was glad of the escape. The hours to herself.

She hurried back up the aisle. Ignored Sister Clea's pathetic call. "Where's Paul? Where's my brother? He said he'd come back. He promised."

And what was a promise worth?

Sabrina had found over and over to her cost—absolutely nothing.

The hunt came so easy. Too easy for Daigh to ignore the obvious. He'd stalked his quarry before. Many times. And turned a skilled and deadly hand to it.

He traced Black Jacket to the village. And from there

toward Clonekilty. On to Bandon, where a frightened publican at the King's Arms assured Daigh a man matching the thief's description had stopped to rest and water his horse and snatch a bite to eat in the tavern's tap before taking the road for Cork. No, he'd not spoken of his business in the city, but he'd a foreign look to him and an impatient air, so a betting man would say he'd been making for the harbor.

Daigh would take that bet. He tracked like a hound upon a blood trail.

Or like one of the *Domnuathi* stalking its next victim.

The truth fired his soul with torchlike intensity. Singed away hope. He'd been fooling himself since waking among the *bandraoi*. Let the calm of days measured in prayer and work lull him into believing he might be normal. A simple man suffering a simple tragedy that time and patience would heal.

Nothing simple or normal about him. And he needed neither time nor patience to heal. It was death that was denied him. Or should he say—dying again. He'd been sent to the grave once already.

But if he now understood what he was, he still didn't know who he was. What dark power had summoned him back from the grave. How he'd ended half drowned upon a stretch of rocky shoreline. What strange presence infected his mind like a violent disease. Those questions remained along with the scattered bursts of so many others pummeling the insides of his skull.

Black Jacket knew the answers. Daigh just needed to run him to ground. Force him to give them up—at the point of a blade, if needs must.

Last night's rain had become today's drizzly mist, leaving him damp and miserable. The road slippery and treacherous. Twice his horse had stumbled. And once he'd had to find a path around a wash where the road had completely vanished under a sea of mud and debris.

Urging the bay into a canter to the top of the rise, he searched the road below as it dipped into a shallow valley. A few carriages. A wagon and team. A farmer in a heavy coat and hat hiking the verge. The rest lost in a gray afternoon twilight.

Turning in the saddle, he looked back the way he'd come. To Glenlorgan. To Sabrina.

I'm back for you. His promise to her. The words coming from some lost place within. A place where he saw her laughing. Loving. The two of them sharing a life. But she didn't belong to him. It had been a mirage. A dream built upon his bones. A desire torn from a life that had ceased to exist centuries ago.

His hands clenched the slick reins.

Nothing solid but for the ache of their separation. That held a pain as real and recent as yesterday.

Sabrina lifted her head after long hours bent over her diary. Squinted against the fast fading light. Rolled her shoulders as she worked out the kinks. And read back the pages and pages filled with impressions, recollections, and conversations, hoping against hope her time with Daigh would make more sense than it had as she'd written it.

No such luck.

In fact her frantically scrawled notes sounded quite a lot like the ramblings of a particularly creative-minded bedlamite.

Memories of a past that didn't belong to her. Daigh's face swimming up through her mind as if it had always been there. And a knowledge of things that shouldn't be hers to know.

Dear heavens, if the *bandraoi* got hold of this they'd shackle her to her bed and hide all sharp objects.

She shoved the book under her pillow. Changed her mind. Stowed it under her mattress.

None too soon.

Jane wandered in, listless and pale-featured. Smudges hovered beneath her eyes, her body stooped as if she sought to protect herself from some invisible hurt.

"Are you unwell, Jane?"

Jane flinched in panic, before her gaze fell with relief on Sabrina. "Don't ever sneak up on me like that. You nearly scared me to death."

"I didn't sneak. I was already here."

She answered with a wan smile. "Were you?" Dipped her shoulder in a limp shrug. "I suppose I didn't notice."

Slouching into a chair before the dressing table, she tore off her kerchief. Even her beautiful red hair was dull and lifeless. Pulling the combs free with shaky fingers, she tangled one. Wrenched it loose with a muttered, "Blast." Tears sliding down her cheeks. Shoulders quivering with dry sobs.

Sabrina threw herself from her bed. "What on earth? Here, let me, before you scalp yourself." Took over from Jane, who merely sat like a life-size doll, allowing Sabrina to remove pins and combs. Brush the heavy fall of Jane's hair, the rhythmic strokes easing her shoulders down from around her ears. Soothing her enough that she closed her eyes. Exhaled on a slow, deep breath.

Was this melancholia a result of the ambush in the woods? How had Sabrina not seen it before? Had she been so wrapped up in her own problems she hadn't noticed her best friend's suffering? Hadn't thought about how the violent attack might have affected her?

Sabrina frowned at her own self-centered fixation. What kind of a friend was she?

Jane attempted a smile. "I'm a mess."

"Certainly not. A good brushing, a few pins, and you'll be fine."

Their eyes met, Jane's red-rimmed and puffy. "Nice try, but you know exactly what I'm talking about. Every time I close my eyes I see that greasy, horrible face and feel that man's breath on my neck. I go all nauseous and trembly, and I can't sleep. Sister Ainnir gave me a sleeping draught, but it tastes so awful, I don't like to take it."

Sabrina smirked. "Sister Ainnir believes anything that doesn't make you gag on its way down must not be effective. A simple infusion of pennyroyal mixed with honey would do more for you than any of her torture potions."

Jane relaxed back in her chair. Already more color to her cheeks, but lingering guilt kept Sabrina babbling. "I wouldn't have let them hurt you."

Her declaration met by a skeptical raising of brows. "And how did you plan on stopping them? You were hardly in a better position."

"Daigh then," Sabrina announced proprietarily. "He wouldn't have let those men harm us. He didn't. He fought. And could have died. All for us." She still didn't quite believe Sister Ainnir's accusations. There had to be an explanation for his departure. Though none she'd come up with so far made any sense.

Jane's mouth twisted in a dry smile. "He really did turn you inside out, didn't he?"

She gave a noncommittal shrug. Pulled a heavy section of hair up and back.

Jane dropped her gaze. Began toying with the pins on the table. "Did you kiss him?"

"Jane!"

A glimmer of a wicked spark. "Did you like it?"

Sabrina jammed a comb in place.

"Ow!" Jane jerked upright. Shot Sabrina a dirty look. "Fine, if you don't want to answer, you don't have to. But don't stab me for asking."

She loosened the skein of hair. Adjusted the offending comb. "Sorry."

A companionable silence fell over the room. Afternoon light slanted long and golden over the bare wood floor. Up the whitewashed walls. Over three sets of plain white coverlets.

Sabrina caught herself comparing the simple unadorned chamber to her sumptuous, peacock-bright bedchamber at Belfoyle. She'd not seen it since . . . well since that last horrendous autumn. Hadn't been home to walk the park or scramble down the cliff path to the narrow stretch of beach. Hadn't stolen fruit from the orangery or curled up in her favorite chair by the drawing room fire.

Would it look the same seen through adult eyes? Would the rooms seem smaller? The grandeur seem less grand? Would she feel like she were coming home, or would it be a stranger who strode the corridors as if seeing it all for the first time? Would the ghosts of her past rise up to walk with her? And what sort of ghosts would they be?

Father with his hot and cold moods?

The patient but distracted hand of Mother upon her shoulder?

Or would it be Brendan who visited her in the tangled corridors and quiet rooms? Explaining away his abandonment and the horrible accusations. Reasoning past her suspicions. Telling her it would be all right. That it wasn't the way it sounded. That the *Ambas-draoi* had it wrong.

He was innocent.

What a fool she was. Twice now she'd been deceived by a man she'd stupidly trusted. Who'd been as false as his word.

Apparently she had quite a talent for seeing a good in someone that just wasn't there.

She shuddered off her daydreams of her lost home by the sea.

She wasn't going back to Belfoyle. Aidan's pleas notwithstanding, she remained committed to the *bandraoi*. Even if that life seemed empty after the upheaval of the last days.

And as for Daigh's betrayal? She'd recover. Thoughts of him would fade in time. Her infatuation naught but cause for future teasing.

"Sabrina? Did you mean what you said the other night? I mean about Daigh MacLir?"

Jane asked this now? Sabrina peered closely at her reflection in the glass. There must be a message tattooed on her forehead. *Moonstruck. Approach with caution.* Or had every priestess suddenly grown adept at reading minds?

She did her best to look breezily vague. "You'll have to be more specific. Which night? And more important, what did I say?"

Jane continued arranging and rearranging the tiny pile of unused hairpins as if afraid to look Sabrina in the eye. "About feeling as if you and Daigh had known each other before? Seeing things?"

Good heavens, talk about sounding like a blathering idiot. She put the finishing touches on the carefully reconstructed chignon. Tried to keep up the appearance of detached disinterest. "It does sound ridiculous when you say it out loud like that, doesn't it?"

Jane flashed her a sympathetic smile. "At first hearing, perhaps. But do you still believe it?"

The memory of the parting in the woods. The gnawing ache of a past separation pressing even now upon her heart. Daigh's fierce certainty they knew each other. His claim he'd come back for her. But back from where? And why for her?

She bought time. Stood back, admiring her handiwork. Touching up here. A stray wisp there. Not bad. If she failed at High *Danu* priestess she could always get a position as lady's maid.

"You're avoiding me."

"I'm not."

"You are. You've rearranged that same curl three times already. If you don't want to—"

"I don't really know what I believe anymore," Sabrina answered in a rush. "But Sister Ainnir is right. The order—and I—need to forget he was ever here. His arrival brought nothing but trouble."

She leaned across Jane's shoulder. Took up the kerchief. Draped it over the dark red brilliance of her hair. Pinned it neatly in place. Sighed. All that hard work, and no one would see it.

"I watched him watching you, Sabrina." Jane craned her neck around, her smile wistful and envious and dreamy all at the same time. But—for now, at least—not haunted. "And you watched him just as avidly. Good luck forgetting that."

Sabrina studied her reflection. Narrow, pinched face. Dark circles. Pursed line of her mouth.

And she worried over Jane? Physician, heal thyself.

A sharp rap on the door, and they turned together to face Sister Brigh's wrinkled scowl. But not her usual world-going-to-hell-in-a-handbasket glare. This held a gleam of suppressed excitement. A hint of victory. Not a good sign. Any victory of Sister Brigh's usually meant torment for some unsuspecting novice.

"Sabrina. You're wanted in Ard-siúr's office. Immediately."

And then she was gone.

No tirade about their lazy duty-shirking? No questioning of the hows, whys, and wherefores that allowed them to be in their bedchamber when honest hardworking priestesses were occupied in the business of the order? Not even a disapproving sniff?

Not good. Not good at all.

Jane's hand found Sabrina's. Her look one of encouragement.

But all Sabrina could think was, this had impending disaster written all over it.

She studied the messenger from beneath properly downcast lashes. Heavy coat and muffler, a hat he ran nervously through sausage fingers leaking water over Ard-siúr's rugs, and a red nose equally damp and runny. But it was his stature that held Sabrina's attention. No taller than a half-grown child, though the crags in his face and the silver-threaded hair spoke of late middle years. What manner of servants was Aidan hiring these days? Probably taken on by that woman he married.

"His Lordship has sent Mr. Dixon, here, to escort you to Dublin. You are to prepare yourself to leave, and be ready to embark no later than the day after tomorrow."

"What?" Sabrina's gaze snapped back to Ard-siúr. "No! I mean I can't leave. Not now. It's impossible. There must be a mistake."

Ard-siúr cleared her throat. Adjusted her spectacles. Read the letter again, with only the slow tick of the case clock breaking the silence. "It all seems quite clear. Lord Kilronan requires your presence as soon as it can be accomplished. He says he must have you with him and his wife in Dublin as soon as can be arranged."

"But why? He certainly never made any push to see me before."

Ard-siúr glanced at the dwarf shifting uncomfortably in the corner. "If you go with Sister Anne, she'll see that you're housed and fed. Our guest quarters are simple, but"—her gaze fell on the dripping hat—"dry."

He bowed, and with a final stream of water trailing from his hat brim, squelched after Sister Anne.

Ard-siúr straightened the clutter of papers on her desk. Actually now that Sabrina was noticing, the clutter extended to the whole room. Not in a noticeable way. But in jarring incremental pieces. An echo of intrusion. A lingering violence in the overwarm air. Even the cat seemed restless. Pacing the floor. Sniffing at a stain that hadn't been there on Sabrina's last visit. Brown. Fresh. And hastily cleaned.

I remember blood. And the mud as I fell.

What had Daigh really been doing the night she'd found him in here? Was it connected in some way to his disappearance this morning? Had she been a gullible little fool? She breathed through her sudden light-headedness. Focused on Ard-siúr to keep the room from spinning.

Ard-siúr removed her spectacles, her gaze long enough to make Sabrina squirm. "I would imagine His Lordship's recent convalescence has spurred this new resolve. Many who glimpse their own mortality as your brother did this spring attempt to set their lives in order. Right past mistakes. Amend what they see as failings."

"So am I mistake or failing?"

"You're his sister. I'm sure he wants to assure himself of your happiness here and be certain that your heart remains committed to a life among us."

"Or does he want to use me to achieve the advantageous marriage he scorned when he married that . . . woman?" She still couldn't bring herself to call her new sister by name. For some reason Aidan's hasty, ill-thought marriage rankled, though she couldn't say why. It wasn't as if she begrudged her brother his happiness. Only that . . .

"Sabrina, you came to us a wounded child. And we allowed you to hide among us. Use the peace you found here to recover. And you have. But now you're a woman, full grown. You must test your strength. Return to a life beyond our walls. Only in that way can you make your choice and be sure of your path."

"But what if he doesn't allow me to return?"

"I'm certain your brother will not hinder you from following your heart and finding the future that is right for you."

"Then you've never come up against Douglas determination. If Aidan wants something, he pounds away until he gets it." Her imminent departure a case in point.

"Ahh, but you share that same tenacity. The irresistible force meeting the immovable object."

How could this be happening? How could Aidan do this to her? Didn't he know what the order meant to her? Didn't he understand her need to remain here among the *bandraoi*? Where she felt a sense of belonging and community? Where she felt safe? But Aidan had never understood her. Never taken the time. It had been Brendan who strove to nudge her out of her shell. Or when needed, crawled into the shell with her and simply let her be her without criticism.

Sabrina clenched the chair back. Focused on the wood, cool and smooth under her hands. The draft of air moving the tapestries. All but one. The wall behind Ard-siúr's desk gaped empty but for a frayed edge of wool caught on a nail. She couldn't seem to tear her gaze from that torn tangle of cloth. Daigh's crime drifting on a breath of wind.

One more man she'd built up in her mind. Though at least this one had fallen from his pedestal over the space of a few days rather than a lifetime.

"Go, child. I will send someone to assist you in packing."

"Yes, ma'am.' Sabrina turned to go, but, struck with sudden inspiration, swung back. "Ard-siúr, did Kilronan send a maid to accompany me?"

"I'm not aware of anyone besides Mr. Dixon. Perhaps His Lordship assumed one of the sisters would travel with you."

"Might I request someone?"

"If we can spare them. Who did you have in mind?"

"Jane Fletcher."

Drumming her fingers, Ard-siúr considered the request. "She has been distracted since the attack. Not quite herself. Perhaps a change of scenery would do her good." Nodded her assent. "Aye, she may accompany you to Dublin and remain until you are well settled."

"Thank you, Ard-siúr."

"I am sure Lord Kilronan feels he's acting in your best interest. You're his only remaining family."

Drunk on her teeny victory and resentment making her reckless, she volleyed, "Are you so certain of that?"

Ard-siúr's drumming stopped, a new awareness in her gaze.

"You once asked if I'd ever received a letter from Brendan," Sabrina brazened. "You believe the *Amhas-draoi,* don't you? You think he's alive."

Ard-siúr spread her hands in a question. "I know only the rumors. Though they strengthen every day, they are still just that—mere speculation."

The tangle of frayed threads caught Sabrina's eye, the knot returning tenfold. "Do you believe he really did those things? That he was as evil and dangerous as they claim?"

Ard-siúr noted the track of her gaze. "And of whom do we speak now?" she asked gently. "Brendan Douglas or Daigh MacLir?"

Sabrina shrugged off her question with her regrets. "Never mind. It hardly matters anymore, does it?"

The wisest and most powerful of the priestesses steepled her fingers against her chin. "I believe to you, Sabrina, it matters very much."

Nine

Cork teemed with life. Crowded, jostling bodies. The rumble and squeak of wheels through narrow streets. A choking press of sound and scents and life that only the salty, brackish sea air kept from overwhelming him. He focused on his quarry. Black Jacket had stabled his horse, threading the roads and alleyways on foot as he made his way through town. Found his way to a snug harborside inn and a private, second-floor parlor. All unheeding of the silent watcher tracking his movements. An ever-present shadow.

The parlor was located at the end of a narrow, rickety outside walkway. Below in the courtyard, ostlers shouted as carriages were hitched and unhitched, passengers chattered as bags were stowed and coaches set to. Horses pawed their impatience upon the cobbles, and coachmen swore and stamped against the damp cold. Din enough to drown out the clumsiest of shadowing. But he wasn't clumsy. And it took a moment's skill to crack the door. Stand idly upon the walk outside as though doing nothing more than enjoying the spectacle below.

". . . better be. Máelodor will have our heads otherwise." Black Jacket's associate. A light urbane voice. Almost effeminate.

"Has to be. I searched that place top to bottom. And look, it's obvious this is the tapestry. The litter. The tomb. The Earl of Kilronan's diary spoke of both."

Daigh's breath caught in his throat.

Kilronan. Sabrina's brother. What the hell had he to do with this? And was Sabrina involved?

It didn't matter. Sabrina didn't matter. Not anymore. He ignored the gnawing ache that had been his since leaving Glenlorgan. The drag of useless emotions. Concentrated on the conversation.

A silence followed, movements within the parlor swallowed by the continuous come-and-go downstairs. Farther down the passage, a door opened. A man and woman emerging, their conversation of weather and passage bookings and the expense of their room seeming out of place among the dark plottings just a wall away. The man tipped his hat as they passed on their way to the staircase, the woman eying Daigh with blatant admiration.

"And Máelodor's creature?"

Daigh strained to catch their words over the arriving blast of a mail coach. The jangle of harness, clatter of hooves, and a fresh bustle from the courtyard beneath him. Like ants from a kicked hill, the inn swarmed with activity, making eavesdropping nigh impossible.

Thoughts of crashing through the door in a storm of deadly violence elicited a thin smile and a twitch of hardening muscles, the serpent stirring from the darkest corner of his soul, but he fought it back.

Better to wait. To follow.

". . . there . . . attacked me . . . not even a *Domnuathi* could have survived that."

". . . fool"—the scrape of drawn chairs—". . . take it to Máelodor . . . tell him about Lazarus . . . what he wants to do with it . . . head to Dublin . . . the *Amhas-draoi* . . ."

Shared laughter.

". . . focus is all on Douglas. Máelodor's dead"—the chuckle of conspirators—". . . information for him. See that he gets it immediately." A clink of glasses. The squeak of floorboards. The meeting breaking up.

Daigh fell back from his position. Slipped up the passage, ducking into the first open door, waiting until Black Jacket passed. Follow him, and he'd find the mysterious Máelodor. The spider at the center of this hideous web.

He'd only just swung back into the passage when the slide of a knife caught him beneath the chin. "Did you catch all that, Lazarus? Or should I fill you in on the parts you missed?" The high tenor of Black Jacket's fellow conspirator.

The knife pressed deep into his neck. Blood dripping upon his collar. No time for the cut to heal before another slide of the blade opened a new wound.

"Inside, if you please."

A slippery, vicious crackle of darkness burned along Daigh's blood. It coursed within him like some foreign evil. Part of him and yet separate. Wanting blood and death and killing. An animal need to obliterate.

"I wouldn't try anything if I were you," the voice warned. "My weapons may not defeat your warding, but my magics can make you wish you were dead."

Allowing himself to be drawn into the chamber, Daigh fought against the storm surge of clawing emotion. Cleared a space within himself free of the ferocious maelstrom. A point of sanity among the madness.

"I told Mr. Bloom you'd not surrender to the grave so easily." The knife sliced deeper. Daigh's flesh parting. His blood flowing faster. It scalded his neck. Seeped beneath his coat, his shirt. "Would you, Lazarus? Not now you've a second taste of life?"

The knife fell away, leaving him cold and shuddering against the well of poison infecting him like a disease.

"Sit, friend. Can I get you a brandy? A glass of wine perhaps?"

Daigh fell into the chair presented. Finally looked upon his assailant. Blond. Young. Features as cool and sweet-natured as his voice. A wiry body holding whipcord strength. Eyes pale and hard as stones. "I've been looking forward to seeing for myself how successful Máelodor was, and I have to say his claims held nothing of the braggart about them."

"So you approve?"

"Oh, yes." His gaze traveled over Daigh with a lingering yet professional eye. "Amazing," he cooed. "Simply amazing."

Daigh's skin crawled. Every nerve jumping. "Who are you?"

"No need to be testy. I'm on your side. But you're smart to ask. Informants could be anywhere." He pushed back one sleeve to reveal a tattoo upon his forearm. A broken arrow and crescent.

Daigh felt his stomach roll up into his throat.

"You recognize the mark of the Nine, Lazarus?"

The name landed on him like a blow. "Aye. But not

Lazarus. It's"—*we can only hope you don't end as he did*—"it's Daigh now."

His correction was met with a razor smile. "Naming yourself? How droll. But fitting under the circumstances. I too have taken on a new name to go with the role that will soon be mine. You may call me Lancelot."

"Are you loyal friend? Or treacherous betrayer?"

A careless shrug. "Remains to be seen."

The man circled him, a hand running casually across Daigh's shoulders. A touch upon the back of his neck. A breath against the heat of his bloody skin. Professionalism vanished beneath a sultry invitation. "You're soaked to the bone. Perhaps you should take off these wet clothes and dry yourself by the fire."

Blood thickened to ice, Daigh's body stiffening as he controlled the queasy turning of his stomach. Gritted his teeth, refusing to crane his neck to keep the man in view. "Where does Bloom go from here?"

Lancelot slid back into his vision. Crossed to pour a glass of wine. Swished it before sipping, his eyes meeting Daigh's over the rim, coolly amused. "His ship leaves tomorrow morning. Máelodor should have the tapestry within a few days. And we shall be one step closer to final success."

"Huzzah for our side." Whoever's side that was. The hell if he knew.

The man placed the glass carefully on the table. "You sound less than enthusiastic."

"I don't count success until it's achieved."

"Oh it will be. Make no mistake. It's been years in the planning. Máelodor is devoted to completing the Nine's unfinished work. Reclaiming the world for *Other* in a new golden age."

A golden age? *Other* dominance? He forced his face into a mask of complete inscrutability. No hint of the wild spin of his thoughts.

"Bloom tells me you attacked him. That you actually tried to stop him from stealing the Rywlkoth Tapestry. Odd behavior from the one sent to procure it in the first place."

Daigh shrugged. Play along. Gain time. Information. "I didn't recognize him. Thought he was there to stop me from stealing it."

Lancelot's gaze narrowed. "He thinks you've gone rogue on us. That you've somehow slipped Máelodor's leash."

"He can think as he likes."

Candlelight flickered like demon-flame in Lancelot's eyes, his hair gleaming in the fire's glow. "Perhaps you should accompany Bloom. Máelodor will be relieved to know his creature is safe."

"Do you go?"

Lancelot offered up a chilly smile, though his eyes continued to burn with a queer, wild light. "I'm flattered, but no. There are rumors Brendan Douglas has been in touch with his family. That he may be en route to Dublin. Máelodor would love to lay hands upon the traitor. Would pay dearly for the privilege of breaking him."

Sabrina's brother in the hands of these men. A long, cruel death would be his. A killing by degrees until the victim prayed for the mercy stroke. An end to the torture. Somehow he knew this. Just as he knew he'd once prayed for that mercy. And been denied.

His hands curled to fists, anger pushing past sound judgment.

The man crossed to Daigh. Stood over him, his gaze

now leaping with a greedy hunger he did nothing to hide. "You know, I'm curious."

"About what?" Daigh pushed from a mouth gone dry.

They met eye to eye. Sweat beaded the man's upper lip, a single drop curling down his cheek. "As one of the *Domnuathi,* you're bound body and soul to your creator. A slave to his every whim."

Daigh's skin grew hot. Bile choked him. Thick, horrible. But he answered in the only way that would keep this man's trust. "Aye."

Lancelot leaned forward. Close enough for Daigh to smell the heavy scent of musk and sweat. See the scrape of a dull razor. A tiny scar at the corner of his mouth.

"So if I did this and told you Máelodor ordered it so . . ." He pressed his lips against Daigh's neck. "Or this . . ." He kissed his cheek.

Daigh threw himself to his feet, violently shaking. Grabbed him by the collar. "You would find yourself without a head."

The man seemed amused rather than alarmed. "Would I?"

Immediately, Daigh's lungs collapsed. His body caught in a snare of invisible magic. Binding him hand and foot. Trapping him like a rabbit in a snare.

The man circled him slowly, flush with success and something more. Something sinister and sexual. "It's like chaining a man-eating tiger"—he slid the coat from Daigh's shoulders—"that would sooner tear you apart"—tugged free his cravat—"than look at you."

Daigh released the beast. Let it rush forth in a torrent of dark mage energy that crisped the very air. A fiery slash of pain seared his brain. Slid along his nerves with serpent speed.

He was free.

His hands went for Lancelot's throat. Squeezed.

And like being cleaved from skull to groin, screamed at the agony instantly scything its way through him. Liquefying bone. Sawing through tendons. He dropped, writhing. The sounds of his weeping and screaming muffled by Lancelot's hand over his mouth.

"Did you really think you could win against an *Ambasdraoi*? Shhh, my beautiful monster. The more you struggle, the more you suffer."

The spell eased. And then the man's mouth was on his. A tongue diving between his lips. Taking from him. Sucking him dry. A twisted, power-mad assault.

Daigh wrenched his head away, but Lancelot gripped him by the chin and took his fill. Released him on a satisfied sigh.

Straightening, he adjusted his coat. Smoothed his hair. Finished his glass of wine in a long swallow. "A shame to end our interlude prematurely, but"—he gave a coy shrug—"tell Máelodor I will do whatever it takes to capture Douglas alive and unharmed. He'll enjoy destroying Kilronan's brother bit by bit. He has such a talent for inflicting pain." A hand upon the latch, he turned on Daigh a final gleam of triumph. "Wouldn't you agree, Lazarus?"

Sabrina took a deep breath. Immediately sneezed.

Dust tickled her nose. Clung to her fingers. Coated the book she read and the table where she sat. Even Sister Ursula, the keeper of the order's texts, seemed as cobwebby and faded as the books, scrolls, and parchments she tended.

Or perhaps she was merely ice-blue from cold.

Teresa had been right. It was freezing in here. A

double layer of petticoats and her thickest stockings, yet still Sabrina's teeth chattered.

"Have you found what you were looking for?" Sister Ursula stuffed a wisp of fine, white-blond hair back under her kerchief. Regarded Sabrina with pale blue eyes.

Sniffling into her handkerchief, Sabrina returned the smile while trying to hide the pages with her elbow. "I have, thank you."

The sister had not managed to hide her curiosity or her surprise at Sabrina's venturing into her domain. And still observed her with a faint sense of confusion.

So perhaps scholarly pursuits weren't Sabrina's habit, but it wasn't as if she didn't read at all. She loved a good mystery. Or a thrilling romance where ghosts rattled chains and the poor heroine wandered about cavernous passages with one stubby candle.

Not exactly the heights of so-called literary achievement, but Sister Ursula didn't have to eye her as if she wouldn't know poetry from prose.

With a vague nod, the priestess glided away, and Sabrina was left alone to try to make heads or tails out of the gibberish staring up at her from the enormous, dusty tome.

She reread the last passage, hoping it would make more sense the second time around. Not a bit. The writer of this tract delved in great footnoted detail into the nature of memory. The biology. The physiology. The psychology. Even the chemistry. There were diagrams, tables, charts, and references to other works by other equally obscure scholars with their own sets of tables, charts, and references. Following the circumlocution ended her right back where she started. A dog chasing its tail.

But still it had been the closest reference she'd found so

far to the odd hallucinations she'd experienced. Not that it mattered. Daigh had disappeared. Whatever had caused her to fall into his memories would stop now that he was gone. So why spend her last hours here browsing endless titles, trying to read ancient texts, and puzzling out unintelligible hieroglyphs?

That was the real question she should be studying.

She sank her chin onto her hand. Peered up into the weak light coming through the filmy clerestory windows, and tried throwing herself into a memory as if diving off the cliffs below Belfoyle. But no odd shifting and spinning of the room took place. No melting of the stacks and shelves into a damp, dripping wood. No Daigh slanting his mouth against hers in an axis-tilting kiss that sizzled her insides like a torch.

She sighed. *Thank heavens.*

And closed the book.

Night closed in. The fire dying back to glowing embers. Cooling to gray ash. The temperature dropping with each passing hour until his breath fogged the chilly air, and his body cramped with cold.

Bloom's ship left in the morning. Daigh had only hours before he'd lose his chance to follow. Find Máelodor. Make sense of what was becoming an increasingly dangerous conspiracy.

He tried rising. Dropped back with a pained moan, nerves flayed raw and even breathing almost more effort than he could muster.

He sought the solace of sleep. Managed only cluttered hideous dreams that left him retching and sick. But awake, he saw only the suffused lust of the man calling himself

Lancelot. Heard once more his blood-chilling avowals of Douglas's torture.

Sabrina's brother. A man he'd never met. But fated for a death as gruesome as any devised.

If the man sought Brendan Douglas he might turn his sights upon Sabrina. Use her as a pawn in the capture of her brother. Surely nothing could harm her while she remained with the *bandraoi.* Not even Lancelot's malignant powers.

Still, Daigh had penetrated the sanctity of their walls. As had Bloom. It wouldn't take much to separate Sabrina from the crowd. Get her alone. Take her captive.

His heart turned over in his chest. His brain alive with images each more terrifying than the last.

He battled back his fear by concentrating on the snatches of conversation. Struggling to fill in the blanks. Bloom and Lancelot spoke of a diary. Kilronan's diary.

Sabrina.

Their first conversation.

You were asking someone for a diary. Demanding it.

Apparently he'd succeeded. But at what price?

A man twisted with hate. A sword arcing silver above him. A battle he nearly lost. And a woman's tearful pleading for mercy. Piecemeal memories surfaced like sharks to feed, leaving him shuddering and sick. He curled into a ball until it passed.

Black faded to gray as dawn approached, and strength returned by interminable degrees. Rolling to his knees. Levering himself to his feet. Straightening against the spine-snarling twitch of fried muscles.

The Earl of Kilronan's diary had told them where to find the Rywlkoth Tapestry. A tapestry kept with the *bandraoi.* A tapestry he'd last seen hanging in Ard-siúr's office.

Sabrina.

Lady Sabrina.

Daughter and sister to the Earls of Kilronan.

Sister to Brendan Douglas.

Sister of High *Danu*.

The clues clicked into place, creating a heart-dropping image.

He threw open the door, almost running over the same couple he'd encountered yesterday. The gentleman's muttered oath and the woman's gasp of wide-eyed fear giving him a good idea of the picture he made.

Scary bordering on terrifyingly insane.

At least he looked the part of monster. Lancelot clothed his evil behind a façade of cultured aristocratic polish.

The heirs of Kilronan wouldn't know they were being hunted until it was too late.

But then—he closed his fist around an invisible weapon—neither would Lancelot.

"The carriage is ready, Lady Sabrina."

She winced at the title used by the shy young priestess sent to retrieve her. Already her exile had begun. The loosening of ties. The move from one existence to another.

She ran a hand over the coverlet on her bed as she took one last look around. The plaster crack up one wall that resembled an upside-down duck. Teresa's dog-eared copy of *The Children of the Abbey* upon a bedside table. The lopsided corner cabinet held closed by a gadget of paper jammed between the doors.

She didn't want to leave, and yet the bedchamber no longer seemed like hers. It had already taken on a stark distance. A week from now would all trace of her be gone?

Heat pricked her eyes. If only she could roll herself in her quilts and play invisible until Mr. Dixon—Aidan's pint-sized dogsbody—gave up and left.

"My lady?"

Sabrina whipped around. "Don't call me that. Ever."

"No, my . . . I mean no, ma'am." At Sabrina's continued glare. "I mean no, I won't. Sabrina." Darted back out the door like a whipped dog.

She sighed. Why did the title upset her? Mr. Dixon had been addressing her as Lady Sabrina unceasingly for two days now. No wonder the sisters were confused.

Standing, she drew on her gloves. Buckled closed her fur-trimmed pelisse. Smoothed the ribbons of her bonnet. All provided by Mr. Dixon with a note from the new Lady Kilronan.

> Excuse the audacity. Aidan insisted I send along clothing enough to see you to Dublin. And you know how he is. If I hadn't agreed, he would have done it himself and who knows what you would have ended with. Can't wait to finally meet you. I've heard so much. All of it good, of course.
>
> —Cat

Catching sight of her reflection, she had to admit—grudgingly—Aidan's wife had style. No one would ever mistake the elegant fashion plate in the mirror with the scrubbed and unadorned apprentice of a few short days ago.

Too bad it was all for naught. She never was nor ever would be the Society man-catcher Aidan wanted her to be. And she'd tell him so the first chance she had.

Catching up her reticule, she sighed. Took one last look around, sending up a heartfelt plea to the gods for guidance.

This exile was temporary. She'd return to the *bandraoi* by spring. No later.

So why did she feel as if she were saying a long and very permanent good-bye?

ten

Lord Kilronan wasn't in town. He was expected, but no, he couldn't say when. Mrs. Norris, the earl's lady-aunt, was not at home to visitors. No, Mr. MacLir was not welcome to leave a note.

The strange little dwarf had been firm. As well as extremely unpleasant.

Unable to pass on his warning, Daigh departed before his frustration turned ugly. Already rage uncoiled from that dark pit in his mind where the presence waited. It fired along his taut nerves. Called to the blackest parts of his soul. Filled his vision with its cold, yellow eyes.

"Really, Sabrina. Lord Kilronan can't be a complete fiend."

A punch to the gut. A spear to the brain. Both served to kick him loose of the presence's mounting spiral of violence. He ground to a stop. Spun around to see two women emerging from a coach drawn up to Kilronan's door.

Rigidly erect. Face marble white beneath the brim of

her bonnet, Lady Sabrina Douglas gazed upon the town house's brick façade with obvious dread.

Ignoring the grumble of passersby as they elbowed their way past him, he watched her ascend the steps. Stared at the closed front door for long minutes after as if willing her to come back and explain herself.

Damn it all to hell. What was she doing here? She was supposed to be in Glenlorgan. Closeted away behind a phalanx of High *Danu bandraoi*. Protected. Safe. Out of harm's way.

Out of his way.

"Darling. You don't know how glad I am to see you."

Aunt Delia sailed down the wide marble stairs, enveloping Sabrina in a lavender-scented hug that left her gasping for breath, but steadied the uncertain whirl in her head she'd experienced climbing the front steps.

"We expected you days ago. I was certain you met with some terrible accident upon the road with no one but that odd little dwarf to act as your protector. Come along, and let's sit for a nice chat. I've canceled all my calls this afternoon, so we have hours to catch up."

She took her hand, dragging an overwhelmed Sabrina into a downstairs salon. Jane waving her ahead while she lagged behind.

"I don't know what your brother was thinking in hiring such a county fair freak, but there you are. He doesn't consult me. I'm only his aunt. Hardly family at all. And if it's a choice between me and that woman . . ." She flitted a quick glance at Sabrina, who'd gone stiff at hearing her own unkind thoughts repeated by her aunt. "Ah, well"—she waved a heavily ringed hand—"if Kilronan wants to enter self-imposed exile by marrying a social pariah, who am I to stop him?"

The salon—like the woman—exuded over-the-top femininity. Cherubs erupted from every tabletop, side by side with statuary of nude, muscle-bound gods. Hothouse flowers scented the already perfumed air, and even the fire glowed with magically enhanced pink and purple flames.

Rendered speechless by the results of Aunt Delia's idea of decor, Sabrina mumbled, "I'm sure Aidan doesn't mean to slight you."

Though now she was here, she could see why her brother might choose to consult with their aunt as infrequently as possible.

Again the droopy wave of a hand. "It's not for me to complain. I merely do as I'm ordered. 'Hire me a town house, Aunt Delia. Furnish and staff it, Aunt Delia.' If it weren't for Kilronan House being little more than a pile of rubble, I probably wouldn't have heard from him at all."

Sabrina cast another shocked glance at Aunt Delia's nightmare idea of style. What on earth would Aidan say when he saw the results of his requests? "You've done . . . wonders," she prevaricated. "The place is truly incredible."

"Thank you, darling. You always were a sweet thing. Biddable. Not at all like your brothers. But that's neither here nor there. Look how you've grown. The last time I saw you, you were sadly lacking in polish. But now"—she leaned back, taking Sabrina in with one long critical gaze—"you're almost pretty."

Sabrina had forgotten Aunt Delia's fondness for hiding poison amid her praise. She smiled through gritted teeth.

"Yes, you're quite improved in looks. I'm surprised. I

would have thought the *bandraoi* would have dressed you in sackcloth and ashes with rope sandals on your feet."

"Lady Kilronan was kind enough to send me these things."

Her aunt raised a pair of painted-on brows. "Was she? I'll give the woman credit. She's got a certain subdued style some might call tasteful."

Since Aunt Delia wore a patterned purple and yellow gown straining against her huge expanse of bosom and hip, Sabrina could only thank her lucky stars her sister-in-law had supplied her with a suitable wardrobe. Had she relied on her aunt for help, she'd end looking like a cross between a flower garden and a circus tent.

"Are my brother and his wife here?"

Please, say they're here. She didn't know how much longer she could endure this inquisition.

"No, darling. I received a letter this morning. They've been unavoidably detained, but will do everything in their power to arrive as soon as possible. I should hope so. I've already had to postpone my travel to Bray. I refuse to alter my plans again."

Sabrina's heart sank. She was to be trapped with only her aunt's company for who knew how long? And here she'd worried she'd be stuck with the new Lady Kilronan. Bad enough in its own way. But this was shaping up to be far worse.

"Speaking of family, let me tell you the latest scandal." Aunt Delia nestled in like a hen upon her nest. "Miss Rollins-Smith has vowed she'll die a spinster rather than marry anyone but your cousin Jack."

"But he's dead."

"Well, of course he is. And didn't the famed O'Gara

luck fail on that sorry occasion? Always knew he'd come to a sticky end. Unstable, he was. Rackety."

Her aunt's face shone with gruesome delight. Not even an attempt at a few crocodile tears for her sister's son. Sabrina could only imagine Aunt Delia's reaction to Aidan's recent brush with mortality. Probably took bets on his recovery.

"The silly girl is just being dramatic," she simpered. "Always was one for the grand gesture. She's been wearing black since spring. Makes her look horribly sallow. And it's not even as if your cousin and she were ever properly betrothed. A wish of his parents, but hardly a fait accompli. Anyway, after word came that Jack had been killed the girl suddenly went high tragedy on us. Acted as if they'd loved passionately from the cradle." She leaned in, dropping her voice to a stage whisper. "Personally, I don't think Jack O'Gara was capable of loving anything more than he did the bottle and his cards."

She spoke as if imparting a long-suppressed family secret, ignoring the fact she'd been skewering the dearly departed for the last five minutes.

Sabrina hadn't known Jack well. He'd been of an age with Aidan and Brendan and on his occasional visits to Belfoyle had ignored his shy younger girl-cousin. Not hard to do. She'd always been a little afraid of the tall, handsome boy with the clever tongue and a devil's penchant for trouble. In response, she'd retreated to pale silence. Disappeared as soon as he entered a room. It was probable Jack hadn't even remembered Aidan and Brendan had a sister.

But Aidan and he had been close. And her brother had taken Jack's death hard. His letters over the summer had been full of self-recrimination and guilt. Though why he should feel responsible for Jack's coach being attacked by highwaymen, she couldn't fathom.

"Are you heeding me, Sabrina?"

She jerked back to attention. "I'm sorry, Aunt Delia. I suppose the journey has taken its toll." She tried to look suitably fatigued.

Aunt Delia clucked her disapproval. "You always did have your poor mother's constitution. It's no wonder she wasted away after your father died. No spirit." She heaved a bosom-jiggling sigh. "Well, if you're fagged, I'll ring a maid to show you to your room. And your companion—she's properly behaved, I hope."

"Miss Fletcher is a perfectly respectable barrister's daughter, Aunt Delia."

"Oh well, I suppose that's all right then. Not exactly suitable company for the daughter of an earl, but no doubt you're used to consorting with all sorts of rabble in that order of yours."

She couldn't wait to tell Jane she was rabble.

"I should have traveled myself to retrieve you, but I did have the house to complete, staff to hire, supplies to lay in, and there was a political dinner at Dublin Castle I simply had to attend. I was sure you'd understand."

"I was quite well taken care of by Mr. Dixon."

"Hmph. That dwarf. Another whim laid at the foot of that woman. I don't know what Kilronan could have been thinking. The stories I've heard . . ." And on the same complaint that had begun this conversation, Sabrina departed in search of Jane.

"Bloom has just ridden in, sir. He says he brings good news."

"Bring him to me immediately." Hiding his heart's leap of excitement behind a heavy-lidded gaze, Máelodor closed the crumbling vellum pages illustrating Arthur's last battle. The final moments of a king brought down by treachery and betrayal depicted in medieval monkish artistry. The *Other*'s golden age destroyed through one traitorous son's fiendish plotting.

A story repeated in gory detail seven years ago. Brendan Douglas's deceit ending in the murder of his father by the *Amhas-draoi,* the destruction of the Nine, and all they'd striven for with one diabolical action.

But soon all Douglas's treachery would be for naught.

Lazarus had obtained the Kilronan diary. Its secrets revealed to one who could break the warding spells and translate the mysterious language.

And now Bloom arrived with the Rywlkoth Tapestry; the map to Arthur's secret tomb.

Only the stone known as the Sh'vad Tual remained unaccounted for. The key to opening the tomb. Recovering the bones of the *Other*'s sacred king.

Secreted away by Brendan Douglas in the final weeks before the *Amhas-draoi* assault, the stone would only be found with his assistance—willing or unwilling.

And if all went as planned, soon he—like the diary and the tapestry—would be in Máelodor's possession.

His body simmered with violent arousal as he pictured the breaking of Brendan Douglas. He hoped the man begged. Wept. Pleaded for mercy then death.

Despair fed Máelodor's appetites as no woman ever had.

And it had been too long since he'd partaken of either pleasure.

He couldn't wait.

A peremptory knock and his man entered. "Mr. Bloom, sir." He motioned in a travel-spattered gentleman muffled in greatcoat and hat, and still muddy from days on the road. Closed the door silently on his way out.

Máelodor lifted a stern face and ceremonial hand to the newcomer. "I assume your return means you've been successful."

"I have, Great One." He dipped a hand into the lining of his coat. Withdrew a rolled piece of cloth. Handed it over, barely concealing the smug conceit of his success.

Máelodor took it. Untied the ribbon. Spread the tapestry out upon the table.

"It was just where you said it would be," Bloom explained. "With the *bandraoi* at Glenlorgan."

The fibers that had once been white now held the stains of centuries. Rust-brown in spots. Other places faded to dull yellow and gray splotches. One corner was damaged, the threads torn and frayed. But the images depicted remained vibrant and alive.

A scene rendered in beautiful shades of crimson, gold, royal blue, and emerald green. A litter borne by six attendants in heavy armor, their helmets raised, their heads bowed in grief. A line of veiled followers trailing behind, also bent with weeping. One had fallen to his knees. Another paused to give comfort. Ahead a tomb's maw within a rock face. One of the same gray-veiled figures stood beside the open cave. Arms lifted high to where a star rendered in a deep blue shone down upon the litter.

Exquisite detail. Artistically brought to life by the ancient hands that had embroidered it. A priceless artifact of *Other* antiquity.

He closed his hand on the coarse linen. Threw the whole into the fire. And turned his full wrath on the man standing frozen and horrified. "You fool! You wormy son of a bastard's whore. You've brought me the wrong tapestry!"

Eleven

The cathedral brooded against the overcast sky, or perhaps it was merely sulking, surrounded as it was by the helter-skelter of dirty alleys and squalid tenements. A breeze tugged at Sabrina's bonnet and twitched at her skirts as she crossed the muddy grounds to the entrance in company with the rest of Aunt Delia's sightseeing party.

Up ahead, the Misses Trimble walked arm in arm with the gentlemen invited to make up the rest of the group. The trio of giggly sisters batted, sashayed, and simpered like seasoned campaigners. Generals knew less of strategy and tactics than these young women. The men didn't stand a chance.

Aunt Delia shepherded her charges inside, a harried young man in moth-nibbled coat and much-darned stockings rushing to meet them.

"Mr. Munsy has kindly agreed to show us around," Aunt Delia chirped. "Wasn't that nice of him?"

The young curate bowed and smiled.

The sisters giggled.

Sabrina rolled her eyes and tried to pretend she didn't know any of them.

The group followed the proud oratory of the flustered curate whose booming voice seemed incompatible with his scarecrow gawkiness. ". . . built originally by the Danes . . ."

Glenlorgan's simple chapel couldn't compare to the grandiosity of the cathedral, but the smells were similar. Candle wax, incense, and wet wool. So too was the serenity that comes of great age and great faith. The mind-clearing clarity infusing the very air. They wrapped around Sabrina like a comforting blanket or a parent's hug. Lifted her burdens of uncertainty, anxiety, and Aunt Delia's incessant prickly chatter. Strengthened her determination to return to the order as soon as possible. Aidan would not win. Not on this. She was not the submissive child of his memory, and she refused to be pushed about like a pawn on a chess board.

". . . oldest building in Dublin . . ."

Above her, choristers practiced their scales to a violin's scratchy accompaniment.

". . . the Welsh-Norman Strongbow . . ."

"I believe our enthusiastic tour guide plans a test at the end of his lecture."

Sabrina flashed a startled look at the gentleman who'd stepped up silently beside her. Tall and lean with an icy crispness, from his wheat-gold hair to the diamond-encrusted fob hanging from his waistcoat pocket, Mr. St. John oozed elegance and wealth from every pore. How on earth had Aunt Delia managed to convince him to join their sightseeing party? And how had the Trimbles let him escape?

"I'm afraid he'll be sorely disappointed in his pupils." She cast her eyes over the bored-looking group. "They don't seem terribly interested, do they?"

St. John motioned toward Jane. "Miss Fletcher seems riveted."

He was right. Jane hung on Mr. Munsy's every word. He blushed his appreciation and doubled his speech-making efforts. Now with arm gestures.

"Unfortunately for the curate, it's sympathy rather than interest," she explained ruefully. "The less the others attend to him, the more Jane will. She hates anyone to feel slighted."

"An admirable quality in a young lady. But I'm sure you're just as endowed with similar gifts."

Did he give her a certain look when he spoke? His smile a bit brighter? His eyes a bit sharper? Was that last pause a beat too long? What did he mean by "gifts"? Did he seek to discover if she was *Other*? Was he merely being polite? Was she being overly suspicious?

She mumbled a response, praying it satisfied him and he'd return to the group, which had made it halfway up the nave and were now admiring the gothic architecture and learning which bits dated to when.

Unfortunately he took her arm, forcing her to accompany him as he strolled. Perfect—now she had to come up with chitchat. She detested chitchat. And his touch was cold even through the sleeve of her pelisse.

She scrambled for anything to fill the awful, awkward silence. "Have you lived in Dublin long, sir?"

"Since early spring. But I hear you're newly arrived. How are you liking the city's delights thus far?"

Nothing intrusive about that. Perhaps she imagined her misgivings.

"To be honest, I'm still gaining my sea legs as it were." She tried catching Jane's eye, giving the universal sign for *Help, reinforcements needed.* No luck.

"Your aunt mentioned your brother and his wife are due to arrive soon." He leaned in, pressing her elbow. Another cool touch sending shivers up her arm. "Lord Kilronan's unexpected marriage put quite a few pretty little noses out of joint." His gaze passed over the giggling Trimbles.

She stiffened, withdrawing her hand. Flashing him a dangerous look. "Odd. They never cared overmuch for his attentions when he stood on the brink of financial ruin."

He smiled a mouth full of shiny teeth. "I took you for a little sparrow, but you've the courage of an eagle. I wish my sisters were as quick to defend me against my enemies."

Feeling a fool now for overreacting—and after all Aidan hardly needed her protection—she made overt gestures behind her back with her guidebook. "I apologize for losing my temper." Cleared her throat dramatically. "I shouldn't have implied . . . I mean . . ." Coughed loudly and repeatedly. "Kilronan hardly needs my assistance. He's quite able to defend himself."

Jane remained engrossed by Mr. Munsy.

St. John, on the other hand, was eying her with alarm. "Are you quite all right, Lady Sabrina? Perhaps a drink? Let me find you one."

He set off in search of water, giving her the opportunity to dive into the nearest stall. Peeking around a column, she smiled when St. John became ensnared by the youngest and sauciest Trimble, who seemed in no hurry to release her prize. He glanced back once. Frowned at the empty spot where Sabrina had been before he was led off by a determined Trimble. The whole group headed toward the stairs leading down to the crypt.

The curate's voice rose above the chorister's growing rehearsal. ". . . dating from the twelfth century . . ."

The Trimble girls gave a chorus of frightened giggles—what else?—and the whole lot of them disappeared.

Finally.

Sliding into a pew, she sought to recover her lost peace. Push aside the embarrassing conversation with Mr. St. John. No doubt her entire stay in the city would be made up of similar humiliating inanities.

After so many years with the *bandraoi,* she'd forgotten the hustle and hazards of the outside world. The constant jostling and noise. The overt, curious stares and the din of raised voices. Already the unceasing barrage of unfiltered emotion battered her mind. Washed against her brain like a steady lapping tide. A few moments to herself was bliss.

The choir began low and uncertain before rising in strength and numbers. A soaring celebration that the stone of the cathedral gathered and spread until the rhythm swam up through the soles of her boots. Hummed along her bones. Filled her head with sound and light and melody and bass. One voice rose above the others. A clear vivid soprano.

She closed her eyes, letting the music and the voice wind its way through her.

A tenor joined the soprano. Dipping in and out of the melody. Picking up when the soprano flagged. Then taking over completely. The tune changed as well. No longer solemn and reverential, now the melody leapt and skipped like the measure of a dance. Latin giving way to a strange lilting tongue she didn't understand though somehow she knew the song spoke of love and heartbreak and loss.

Opening her eyes, she gasped her dismay. No. Not again. It wasn't possible. This wasn't supposed to happen now that Daigh was gone. She wasn't supposed to be sitting beside a hissing fire. Its dim light should not be gilding his hair with a fiery glow as he sharpened his blade. She could not be hearing the rhythmic slide of his stone up and down the heavy sword or a harper's agile fingers and clear bell-like singing.

But she was.

Daigh slid the sword back into its sheath. Stood, drawing her up beside him where she encountered not his usual empty black gaze, but eyes, clear and gray-green. As yet, unchased by shadows.

"I leave for Caernarvon at dawn. There's trouble brewing, and Prince Hywel has asked I attend his father there."

She frowned. "Then I go too. I've seen those women at court looking at you. Like a feast."

He laughed. Planted a kiss on her cheek. His chest rose and fell beneath her palm. His heart a rapid drumbeat. His voice vibrating in a deep rumble she felt all the way up her arm. "Jealous? I'm flattered, but I can't take you. Not this time."

The harper ended his song, the last plucked strings quivering to silence.

She opened her mouth to argue just as a hand clamped her quiet. An arm held her close.

And she came terrifyingly awake.

Success.

Máelodor opened his eyes, though even that tiny action tired him. His heart crashed against his ribs. Pain squeezed his chest, shooting down his arms. His breathing came in wheezy bursts. Every gulp of air cramping his straining lungs.

He'd crossed distances and dimensions. Tracked the murkiest paths. Followed the trail into the deepest abyss and back out. The *Unseelie* sensed him as he passed. They called to him. Beseeched their release. He ignored their pleas. They would need to wait for their reward. It was not yet time.

Instead he reached ever outward. Mind to mind. Pushing himself far past his normal breaking point. But his efforts had been rewarded. He'd succeeded. Felt an answering touch. Sensed the mage-bond between master and slave. Stretched taut. Barely functioning. But intact.

He would rest. Recover. And when next he attempted the crossing, he would repair the connection between the *Domnuathi* and himself. Reinforce his supremacy. Regain control.

"You nearly scared me to death."

Daigh rested his arms on the back of her pew, his eyes burning in a stricken, haunted face. "I didn't want a scene."

"Grabbing and gagging me was supposed to keep me calm?" She frowned, trying to pull her mind back from the vision still haunting her of Daigh as he'd been in her dream. The teasing smile. The kiss. The warmth of his body beneath her hand. She massaged her temples. Why was this happening to her?

The Daigh in front of her now looked ready to go up in flames. He fumed with suppressed rage, his body radiating violence. "No, I meant only to keep you quiet." He leaned toward her, running a thumb over her cheek. "You're crying."

Disconcerted, she put a gloved hand to her face. "Am I? A dream I had. It was nothing. And certainly not about you."

Amusement lit for a moment the scouring intensity of his gaze. "Tell me about this dream that had nothing to do with me."

She would not let him drag her back under his spell. He'd lied to her. Made her feel a yearning she didn't want to feel. Made her picture a life that wasn't hers, yet one she began to long for with every new encounter. Then made a fool of her for even imagining.

She tipped a stubborn chin in his direction. "Very well. We were talking. You . . ." She paused, embarrassed. "You kissed me."

Grief dimmed his smile. "Then what?"

"You told me you were being called back to Caernarvon. That Prince Hywel needed you."

His gaze fled inward. His voice coming low and certain. "There was to be a meeting with the English. I was summoned to translate. To spy."

At once, his shoulders hunched as if he'd been struck. Sweat sprang out upon his forehead, and he slumped heavy against the pew.

"Daigh!" She reached for him, but he shook his head. "It happens when I remember. It passes soon enough."

He closed his eyes. Breathed deeply through his nose. Teeth chattering. Body shaking.

Her eyes burned, a tear sliding down her cheek. "Spy on who? The English? Are you French? A soldier for Napoléon? That's it, isn't it? Oh gods, I'm harboring a war fugitive."

"Nay, Sabrina," he coaxed her back from the brink of hysteria. "You needn't add that fear to your others."

"But what I dreamt. It was a memory. Your memory. Just like the last time."

"Aye."

"Then you can tell me who Hywel is? Prince of what? Why am I dreaming *your* memories? As if I was there and a part of them?"

He turned away, his jaw clamping. Eyes distant. Voice cagey. "I can't explain. I don't know."

She didn't believe him for an instant. Even if she hadn't felt his tension thicken like a cold fog, there was a tone in his voice telling her he lied. "What are you doing here, Daigh? Are you following me?"

"Not you. The man you were with. What did he want? What did he ask you?"

"Mr. St. John . . ." She paused, her brows drawn into a frown. "You know him?"

"We've met before." He flinched, spinning away. "And if I didn't need him alive, I'd put a bullet in him right now."

She grabbed his hand. "Daigh, what's going on? Why did you run away that night? And why are you acting as if Mr. St. John were the devil's henchman?"

"As if? The man could show Satan a trick or two."

"That's not answering my question."

"How did the sisters explain my disappearance?"

"They called you a thief. Said you broke into Ard-siúr's office. Stole things."

"And the blood?" So casual, as if his life hadn't been spattered from wall to wall. And yet here he stood. Whole and infuriatingly uninformative.

"A quarrel among thieves," she answered.

The corner of his mouth twisted, his expression hardening. "Right enough as far as it went."

"What's that supposed to mean?"

His features rearranged themselves into cool impenetrability as he answered questions with questions. "My turn. What are you doing in Dublin? Damn it, Sabrina. You're supposed to be safe at Glenlorgan. Not here. And certainly not with that villain."

"My brother sent for me."

He went rigid, every inch of steel reasserting itself. Now he towered over her like an erupting thundercloud. Menacing. Powerful. Dangerous. "The Earl of Kilronan? Sabrina, did he say why? Or ask you about a tapestry? It was kept with the *bandraoi*."

The blank wall. The frayed threads. "You stole it. Sister Ainnir was right."

He spoke over her. "Listen to me, Sabrina. Did Kilronan mention a tapestry? Someone named Máelodor? Or your brother Brendan?"

"How could you take from—" She drew up short. "What did you say?"

"Did Kilronan mention Brendan Douglas? That he'd seen him? Been in touch with him?"

How did it all come back to Brendan? It was as if in writing about that horrible long-ago day she'd summoned some dark, threatening evil from the past. She stared at him blankly. "What have you heard? What do you know of Brendan?"

Footsteps and voices growing louder. Aunt Delia's voice hallooing as if she were on the hunting field. "Sabrina! Darling! Where've you taken yourself off to?"

She turned to leave. "I've got to go."

He grasped her hand. Pulled her close, his face inches away from hers. "Stay away from St. John. Don't talk to him. Don't trust him."

She nodded dumbly. The black of his eyes drawing her in until the heat of a fire, the song of a harpist, and the rasp of stone on steel filled her head. She need only let herself be swept into that gaze to be back in that place.

"I'll see you soon." He released her, shocking her out of the moment.

"Promise me?" Challenge in her tone.

He did not—or could not—answer.

twelve

Daigh tossed back his wine. Poured another from the bottle left by the publican. Sought to gather the lost pieces of his life. Hywel. Caernarvon. Sabrina might not have known the significance of those tossed words, but he did. She had triggered a cascade of images. Two lives sliding simultaneously through his fractured mind.

A man honor bound to his prince and liege lord, whose mixed lineage made him an asset to Gwynedd's court.

A man slave bound to a gnarled, haggard master-mage with a malicious nature whose hands dealt excruciating pain. Whose mouth spewed mind-twisting poison.

Máelodor. The *Other* who'd unearthed his bones. Had pulled his spirit from the abyss of *Annwn* and bound him once more to this plane as a *Domnuathi,* a soldier of Domnu. To a life splintered and broken where memories brought with them body crushing pain, and where a dark force always lurked just beyond his consciousness. An evil that was both a part of him and a way to control him.

The black rage had almost conquered him this afternoon. His nightmare come true. Lancelot, or as he now discovered, St. John with Sabrina. The whoreson touching her arm. Whispering his nauseating filth in her ear. Close enough to steal her away to be used as bait.

Seeing them together nearly destroyed every wall he'd struggled to build between sanity and the howling storm of madness. Awakened his killer instinct, narrowing his vision to a pinprick, icing over a soul black with hate.

What had pulled him from the brink? What had fed the demons pursuing him, allowing him to escape?

He closed his fingers over the lacing of scars across his palm. Pushed himself back from the table to stand.

A memory. A dream. A precious moment from a life that couldn't have happened.

Sabrina.

This time the misshapen dwarf barely cracked the door open before tossing him a belligerent scowl. "Lord Kilronan's still not at home."

"I know," Daigh said, jamming his foot in the door before the man could slam it shut. "It's Lady Sabrina I want. Tell her Daigh MacLir calls for her."

He might as well have told the man to strip naked and paint himself blue. He eyed him like a disease.

"Lady Sabrina's not at home," he answered in an imperious tone. "But even if she were, she's certainly not available to persons what look as if they're straight from Newgate."

Daigh's temper flared. "It's urgent."

The man stood his ground, though his voice came shakier than before. "Urgent or not, if I was to let every

Tom, Dick, and Harry in here what says they know my lady, I'd soon be out of a position."

It wouldn't take more than a mere shove to propel himself inside. But what if the man spoke the truth and Sabrina had gone out for the evening. He'd gain nothing and be worse off than if he withdrew gracefully and tried again later.

Removing his boot, Daigh said, "Thank you for your help," not even trying to hide his sarcasm.

The dwarf snorted. Slammed the door. Slid the bolt home with a resounding thud.

So much for coming in by the front door.

He stared up at the town house. A light shone from an upper window, but the lower floors remained dark. A narrow alley ran beside the house. Stairs led down to a locked door. An iron gate—unlatched—beyond which shrubbery crowded in a tiny patch of garden at the back of the house.

Light from a second-floor window threw squares of yellow across the lawn. Thick vines climbed a trellis along the back wall, a few summer roses still faded and clinging.

He withdrew silently.

But he'd be back.

Half asleep, she rose from bed, drawn to the window by an undefined apprehension. The icy floorboards chilled her fully awake, the sharp air she inhaled pulling her from the last of her dreams.

Crossing the room, she tried ignoring the troupe of cherubs cavorting upon her mantel and the winged Hermes in perpetual flight upon her desk. But Aunt Delia's odd bent in objets d'art only seemed to emphasize the world Sabrina had been shoved into against her will. A world as alien to her now as if she'd never been born into it. Never known the life of the earl's daughter. Only the *bandraoi* apprentice.

The city seemed to rise around her. Hemming her in. Drowning her out. So many voices. So many feelings. Humming and buzzing through her mind like an angry swarm of bees.

Pushing the heavy drapes aside, she stared down into the garden. Leaves clung to the slippery wet branches of the trees despite the stiff wind. A cat yowled its desire to be let in. Raucous laughter echoed up and down the street from a few young bucks making a late night of it.

She felt as if she were shrinking with each hour that passed. Stepping back to the time when she couldn't speak without stuttering. Couldn't move without stumbling. Couldn't exist without feeling that every eye was upon her, waiting for her next embarrassing misstep. Even the fingernail moon riding low in the west seemed to wink at her in disdain.

The days spent in Aunt Delia's company hadn't detracted from that feeling. Only intensified it. Her aunt's greatest pleasure seeming to be ripping family and friends to shreds over the evening meal.

Tonight for instance.

Jane had smiled and eaten, now and then shooting Sabrina glances of shared amusement. Mouthing the word "rabble" at inconvenient intervals. But beyond that, she'd been absolutely no help in deflecting Aunt Delia's attention or breaking into the one-sided chatter—her aunt more than able to hold up all sides of any conversation.

Just as well. Sabrina's mind swung from thought to thought like a pendulum, catching a comment here and there while wrestling with the echoes of her last conversation with Daigh.

Aunt Delia recounted Aidan's wife's less-than-stellar origins . . .

"A brewer's stepdaughter of all things, darling."

Did Kilronan mention Brendan Douglas?

The scandal with an as-yet-unnamed gentleman that sparked her fall from Society . . .

"Some say she was actually with child, though I don't countenance such vulgarity. Aidan would never tarnish his family's name by marrying another man's whore."

What do you know of Brendan?

The rumors about her lost years that included, of all ridiculous charges, life as a thief in the employ of a murdered archrogue . . .

"They say he was slaughtered. Not enough pieces left of him to bury."

Stay away from St. John.

Aidan's besotted love that had exiled him to the remote reaches of Belfoyle where Lady Kilronan's lack of social entrée wouldn't be an issue . . .

"Not seen him since Kilronan House burned. Married by the village priest. No family present. Not even a proper wedding breakfast."

Don't talk to him. Don't trust him.

By the time the servants had removed the dessert course, Sabrina's sympathies lay squarely in Lady Kilronan's camp. And she almost looked forward to meeting the colorful and much-maligned countess. Anyone who could ruffle Aunt Delia's feathers couldn't be all bad.

Still, it made Sabrina acutely aware of the scrutiny she'd undergo while under her aunt's chaperonage. What on earth would happen if Daigh showed up here? Would it be better if he didn't?

She shivered, recalling the warmth of his touch, his full, sensual lips, his hard, brutal beauty. She swallowed around the knot in her throat as heat pooled low in her stomach. And most important, how would she handle her growing attraction to a man whose past intruded into her mind with the clarity of memory?

I'll see you soon.

What unknown force brought them together?

What unknown link bound them together?

And what unknown trouble would they face together?

For trouble was coming. She felt it in the crisp November breeze. In the flutter of blood beneath her skin.

She dropped the drapes back into place over the window. Crossed to the desk. And, scowling at winged Hermes, opened her journal. Put pen to paper in an attempt to fight off the realization that what she'd taken for the storm had only been the calm before the tempest yet to come.

The wall, the trellis, and poorly pointed brickwork. Daigh was in.

Sabrina's scent hung in the air. A dying fire glowed red in the grate. The bed a jumble of gray against the darker shadows.

He took a step farther into the room, and the world exploded behind his eyes. His legs crumpling. The floor rushing up to meet him.

"You!" Sabrina hissed.

He rolled over, touching his head. His fingers coming away sticky. "Bloody hell, woman. Are you crazed?"

She glared down at him, still holding the heavy marble

statue she'd used to crack him over the skull. "I'm not the one breaking into a lady's bedchamber in the middle of the night."

Already regretting the reckless impulse bringing him here, he shoved himself up onto an elbow, wincing against the room's dizzy whirl. "You asked me to come."

"Not like a thief in the night. That's twice now you've nearly frightened me out of my wits."

"I needed to see you."

"You've certainly managed that." She cinched her robe closed more firmly around her waist, but it only highlighted the shapely curve of her hips, the smooth skin showing above the collar of her shift, hair atumble down her back, wisps framing the narrow oval of her face. The fire reflecting in her eyes like flames upon a dark sea.

Her face haunted his memories. He'd caressed the silk of her cheeks, kissed her sensual lips, caused laughter to brighten her eyes.

Why did he remember her this way? Was he going mad? Was he already there?

"If my aunt finds you here . . ." Her gaze darted toward the door.

He shoved his thoughts away. They brought him nowhere. Whatever past he recalled, it was one he could never recover. Whatever woman he remembered was naught but dust. "She won't. If you disarm, we can talk. Then I'll leave. No one will know I was here."

She eyed the statue uncertainly. Placed it on a nearby table, though within reach.

He dragged himself upright, the room staying comfortingly in one place. He touched his scalp. No bleeding and barely a bump. This hadn't been the wisest of plans. But it had gotten him inside. And with Sabrina. Alone.

He ground his jaw. Refused to let his mad sexual fantasies get in the way. He needed information. That was all. Nothing else.

He inhaled a shaky breath.

"I didn't hurt you too badly, did I?" Eying him contritely, she fiddled with the tie of her robe.

"Nothing permanent." He grimaced.

"Of course." Her voice sharpened. "Then you can explain why you broke into my bedchamber."

Pacing a few steps, he leaned against the mantel. Stared into the slumbering fire. "Tell me about Brendan." She gave a little gasp. He whirled to face her. "Then I'll tell you what I *can*."

Her gaze narrowed at his choice of phrase, but she didn't argue. Instead, she dropped into a chair. Her profile etched in soft charcoal lines. "What do you want to know?"

"Anything. Everything."

She shook her head as if it pained her. "He disappeared seven years ago just before my father's murder. But—"

"Murder?"

She flashed him a scorching glare. "My father was executed by the *Amhas-draoi*."

He jerked in his seat, a flush of heat then cold queasing him from head to foot.

Did you really think you could win against an Amhas-draoi*?*

Lancelot's taunt curled up from a corner where he'd shoved the man's predatory sexuality. The scouring taste of his mouth crushed to his. The nerve-disrupting blast of magic that had left Daigh praying for death amid his own vomit.

Sabrina continued, unaware of Daigh's struggle against the cloying chilly sweat. Still with her eyes locked on her lap. Her words lacking any emotion as if she spoke of strangers. "Father and his associates were hunted down and executed."

Were Máelodor and St. John after Douglas as part of some *Ambas-draoi* operation? No, couldn't be. They'd been too wary of discovery. And St. John had spoken of their plan. *Other* dominance. The Nine.

He followed a hunch. "Did Máelodor suffer the same fate?"

She looked up. A line between her brows. "I've never heard that name." She gave a slight shake of her head.

A roadblock. He detoured. "What were your father and his friends doing to have the *Ambas-draoi* after them?"

"Daigh, tell me what's going on?"

"I will, but first—what were they planning? What crimes did they commit that ended in a death sentence?"

She subsided, but fear finally stole over her face. "The *Ambas-draoi* came to me at Glenlorgan. They asked me questions. Over and over until I wanted to scream. Then they told me horrible stories of Father and Brendan. I didn't want to believe them, but they said they had proof."

Daigh watched as the past took hold of her. Her body fading into the dark as if hoping none would find her there. The world and the memories might pass her by.

"They claimed Father and the others twisted their mage energy into dangerous paths. Worked dark magics. Experimented with things they shouldn't have."

Summoning *Domnuathi* perhaps? He pushed that thought away as being of little use.

"Your brother disappeared," he mused.

She stiffened, her face once more achingly alive. Fever bright with unshed tears. "It was just before Father's murder. He said he had to leave for a time. Then he never wrote. Never tried to contact me. After all these years, I just assumed he was dead. Like Father and Mother. Like all of them." Did she seek to convince him or herself?

He took her hands in his. The bones fragile. His work-roughened skin at odds with her dainty femininity. "He's not, Sabrina. Brendan Douglas is alive."

Her lashes swept down to shield her thoughts from him, her face averted. "How can you be certain?"

"The night I disappeared from Glenlorgan I surprised an intruder in Ard-siúr's office. He'd been sent by a man named Máelodor to steal a tapestry from the *bandraoi*. I followed him as far as Cork before he escaped, but I overheard him speak of Brendan. He'd been seen in Dublin and was thought to be trying to contact the Earl of Kilronan."

Her face went rigid, her hands clenched in her lap. "And you think that's why Aidan summoned me to Dublin?"

Their eyes met, hers so deep a blue as to be painful. A bottomless well in which he might forget the horrors of his existence. The truth of his monstrous origins. Tears illuminated the indigo brilliance of her gaze. Quivered on her lashes. A silver track sliding down one pale cheek.

He turned back to the fire. Suddenly needing to put a distance between them. Space for him to breathe. Gain control. Remember what he was. And what could not be. "I don't know. But it all fits together. The tapestry was housed with the *bandraoi*. You've been called to Dublin, where Douglas was last seen."

"It does make sense." She rose to join him at the hearth.

He stared down into her upturned face. Full lips curved in a hesitant smile. Dark brown hair crackling and wild around her head. Smelling wind-sweet. A shock wave of raw arousal burst through him.

He couldn't help himself. He traced the line of her jaw. The long swanlike column of her throat.

She didn't move away, but he caught her broken breathing. The pulse leaping at the base of her throat. Saw his desire mirrored in her eyes.

What would it be like to come over her skin on skin? To stroke her sleek body until she cried out for release? To bury himself in her welcoming heat and feel his own nerve-sizzling climax between her legs? And why did he feel he should already know?

He dropped his hand to his side where it curled into an angry fist. "I must leave you."

She gave him a curious look. "Daigh, you could have stayed with the *bandraoi*. Explained to Ard-siúr. She would have understood and helped."

"There were reasons it was best to leave."

A regretful quirk of her lips. "Which you're not going to explain."

"I can't, Sabrina. You'll have to trust me."

"Was the man you surprised in Ard-siúr's office Mr. St. John?"

"No. But St. John is part of it."

"Part of what?"

"I don't know. Yet. Just stay clear of him, and if you hear from your brother, warn him. Tell him he's being hunted. Máelodor is after him. Maybe he'll understand better than I do."

He took a deep breath in an effort to shake himself free of this woman, this room, this fantasy where Sabrina remained within his heart's reach.

Bloom had called him a demon. Lancelot had labeled him monster. And were they far wrong? Sabrina, alone, had looked on him without worry. Without fear. Without loathing. A heat in those deep blue eyes that warmed even the parts of him that held the taint of the grave.

A heat that would vanish if she ever learned the truth. That Daigh MacLir was a myth.

Lazarus the reality.

thirteen

Daigh wasted no time tracking down St. John.

He'd entered the building across the street last night. Had yet to leave. In the interim carriages deposited their rain-soaked passengers at the steps leading up to a fan-lighted bright green door. Other cabs clattered to a halt to pick up the umbrellaed gentlemen emerging into the autumn downpour.

When Daigh had taxed a passerby on the building's purpose, he was given a quick fearful once-over and a stuttering confession that it housed a gentleman's club.

So that begged the question: Why did a fashionably dressed young woman descend the steps?

High-class whore? Perhaps. She'd not the usual look of a light heel in her well-appointed outfit and the proud set of her head, but then he didn't expect the type of gentlemen he'd seen over the last day to settle for a greasy-haired slattern in a gin-stained smock.

As he watched, she checked the street with a frown of

displeasure before making a hasty retreat toward a nearby hackney stand.

He drew in behind her. A whore might be the easiest way to gather the information he needed. Pillow talk spilled for a discreet bribe. Hardly an inspired plan, but he'd already suffered St. John's brand of pain. Had no wish for a repeat of his repulsive appetites.

She slowed as they neared the corner, and he quickly drew into an alley. If she knew she were being followed, she might duck into one of the many shops lining the street, and he'd be back to playing the waiting game.

After a few moments, she resumed her pace. Hailed the cab with a businesslike shout.

The driver bowed her in. Shut the door, taking his seat on the box behind a dagger-hipped nag with a weary air.

At the slap of the reins, Daigh made his move. Threaded the few rain-muffled pedestrians. Jumped for the hackney, unlatching the door with a menacing glare for the driver, who chose cowardice over duty and ignored the trespass. He slid inside, shaking the rain from his coat.

"So glad you could join me, sir." The woman smiled coquettishly as she leveled a snub-nosed pistol at his chest.

Miss Helena Roseingrave strode the room like a field commander. A steel gleam in her dark eyes. A testament to the warrior goddess Scathach's training from the breadth of her shoulders to the belligerent jut of her chin.

"Why should I believe anything you tell me?" she spat. "You're no more than Douglas's conjured killer."

"Ask Lady Sabrina yourself."

She regarded him with an intense stare that—more so than the weapon—had held him immobile through their short cab ride and the exchange that followed. "Perhaps I shall."

"It's Máelodor you should be hunting. Not Douglas," Daigh growled.

"We executed Máelodor in Paris years ago. Douglas, on the other hand, is still a wanted fugitive. Gervase St. John is no rogue bounty hunter, he's a trusted member of the brotherhood."

"So you'll ignore my warnings as the ravings of a madman?"

"You're worse than a madman, aren't you . . . Lazarus." She smiled with glacier warmth.

The presence screamed its pleasure. Punched against the insides of Daigh's skull with a fist like a mace. He jerked in his chair. Bit back a grunt of pain. Sweat beading his brow. He'd not let it take him over. Not let it win. It was what Máelodor wanted. Control. Domination. Damnation.

She watched his inner conflict with scientific indifference. "He lives inside you. His blood fed your creation. His madness lit the fire beneath your bones. And while you both exist, he'll always be there, infecting your mind with his evil."

"I'll fight him off."

Another sharp shrug. "You can't hold out against his will. He's your maker."

"So end my misery. Kill me."

Her eyes flew to his, the longing to do just that starkly apparent. "Much as I'd like to, I can't. As a *Domnuathi* and warded by Douglas's *Unseelie* spells, you're inviolate to all but the most powerful magics. Those wielded by the *Fey* themselves. You're enthralled to your master until he tires of you."

His flesh crawled against the venom of St. John's hissed

words. His seeking hands. His sickening kiss. "I'm no man's slave," he snarled.

She cocked her head, gazed upon him with steel-dark eyes. "You're the twisted sum of your creator's ambitions."

"As will Arthur be if what you say is true and their goal is to resurrect him." *And by the gods, what a thought.*

"It won't get that far. We'll find Douglas before he can locate and breach the High King's tomb."

"And after you capture Douglas? After you realize it's Máelodor you should fear? By then it'll be too late."

She remained infuriatingly placid, but all the colder for it. "A chance the brotherhood will take."

Her words, uttered in such a calm manner, gave no hint to the crash of mage energy she unleashed.

It toppled him from his chair. He screamed, writhing like a beast caught in a trap. And gave himself to the uncoiling power of the presence. Let it pour from him in a scalding torrent of magic and strength.

Scrambling to his knees, he deflected her spell with a curse of his own that had her reeling. And left him stunned.

He could wield that much magic? Another secret lost in the unreachable depths of his forgotten memories.

But once discovered, the powers flooded his senses. Ability and then instinct controlling the mage energy surging along his bloodstream like oil burning on water.

He sucked air into his collapsed lungs as he parried the strongest of Roseingrave's attacks while tempering his own response. Difficult to do as she pummeled him with spell after devastating spell, but he would not be goaded into retaliation. He needed her alive. Needed her willing to listen.

"Why?" he squeezed through teeth clenched against the searing pain centered at the base of his brain.

"I'm sworn to protect humanity from things like you."

As if she'd conjured it from air and speed, she fisted a dagger. The blade's flash caught out of the corner of his eye. The weapon's descent barely missing him as he dodged out of its path.

In response, he slammed her to the floor with a blaze of mage energy pulled from some hidden recess of knowledge. Held her there.

She glared up at him, loathing visible in the strained muscles of her neck, her white, bitter features as she lunged for the weapon.

He tore the dagger from her hand. Touched it to her throat. "Will you surrender all for vengeance? Máelodor's got the tapestry. All he needs is the stone and Arthur will be his."

Her mage energy battered at him like a hurricane tide, and only his newfound battle-magic kept him on his feet and dead-steady.

"If St. John and Máelodor succeed in starting this war, it's the end of the *Other*."

He saw her mind chewing over his words.

"The *Duinedon* are too numerous. Too strong. They'll slaughter you all."

Her spells eased. Just enough so his every breath didn't come laced with broken glass. He used the respite for one last appeal. "What do you stand to lose?"

A tense moment followed, suspicion vivid in her gaze. Finally, she spoke through a hissed indrawn breath. "What's your proposal?"

He pulled her to her feet. "Aid me. If I'm wrong, I'll accept any punishment the *Ambas-draoi* mete out."

"And if you're speaking truth?"

Scathach. Warrior goddess. Head of the Order of *Ambas-draoi*. True *Fey*.

A thought hit him like a blow. A flash of inspiration. "Scathach sends me back."

"You want her to—"

"Kill me. Aye."

She raked him with a long prescient look. "So right or wrong, you end with what you want."

He thought of Sabrina. The damaged memories she'd loosed. Of her. And him. And a past that could never have happened. The fragile dreams she'd evoked. Of the two of them. And a future that would never be theirs.

"Do I?"

She didn't answer right away. Instead, she strode to the window. Looked out on the night for long quiet minutes. When she turned back, her face held a frightening and grim determination. "You have a deal. I'll see what I can find out. But you must do something for me."

"Go on."

"Help me find Douglas."

"If the *Ambas-draoi* haven't found him in seven years, what makes you think I can?"

"Simple." She lifted a brow in coy suggestion. "Ask Lady Sabrina."

Aha! Just where the clerk told her it would be. Sabrina pulled the book from the lending library's shelf as Jane appeared from the next aisle over.

"Have you found what you were looking for?"

Sabrina held up her one fat volume in answer: *A Full History of Wales As Recounted by a Most Learned Professor and Traveler of That Fine Country.*

The title had been squashed onto the spine in a font so tiny one needed a magnifying glass to make it out.

Jane cocked her head. Grimaced. "Yikes. Trouble sleeping?"

Did she ever.

Daigh's pounding questions and stunted explanations set her mind spinning off into unexplored possibilities. None of them heartening. A stolen tapestry? Máelodor? Her father's death? Brendan's return? How were they all linked? And where did Daigh fit into that puzzle? And did any of it explain the mysterious pull of Daigh's memories? The life she saw as hers with a man she'd only met weeks earlier?

Days and nights of an endless circle of unanswerables had unraveled her, Jane finally coming to Sabrina's room with a dose of her own medicine.

"Here." She handed her a cup. "This was given to me by a talented healer. It helps when you're having trouble sleeping."

She'd almost spilled her worries to Jane right there. But in the end had kept quiet and accepted the draught. She didn't want to worry her friend now that she was finally losing that frozen rabbit look. And what would Sabrina say? *By the way, the man I'm hallucinating about is back. And he's warned me my dead brother is alive and being hunted by someone named Máelodor?*

Not exactly conversation of the sane.

Aunt Delia would be no help. She'd long ago renounced the *Other*-born part of herself. Had seen no social advantage or monetary gain in her *Fey* blood. And only used the simplest of magics—those manifested in chubby cherubs and fires that smelled less like smoke and more like rosewater.

Sabrina had even tried penning a letter to Ard-siúr, the

first draft ending in the fire along with the four versions that followed. The head of their order had asked about Brendan. But did she ask because she assumed his guilt or because she believed his innocence? Sabrina had no way of knowing, and if her brother ran for his life, she'd do him no favors by giving him away.

Sabrina clutched the book to her chest. "I've always been interested in the history of Wales."

"Since when?"

"Oh ages and ages." She waved vaguely, praying Jane didn't push. The trouble with having a friend who'd known her so long.

"If you say so. I'll meet you by the door when you're finished."

Bless Jane and her lack of curiosity. Sabrina beamed at her in grateful thanks.

Finding an empty desk, she sat down. Opened to the table of contents and ran a finger down the page. Here was one mystery she could solve on her own.

Topography.
Flora and fauna.
Population.

No. No. And no.

The list went on through early inhabitants. Religion. Folklore. Food.

Finally toward the bottom. Powys. Dyfed. Gwent. Gwynedd.

Kings.
Lines of descent.

She ran her finger down the list until she came to Hywel ab Owain Gwynedd. Son of Owain Gwynedd. Killed in 1170.

She blinked. Read it again.

Killed in 1170.

At Pentraeth.

Ambushed and murdered by his stepmother's sons.

Ambushed. Murdered.

She slammed the book closed. Took a deep calming breath while terror scissored her insides and her mind refused to believe. Refused to think beyond the date. The name. An explanation.

The library air grew damp and heavy with wood smoke and leaf mold. An acrid musty autumn smell. Her head swam, and she clutched the table for support. But the table was gone. The shelves naught more than ghostly outlines. The building fading to a foggy swirl of damp cloud.

She staggered for balance and caught sight of her hands. Browned by the summer Welsh sun, clutching long woolen skirts. A belt of ornamented leather hung low from her waist. Keys dangling at her hip.

As she hurried across the yard from the byre to the house, thoughts scurried like field mice through her head. The cows needed milking. The spinning was woefully behind. Astrid was down with fever. And Daigh was gone. He'd traveled to meet the prince despite her pleas that he remain with her. Instead he'd insisted. Had spoken of loyalty to his liege. His need to aid Hywel in securing a throne usurped by his conniving stepbrothers. And none of her warnings swayed him. *Please,* she begged the gods. *Please bring him safe back to me.*

Her head throbbed with broken mirror images of herself, but the only thought that surfaced was Hywel. Killed in battle. Dead in a slaughter that left few alive to flee. Including Daigh.

A hand came around her shoulder. Corded. Scarred. The tip of one finger missing. Closed the book on a sigh of fluttering pages. "A woman's curiosity is a dangerous thing."

The lilting accent wrapped around her. Dragged her back into the present on a tunneling tidal surge of emotion.

She spun in her seat, ribs pressed into her lungs. Breathing shallow and fast.

He took the chair beside her without invitation. Gazed on her calmly, though she felt the bash of his emotions like a hammer against the inside of her skull. His body vibrated like a stretched bowstring, though his face remained carved in solemn resignation. "Now you know the truth."

She studied him covertly for the signs she'd missed. But nothing screamed dead man ahead. No hint of the tomb in his bronzed skin or thick dark hair. In the titan strength of his frame or his soldier's agility.

"Are you a ghost?" Her voice came out in less than a whisper.

His eyes darkened from midnight to witching hour, and he shook his head slowly as if it pained him to move any muscle. "Nay. No spirit. But flesh and blood and bone. As human as any."

"But you were"—she tried opening the book, but he trapped it beneath his hands—"there. With Hywel."

"Aye. I died with him at Pentraeth."

I remember the blood. And the mud as I fell.

"How?" Her head swam, and she thought she might be

sick. She tried to breathe through the nausea. Managed a squeaking, "That would make you over six hundred years old." She couldn't stomach it. Turned away, but he caught her chin. Refused to let her hide her horror.

"What have you seen?" His eyes laid bare his pain. His grief. The bones of his face lay stark beneath his skin. Lips pressed grimly together. In the hollow just beneath his jaw, his pulse beat a frantic tattoo.

"I was there. I waited for you even though I knew what would happen. I knew you'd never return." She dug her nails into her palms, letting the sting anchor her securely into the here and now. "Until now, I've only ever seen your past. But this time you weren't there. You'd left, and I was alone. It was my past—my memory—too." She gave a frustrated shake of her head. "Whatever is happening, it's changing. Showing me memories that are clearly not mine to know. If you hadn't noticed, I'm not six hundred years old. I'm not a ghost or a spirit or . . . or . . . anything like that."

"You're *Other*."

She shot him a *your-point-being?* glare.

"You carry the blood of the *Fey* within you. Perhaps the answer lies there. Part of your gift."

"My gift is healing. A gift we've already established you don't need."

"Not all healing is of the body." His gaze drew her in. The yearning she'd glimpsed from the first moment she'd met him, charged with hopelessness.

Without thinking, she reached out. Threaded her fingers with his. Squeezed her reassurance.

He glanced at their linked hands but did not draw away. His grip was firm and warm and lightning charged.

"What are you, Daigh?"

A long silence followed, broken only by the murmur of patrons. The tinkle of the front door bell. A visitor's rather loud insistence on the clerk finding her a copy of *Fanny Hill* that did not have pages seventy-three to eighty-four missing.

Daigh smoothed the book's leather cover with a broad, calloused hand, and she felt it like a caress against her own skin. Skimming her hips. Gliding across the tops of her breasts. Stroking her in all her most secret places until desire quickened to need. She squirmed, fantasizing and remembering and dreaming that hand on her. It was like being the worst sort of voyeur. Watching and experiencing simultaneously. And left her mouth dry and heart galloping.

"Do you know of the *Domnuathi*?"

She shook her head, unable to speak. A horrible heat spreading up from her center to color her face.

"We're men born from our unearthed bones. Soldiers of Domnu. Alive only by the grace of our creators and the blackest magics." He paused. Gritted his teeth. "Monsters."

"So the life you remember is one that ended—"

"Centuries ago. Aye." His hand closed into a slow fist, the roped veins blue against the bronzed weathered skin. Violence deferred but always present.

"How?" she asked in a thready whisper.

"A master-mage named Máelodor." The man he'd asked her about. The man hunting Brendan.

Every time she thought she'd gained a hold on the increasing chaos, a new piece of information turned her topsy-turvy. She latched on to the one constant between them. "You said you remembered me. That I was the face in your dreams. Even that first night you said that. How? If the life and the faces you remember are those of—"

He glared at the book as if his answers might be between the pages where his death read in four short lines. "I don't know, Sabrina. I don't understand. I'm as lost and confused and afraid as you. When I close my eyes I see you as clearly as if those moments between us happened yesterday. Why you see them too?" He shrugged. Drew a heavy, sorrowful breath. "Your brother Brendan knew Máelodor. Perhaps he would be able to answer our questions. Have you heard from him? Any word?"

"No."

His gaze sucked her in like a whirling black hole. Empty of light or warmth or humanity, they were a glimpse of the eternity he'd been denied. But she recalled the gray-green eyes of her dream. Vibrant. Passionate. And was not afraid.

He gave a bark of humorless laughter. "At least now we know why I can't be killed. I'm already dead."

The healer in her needed to ease his suffering. Needed to show him he was more than what Máelodor had created. Without thinking, she placed a hand upon his chest, the warmth of his body and the steady thump of his heart igniting a slow heat low in her belly. Then taking up his hand, she placed it over her heart, embarrassed at the runaway gallop drumming her insides.

Their eyes met for a long, quivering moment. "Tell me, Daigh"—she offered a shaky smile—"where the difference lies."

fourteen

"I won't drag her into this. Not for Máelodor. Not for you."

Daigh stalked the narrow confines of Miss Roseingrave's parlor. Ran his hand along a shelf. Snatched a glance at the flat, charcoal sky beyond the window. Pain dogged his every thought. A dragging weight, as though his brains were being pulled down into his spine. It had been this way since he'd risen at dawn. Muscles cramping. Nerves jittery as a drunkard's. His vision splashed in grisly shades of violence. Whatever evil lived within him woke and woke hungry.

Miss Roseingrave glared at him. "She's a Douglas. She's already involved whether she likes it or not."

"Sabrina will think I betrayed her."

"That's not my problem. I've asked what questions I could of the people I trust. So far, there's nothing connecting St. John to Máelodor other than the fact the *Amhas-draoi* was present at the execution."

"Keep digging."

"If I'm to risk my reputation in mad accusations, I need more. If Máelodor wasn't executed, who covered it up? Where is he now? How was he able to summon a *Domnuathi*"—she curled her lip—"when all my sources tell me it can't be done? Who besides St. John might be part of this conspiracy? How widespread is it?"

"You'd do better to ask these questions of St. John. Forget Douglas." The presence glided between the chambers of his mind like an intruder. Knowing his thoughts. Feeling his fear. Thriving on his pain. He flinched, sucking in a sharp breath.

"Douglas was part of the failed Nine. The group formed and headed by his father, the last Earl of Kilronan. He'll know." Strolling across the parlor, Roseingrave wrenched open the door, almost pulling the figure huddled at the keyhole right off her feet. "Isn't that right, Grand-mère?"

The hobbled, bent old woman straightened. Tossed a golden-yellow scowl at her granddaughter before shuffling into the parlor, plopping onto a sofa with a huff. "What would I know about such things as that, *ma minette*? Firestarters and rabble-rousers, the whole group of them. And so I told Henry Simpkins when he sought me out with his sly good looks and his snake-oil sweet talk. Calling himself Máelodor as if that might make him seem grander than he really was. I'm too old and ugly for such tricks to work on me. I sent him off with a flea in his ear."

Roseingrave's eyes gleamed with tender amusement. The first glimpse of humanity in an otherwise armored exterior.

"I couldn't help you even if I wanted to," Daigh said. "Sabrina's hemmed in by chaperones. There's no chance to speak with her privately."

"She goes out, doesn't she? Then we go where she goes. Sir Lionel Halliwell is hosting a ball in a few days. You can corner her there."

"How do I get in?

"With me."

"Why go to such lengths? Why not gain her confidence yourself?"

"The Douglases don't trust the *Amhas-draoi*. No doubt Lord Kilronan has filled Lady Sabrina's head with his suspicions of our intentions. But you"—her lip curled in a cynical smile—"she trusts you. Flex a few muscles, and she'll tell you anything."

"Can you blame her?" Grand-mère piped up, a girlish flush to her withered features.

"Fine," Daigh snapped. He was backed into a corner. To expose St. John he needed Roseingrave's help. And once St. John was exposed, the rest would fall into place. The *Amhas-draoi* would realize where the true danger lay and Brendan Douglas's innocence would be revealed. Sabrina would understand. "I'll ask her what she knows, but Douglas goes free after. I want your word."

"I can't agree to that. What would happen if Scathach and the brotherhood discovered I let him escape?"

He bared his teeth in a rapier grimace. "That's not my problem."

Frustration strengthened the beast sharpening its fangs on his bones. The room pitched beneath his feet, his vision blurring, a stabbing blaze of pain to the base of his brain like an axe to the neck. He bit back a moan, only the firm chill of the wall holding him upright against the whirlpool opening at his feet. The presence swelling to a crackling roar as it sought to drag him in. Drag him back.

When he opened his eyes next, he stared up into the old woman's shrewd, yellow gaze. She bent over him, a hand to his forehead. Another placed flat against his chest where his heart thundered.

Behind her, Roseingrave watched. Her contempt clear in her posture and her expression. "I told you it would be impossible to hold out for long. He controls you body and soul."

"No!" he roared, fighting to rise. Restrained by the old woman. He must be weaker than he thought. He fell back with a curse.

Her mouth wrinkled into a white-lipped frown. "Your creator's mage energy is potent. Dangerous. He tries to win you back to his cause using all the dark magics at his disposal. It would take a more powerful man than you to resist."

He closed his eyes, suddenly battle-drained, limbs weighted, head spinning. "I feel him always. But today . . . something's different. Almost as if he's here beside me. In this room."

A prickly silence followed as if each of them strained to catch a glimpse or hear the stir of breath that would reveal Máelodor's presence.

Roseingrave's grandmother broke the tension. "Fight him," she commanded. "Show him you're not afraid. He thrives on death? Choke him on life. Glut him until he's crushed beneath a mountain of beauty and friendship and love and faith."

He searched his mind for some glimpse of a moment. Anything to drag himself away from the maw at his feet where Máelodor waited.

Nothing.

A screeching metal-on-metal buzz filled his head. He couldn't think. Couldn't concentrate. Couldn't breathe. "I can't . . ."

The old woman's shriek reached him over the din. "Reach deeper."

He folded his attention inward and inward again. Fed the presence on the few broken, shattered memories left to him.

Men's faces ringing a table, cups raised in good cheer. An iron-gray stallion, neck arched, ears pricked as it nuzzled his hand.

The presence devoured these images, leaving jagged blackened holes where Daigh's past had been. But in return the pain eased. He could breathe again.

But now he knew it for what it truly was—a temporary reprieve.

There would be no freedom until he killed Máelodor.

Or Máelodor killed him.

> Sorry for the delay. Expected to be in Dublin before you. Hope Aunt Delia hasn't drive you around the bend yet. Cat and I will be there as soon as possible. There are things we all need to discuss that can't be decided in a letter no matter how long.
>
> Aidan.

Her brother. The king of understatement.

Sabrina refolded the letter. Tucked it into her journal. Flopped back on her bed with a frustrated sigh.

By "things" did he mean her speedy return to Glenlorgan? His out-of-the-blue marriage to a scandal-ridden young woman of no fortune and dubious morals? Brendan's rumored return to Dublin? Máelodor? A tapestry? The list went on and on.

Could he be any more enigmatic?

She rolled over, her gaze landing on the volume of Welsh history she'd brought home with her from the library. It seemed to crouch on her desk. Waiting for her to pick it up. Turn to the bookmarked page. Read the sentences over and over as if somehow they might reshape themselves into a history that didn't end with Daigh's death centuries ago.

They never did.

If Daigh told the truth, the words she read and the moments he recalled were one and the same. Could it be? There was no reason for him to lie. And the few stolen memories of Daigh's she'd fallen into certainly suggested it was so. The whole situation haunted her like a bad dream. And she'd been having a lot of those lately.

At least Aidan's letter had diverted her from the whirl of her thoughts. Kept her from thinking about her impulsive and reckless behavior at the lending library. Daigh's hand upon her chest. His touch zinging excitement through her from the top of her head to the tips her toes. Her heart threatening to beat right out of her chest. And yet he'd simply watched her with that same steady, soul-scouring stare she could drown in forever. Said nothing. Given no hint of his thoughts.

Apparently her brother's letter hadn't diverted her enough. She was right back where she started.

She flopped back a second time, groaning. By the gods, could she have acted more outrageously? Had she taken complete leave of her senses? She should be grateful to Jane for taking that moment to drop an armload of books. A mood breaker for certain. And one Daigh had used to vanish as completely as if he'd wrapped himself in the invisibility of the *feth-fiada.*

And really, she should be shocked. Appalled. Utterly and completely bowled over with disgust. He was walking dead. A man who until recently was naught but bones in a churchyard. An animated cadaver. One of the *Domnuathi.*

She should not have butterflies the size of vultures banging around her insides. Or be prickly with anticipation for their next meeting. She fisted a hand against her forehead. What was wrong with her?

Staring up into the bed curtains, the sounds of the household drifted up from below. Aunt Delia's shrill commands to her dresser as she prepared for the Halliwells' ball tonight. The soft shush of a maid in the corridor sweeping. The jangle of a bell pull. Steps on the stairs.

It had taken days to grow used to rising without the aid of the convent's tolling bells. Longer to stop looking over her shoulder for Sister Brigh's scowling face. Even now, dozing for an extra fifteen minutes seemed almost decadent. And time not spent in work, study, or reflection felt utterly frivolous.

She hated to admit it, but she found her leisure a wonderful respite. It made her recall the relaxed boredom of her life as it had been before her withdrawal into the order. A freedom she hadn't appreciated.

"No, perhaps the lilac with that lovely gold overskirt and the lace up the sides." Aunt Delia's indecision floated between the walls. "When you're done here, see to Lady Sabrina. I want to be sure she stands out. She's such a mousy little thing."

Sabrina grimaced at the sobriquet. What was so wrong with mousy? And why stand out if she planned on returning to Glenlorgan by June? She knew why. And it all went back to Aidan's letter. Things to discuss. Whom was she fooling? She knew what he wanted. Her sparkling debut into Society followed by an advantageous marriage to some proper peer with deep pockets and a respectable reputation. Both assets the Douglases of Kilronan had lacked for longer years than she could count.

She was to be Aidan's latest throw of the dice.

Or so he thought.

A knock brought her from that rebellious line of thinking.

Oh no. Aunt Delia's maid come to work miracles.

"May I come in?" Jane poked her head around the door.

Sabrina sat up, smoothing her face into a calm smile.

"Nice try, but you're picking your fingernails. And the mulish set to your chin is showing." A shawl clutched to her shoulders, Jane took a chair by the fire. "What's wrong?"

Hiding her hands in the folds of her skirt, Sabrina let her expression relax back into a frown with a sigh of relief. "If I'm not careful Aidan and Aunt Delia will have me married off to Sir Moneybags Stiff-and-Boring before summer's end. Farewell to my life with the *bandraoi*."

Jane stretched her feet to the hearth. "Surely Kilronan won't stand in the way of your return to Glenlorgan. Not if you show him it's what you really want."

Sabrina snorted her doubt, her gaze falling once more on the brooding Welsh history.

Jane caught the track of her gaze. Lifted an eyebrow. "It *is* what you really want, isn't it?"

Sabrina bristled. "Of course. Haven't I always said so?"

"Yes, but you also used to fill the school dormitory with tales of princes and princesses. Stamping chargers.

Wicked villains. Romance and derring-do and happily ever afters."

"What's your point?"

"Perhaps—just perhaps, mind you—you're thinking you may have stumbled on your own once upon a time." Her face reddened, or were her cheeks flushed already?

Sabrina threw herself out of bed. Crossed to the desk, grabbing up the book. Shoved it into a drawer where it couldn't stare at her. Leaned against the desk confronting Jane with grim resolve. "It doesn't matter. Daigh MacLir is not my happy ever after. He's not mine to want."

"He followed you to Dublin."

"No. He fled Glenlorgan and happened on me in Dublin. That's different."

"Remember once you said—"

Sabrina wouldn't let her finish. It was too humiliating. "Only too vividly. Don't bring it up. It was silly and ludicrous. Fate, destiny, even love at first sight aren't real."

It was Jane's turn to look stubborn. "If you say so. We won't speak of it again."

"Thank you."

"But has he kissed you?" Jane grinned, a naughty twinkle in her eyes.

"Jane!"

"Very well." She sighed. "If you don't want to discuss Daigh MacLir, we'll speak of Kilronan's intentions. If you're so alarmed, what do you propose to do?"

"I don't know yet." She caught herself gnawing the edge of her finger. Swiped it behind her back before Jane could reproof her. "But if Aidan wants a fight, Aidan shall have one. I'm not as docile as he remembers."

Jane giggled. "Ard-siúr was right. Setting you loose has

done wonders for your confidence. And your stubbornness."

"Ard-siúr spoke to you about me?" She wasn't sure whether she was pleased or annoyed.

"Only to say if you came back to us, you'd be twice the priestess you would have been had you never left at all."

"Did she now?" Sabrina's back went stiff as she pushed off from the desk. "I'll show her then. Twice and thrice the best."

"And Daigh?"

"You weren't going to discuss him." Disappointment lodged deep within her chest. A hard, cold rock that seemed to expand until all of her felt weighted and achy. "He's not my future." She thought of his certainty. His intense near anger as he swore he knew her. She was his dream. But it couldn't be. No matter how much her heart began wishing it were so. "And no matter what he says, I'm not his past."

fifteen

The musicians struck up a jaunty Scotch reel. Couples forming while Sabrina watched from her place hidden behind an entire grove of potted palms.

Aunt Delia had wandered away shortly after their arrival at the ball. A welcome respite. She'd spewed her poison praise during the entire carriage ride and only subsided upon stepping into the marbled entry hall of Sir Lionel Halliwell's home at which time she became all that was charming and urbane. Her final parting shot as the powdered footman handed them down to the pavement outside the town house, "Never fret. You'll be fine, darlings. There's always a few simpletons just arrived in town in need of partners for the dancing."

Sabrina answered with a proper smile and thereafter began her subtle drift toward the nearest stand of greenery. Pausing to down restorative clarets at every tray-bearing servant's pass.

The music began. Ravishing in a gown of cream silk

with her beautiful red hair piled expertly atop her head, Jane stood opposite a paragon of masculinity in full scarlet regimentals who'd begged a dance within moments of their arrival.

Sabrina had received no such invitation much to her aunt's chagrin and her own relief. She couldn't imagine trying to conduct small talk while keeping to the steps of the dance. It had been too many years since dancing lessons at Belfoyle. And she hadn't been all that proficient then.

Ahh well. At least here she needed all her energy to keep from making a fool of herself, while if she were at home, she would not be reading her history of Wales, not imagining Daigh as a six-hundred-year-old armored warrior—despite the pleasing picture a battle-armored Daigh made—not thinking of his heated, black gaze locked on hers, and definitely not reliving their one and only kiss that still sizzled her insides like a torch.

Dancers moved in precise pairs. Locked eyes. Spun. Joined hands.

What would it be like to have him kiss her again? Or to have his arms around her? His hands upon her . . .

She closed her eyes, taking a deep breath. What was happening to her? What was it about Daigh that turned her inside out?

She'd always been drawn to the wounded even as a child. The bird with a broken wing, the cat teased by the gardener's sons, the dog with the bony ribs and imploring eyes that followed her home. All of them had found a place in her heart. And was Daigh so different? The haunted desperation at the edges of his gaze? The grim intensity in his muscled frame? The misery etched into the sharp angles of his face?

Was he simply her latest stray?

Men and women moved in rhythm and time. Closed and separated. Hands clasped then released with a smile.

She swallowed the last of her claret. Searched the room for a convenient servant with a refill. Stiffened at the familiar smiling sophistication of Mr. St. John. He and her aunt chatting and peering at her from across the room with twin looks of delight.

Their differences could not have stood out more. Mr. St. John's stark black and white elegance in blazing contrast with her aunt's ghastly lilac and gold gown.

"There you are, darling," Aunt Delia cooed as she pushed her way into Sabrina's grotto. "What on earth are you doing skulking in the bushes? I told you in the carriage not to worry. The powder does a fabulous job of concealing your spot."

What was the punishment for auntricide? Any magistrate who knew Aunt Delia would probably let Sabrina off with a medal for exemplary conduct.

"If only your gown was as inconspicuous," she muttered into her fan.

She glanced out at the crowds jockeying for the next set. Jane had already been claimed by a consumptive-looking gentleman who gazed upon her with melancholy eyes.

Where were those servants with the claret when she needed it?

Aunt Delia tugged Mr. St. John forward. "Look who I found loitering about in the card room. You remember Mr. St. John from our outing to the cathedral."

"It's a pleasure, Lady Sabrina." He sketched a bow with ballerina grace. Took her hand, offering her an air kiss. His touch as cold as ever. A shame his gaze wasn't. It rested on her bosom with warmth enough to bring an unwelcome crawl to her skin. "I just told your aunt how I'd hoped to get a chance to see once more the most beautiful woman in Dublin."

Daigh had warned her to beware of this man. To stay as far away from him as possible. Trying not to be too obvious, she slid her fingers away and adjusted the wisp of silk that passed for a shawl more firmly over her cleavage. "My aunt has always been considered a diamond of the first water. I'm sure she was flattered."

Aunt Delia giggled into her handkerchief while a flicker of displeasure passed over St. John's features before the placid smile returned. "But you're family. And as such the resemblance is striking. Same luminous eyes."

Aunt Delia's seemed to have been tinted amethyst for this occasion.

"Same shimmering hair."

Her aunt's shocking pink and curled into girlish ringlets.

"Same lithesome body."

Aunt Delia hadn't been lithesome since the last century. If then.

"Two great beauties. And I have the pleasure of both of you to myself."

The man was either a consummate liar or bat-blind.

"Oh, there's Lady Townsend." Her aunt interrupted by waving madly across the room to a skeletal female in a dark blue gown, saving Sabrina from trying to fill the sudden awkward silence with a sparkling witticism. Which was good because her mind had gone completely blank. "Has she lost weight? She looks positively sickly, poor dear. I better go deliver my sympathies." Aunt Delia jiggled her delight. "I'm sure I can trust you, Mr. St. John, not to take advantage of my niece's naiveté while I'm gone."

"Complete discretion, madam." He sketched another gallant bow that had Aunt Delia batting him with her fan and tittering.

She bounced away with a sway to her backside that drew every man in the room's eye. Only Mr. St. John seemed impervious. His attention rested solely and uncomfortably on Sabrina. "Has your anticipated reunion with your brother happened yet? At our last meeting you seemed quite keen on his arrival."

Had she? She couldn't recall, but she would hardly reveal to him how un-keen she was to see the brother who'd ordered her here against her will. "I'm afraid Kilronan's been delayed." She plucked a drink from a passing tray. Dutch courage when all her instincts—and Daigh—warned her to avoid St. John.

"A shame, but perhaps your other brother is taking your mind off His Lordship's continued absence." His eyes gleamed like pale glassy marbles.

She nearly choked as flames chewed their way down her esophagus. Good heavens. Had that been brandy? "My other brother?" she sputtered.

"The gentleman I saw you in company with at the cathedral?" He smiled with concern as if he'd caught her in an indiscretion. "I hope I'm not being intrusive. I didn't get a good look at him, but you seemed very close."

"Oh." She held her breath. Took a second time-buying swallow of the hell-broth. It hit her stomach with a thud. "That wasn't a brother. It was a . . . a cousin. My cousin Jack."

"Would that be Jack O'Gara?" he asked, maneuvering

her deeper into the palms. Behind a column and farther from the eyes of the other guests. Every Lothario move down pat.

"You know him?"

Again that toothy Cheshire grin. "Only by reputation."

She resorted to her fan. Snapping it up and open. A curtain wall between herself and this daring scoundrel's practiced seduction.

"Yes, well, he was very sorry he couldn't stay and be properly introduced."

He swirled the wine in his glass round and round. Watched her over the rim. "I'm sure he was."

She went from stiff to paralyzed. Oh lord, why had she used Jack's name? He probably knew of Jack's death. She'd be caught in a lie and have to explain herself. Humiliating, and, if Daigh was right, dangerous.

Flapping her fan nervously while reaching out with her mind, she sought to catch any hint of his thoughts. Like hitting a wall, she came up against a consciousness shut and barred to any intrusion. She pushed deeper, but met only a frozen, slick emptiness. A burn like ice. Breaking contact, she fell back into herself with a dizzy lurch and a flush of heat staining her cheeks. This man was expertly trained. No cracks through which she might steal a thought.

"The refreshments are quite potent tonight," he said, taking the empty brandy tumbler from her hand to place it on a low table nearby. "You might like to switch to lemonade instead."

His eyes sparkled, a keenness to his sweet face. Had he felt her mental touch? Was he now laughing at her failure?

Her mouth went dry, the room suddenly stuffy and over warm. Her gown seemed to cling, her stays to bite into her ribs. She tried inhaling, but the hot, sour odors of warring perfumes and sweat and alcohol all combined to turn her stomach and thicken her brain. She squinted, trying to focus at the now-wavering face of St. John. Was she drunk? She hadn't had that many glasses, had she?

"Perhaps lemonade would be best. I don't feel quite right somehow." She glanced about her for a bench or a chair. Somewhere to sit and collect herself, but no one had thought to place seats in this out-of-the-way corner. "If you'll excuse me, I think I'm going to find a quiet place to catch my breath."

But he wouldn't let her escape. He took her hand. Led her toward an even more secluded alcove. "I'm sure your aunt wouldn't want you left alone if you're unwell."

"She won't be alone."

She and St. John went rigid in unison. His hand closing around hers until she winced. His ring cutting into her fingers.

The room wavered and spun, the floor dropping from under her, the walls bleeding into a smoke-filled hall full of low, confused voices. Men and women moved like wraiths, their eyes weary, their bodies crouched and distressed. He stood just beyond the firelight. She knew his stance, the cock of his head, the quiet intensity behind every gesture no matter how slight. He stood amid a crowd of rough-looking men dressed as if they'd only arrived. Mud-spattered. Breathing hard. For a moment he looked her way, the flames' flicker dancing across his eyes. His gaze sharpened on her face.

With a crack like thunder, the world settled back into its usual shape, leaving her sick and dizzy but clearheaded enough to recognize the colossus blocking their path.

Daigh: dark, gorgeous, and absolutely ablaze. His gaze threatened to torch her to cinders, the glare he settled on Mr. St. John even more deadly.

St. John never even flinched. His smile was if anything more brilliant. His eyes gleaming with almost fiendish excitement as his hand slipped from Sabrina's. And he stepped back with a flourish of surrender. "I see, sir, that you missed your ship."

"Did he hurt you? Tell me, Sabrina, I'll rip his head off and stuff it down his neck."

Daigh's gaze and hands ran over her as if seeking reassurance she was in one piece and breathing.

An unsettling heat flooded her, and she stepped out of reach. Tipped her chin to meet him eye to eye. She must put the proper distance between them, especially after her outrageous impetuosity of their last meeting. "What are you doing here?"

"I came looking for you." He darted a glance across the room to the back of a tall, slender woman in wine-red silk and gold-lined pelisse. Went stone-still and narrow-eyed. Turned his attention back to Sabrina. "We need to speak."

Without waiting for an answer, he took her elbow, the heat of him warming every place St. John's arctic touch had chilled. Steered her deeper into the foliage. Out the back of the alcove. Down a corridor. Up a small flight of stairs. And through a pair of French doors to a terrace that opened onto a tiny pleasure garden. Or what would be a pleasure garden in spring and summer. In December, it was more like an icehouse. Rain had frozen onto every surface to create a crystal-encased landscape. Lights from the windows sparkled against the bushes and trees and paths.

Golden pools shimmered across the lawn. Music and the rumble of conversation floated on a cool breeze.

If she weren't freezing, she'd have been enchanted.

"You're shivering." Daigh shrugged out of his coat. Draped it over her shoulders. Buttoned her into it like one would a small child. Though she couldn't recall a single instance of either of her parents ever performing such a simple yet caring gesture.

It draped almost to her knees, and she burrowed into the warmth, inhaling wool and claret and soap and man until she grew dizzy on it. Fresh air mixed with Daigh working to muddle her already tipsy brain rather than clear it.

Shaking off her befuddlement, she drew herself up. "What are you thinking? Accosting me in a ballroom? Dragging me out here alone?"

"It was that or allow St. John to finagle his way into your confidence. I warned you. Stay away—"

"What did you intend for me to do? Give him the cut direct? I don't even know why I'm avoiding him."

"Because I told you to isn't enough?"

She gave him a *what-do-you-think?* stare. Was relieved to see the tamped rage diminish and even a spark of amusement flash in his dark eyes. "Women haven't changed much in six hundred years. Still pig-stubborn."

She scoffed her annoyance. "Neither have men. Still bossy and overbearing."

"So now that we've established your obstinacy and my arrogance, stay away from—"

"You're doing it again."

He snapped his mouth shut until she swore she heard his teeth grinding.

"Please, Daigh. I know in your own manly way you're trying to protect me. At least I'm assuming that's why, but I don't know from what. Or why I even need protecting. What does St. John have to do with Brendan's return and a stolen tapestry? Are you afraid I won't be discreet? Or that I'll be more shocked than—"

"He's Máelodor's man," he blurted.

"Your crea . . ." she trailed off into a silence as brittle as the ice upon the trees.

"Creator. You can say it, Sabrina."

She hugged the warmth of the coat to herself. The scent of him heightening the stupid need to throw herself into his arms. But she hardened her heart against the swamp of emotion. She'd not repeat her previous mushy sentimentality.

Besides, Daigh didn't look in the mood for comfort. He'd gone stone-rigid, his eyes glowing stern with refracted moonlight. "St. John's a member of the *Amhas-draoi*."

It was her turn to go stiff, her stomach plummeting into her slippers.

"Máelodor is using him to find Brendan. He seeks to pay your brother back for a past betrayal. It's all part of what I can't remember. Whatever accident left me washed up on your beach took most of my memories of this life, but left those of my days with Hywel. I catch impressions. Hints of things. But most is gone, and I'm left to piece it together like a shredded quilt. That's why I need St. John. Alive. He can lead me to the master-mage."

She couldn't swallow.

"Sabrina, if Gervase St. John finds Brendan, your brother's death will not be quick. Máelodor has made suffering an art."

Couldn't breathe. "How do you know this?" she whispered.

He wouldn't meet her gaze as his voice rasped out the words. "You've seen the proof, Sabrina."

Of course. The scars. Thousands of them. Covering Daigh's body. A canvas for another man's inhuman cruelty. She wanted to be sick. Who was the monster? Daigh who strove to stop a killing, or Máelodor who sought more torture and death?

And why oh why had she asked? Not knowing was so much better. Manly protectiveness definitely had its place.

"Your brother won't be free until Máelodor's dead." He stalked away.

Nor would Daigh, though she didn't say it.

He prowled the garden. Moved silently in and out of the shrubbery, muttering soldier obscenities before coming to a halt in the middle of the garden, head thrown back. Eyes trained on the night sky.

She caught her breath as once more she felt herself falling into a world not her own. A strange shifting of light and shadow and air and earth. A ripping loose of her mind as reality and illusion mixed in a crash of jarring, overlapping images. But this time as quickly as it began, the rushing free fall into memory ended back on solid ground. High ghostly stars. And a cloud of air at every shivering breath she took.

Daigh's fists uncurled. He rubbed a hand across the back of his neck. Returned to her, gratitude brightening his obsidian eyes. "You're still here. I thought you'd take the first chance to run."

She held out her arms, coat sleeves drooping over her hands. "I can hardly return to the house dressed like this.

And I was"—*afraid for you*—"enjoying the air out here. It's wonderfully refreshing."

He rubbed his chin, a smile hovering. "You're a horrible liar. I can hear your teeth chattering. Let me take you inside. I may not be of this time, but a man and a woman and a dark garden spurs the same scandal in any age."

The idea struck with the force of a backhand. Of course. Aidan and Aunt Delia's plans be damned, she refused to be harried into a marriage simply because her brother thought it in her best interest. And here in front of her stood her answer. After all, what husband would want her once she'd soiled herself out of wedlock? She'd be gloriously, perfectly ruined. Aidan would be shoving her back at the sisters with a hearty good riddance. Happy to dispose of a sister no longer marriageable and therefore no longer of use.

It was a dangerous plan. Dangerous and reckless and insane. But Ard-siúr had told her to find her future. To risk life before she made the ultimate decision about joining the sisters of High *Danu*. Daigh was the ultimate risk with his brutal good looks and a power in his soldier's frame that sent delicious heat pulsing straight to her center.

Her resident butterflies swooped and plunged, a summer burn overtaking the tingling numbness in her chilled body. That was all this was. A way to return to Glenlorgan. It had nothing to do with the crazy surge of reckless feelings Daigh provoked in her. Nothing at all.

Now if she could just convince Daigh to go along.

With a tip of her chin, she made her decision. "I'm not going inside. I can't stand one more moment of Aunt Delia's sugar-coated insults, and if Mr. St. John is as determined as you say, he won't allow me to escape as easily a second time."

"You can't stay out here."

Hands on hips, she faced him down. "Has anyone ever remarked that you sound like the primmest of chaperones? I didn't say I necessarily wanted to stay out here."

A wary frown, but he hadn't laughed in her face. So far. So good. In fact, he looked downright intrigued. "What do you propose?"

"Take me with you. I don't want to go home. I don't know where I want to go. I just want to be with you a bit longer." Her jaw stiffened in a bulldog jut before she realized she was supposed to be looking seductive. Trouble was she didn't know how to look seductive. Wouldn't know flirtatious if it bit her. She pouted her lips. Batted her lashes. Immediately felt a complete fool.

"Sabrina—"

"I know I shouldn't ask. I know you're only here with me because you want to keep me safe from St. John."

"You've no idea of what I want." His voice cold and almost angry.

She plowed ahead before she could come to her senses. "I can't face them. The curious stares. The pointed questions. Not now. Not yet."

Was it working? Was he regarding her with something more than exasperation? The heat spread to her face. Blood pounding in her ears.

His gaze knifed through her. "Are you certain this is the path you would choose? There is no going back."

Was she certain? She focused on Aidan's letter. All of Aidan's letters actually. The ominous upcoming discussion. His desire to pull her back into the family fold. Her wish to get back to Glenlorgan. Gather up her old life where she'd left it. Taken all together, they gave her courage when common sense told her she played with fire.

She squared her shoulders. "I am."

He opened his mouth as if to argue, but settled under the determined stare she leveled at him. Surrendered with a quick wry smile. His dark hair gleaming blue. His body bearing a blast of inferno heat she felt to her toes as he walked her through the garden to the gate and the mews beyond. His hand upon her back like a brand. The damped fire of his gaze as he beckoned to a waiting carriage shooting sparks into his eyes.

"Where do you wish to go?"

She shook her head, unable to form words. Unable to think beyond being here with this man who unsettled her just by being next to her. "I don't care."

Settling her in her seat. Tucking heaping lap rugs around her, he rapped on the roof and with a bark of command, ordered, "Drive."

Ruined it by shooting her a look that was anything but commanding.

Sixteen

He watched her from the carriage's opposite seat, his arm lying casually across its back. If not for the battering crush of his mind against hers, she'd have believed his pose of nonchalance.

But now that she'd committed herself, she wasn't sure where to go from here. Would he envelop her in a passionate embrace? Did he wait for her to make the first move? Was it her, or was it extremely warm in here?

"At the Halliwells' . . . I felt it again, Daigh. It was like all the other times."

"A dream?"

"I wasn't asleep."

His hand clenched to a fist but in no other way did he show his agitation. "Tell me."

"I was in a hall crowded with people. They were nervous. Upset. You were there in company with a group of men. I was . . ." Her hand fell to her stomach, and she caught back a gasp. Her eyes flew to his. She said nothing, but kept her hand resting lightly across her abdomen as if protecting it.

With every word, his face hardened, his mouth thinning to a tight line, the shadows fighting for control. "When I saw you with St. John. I was this close . . . I fought it back the only way I could. There was a memory of . . . I don't know. Hywel had already escaped to Ireland after his father's death, but there was word he planned to return. I . . . damn it, I can't remember any more. The darkness swallowed it as it has all the others."

"But some remained. Enough to see that your memories connect us. I'm seeing what you're remembering. As you're remembering it."

"So am I causing your visions? Or are you triggering my memories?"

"I wish I knew." She fought to keep the waver from her voice.

He swung across to her seat. Nestled her closely against him. His heart thundered in his chest. Slammed against her palm. Thrummed in the chilled air of the carriage.

A man and a woman. A kiss. A promise. A tumbled bed where lovers wrestled. She suddenly realized she wanted these memories. Not just to recall them, but to relive them.

"It doesn't matter the how or why, Sabrina," he said simply. "Only that it is. For without these memories, the presence would have long since devoured me from the inside out. They are all that stand between me and Máelodor."

He fell silent, only the sound of his breathing and the occasional creak of the coach to break the quivering tension. The pressure of his emotions built around them like ice upon a dam.

She curled into the crook of his shoulder, using all her empathic gifts to settle the tangled roil of his thoughts, ease the angry questions straining against his heart. Slowly his body relaxed beneath her while his mind calmed from the storm-angry churn of confusion.

"You've been given a gift, Daigh. A second chance. An opportunity to reclaim what was stolen from you six hundred years ago."

"Everyone I remember is dust, Sabrina."

Her heart turned over at the grief in his voice. She leaned in. Let her hand glide over the ripple of his chest. Delighted in the shiver of his muscles. Finally found the words she was looking for. "Not everyone you remember."

Miss Roseingrave's carriage was well sprung and well cushioned, but every jostle still sent Sabrina's body swaying against his, the wind-scent perfume of her hair making him want to bury his nose against her neck and inhale.

A voice in his head urged him to take her up on her oh-so-obvious proposition. She wanted him. Who was he to deny her? Besides, it would make extracting the information Roseingrave wanted that much easier.

He shifted uncomfortably as the carriage rounded a corner, almost tossing her into his lap.

No, he should be chivalrous. Refuse the lecher that wanted her astride his lap and panting. To hell with Roseingrave.

Another corner. Another press of her soft body to his ribs. A hand against his leg as she braced herself. A hand suspiciously fluttery and warm before it was withdrawn.

He looked up to see the same blaze of hunger he knew existed in his own gaze.

"Aunt Delia told me there'd be some simpleton newly come to town who'd be content with having me as a partner." Her shy smile doing far more than her clumsy attempts at bold allure to goad him to action.

"Your aunt was right."

She gave an uncertain laugh. "Probably the only time in her life."

Leaning in, eyes closed, her face turned to his with such pure innocent yearning that a twist in his gut rose to his heart. His finer instincts trampled under the crush of desire. He tipped her chin with one gentle finger. Pressed a kiss upon her. And surrendered.

He flicked his tongue against her lips. Then within. Tasting. Teasing. Enticing her ever further forward in this sweet seduction.

She answered by caressing his cheek. Smoothing the hair back from his forehead. Tracing the line of his jaw. Dropping to splay a hand over his chest. Her breasts crushed to him beneath the heavy wool of his coat. Her actions came tentative and unskilled, but flared through his body with raw force.

He pulsed with arousal, alight with a dazzle of lush wild heat.

"It's like the memory of us," she murmured. "And not."

"Mmm." He could barely talk. Only feel. "Not real. Only a ghost. Like me."

She giggled. "An awfully solid ghost."

He pulled her into his lap. Dragged his coat off her, revealing the white of her shoulders, the sweep of her collarbone. The rounded mounds of her breasts. Taut. Sweet. Straining against the silky fabric of her gown. He cupped them. Thumbing the nipples taut. Easing the collar lower.

Skimming the slope of her throat. Tonguing the creamy flesh inch by exposed inch. Slowly. Gently. Giving her every chance to change her mind.

She trembled but didn't pull away. Rather, she leaned into his touch. Followed his lead. Her own hands growing ever more adventurous. His cravat discarded. His shirt untucked. Then on the seat beside them.

"Oh, Daigh," she mourned, tracing the puckered silver tangle of scars.

He shivered, gooseflesh following the path of her fingers. Slanting his mouth over hers. Gliding a hand up her calf. Her thigh. To the junction of her legs.

She squeaked, her eyes flying open. He moved no farther, letting her adjust to this new sensation. Taking his time, though it cost him to do so.

Slowly she relaxed under his steady, sultry kisses. Her body melting into his. Her hands coming round his neck, pulling him close. Threading through his hair.

She was wet for him. It would take little more on his part to have her aching. Just as he ached.

She lifted her head to stare deep into his eyes, a siren's smile playing about her bruised lips. "Don't stop, my love," she whispered.

He didn't breathe. Didn't dare move. Afraid to break the spell of that whispered endearment. It wasn't true. But it felt so good.

He was reminded of their conversation at the cove. The way she stared at the sea with a wistful longing. The slender poignancy of her movements as she lifted her face to the wind. The nascent courage in her bluest-of-blue eyes. Like a jessed hawk. Tethered to her perch, yet yearning to try her wings.

Then she kissed him, and the spell dissolved in a blinding flash of reality. What he was. What he could never be.

Did he care? He could satisfy the greedy hunger he'd harbored since that first long-ago kiss. Could drive himself deep within her velvety heat. Bruise those coral lips with his kisses. She was willing. It would take naught but a few skilled moves on his part to have her beneath him. And since when had his conscience carried the day?

He couldn't remember. And there lay the heart of his dilemma.

He couldn't. Sabrina could. She remembered him. And trusted him. Could he really break that trust for a quick bedding?

He caught her hands. Drew them from around his neck.

She frowned with confusion. "Daigh?"

Sliding from underneath her, he shrugged himself back in his shirt. Tucked her skirts round her in demure virginity. Rapped once more on the carriage roof to signal the driver. "Return to the Halliwells'."

She grabbed his arm. "What are you doing?"

"Not making love to you," he answered through clenched teeth. "You can thank me some other time."

For reasons of his own, Daigh refused to let her slink away with at least the tattered shreds of her dignity intact. No, he decided to play the gallant to the hilt. Handing her down from the carriage. Escorting her through the icy garden, still blessedly empty and silent. None to witness their illicit arrival. None to see the burn of embarrassment scorching her cheeks. If only he'd leave so she could find Jane, plead a splitting headache—not a fib—and go home to be mortified in the privacy of her own bedchamber.

Back through the French doors. Down the stairs. Up the corridor. Into the alcove. And smack into Jane and Aunt Delia who stood heads together, trading worried glances.

"There you are, darling." Aunt Delia sighed with audible relief. "We wondered where you'd scampered off to." Her gaze traveled up Daigh, brows drawing into a scowl. Sabrina could almost hear the wheels spinning. Perhaps her chance hadn't been lost. She didn't have to say anything. Aunt Delia's filthy little mind would fill in all the blanks.

But before she opened her mouth to ask the obvious, Jane threaded her arm through Daigh's. Grabbed him by the ear, drawing him down to buss him on the cheek. "Daigh, you beast. You did come. And you've found Sabrina already." Swung around to Aunt Delia. "Mrs. Norris, may I present my brother to you. Mr. Fletcher is newly arrived in Dublin."

That twinkle of amusement was back in Daigh's eyes. And he actually smiled as he bowed over her aunt's hand. An expression to turn any woman's head. "I found Lady Sabrina at the punch bowl, complaining of a headache. Perhaps it would be best if she were taken home."

Aunt Delia was no exception. She fluttered like a schoolgirl. "She always did have her poor mother's constitution. The merest breath of wind would send her to her bed with a cold."

"If you would allow it, I'm happy to escort the young women home."

Sabrina's head snapped around. Please no. She couldn't take another moment of Daigh's company right now.

"That would be perfect. Thank you, young man."

Sabrina shot Jane a glare. Perfect was just what it wasn't.

"Brother?" Sabrina complained. "Brother? What were you thinking?"

"I was thinking of your reputation. Something you obviously weren't."

"That's exactly what I was thinking of. Or rather the destruction of it. It would have worked. Aunt Delia would have been sure to tell Aidan. And Aidan would have been suitably horrified. Enough to send me back to Glenlorgan with the speed of a cannon shot."

"That was your plan? A scandal with Daigh MacLir?"

"It would have worked if . . ."

"If what?"

"Never mind." She rubbed her temples.

"You two were gone quite a while. Did he . . . and you . . ."

"Jane!"

"He is my brother," she answered smugly. "I have a right to know."

"You want to know what happened? The whole ugly, sordid episode? I'll tell you. I threw myself at him. Did everything but stake myself out for his pleasure. Do you know what he did?"

"By the sounds of it—"

"Nothing! Not a thing. He was—more or less—a perfect gentleman. Drat him."

"Is it the more or the less you have a problem with?"

Sabrina closed her eyes. Saw once more the hard, arrogant beauty of the man as he'd caressed her. Experienced again the persuasiveness of his kisses. And remembered the complete contentment she found in his arms. As if she could live her life within that powerful embrace.

"It doesn't matter. It was a stupid idea."

Daigh paid off the hackney. Still four or five blocks from the room he'd taken in Wood Street, but he needed the air. The time. The space to think.

He'd held a dream when he held Sabrina. Insubstantial as cobwebs. Fragile as foam upon the waves. It didn't matter how certain he was of her place in his previous life, she was as out of reach as his half-forgotten past.

A blast of wind curled down his collar. Rattled shutters. Trash skipped and swirled down the street. But beneath the normal night sounds came a faint rattle. A slide of a broken footstep. A held breath.

He sensed it all between one heartbeat and the next. Battle intensity reining him to a quivering tension of muscles in anticipation. Passing an alley shrouded in wraith-like shadows, he glanced within. Someone watched. Someone followed. His hand fell to the dagger at his waist, but he kept his pace even and unhurried.

A carriage clattered to a stop at the next corner, and a man stepped down into the light of the pavement lamp. The coachman slapped his reins, the carriage barreling off.

Bile chewed its way through Daigh's gut. A horrible, crawling, humiliating disgust, but he faltered for only a moment before resuming his long, easy stride.

"Did you see our little sparrow home?" St. John's smile beckoned with angel innocence. Only his pale eyes, reflected in the glow from the lamp, chilled with their malice. "How chivalrous of you."

Daigh collared him. "Come near Lady Sabrina again and I'll take you apart piece by bloody piece."

"Don't tell me you have feelings for the girl. Fascinating. The monster in love. Does she know what you are, Lazarus?

Can she smell the reek of the grave you give off? Or is she smitten by that sensual animal beauty of yours and doesn't care?" He raked Daigh with a gaze that held the leering sexuality of Cork, leaving Daigh nauseous and shaking with rage and embarrassment. He released him on a muttered oath. "Easy to lose one's perspective when confronted with six and half feet of pure animal magnetism. I should know."

Daigh snorted his lack of concern. Began walking, but St. John wouldn't allow his escape. Kept apace with him.

"Does she know where Douglas is hiding?"

"Leave her alone, St. John," he growled.

"Perhaps I will. Perhaps I won't. It all depends on you. You've maneuvered your way into the little sparrow's confidence. So, you can find out what she knows. Lead me right to Brendan Douglas."

"You're the bounty hunter. Find him yourself."

St. John opened his arms in a surrender gesture. Sighed. "He proves more elusive than expected. But with Lady Sabrina's assistance—willing or . . . unwilling. And perhaps unwilling might be more fun—I shall capture him."

Daigh grabbed his shoulder. Spun him around. Pulled him close. "Touch her, and you're dead as I was. And no Máelodor to bring you back."

St. John's mage energy crackled along Daigh's nerves like acid. Burst at the base of his brain like a hammer blow. He saw nothing but a crimson haze. Heard nothing but St. John's hissed curses. Felt the glide of a cold hand upon a chest that only minutes earlier had burned with Sabrina's tender touch. Cold lips pressed to his mouth, making choking vomit rise into his throat.

He fought back. Broke the binding restraining him. Tore himself free of the hands gliding over him with a sexual insistence. He doubled over, retching into the gutter. Heaving. Sick. Furious.

"See? You do care." His hand rested possessively upon Daigh's back. "My sweet deathless beast, you forget what you've so recently learned. That I can bring you a pleasure no woman ever could. Or I can break you." Again the cool fondling hand, but this time it hardened. A weapon appeared. A dagger. It punched into Daigh's gut. He arched away from the explosion of pain. But it came again. This time to the small of his back as he fell. And again to his ribs.

He dropped to the ground. Blood running in rivers from his wounds, the hurled curse slowing his healing. Pushing him toward shocky numbness.

St. John bent over him. Stabbed him between the ribs.

Nowhere for Daigh to escape. To recover.

Blood filled his mouth. His vision closing in on him until all he saw was St. John's pale soulless eyes. His gleaming angelic demon smile. "Lady Sabrina will find me Douglas one way or another."

"Whoreson," Daigh mouthed.

The kick that followed brought a scream to his lips. He reared up against the inferno of agony. His lungs starved for air. His nerves shriveling against the next attack.

"You search for Douglas?"

A deep voice sounded from somewhere to Daigh's right. St. John's attention shifting immediately to a nearby alley.

"Then you've found him. But finding and catching are two different things." The words taunted their challenge yet held an unyielding strength. Whoever this was, he was well able to take care of himself.

Daigh tried moving his head. Couldn't even breathe

without whimpering. Mage energy infected his blood. Coursed its black power along his veins. He was trapped in a web of pain until it subsided.

St. John vanished from his side. Power throbbed the air. Shot in ribbons of light from street to street. A shout. A curse. And silence as the antagonists receded.

The dark alley. The quiet steps. Douglas had followed. Douglas had watched. And he'd interceded to save Daigh. But not before he'd heard the whole. Knew Sabrina's danger. St. John's evil. And Daigh's ultimatum.

He lay alone on the pavement. Stared up into the coal-thick night. Felt the torture of healing as his body—now free of the *Ambas-draoi*'s interference—knit itself together. Tendons. Muscles. Arteries. Bone.

St. John's threat the only wound that would never heal.

Seventeen

Máelodor heaved himself into the carriage. Allowed the hovering manservant to settle him comfortably under half a dozen traveling rugs. Place heated bricks on the floor. Still the icy air cramped his joints and settled in his bones until he had to grit his teeth against the ache.

Bloom's failure had spurred this trip. Bloom's body scattered to the dogs.

He'd not fail Máelodor again.

"You should be at the coast by nightfall, sir." The unctuous groom piled on an extra rug. "And in Dublin within a day or two if the weather holds."

Máelodor waved off the annoying little toad. "And word's been sent to St. John of my arrival?"

"Aye, sir. We've ordered him to meet you."

"And Lazarus?"

"Nothing yet, sir."

He closed his fist around the head of his cane.

Máelodor's wards kept the creature whole. His magics

kept him subservient. So where was he? Why hadn't he sent word?

He'd already shown the *Domnuathi* in graphic and violent detail what happened to those in his service who showed a disappointing lack of obedience. He smiled. How much more exciting and gratifying when the pain could be strung out forever. No inconvenient death to mar the perfection of the suffering. It would be a fool who tempted a repeat of the process. And whatever Lazarus's flaws, fool was not among them.

Máelodor's raising of a soldier of Domnu had started as an experiment. But it had paid out with so much unexpected new knowledge. The second summoning would be all the greater a success for what he'd learned.

Arthur would be tied to Máelodor just as Lazarus was. Inviolate against death. Enthralled to his creator. A perfect tool to create a perfect world.

Daigh opened his eyes, not on the woman who haunted his fevered dreams, leaving him drenched with sweat and heart racing. But on the hard-bitten beauty of Miss Roseingrave, who regarded him with a mixture of revulsion and ridicule.

"How did you get in here?" he growled.

"Your landlady let me in." Her critical gaze wandered the barren, dusty garret. "You left the Halliwells' suspiciously early last evening. I assume you've something to show for it besides Lady Sabrina Douglas's deflowering."

"Jealous?" he sneered, tired of Roseingrave's hostility. Swinging out of bed, he drew his shirt over his head. Combed an agitated hand through his hair.

She flushed, lips pursed, eyes flashing violence. "Hardly."

"Then aim your vitriol at me. Not her. She's done nothing to warrant your claws."

"Hasn't she? The Douglases lie at the center of a violent whirlwind. Their father began it with his demented ideas of *Other* supremacy. And the heirs of Kilronan follow in his steps like lemmings. Brendan Douglas threatens our world with exposure and destruction. And if it weren't for Lord Kilronan's stubborn stupidity, the *Amhas-draoi* would have his father's diary, and his cousin would still be alive." She sucked in a ragged breath. Her eyes burning with tears, her face twisted into paroxysms of rage and grief.

He put a hand out in an awkward attempt at comfort, but she whirled away from him.

"Don't ever touch me," she warned in a cold, ringing voice. "I'm not some untried virgin dazzled by your Hercules looks. And no doubt, if Lady Sabrina knew the truth, she'd be as horrified by you as I am." She drew herself up, tall and athletic and radiating violence.

"She does know the truth."

"Does she?"

"What the hell is that supposed to mean?"

"It means I don't care how you do it, but find me Brendan Douglas."

"And St. John?"

"He arrived in Dublin last spring."

"That's it? I knew that much already. What of his movements before last spring? What of the brand on his arm?"

"I've seen no brand and I can't exactly ask him to strip for me. As for his movements, bring me news of Douglas and we'll talk."

As much to keep his hands from around her neck as

anything else, he plunged them into the icy water of his washbasin. Splashed himself awake. Cooled his growing temper.

"Do you want Scathach's help or not?" she demanded.

When he turned back, she'd gone.

Both hands braced against the edge of the nightstand, he stared into the speckled, cracked mirror. Looked for some vestige of the man he'd once been in the stern angle of his jaw, the cruel set of his mouth, the empty hell-black of his eyes.

Dragging back his sleeve, he glared at the brand on his forearm. The crescent pierced by a broken arrow. Máelodor's signature. His mark of ownership. As binding as any slave collar.

His mind made up, he turned the mirror inward. Rolled his sleeve back down.

Helena Roseingrave was right. Sabrina didn't know anything about him.

Nothing at all.

Sabrina left the Ogilvie townhouse on St. Stephens Green with the same stunned exhaustion experienced by battle-sick soldiers. A sort of heavy torpor and a feeling as if her very brain had shaken loose from its moorings. The incessant questions. The hidden pitfalls. The constant search for imperfections. In her dress. Her speech. Her manners.

"That went well," Aunt Delia chirped as they were shepherded into a closed carriage for the few short blocks to home. She huffed into her seat, wrapping a pink striped shawl over her shoulders. Fiddling with the string of pearls choking her double chin. "The Misses Ogilvie are always so pleasant. Though they have to be, don't they? Miss Ogilvie with that horrible flat nose that makes her look like a toad. Miss Henrietta with that sallow skin and those dark circles. Their mother's at her wit's end, trying to secure proper marriages for them."

"I thought their mother was your especial friend."

"She is, darling. Letty Ogilvie and I were at school together. Had our come-out the same year. But really, she could have done so much better for herself."

"And you told me you wanted me to take my cue from the Ogilvie girls."

"Well, of course. They may have little in the looks department, but they're well regarded. And it wouldn't do your countenance any harm if you were seen in their company. You'd shine like a diamond between two coals, darling."

What on earth did her aunt say about people she didn't like? Sabrina shuddered to think.

Her shoulders quivering in silent laughter, Jane took a sudden unwavering interest in the doings of a man selling hot spiced gingerbread.

At least this trip to Dublin had achieved one thing: Jane no longer carried a haunted air, nor did she jump at shadows. Sabrina would cling to that positive. With white knuckles.

Arriving back at Upper Mount Street, Sabrina shed her pelisse and bonnet onto the waiting footman, frantic to escape Aunt Delia's barbed comments and incessant pettiness.

The man gave a subtle clearing of his throat. "Excuse me, Lady Sabrina, but there's a gentleman to see you. He's waiting in the upstairs parlor."

Daigh. Had to be. A wild fizz spread up from her belly until she buzzed with stupid excitement. Made more stupid by his embarrassing rebuff.

"Thank you. I'll see him right away."

Lifting her skirts, she took the stairs slowly, gathering herself together. She'd be dignified. Distant. Show him she didn't care.

At the closed door, she drew up. Smoothed her skirts. Checked her hair. And grasping the knob firmly, opened the door.

To an empty room. An open window. And a card upon a table.

Had to run. Back when I can.

B.

"You again." The little man glared, but his heart wasn't in it. Perhaps persistence had begun to wear him down. "Haven't I told you to clear off? His Lordship's not home. Mrs. Norris is out, and I'll not—"

"Tell Miss Fletcher her brother is here." He shrugged himself deeper into the doorway and out of the misty drizzle.

The man must have thought Daigh was planning on storming the castle. He threw himself into the breech, his height in no way detracting from his bulk or his strength. "Brother? Thought you said your name was MacLir."

"Half sister."

"Mm-hm," the man grunted, clearly unconvinced but allowing him to step out of the weather and into the entry hall. "Wait here. I'll see if she's home to"—he raked him with another fearsome glare—"half brothers."

Daigh would be quick and clear. Ask Sabrina about Brendan. Pass on the information to Roseingrave. Stop St. John before he could carry out his threats. Get Scathach to send him back to the grave.

He would not put forward explanations or apologies for last night. He would not imagine Sabrina as she'd been, glassy-eyed with desire, her flesh like silk, her curves perfect in his hands. Nor dwell on the hazy mirage of an impossible past where he'd enjoyed all that and more.

Didn't matter. Didn't happen.

There'd be no regrets to worry over in the grave.

Sabrina read the note over though she knew the few words by heart. Examined for the hundredth time the front and back as if somehow an invisible message might be hidden there.

Obviously Brendan and Aidan had taken the same course in letter-writing. Be brief and ambiguous as possible. But why now? Why after seven years with no word?

"My lady?"

Mr. Dixon stood at the drawing room door, looking grouchy and flustered. "There's a gentleman below."

Brendan had returned. She shoved the note into her apron pocket.

"Says he's Miss Fletcher's half brother."

Daigh.

She flushed crimson. What on earth could he want?

"But she's out with Mrs. Norris. Should I be sending him on his way?"

"No. Yes. No," Sabrina stammered. "That is to say, I'll see him."

Mr. Dixon's lips thinned to a disapproving line, but he nodded.

Sabrina had moments to compose herself and then he was there. His giant's frame filling the door. His dark head ducking beneath the lintel. His face pale and sullen in the gray afternoon twilight.

Her excitement hadn't subsided. Instead it had increased tenfold alongside her mortification, and she rose to greet him, hoping she didn't look as discombobulated as she felt.

"I didn't expect to see you again." She forced herself to meet his gaze, though her cheeks burned. "Or did you catch sight of St. John skulking at the corner?"

Her attempt at blasé fell flat. His hands curled to fists and, if possible, his features darkened.

Her throat constricted, nerves making her insides squirm. How did she ever think she could get through this encounter without feeling a fool? She'd begged him—and wasn't that humiliating enough?—but no, it got worse. He turned her down. What normal male turned down easy sex? None according to what little she knew of the male species. Which said what about her charms? It was a good thing she was destined for a life devoted to the *bandraoi*. If she couldn't attract a man by throwing herself at him, how was she ever supposed to attract one with nothing but small talk and coy smiles? Perhaps she was safer from Aidan and Aunt Delia than she thought.

"Please, sit down." She gestured to a chair.

Daigh glanced at it but made no move to accept.

Her annoyance erupted into full-fledged anger. And she blurted the first thought that popped into her head. "You're safe from any unwanted overtures. I promise not to push my odious presence on you again."

"Your odious . . ." He gave a bark of grim laughter. "Is that what you think?"

"What else am I supposed to think?"

"That I'm not a lust-crazed scoundrel who'd ruin your future for my own pleasure?"

He sank into a chair across from her, and she noted the tired lines dragging at his features, a strain pulling at his body and his emotions. He drew close to breaking.

He rubbed at his left forearm as if scrubbing away a stain. "Sabrina, I don't know how or why, but you're the woman I see when I close my eyes. I know your scent. I recall the sparkle of your smile, the way your body feels as it moves beneath me. And the way mine feels when I take you. Flashes of an impossible life with you fill my head. I can't stop them. I don't want to. But it's just that—impossible. I won't let you throw yourself away on me. Not when your future still lies before you."

She swallowed around the knot choking off her breathing. He dreamt these things. As had she. They were as much a part of her memories now as his. Perhaps that's why it had been so easy to let her desires overpower her sense. He was no stranger. He'd already been lover, husband, and friend. Impossible, he'd said. And she knew it. But it didn't make the memories of that life she'd glimpsed any less powerful.

"He hasn't come right out and said it, but my brother wants to marry me off."

His body barely flinched before he answered smoothly, "You'll make someone a very lucky man." A corner of his mouth tipped in a rueful smile. "But it won't be me."

She hardened her heart. "It won't be anyone. I don't want to marry. Ever."

"That would be a shame. You have much love to offer."

She had no answer and couldn't speak anyway.

He pulled himself to his feet. "I came to ask one thing,

and then I'll leave." He paused, his jaw hardening. "Your brother Brendan—have you heard from him since you arrived in Dublin?"

She caught back a breath. Her hand falling unconsciously over her apron pocket. Did Brendan's return and Daigh's arrival fit together somehow? Could her brother be preparing to create his own *Domnuathi*? No, she wouldn't believe it. He could never initiate such madness and misery.

"If I'm going to stop Máelodor and St. John, I need to find him, Sabrina. Soon."

"You think he's part of all this?"

"I don't know and I don't care. It's Máelodor I want. I think Brendan can aid me."

Seven years and her family still sought to drag her back into its destructive orbit. Suck her into the tragedy and the heartbreak and the agony she thought she'd put behind her when she entered the order.

Would she ever be free of her father's sins? Her brother's crimes? The long shadow that still seemed to hover above them all?

"Have you had word from him?" Daigh prodded. "Anything."

Her hand dug into her pocket. Crushed the note, the edges of the paper biting into her fingers. Brendan was alive. He'd come home. But was he any safer than he'd ever been? The *Ambas-draoi* still hunted him. So now did Máelodor and Gervase St. John if Daigh spoke truth. Would revealing what she knew help or hinder? Not that she knew much more than she ever had. Except that he'd be back. Hopefully bearing explanations.

Daigh's intensity charged the air. Crackled over her skin.

Sparked against her mind with dread and anger and fear and shame.

Should she? Shouldn't she? She closed her eyes, sending up a prayer for guidance.

The front door opened and shut.

"Sabrina, darling! We're home!"

The gods—and Aunt Delia—had spoken.

Eighteen

Lord and Lady Kilronan arrived in the middle of the night. Sabrina had vague recollections of voices and steps in the hall, orders being given, and harried servants to-ing and fro-ing. She'd ignored it all by shoving a pillow over her head and burrowing deeper into her bedclothes.

This morning she could no longer ignore it. She'd been dressed, styled, and prepared for sacrifice by her lady's maid, who seemed to think His Lordship's marriage had been oh-so-romantic. A grand passion just like that Romeo and Juliet couple.

She decided to forego informing the poor, deluded woman how that relationship had ended, and rose from her dressing table with the grim smile of the condemned.

Aidan was happy. That was Sabrina's first startled sense, peeking around the drawing room door. Not beaming and goofy grinning happy, but a quiet satisfaction that eased his usually stern features and softened the intense light in his gold brown eyes.

He stood braced in front of the hearth, hands clasped behind his back, gaze wandering in horror over the cottage flower wallpaper, the dainty, lace-encrusted furniture, the herd of cherubs whose painted eyes all seemed to focus on a nearby sculpture of Zeus in naked splendor, thunderbolt in hand.

Despite his otherwise relaxed exterior, Aidan looked as though he'd like to hurl a few thunderbolts of his own. "What was she thinking, Cat? It's like a damned Paris brothel in here. And what is that horrid smell like overripe fruit?" He sniffed the air by the mantel where purple and blue flames glimmered in the grate. "I knew I should have arranged things myself."

From the far corner out of Sabrina's restricted line of vision came the amused reply, throaty and smooth as velvet before breaking into a girlish giggle. "She does have a certain unique taste."

"It's not funny," he grumped.

"You can laugh or you can cry. I choose to laugh. I've spilled enough tears for a lifetime."

Aidan glanced at his watch. Paced a strip of rug, fumbling with his fob. "Where is she? I sent the maid to wake her over an hour ago."

"Stop fretting. She'll be down soon enough."

"I'm not fretting."

"You're nervous as a kitten in a thunderstorm. Relax. She's your sister. It'll be fine."

"You don't sound nervous at all."

"She'll accept me or she won't. I've gotten quite good at not caring overmuch."

"No, you've gotten good at hiding that you do care. Different entirely, *a chuisle*."

Love and intimacy and tenderness weighted his words, and Sabrina felt like an intruder on some private moment.

Backing away from the door, she cleared her throat. Took a few heavy steps. And glided into the room as if she'd only just arrived.

Daigh stalked the narrow garret. "I've tried. And failed. If you want Douglas, you'll have to find him yourself."

"And you? Given up trying to implicate St. John in this business? Or has Kilronan's sister changed her views on bedding a corpse," Roseingrave stormed. "Perhaps she finally found out what you'd done. To her. Her family."

His gaze narrowed. "What are you talking about?"

Her look tore through him with spear-point intensity. "You're Lazarus. No matter how you pretty up the reality, you're a creature of death. And you deal it as casually as any animal." She gave a hard, brittle laugh. "Did you and Brendan Douglas share a toast when you told him you'd murdered his cousin?"

"Damn it—"

"You killed him. Didn't even flinch. Didn't even wait to see if he suffered. Just left him in the road, drowning in his own blood. Did you care? Did you even suffer a pang of remorse?"

"I never . . ." Or had he?

A dark road, sloppy with rain. A carriage and a man with a gun. The Great One's orders, commands Lazarus could not deny.

The explosion of images rocked him back on his heels.

Fear. Surprise. And the dead weight of a body toppling silently and softly into the mud. A woman's scream ripping across the storm.

He dropped to the bed, his hands clutching his head. Bile and vomit scouring his throat raw. His body numb and cold with sweat as images flashed like lightning through his brain. A deadly hunt from Dublin through the Slieve Aughty mountains to the barren, coastal cliffs of County Clare. A battle rippling with flame and *Unseelie* magic. Lord Kilronan's vicious hate. Lady Kilronan's pleas for a final mercy. And a diary. A diary he'd captured for Máelodor in his quest to resurrect Arthur for his own violent and twisted ambitions.

"Live with that, Lazarus," Roseingrave mocked. "I do."

He remembered. Everything. In one cataclysmic flooding of memory, it all came rushing back.

The presence slipped and slid through his brain, scales flexing, eyes burning, rage scorching its way through his body as if he were being consumed from the inside out. Seeking, hunting, gathering what it could from its growing control. With every beat of Daigh's heart, Máelodor's poisonous mage energy intensified. His powers and Daigh's strength forming one monstrous being. He held it back as best he could, but it was like holding back the tide.

"You play with a dangerous weapon, *amhas-draoi*," he snarled. "What makes you think you won't end as dead as Jack O'Gara?"

"I don't scare easily, Lazarus."

He grabbed her arm, pulling her in close enough that she tilted her head back to meet his gaze. She remained unflinching, but he sensed her uncertainty and perhaps even a hint of fear. As it should be.

"Then you're a fool," he said, letting her feel the killing weight of his regained powers.

She struggled, but he gripped her, his fingers biting into her flesh.

His mage energy flooded him. Tangled her heart in its serpent grip. Coiled around it. Slowed it beat by beat by beat until she gasped and went limp. Releasing the spell, he dropped her into a chair to recover before spilling his stomach into the slops jar. His legs barely holding him up, his body wracked with uncontrollable spasms as the presence retreated once more.

"I'll do what I should have done from the beginning." A clean shot to the head. A simple kill. Sabrina and her brother would be safe from St. John.

He no longer needed to worry about finding Máelodor.

His master would find him. He already had.

Aidan rested his chin on his hands. Gazed on Sabrina with older-brother exasperation that set her teeth on edge. "This isn't exactly how I anticipated our first meeting." He sighed. Shot a despairing glance at the unwelcome addition to this little tête-à-tête, sitting silent and watchful in the corner.

Sabrina braced herself against the unconscious fall into little-sisterly submissiveness. Felt Lady Kilronan's scrutiny like a pricking up and down her spine. "Did you think we'd enjoy a nice reminisce over tea and cakes, Aidan? Tease each other over our misspent youth and compare notes of the past seven years?"

"Aye. Something along those lines." Aidan smothered a smile behind his hand, but his dancing eyes gave him away as he shared a private joke with his wife.

For some reason, that just made her dig her heels in further. "You commanded me, Aidan. Like one of your servants or a dog brought to your side with a whistle. Did you ask whether I wished to leave the sisters for Dublin? Did you take into consideration what I might want?"

"How could you possibly know what you want when all you've known for the past seven years is Glenlorgan and the life of a priestess?" His features fell into more serious lines. "You've been closeted in that place long enough. You've not been home to Belfoyle once since Father and Mother died."

"I don't want to go to Belfoyle. What's there for me now? It's a house, Aidan. Not a home. And hasn't been for the last seven years."

"It could be." He shot another exclusionary glance in Lady Kilronan's direction. Obviously obtained the silent answer he was looking for since he turned back to Sabrina with new resolve. "This isn't how I would have broached the subject, but now we're hip deep in it, I might as well wade further. Cat and I want you to come with us when we return to County Clare, Sabrina. To live. I want you to get to know her. To see her as family. As a sister."

That woman? Not bloody likely. She spun around to finally face the nervy hoyden who'd seduced Aidan into marriage. Found herself eye to eye with a young woman perhaps only a year or two older than herself. Slender. Slight. A sheen of jet black hair. Feline green eyes. Not exactly the blowsy hips and bosoms Covent Garden wares Sabrina had scornfully imagined bear-leading Aidan to the altar. But there was a spark of something in the way Lady Kilronan returned the unblinking stare. A maturity to her solemn features. Experience in the tiny lines dimpling the edges of her turned-down lips.

Rather than an overfriendly smile or oozing goodwill, she regarded Sabrina with the same wary watchfulness she received. Head cocked a bit to the side. A lip chewed between her teeth.

Nervous. Proud. Hopeful. Sad. Sabrina felt all these

things when she looked upon Aidan's wife. A twining of emotions showing only in the flicker of her eyes and the poised way she rested her hands in her lap.

No. She didn't want to like her. Didn't want to know her. She needed to stand firm. Stand fast. She wasn't the eager-to-please baby sister any longer, and Aidan—no matter how much he shoved—couldn't fit her back into that mold.

"My family are the priestesses of High *Danu*," Sabrina bit the words off in staccato syllables. "And my home is Glenlorgan. The sooner you both understand that, the sooner we can end this farce of a family reunion and I can leave."

Before her courage faltered or either of them could talk her around, she fled.

Cat's sardonic "So, should we take that for a no?" echoing faintly after.

Sabrina smoothed out the note. Read it once more. Traced the ornate, swoopy handwriting. As flamboyant, showy, and enigmatic as Brendan himself.

Where had he been all these years? Why hadn't he tried contacting her before now? Why had he let them all think him dead? And what did it all have to do with Daigh and Máelodor and St. John and her father?

She'd toyed with the idea of going to Aidan with the note right up until the moment he'd begun harping on Glenlorgan and his grand plans for family reunification. Her intentions had shriveled on the vine. He wouldn't listen. He'd bull his way past her explanations and her questions, ignoring her. Treating her like a child with a pat on the head and careless condescension.

So whom did that leave?

Her fingers brushed over the ink. Held the edges of the card. Brendan had touched this. Brendan, the brother she'd wept over for nights too numerous to count, whose face haunted her dreams for long years after, who'd taken a part of her heart with him when he left.

Daigh asked about Brendan. Needed his help. And sought to warn him about St. John and Máelodor.

Perhaps she'd misread the sign from the gods. Perhaps they hadn't been telling her to keep quiet about Brendan at all. Perhaps they'd been warning her of the life awaiting her if she didn't speak to Daigh.

Perhaps she needed to stop relying on the gods. They were singularly unhelpful.

A milky sky blanched the world to a monotonous gray. Blunting the edges of buildings. Bleaching the men and women passing through the streets. Dulling even the air to a soggy, misty miasma of smoke and rain.

Hands clenched and heart racing, Sabrina stood across from the Wood Street lodging house. Stared up at the blank windows. What on earth was she doing here? Had she taken leave of her senses? She'd wanted reckless. But this was beyond a fool's errand.

The front door opened while Sabrina stood pondering her next move. A woman emerging grim-faced, glaring, and as devoid of color as the faded day. Her face rang familiar. But from where?

The woman called over her shoulder to someone inside, her words indistinguishable amid the normal morning street hustle. But when she turned back, her eyes fixed on Sabrina like twin daggers.

Stepping down to the pavement, she crossed to Sabrina's side of the street. On closer inspection, her brittle demeanor seemed even more fragile. Her movements overcareful as if she were ill or in pain. "Lady Sabrina Douglas, isn't it?"

Sabrina met and matched the woman's arrogant condescension with her own noble bearing, rickety as it was. "You've the advantage of me. I don't believe we've been introduced."

"Miss Helena Roseingrave. I met Lord and Lady Kilronan in the spring." Her gaze flickered with some indefinable emotion. "And I hope someday to meet your brother Brendan."

Now why did she say that? As if she knew why Sabrina was here? As if she were as involved in this business as the rest. Sabrina's hackles rose. "In that you may be disappointed. He died a long time ago."

Miss Roseingrave's smile never reached her eyes. "There's death. And then there's death. As I'm sure you're aware, Lady Sabrina. You're well acquainted with both the permanent and more temporary variations."

Sabrina locked her knees to keep them from buckling. Dug her nails into her palms to keep them from this nasty woman's face. "As intriguing as this conversation is, I'm afraid I haven't time to prolong it. But if you do unearth my brother, give him my regards, won't you?" And with that conversation killer, she sauntered away. Head up. Eyes knife-bright and shining with tears.

Roseingrave's gaze gleamed with the keenness of a blade. "Right before I execute him for his crimes, I'll impart your warmest greetings."

Sabrina swallowed back the sudden choking dread.

Shook off the clammy snaky sweat that clung to her skin. And half ran, half sobbed her way across the street. Up the steps. Pounding the door with the side of her fist. Hugging her body in an attempt to stop the chills Miss Roseingrave's words had produced.

Daigh had to be here. He just had to be.

Nineteen

Sabrina. Here. Now. His descent into hell was complete.

He squeezed his eyes shut. When he reopened them she'd be gone. Had to be. But she wasn't. And in fact, she stood within a halo of herself. Two overlapping images crowding his brain.

Six hundred years old.

Seconds fresh.

A marcher lord's dimly lit solar.

A dusty, smelly Dublin garret.

She stood gawking with gem blue eyes, face creamy as marble, expression doe-shy and stretched with appalled concern as she flew to his side.

He curled himself more tightly against the gut-seizing cramps accompanying this new flash of remembrance.

"Did she hurt you?" she fumed. "So help me . . ." This forceful, outraged Sabrina burst through the pallid ghost-version like sun against fog. Eradicated it with the vibrant energy of the living.

"That was my line," he answered, scrubbing his mouth with the back of his hand. "And you once said I didn't need your healing."

She pushed his hair back off his face. Tutted over his fever heat. "How was I to know you were going to run afoul of a hateful, fire-breathing gorgon?"

"I think they turn you to stone."

"Who?" she asked absently as she quickly and efficiently arranged blankets, smoothed tousled clothing, eased him back against his pillow.

"Gorgons. Dragons breathe fire. Gorgons turn you to stone." Already he felt knotted muscles easing, though his brain remained burnt and blistered with the full knowledge of his sins.

Hands on hips, she scowled at him with a gifted healer's skeptical eye. "Why are you babbling about gorgons? What on earth did she do to you?"

He looked to the window. To the floor. Anywhere but at her. "Miss Roseingrave merely filled in the blanks."

Sabrina drew up his one and only chair. Settled herself with experienced professionalism. But he was aware of the smooth, cool flesh beneath that proper high-collared exterior. The sweet taste of that mouth and the dreams filling that sapphire gaze. It made him want to howl his anguish. Pull the world down around him and crush out the pain of this new exile.

She childishly chewed the edge of one finger. "She claims she's going to kill Brendan if she finds him." A wobble threaded her words. And now you're hurt . . ."

"Miss Roseingrave is *Ambas-draoi,* Sabrina."

She sucked in a frightened breath, her face going chalk white, brows snapping into a frown.

He pressed the heels of his hands to his eyes. "Puzzled it out, have you? She wants me to hand her Brendan Douglas's head on a platter. Or at least his whereabouts."

"That's why you kept asking if I'd heard from him. You planned on—"

"Trading him for a clean, quick death. Aye."

"You want so much to die?"

He opened his eyes to see her glowering down at him from eyes bright with outrage.

"I want to be free," he answered firmly. "The form of it makes no difference."

She gazed at him for long unbearable minutes, her words when they came soft but certain. "So what made you change your mind about Brendan?"

"What makes you think I have?"

"You'd not be telling me otherwise."

He swung his legs over the side of the bed. His stomach rolled, but the room had stopped the wild spinning of earlier. "Perhaps it's all part of my wily plan," he said, running a hand over his chin. "Make you think I'm on your side when the only side I'm on is my own."

"I don't believe it. You're too forthright. Deception and conniving aren't your way. You face your enemies head-on."

He straightened, shooting her a sarcastic look. "Your empathic gifts are so great you can read my character?"

A dogged glint flashed in her eyes. "It's naught to do with empathy. I read the man as he's shown himself to me over and over." She leaned forward. "Honorable. Principled." So close he counted the freckles upon her nose. Drowned in her jewel blue irises. "Compassionate." She barely pressed her lips to his.

His body shuddered, this time with suppressed need.

"This isn't a game, Sabrina. I can't save you. I can't even save myself."

"I'm not asking to be saved." Such a serious face. Determined. Almost angry.

No. He knew exactly what she was asking for, and it was becoming harder to deny her. And why should he? His villainy had been firmly established.

"It wouldn't be our first time," she cajoled. "You know it. You remember."

All too well. Sabrina, smiling as she teased him to arousal. Wanton and passionate, her body sleek and soft beneath him. Spooned against him as she slept after. The picture burned in his mind.

"It never happened. Couldn't have." He denied his memories. Yet here she was before him. An impossible reality. But then—as death undone—so was he. Perhaps two impossibilities created their own mysterious magic.

He reached for her. Felt her shiver beneath his fingers as he drew her up and against him. For all her brave talk, she remained fearful.

He cupped her face in his hands, sliding his tongue along the seam of her lips. She opened to him, letting him dip inside. Quick flicks to entice. To tempt. While she stood without moving, hands splayed against his chest as if unsure where to go from here.

Taking the decision away from her, he caressed her shoulders, the curve of her breasts, down her sides, settling his hands on her hips. Gathering her close.

As she relaxed, his kisses deepened. She tasted velvety sweet, her honey heat acting on him like a drug until he hungered for more. Hunger for her congealing into a devastating greed. He wanted not just to recall their passion. But to relive it. Sabrina belonged to him. Body and soul. In this life and the last.

Buttons. Knots. Ribbons. Each article of clothing discarded with wicked eroticism until he throbbed with impatience, and her breathing came quick and gasping with every touch of his hands upon her flesh.

There was an instant when he stood before her naked, his uncountable scars ice-white and puckered against the bronze of his skin. Shame and cowardice and the burning knowledge of his crimes flared through him once more.

Sabrina would find out. Sabrina would hate him.

Then she bent, kissing his chest. Tracing the myriad paths of Máelodor's cruelty, her gaze bright with unshed tears.

Courage. Strength. Compassion. Generosity. She possessed them all.

Heart beating painfully, he swept her up and into bed to lie atop him, her sun-drenched brown hair spilling over him, her skin silken soft and blushed pink and gold like a sunrise. With ever-increasing abandon, she kissed him, tugging at his bottom lip with her teeth, darting a tongue inside, matching his temptations with her own.

Urgency ignited his blood, his cock hard at the junction of her legs. It would take seconds to bury himself deep inside her. Instead, he spun out his seduction. Enjoyed her body inch by melting inch. Treated this time as precious and never to be again.

She moaned her yearning into his open mouth, begged him even when she knew not what she begged for. Her body sinuous, sinful perfection.

Rolling her beneath him, he spread her legs, kissing his way down over her breasts, alternately laving and sucking her nipples until she trembled. Preparing her for him with skillful gentling as if she were indeed the self-conscious wild creature he'd first envisioned upon that rocky mile of lonesome beach below Glenlorgan.

So when he entered her with a tender stroke, her body curved into his, hands twined around his neck, hips arched to meet him.

She gasped, eyes wide as he remained poised above her. But only for a moment before she smiled, spurring him onward with a siren's invitation. Taking him deeper within her until it was his turn to tremble, his body closing fast toward a dangerous edge.

He slowed the tempo, savoring the pleasure. Knowing it for what it was. A beginning and an end.

She may not have understood the significance of his actions, but she responded with a sweet eagerness that had every nerve in his body leaping to new heights of attention as he thrust deeper.

Sabrina wound her arms around his back, face dappled with light and shadow, breasts high and round, tips pebble-hard. Pressure built within him. Pooling low. Radiating outward. The pleasure-pain of their joining increasing with every thrust.

Her eyes fluttered open, meeting his steady gaze with a diamond-blue rapture. And it was as if he were back where he began. At the ship's gunwale, staring deep into the heart of the sea. Praying to any god he could to be allowed to rejoin his lost lover in *Annwn*. Had this then been their answer? Had the gods heard him after all? And was this one moment with Sabrina his reward?

Or his punishment?

Desire coalesced down to a focused instant. Boiled high

in a brilliant shockwave as he exploded inside her. Kissed her as she moaned her bliss into his mouth.

She dug her hands into his shoulders, head thrown back, breath ragged. Whispered his name over and over as she climaxed around him. Achingly star-bright and beautiful in ecstasy.

Later, they lay nestled together, neither one ready to gather the discarded proprieties they'd shed with their clothes. The day lingered into twilight as they talked and dozed and talked some more. He should release her. Let her go. Force her out of his bed and, even if she didn't realize it, out of his life. Instead, his arms wrapped around her, his chin resting against the top of her head, the heat of her warming every dead place within him.

"Will you return to Glenlorgan?" he asked.

She shifted in his arms until they faced one another, a crease between her brows. "Not if Aidan has his way." She curled closer into him. "He wants me to return with him to Belfoyle. He thinks going there will make me forget the last seven years. As if we can re-create the life we had before Father's murder, and I'll suddenly realize his plans for my future are the best."

"Perhaps going home would help you lay aside your grief. You can see things as they are now. Not dwell on what was."

"Once he's got me safely hidden away at Belfoyle, he'll never allow me to return to take my place among the sisters. I'll be fitted out as the latest Douglas up for sale on the marriage market. Healthy, all my teeth, and the rents from an estate or two thrown in for good measure. What gentleman could resist?"

"Love can sometimes be found even in the most practical

of alliances. You may be lucky in your brother's choice." Like picking at a half-healed wound, he tormented himself with the statement, imagining Sabrina with another man.

"Even if I did, what use would my healing abilities be in this world? I'd be trapped in the role of good little hostess and breeder of sons. Never allowed to utilize the gifts I've been given. I couldn't stand that."

He pushed her hair off her face. Kissed her forehead. "Your brother sees happiness in marriage and family. And who can argue? Not many men are blessed with a woman as courageous and spirited as Lady Kilronan."

She lifted her head, her crease deepening. "You know her?"

He shrugged, answering quickly, "By reputation only," hoping that satisfied her.

It seemed to. She lay back down. "You think I should listen to him and return to Belfoyle."

Isolated. Warded. Far from Dublin and St. John and Máelodor.

And him.

Belfoyle was exactly where she needed to be.

"I do," he answered.

She snuggled into his chest, almost as if she were burrowing in. Her body sending tingles of renewed heat straight to his groin. He clenched his teeth, knowing if he surrendered to his body's increasing demands, she'd be fortunate to arrive home before dawn.

"And if I shocked you by asking to stay?" she murmured. "With you?"

"Don't, Sabrina."

She rolled up onto an elbow. "That sounds very much like a thank-you but no."

He ignored the scraps of heart left to him. Cracked his mind to the presence as a way to fight back against the temptation of her proposal. Immediately, the ominous brimstone anger overwhelmed his lust. Black emotions scorched the insides of his skull, leaving naught but the charred remains of his earlier desire. "I can't protect you. I'm who you need protecting from."

He stared at her. Without speaking. Unable to breach a gap of inches. No way around the dead bodies lying between them. No way over the mountain of sins he'd committed for the sake of his master. His creator. The Great One.

"Mr. MacLir." A rap upon the door broke them both free. "There's someone downstairs asking for you. A rather foul-tempered gentleman with a pistol and an unstable eye."

St. John? Here? Could it get worse?

"Says he's the Earl of Kilronan."

Bloody hell. He'd had to ask.

Sabrina dressed in a frantic race, ears tuned to clomping footsteps on the stairs or a pistol report. Neither occurred, and she entered the parlor, more or less in a presentable and unfrenzied state. Hair bundled into a loose chignon. Stays abandoned, but stockings in place and gown right way around and buttoned correctly.

She hoped.

"How did you find me?" she demanded, pretending a bravery she didn't feel.

Aidan swung around, brows drawn down over narrowed eyes, body radiating violence. "Recognize this?" He slammed her journal on the table.

She cringed, wracking her brain. Surely she'd hidden it

away. She never left it out. But she'd stayed up late, jotting as much down as she could. Every moment. Every kiss. And this morning, Aidan's arrival had surprised her from her normal routine. She must have forgotten . . . A weight pressed on her chest, making her fight for every breath.

All her thoughts. All her actions. Spread across page after page for anyone to read. Anyone and Aidan, who now looked primed for murder.

"Don't even try the holier-than-thou act. Not when your own wife—" She swallowed back her words at the vicious glare centered on her. "It's not the way it looks," she finished lamely, though it was exactly how it looked. And Aidan knew it.

"Where is he?" Aidan seethed. "Has the monster left you to face the music while he skulks back to his master gloating over your maidenhead?" His hand gripping the pistol shook.

"Have care with your insults, Lord Kilronan. My rage can be fatal."

The deep, velvety baritone slid along nerves still jumping with aftershocks of their lovemaking. She inhaled the sexy man scent of him. Reveled in the warmth of his body. If she stepped back, she'd be in the circle of his arms.

"Lazarus." That one syllable filled with enough venom to kill. "I should have murdered you when I had the chance."

Daigh stepped around her, the towering strength of his body emphasized by the tiny parlor. She'd forgotten how big he was. How he seemed to pulse with a savage light. How his very presence sucked every bit of air from a room and his gaze could smolder with enough heat to singe. "As I remember, my lord, you tried. And how is your lady wife?"

Wait. Daigh? Aidan? Aidan's wife? Did they know one another? Apparently knew and loathed by the killer stare her brother focused on Daigh.

"Did you think to attack me through Sabrina? Were you planning on taking her to Máelodor for his pleasure once you were finished with her?"

Aidan looked in danger of exploding. His face purple. His eyes burning with a dark intensity she'd never seen before. Almost as if the shadow of another crouched waiting in the ruthless gaze. He brought the pistol up to level it at Daigh's chest. The shadow overtaking him. His stare as soulless and empty as if someone else controlled him. Inhabited him.

Daigh never faltered. "That will avail you nothing."

"You forget, Lazarus, I carry within me a little piece of my own monster. My own hell, thanks to you."

"And would you summon it here? Risk losing yourself to the evil of the *Unseelie*?"

"A risk worth taking," Aidan snarled.

"Stop! Stop it now!" Sabrina stepped between them as if she could fend off the inevitable. "Do you hear yourself, Aidan? Is this even about me?"

"What do you think, Sabrina? Or did you think at all when you took up with this thrice damned savage fiend? He's a freak of nature. A cursed, hellish experiment."

"Careful, my lord. I've killed men for less."

"I'm well aware of the men you've killed."

Like two curs circling, teeth bared. Did they even hear her over their chest-thumping brinksmanship?

She grabbed Daigh's arm. Dragged him around long enough to focus on her. "What's this about?" A question she seemed to ask with maddening regularity. But confusion had become her permanent state of mind. And she tired of it. "Why are you ready to tear each other apart?"

Daigh offered her a mad dog stare, a feverish, implacable rage burning in his jet-black eyes. Emotion flooded her senses, but instead of the unstoppable rush of memory, she came up against a wall, stark and impassable. She read nothing of his thoughts. Saw nothing of his past. Only a black, dizzying emptiness like a razored maw. An unblinking serpent's eye. She shuddered under that malevolent, unyielding gaze. Fell back with a startled cry.

"You once said I was given a second chance, Sabrina. But that chance came with strings. The diary I dreamt about? The visions of death and destruction?"

"What about them?"

"Your brother. His wife. Your cousin. Your house. I destroyed them all. Or tried to at my master's bidding. I am a creature in thrall to a madman."

Aidan's injuries in the spring. They'd told her he'd had an accident climbing the cliffs below Belfoyle. Jack dead at the hands of highwaymen. Kilronan House burnt to the ground from a dropped candle on a carpet. All of these had been caused by Daigh? No. It couldn't be. She would have known. Would have seen. Would have sensed it.

But she had. She did. And she'd refused to give any of her concerns credence. Too caught up in her girlish fantasy of Daigh riding to her rescue. Her black-eyed paladin swooping in to save her. It had been just that—fantasy.

Her body went cold then hot. She hugged herself against the shudders wracking her body.

Aidan grabbed her arm. "Come, Sabrina."

"I don't believe you," she whispered, praying for a denial.

"Believe me. It is so," Daigh answered.

Aidan's grip tightened as he pulled her away.

"You wouldn't hurt me. You couldn't." She reached for Daigh, but he shrugged her off with a quick, angry gesture.

"You're a silly child," he snarled, averting his gaze. Refusing to look her in the eye. "A fool."

His insults struck her with the force of blows, but she was already numb and barely staggered beneath them. "And what I saw of us? The images of you and me?"

He lifted his head, raking her with a greasy, ugly stare. "A virgin's infatuation." His lips curled in a scoundrel's smile. "But we took care of that, didn't we, pet?"

Aidan went rigid, his expression thunderous. "Lazarus, you son of a whore's rotten—" Jerked his hand up, squeezing off a shot.

"No!" Sabrina screamed.

The windows rattled, smoke stinging her nose, making her eyes water.

Squinting through the blur of tears, she dropped to her knees and the man crumpled on the floor, bloody hands clutching his stomach.

"Daigh! By the gods, Aidan. Why?"

He loomed over them, white-faced and shaking. "It may not kill him as he deserves, but it sure as hell makes me feel better."

Daigh's chest rose and fell with shallow, painful breaths. Each inhalation pushing fresh blood between his fingers. His lips curved in a faint grimace. "Glad to be of service, my lord."

"Come, Sabrina." Aidan dragged her to her feet. "If I so much as catch a whiff of your stench again, Lazarus, I'll risk any damnation to see you suffer."

In shock, Sabrina shook her head, unable to voice any of the tangle of thoughts beating against her except the inane, "His name is Daigh, not Lazarus."

A stony remoteness entered Daigh's expression as if his humanity had been obliterated. And she knew at last how and why he'd ended in the sea. The lengths he would go to gain what he saw as his only peace.

"No, Sabrina. Not Daigh. Nor Lazarus. My true name is lost. As am I."

"May I come in?"

Sabrina looked up from the hearth where she knelt before one of Aunt Delia's floral scented fires, feeding journal pages to the purple flames. Lady Kilronan's pixie face peered at her around the corner of the bedchamber door. Her first visitor since Jane had darted in long enough to give her a fearful and slightly awed look, grasp both her hands, and murmur, "Don't blame yourself . . . you couldn't have known, Sabrina. And if he ever comes near you . . ." She drew herself up like Joan facing the English army before slinking away at fresh shouting downstairs.

That had been around noon. It was now—quick check of the clock—eight in the evening. She'd been sequestered for over a day while her fate was argued below in loud, carrying tones.

"Have you been sent up to speak to me about the error of my ways?" she grumbled. "A life lesson from one experienced in these matters?"

A shadow passed over the other woman's features, giving Sabrina a twinge of guilty conscience. It wasn't Aidan's wife's fault Sabrina's world had once again come toppling down around her ears. Tears caught in the back of her throat, and she stood in a rush of skirts and apologies. "I'm so sorry. That was ill said, and I didn't mean it. Really. Come in, my lady."

She beckoned her sister-in-law into the room with a watery smile.

"It's Cat. 'My lady' sounds horribly stiff. As if we were strangers."

"Aren't we?"

"For now. But I hope that one day we may count each other as the best of friends." She smiled warmly despite Sabrina's lack of manners. "You'll be pleased to learn we've convinced Aunt Delia you went on a long walk with your maid and two heavyset footmen and lost track of time." She cocked a glance at Sabrina's dismembered journal. "Are you certain you want to do that?"

Sabrina fingered the wreckage. Tossed the rest onto the fire. Watched the book blacken and wither. Wished she could erase the events as easily.

"It was a mistake to keep such a diary," she answered through clenched teeth. "It left me exposed to the worst sort of snooping."

She dusted off her hands. Ignoring the twinge of pain at losing what had been, until this morning, her truest sanctuary. Not even Jane privy to all that lay within her heart.

She made a conscious effort to take a chair facing away from the fire. Arranged herself carefully. Skirts. Limbs. Fussing over shawl or no shawl. Rearranging the pillow. The candle at her elbow. Anything to forget the journal and the ordeal of having to talk to—of all people—her brother's wife about it.

"May I sit?" Cat motioned to the chair opposite.

Sabrina shrugged her acceptance. It took effort to fight.

"If it's a choice between you or Aidan ringing a peal over my head, I choose you."

"I'll take that as a compliment." Cat pulled a face. "He does have a knack for making one's fists itch, doesn't he?" She laughed, and for just a moment, Sabrina had a glimmer of what it might be like to have a sister. Someone besides Jane who, while a bosom friend, wasn't a part of Sabrina's family and couldn't understand the horrible aftermath still rippling outward from that long-ago November day.

She eyed the new Lady Kilronan through downcast lashes. Not the arrogant, dark-eyed frostiness of Helena Roseingrave. Nor the simpering malice of Aunt Delia. Cat had an approachable elegance, a kindness in her face that made Sabrina blush with shame at her earlier unkind opinions. She should have known Aidan wouldn't marry a title-seeking conniver. He'd far too much sense—and cynicism—for that.

And Sabrina had far too little.

"Forgive me for behaving so badly . . . Cat." She liked the familiar name upon her lips. "I've been an absolute shrew. None of this is your fault. You don't deserve my vitriol. It's Aidan who spied on me."

She fumed just thinking about his violation of her most private thoughts.

"He worried over you," Cat supplied matter-of-factly. "He didn't know where you'd gone. Neither Miss Fletcher nor your aunt could offer him any suggestions. Your journal was his last hope."

"That's no reason for his trespass."

Cat sighed. "No, it's an excuse, and not a very good one. But the only one I have. Aidan loves you. He feels responsible for you. A duty to the only family he has left.

And to that end he'd justify almost any action. To him, family is strength. He's come to see the heirs of Kilronan as a bulwark against the world."

"Against Máelodor, you mean."

Cat brushed the charge aside. "Against any hurt. You mayn't believe it, but Aidan was as rocked by your family's disintegration as you. He was left alone to pick up the pieces as best he could. Just as you were."

"He didn't do too badly. He ended with you."

Cat grinned. "I was merely serendipity."

A question hovered. One Sabrina needed to ask. Not out of spite or any wish to wound, but because she and Cat had more in common now than just Aidan. Still, how to ask without sounding like a mean gossip. Direct was best.

Soonest asked. Soonest answered.

She squared her shoulders. Exhaled her words in a gasp of breath. "Do you regret what you did with . . . ? When . . . ? I mean they say—not that I care what a bunch of tattle-merchants say, but—that is . . . do you regret what you did?"

Embarrassed heat shot straight to her toes. Especially when Cat's smile faded. Her stare turning inward, body stiffening, hands clasped palm down in her lap.

"No regrets. Not any longer. Aidan's love brought me to this blessed point." Cat reached across and took Sabrina's hand in hers. The gold and garnet Kilronan wedding band winking on her ring finger. "He saw firsthand the pain giving my heart to someone unworthy of it caused me."

Sorrow lodged deep within Sabrina's chest. Is this what people meant when they spoke of being heartbroken? This hard, cold rock that seemed to expand until all of her felt weighted and achy? She pulled a shawl up over her shoulders, even though the room was overwarm and stuffy from the fire. Gazed for a moment at the rainy night beyond her window where the stifling press of the city seemed to add to her already throbbing head. "Daigh said he tried to kill you. Is that true?"

"Is that what he's calling himself these days?" Cat focused on the fire as if the past could be seen within the dancing flames. "I wish I could tell you differently. If it weren't for Miss Roseingrave, Aidan and I wouldn't have survived."

Sabrina went rigid. "Miss Roseingrave? That she-viper?"

A hint of amusement touched Cat's sad eyes. "Aye. She and your cousin Jack prevented Laz—Daigh from gaining the diary. I miss Jack. I believe she does too."

"Jack wasn't set on by robbers, was he? He was another victim."

"Jack sought to protect me and died for his bravery." She paused, her face drawn and pale. Worry carved the corners of her mouth. Between her brows. "In the end, Daigh could have killed Aidan and me. He was a sword stroke away from ending our lives." She bit her bottom lip. "But he didn't. Something stopped him. Perhaps it's the same something that caused you to love him."

Sabrina stiffened, eyes wide, brain racing. Did she love Daigh? She had once. Long centuries ago. And though he sought to dismiss her visions as a virgin's foolishness, they were more than that. Much more. She tucked her arms beneath her breasts against the squeeze of pain. An all-too-familiar grief. A loss she seemed doomed to repeat again and again.

"You think I was mad to care for him. I see it in your face."

Cat shook her head. "You stumbled in over your head. But take it from someone who's been there, the heart mends. It may be impossible to believe now, but the fall into love isn't fatal." She twisted her wedding ring round and round, the ghost of an old grief hovering beneath her pale skin. "Not if there's someone to catch you at the bottom."

With a hand plowed into his thick auburn hair, Aidan bent over his library desk, pen scratching madly across the page, a grim set to his angular jaw, his expression forbidding in a way she'd never seen before. In fact her brother was as unfamiliar as a stranger. The Aidan of her childhood had been an irresponsible scoundrel. A brother revered as exciting and reckless. Certainly not this cynical, stern-featured autocrat.

Drawing in a fortifying breath, Sabrina tapped on the open door.

Without raising his head, he put up a hand. "Hold one moment, Cat, or I'll lose my train of thought."

"It's not Cat. It's Sabrina. We need to speak."

His head shot up, brows contracting in a wary scowl. "I'm busy. We'll talk later. Once I've calmed down. Right now I'm still ready to tear that bastard's thrice-damned head off and shove it up his—" His pen snapped in two. He tossed it onto the desk with another muttered oath. "Didn't I warn you? Now's not the time."

Ignoring his display of temper and his abrupt dismissal, she stepped into the room, closing the door behind her. "If you're trying to scare me into leaving, it won't work. And I don't give a . . . a . . . damn for your temper," she brazened. "We'll talk now."

He seemed as stunned as she by her outburst. But it worked. He gave her his attention. Rubbed his chin, eying her with an arrogant droop of his lids. "A foul mouth to match your easy virtue. What else can I thank the *bandraoi* for?"

She gritted her teeth until she thought they might crack. "Do you really want to go down that path, Aidan? Because I'm certain your wife would be interested in hearing your opinions on a woman's virtue."

His jaw clenched, contrition instantly flaring in his bronze brown gaze. "Did you ever think it might be because of Cat that I'm as furious with you as I am? One misstep. One hint of scandal and they'll pounce. Shred you to bits with their gossip and their barbs and their hypocritical outrage. Tear you down until there's nothing left. I don't want you to suffer what she has."

He scrubbed his hands through his hair in an impatient and frustrated gesture, and for the first time, she noticed the gleaming silver strands among the gold. The worry lines creasing the corners of his eyes. The tension thickening the very air around him. Much had happened to her oldest brother while she remained oblivious within the sanctuary of the order. Desolation. Suffering And horrible pain. Hints of them plagued him still. In the darkness of his gaze. The solemn austerity of his expression.

"Is that why you and Cat avoid Dublin?" she asked.

He shrugged. "In part. Cat's memories of the city are painful ones. And for myself, I lost interest in the gilded dog pit that is the beau monde years ago. The loss of Kilronan House offered a good excuse for our exile." He shook his head. Sighed again as he toyed with the jagged pieces of the broken pen. "Sabrina . . . how . . . what would ever make you . . . knowing what he is . . . that's what I don't understand."

His troubled gaze wandered over her as if he didn't recognize her. Perhaps he shared her sense of confronting a stranger. She sank slowly into a seat, exhaustion rushing in to replace her earlier hostility. "He cared for me, Aidan. I know it's hard to believe, but he did. I would have detected deceit or treachery."

But would she? Or had he hidden his true intentions behind the blast furnace of emotion that scoured her brain with such frequency? Had his mind's churning turbulence obscured the real purpose behind his attentions?

Aidan leapt to his feet. Hand tapping nervously against his bad thigh. His limp hampering his angry strides back and forth across the carpet. "Lazarus cares for nothing. He's guided by Máelodor in all things. And if he made you believe he cared then it was only because his master bid him do so."

"No. I won't believe that." She couldn't because that meant she'd been wrong. Stupid. Naive. And Daigh's insults had been true.

"You forget. I've crossed paths with him before." He placed a hand over his heart with a wince hardening the already sharp lines of his face. "I could show you the scar."

She lifted a stubborn chin. "And Daigh's scars? Máelodor has tortured him into subservience. Has infected him with evil. It's not Daigh's by right. Not his by choice." She fisted her hands together. Sucked in a ragged breath. Was this her chance? Could she tell Aidan about her visions? Would he believe her, or would he dismiss the connection as a girlish fantasy as Daigh had?

Brendan would listen. Would believe. But Brendan

wasn't here. Aidan was. And for better or worse he was her only family. Perhaps he'd even understand what was happening to her. She surely didn't.

Her voice dropped low as she struggled against the weight in her chest. "I've met him before, Aidan. Known him. Not as he is now, but as he was. Before Máelodor's summoning. Before he was brought back against his will."

Aidan paused, one hand upon the mantel, his gaze fastened on the refreshingly fire-colored flames. A tiny victory amid Aunt Delia's decorating extravaganza. "What are you talking about?" he growled.

"Daigh." When he tried to interrupt, she rushed ahead. She had to speak of it. To explain herself. To make him listen and not just push her story away as a child's silliness. "I know it sounds like insanity, but I've traveled into Daigh's past. I've walked with him. Spoken with him. Loved him. At first I thought I was dreaming, but Daigh remembers me too. He remembers us together. I don't know how or why, but when I'm in Daigh's past it's as real to me as this moment."

He cast aside her words with a careless wave of his arm. "More of Máelodor's black magics. You see what he wants you to see."

She hadn't thought of that. Could it be? Could Daigh have cast some demonic spell over her? No. Her visions were too full of hope and life and affection to be the work of dark powers.

"Máelodor will stop at nothing to gain his victory. And if it includes destroying an innocent girl, so be it," Aidan scoffed.

"What does Máelodor want? Who is he? You talk of his malice. Daigh spoke of his evil. Even Cat trembles when she speaks his name."

"It doesn't matter. You'll leave for Belfoyle, and that will be an end to it."

She stiffened. "If I go anywhere, it shall be back to Glenlorgan."

He sank into a seat nearby. Stretched his bad leg in front of him, kneading his thigh. "Rejoining the *bandraoi* is out of the question. Father's murder won't continue to splinter our family as it has for the past seven years. You're my sister. You belong with me."

"I may be your sister, but I'm not your child. So stop acting as if I am. My future is my own, Aidan. And if I choose to return to the *bandraoi,* there is nothing you can say. I'm a healer. It's my birthright and my calling. It's who I am. I can't turn my back on that gift any more than you could . . . could turn your back on Belfoyle or the earldom."

He lifted his head, crossed his arms. The picture of unyielding obstinacy. Any more arguing would only set his back up higher. She subsided. For now. "You haven't answered my questions about Máelodor."

"Tell her, Aidan."

Sabrina hadn't heard her sister-in-law enter the room, but there she was. Her black hair and green eyes emphasizing her ghost-white skin. She crossed to Aidan's side, resting upon the arm of his chair. His hand came up to run over her back. Rest there possessively.

Their affection made Sabrina hurt with a jealousy she couldn't put into words. If her visions were of Daigh's true past, she'd had this same closeness once. Had it and lost it.

"Sabrina's as involved as any of us," Cat urged. "And as she's found at great cost, what is unknown can be as dangerous as what is known."

Sabrina added her arguments to Cat's. "Máelodor has

tried to kill you. He's used me to find Brendan. What does he want from the Douglases? What have we done to be singled out for his animosity? Please, Aidan. Tell me."

Aidan glanced at the door. Hunched deeper into his chair. Stared long and intently into the flames before giving a faint nod as if coming to a decision. He paused, seeming to weigh his words. "Máelodor was one of the mages who studied with Father. Driven by the same sinister ambitions. The same hellish dream as Father and all of his associates. They believed in a world where the race of *Other* would not only be free to live without fear of persecution, but would control that world and the destinies of the *Duinedon* who served us."

A cold wave of nausea washed over her. "Impossible. It could never happen."

"Father believed it could if the *Other* were united under their last and most legendary king. A warlord who wielded his considerable power during the last golden age of *Other* dominance."

"Arthur. But how on earth . . . Arthur's dust. He's . . ." She clamped her mouth shut. Of course. A soldier of Domnu. One of the *Domnuathi* built from the bones of his former life.

Aidan nodded. "Father and the mages he'd turned to his cause strove to resurrect Arthur as a new leader—literally. To use him as a rallying point for all *Other*. Máelodor searches for the map that will lead him to Arthur's tomb and the stone that will open the protective wards. Once these treasures are in his possession, he'll have all he needs to complete the Nine's work and bring the High King back from the dead."

A question she hated but had to ask. "Brendan was

involved, wasn't he? The *Ambas-draoi* didn't lie when they accused him."

"No. They didn't lie."

The days leading to Samhain. A pile of dead wood heaped in the inner courtyard in preparation for the bonfires lit to signal the day of the dead. Brendan in a quiet but heated discussion with Father, both men staring at each other, eyes matching in intensity and cold arrogance. A hand upon Father's arm shaken off. Brendan disappearing into the stables. Father closeting himself in his library. Unease blanketing the house. Shortening tempers. Filling reproachful silences. Brendan's sudden departure from Belfoyle only adding fuel to the gathering storm.

Aidan continued, "But the *Ambas-draoi* don't know the whole truth either."

The note. The open window.

"Is that why you came to Dublin?"

"The *Ambas-draoi* are searching for Brendan. They believe he, not Máelodor, is behind this new threat."

"Máelodor has dispatched a rogue *Ambas-draoi* named St. John to capture Brendan."

Aidan started forward in his chair, his hands grasping the arms with sudden excitement. "Gervase St. John? Is that who you mean? How do you know?"

"Daigh warned me."

"Why would that devil care what happens to Brendan?"

Swallowing back the sudden lump choking off her breath, she met Aidan's critical gaze head-on. "Because he knows—more than anyone—the pain of being Máelodor's victim."

twenty

The *Ambas-draoi* knelt before him, golden head bowed, a hand to his heart. "I'm honored you sought me out for this task, Great One. I'll do my best to justify your faith in me."

Máelodor placed a hand upon St. John's shoulder. "If you truly desire a place at Arthur's side, I expect better than your best. The High King will need trusted companions to guide him as he gathers his army. Prepares for the uprising. Bring me the Rywlkoth Tapestry, and you shall ride at his side at the final battle. There can be no higher reward."

"How will I recognize the tapestry?"

"Kilronan's suspicious nature led him to disguise it, and though I've studied his diary thoroughly, I've found no description of its alterations. I'm therefore left with only the original inscriptions to go by. These you have."

"A puzzle within a puzzle."

"Hidden somewhere within the concealing design are the clues to lead us to Arthur's tomb."

"It could be anywhere within the *bandraoi*'s precincts. Those shriveled up old besoms aren't likely to invite me in to poke around," St. John said.

"Is this task beyond you? One of Scathach's vaunted warriors?"

"It shall be difficult and time-consuming."

"All worthy goals carry a degree of difficulty. A true peer of the High King would not flinch. Nor would he snivel like a coward."

St. John went rigid with insult—as expected. So quick to take offense. So needy to prove himself worthy. Control lay in knowing what strings needed to be plucked to make the puppet dance. The *Ambas-draoi*'s had been obvious from the first. His inadequacies so close to the surface.

"I shall find a way, Great One," he responded in a clipped tone.

Máelodor nodded. "There is always a way."

Exhaustion and brittle bones undermined him, and he leaned back in his chair, gasping to catch his breath. Ease the pains in his hips and back. The journey from Holyhead to Dublin had been more wearying to his aged body than he cared to admit. He needed to conserve his strength. It wouldn't do to fail just at the time when he most needed his powers.

St. John lifted his head. "And what of Douglas? Is he still a priority?

"Oh yes. Brendan Douglas must be found. He is the only one who knows where the Sh'vad Tual is hidden. He must be made to surrender that information."

"And after?"

Máelodor sensed the man's quiver of excitement. It touched a chord deep within himself. A slithering curl of eagerness that kindled the physical fusion of fetch animal and man known as the Heller change. He'd not done it in years, but now and then a moment of stimulation brought to the surface hints of the serpent. A calculating ruthlessness unmarred by weaker human emotions. And now was not the time for weak emotions. Not when the world of *Other* remained under siege by a growing *Duinedon* malevolence.

Brendan had surrendered to cloying sentiment. He deserved his fate.

He shivered against the bone-deep cold that accompanied the Heller's emergence. "As long as he comes to me still breathing, you may do as you wish." He motioned him to rise. "But right now, all your skills must be bent toward capturing the tapestry. Bloom has failed. Lazarus has vanished. It lies now in your more-than-capable hands."

A glittering excitement fired the *Ambas-draoi*'s eyes. "I've seen the *Domnuathi*."

"Where?"

"Here in Dublin. But he may no longer be an asset to your work. He's grown dangerously unstable. Has strayed from your purpose."

"We shall have to remind him of his indebtedness to us. It's rare to be given a second turn upon life's wheel." He ran a tongue over his lips, his hands curling into fists as he relived their last cautionary encounter. This time Lazarus would realize his gratitude. Or suffer still greater agonies than previously.

"He could still be useful."

"In what way?"

"He's formed an attachment to the Douglas girl that could be valuable if played correctly."

"Has he?" Máelodor's smile stretched his sagging skin taut. "Perhaps his game may be deeper than we know."

Leaning against his staff, he groped to rise, his frailties slowing him to a snail's crawl. His body weakened, every day a new pain. Every night an empty hole where a piece of his soul used to be. It would all be worth it, though. When Arthur bowed before him in sun-rayed splendor. When the *Duinedon* scattered before the combined might of the *Fey*-born *Other* until surrender or slaughter was their only choice. When Arthur, with Máelodor at his side, presided over a new golden age, none of the aches and embarrassments of his broken body would matter.

He would succeed where the Nine had failed.

It would truly be his golden age.

But until then—"Assist me to my carriage."

St. John hurried to his master's side, guiding him down the narrow stairs. Across the hall and out to the waiting barouche. A break in the rain had thickened the crowds. Máelodor leaned heavily upon St. John to keep from being knocked down by the rushing passersby. Gentlemen with umbrellas, bundled against the damp. Women in dark woolens, their hats and bonnets drooping against the drizzle.

A woman in black, her face obscured by a heavy mourning veil brushed past him, shooting a tingle of mage energy up his arm where they touched. He glanced back, but she'd disappeared into the swarm of pedestrians, and then the coachman was there. Opening the door. Letting down the steps. Bundling Máelodor into the warmth of the carriage.

St. John bent close. "I shall not let you down."

Máelodor let the full force of his power harden in his gaze. "See that you don't."

"You can't, Sabrina. They'll find out," Jane pleaded.

"They won't find out anything." Sabrina turned a deaf ear and continued stuffing her satchel. Extra gown. Pair of slippers. Two shifts, a shawl, and a third pair of stockings. Looked around for anything she might have missed. "I've arranged it all." Removed the shawl. No room. "Aidan and Cat think I'm leaving with Aunt Delia for Belfoyle. They agree I should get away and rest." In other words, retire as far away from Dublin and any hint of scandal as soon as possible. "And Aunt Delia believes I've taken suddenly ill and must remain here. She's leaving for Bray to visit a friend of hers."

"You put that idea in her head, didn't you?"

"I might have hinted, but she was more than happy to go. I think she's had it up to her ears with Aidan's black looks every time they meet. She's never forgiven him for breaking that statue of Ares in the drawing room. Swears it was on purpose. I think she's kept the pieces."

Jane giggled before stifling it behind a suitably stern look. "I still don't think this is a good idea. How will you travel? Where will you stay along the way? What will people think? Lord and Lady Kilronan will kill me when they find out. And I'm too young to die."

Sabrina ticked off her answers on her fingers. "One—I'll go by mail coach. It leaves from Sackville Street every evening. Two—I have money enough to pay the fare and extra for food and lodging. Three—People will think whatever they want to think. And four—I'll write telling Aidan where I am once I reach Glenlorgan." She huffed the hair from her eyes. Stood back, studying her satchel. Did she take enough? Too much?

"At least let me come with you. I can be ready in a half hour."

"I need you to stay behind to allay any suspicions. Tell them I'm not well and need to be left alone."

"And when they discover you missing?"

"Claim you didn't know anything about it. Or that I threatened you with physical harm if you told."

Jane twisted her handkerchief in her hands as if she wrung a neck. Probably Sabrina's. "Can't you simply ask Aidan to take us back himself and save all this subterfuge?"

"I have. And he refused. More than once. He's said a return to the *bandraoi* is out of the question. He wants me at Belfoyle where I can be properly looked after. His idea of properly being a guard at my door, meals of bread and water, and Aidan prowling the house like a fire-breathing gor—dragon."

Dragons breathe fire. Gorgons turn you to stone.

She swallowed back tears. Ard-siúr had termed Daigh a wounded animal. Warned Sabrina what would happen if she followed her heart and tried to save a man who was beyond saving. She'd no one to blame but herself if her life lay scattered and broken around her.

She missed Ard-siúr, Sister Ainnir, even Sister Brigh. Her cluttered, crowded bedchamber. Long nights in the infirmary and long days in study or working. Her friends. Her life.

She wasn't brave. Or independent. Or mature and worldly wise. She'd made a complete hash of everything. And now she just wanted to go home.

"He should be relieved if I retire into the order. All I've given him is trouble. He can write me off as another disappearing family member."

"You can't keep running away, Sabrina. From your family. Your past. It lives inside of you. They're what makes you, you."

"If you're going to tell me I'm using the *bandraoi* as a way to hide from myself, join the queue. Why won't anyone believe that the life of a High *Danu* priestess is what I want? Is it so hard to believe?"

Jane pulled a face. "In short—yes."

Daigh slammed his knife back into its sheath. Breathed deep to allow himself space to recover from the crumbling cliff edge of insanity. He'd come here ready to free himself once and for all of St. John's threats. After storming from room to room, it became clear he'd come too late. Furniture had been covered. Beds stripped. Hearth black and cold. The *Ambas-draoi* had fled. Yet his scent lingered in the air. Heavy. Musky. Stomach-turning. Just inhaling sickened Daigh.

He sank down on a chair. Dropped his head in his shaking hands. Fought back the nausea and the rage and the bitterness. Would these feelings end with St. John's death? Máelodor's? Or was he doomed to know only the darkest of emotions? Live only among the shades of his shattered past? A deathless specter unable to escape this world for the next?

The presence called to him. It locked onto his despair, feeding it with ever greater torment until his vision narrowed to a pinprick. His muscles twitched with denied violence. It would be so easy to allow Máelodor complete control. Lose himself in the mindless cruelty that was the master mage's wish. It would be quick. Safe. Much less painful. Already his head pounded as the dark mage energy swam through his body. As the brutal *Unseelie* magics tried to take hold.

He drew in a ragged breath. Fought back as the old woman had shown him.

Offered up Sabrina.

Standing upon the rocks. The sea lapping at her bare feet. Hair loose and free of its kerchief. Head raised to the wind. She turned to him, smiling. Her blue eyes as clear as the sky, aglow as if someone lit a fire within her.

It had been a single second in time. But he remembered it. Used it to feed the beast rooted beneath his skin. Ease the jagged press of Máelodor's possession.

There would be no more to take its place. He'd made sure of that with his cruelty. But better she hate him than grieve for him.

He hardened with newfound purpose. He'd turn his new knowledge back upon his tormentor. Use the very attributes Máelodor had gifted him to thwart the master-mage's plans. The Rywlkoth Tapestry lay with the sisters of High *Danu*. He'd seen it, though he'd not understood its significance at the time.

But times were different.

He would retrieve the tapestry as originally instructed. But Máelodor would never lay hands upon it. Not as long as Daigh held to life.

And thanks to the dark mage, he always would.

He held his breath at the creak of the outer door opening. A squeaky floorboard. Quiet breathing.

St. John returning? Would Daigh have his chance at vengeance after all?

Unfolding from the chair, he took up position behind the door. Slid his pistol free. Cocked it.

In one gliding flow of motion, he swung around the door. Targeted the man in his sights. Leveled the gun. And squeezed off a shot, jerking the weapon aside at the last moment as the intruder spun around, his own pistol raised to fire.

Daigh's bullet went wide, exploding into the wall.

Lord Kilronan's aim was true. It slammed Daigh backward as it tore through his ribs.

He lay upon the floor, blood pooling beneath him, the fire of healing as painful as the wound itself. He tried breathing around the knifing pain but couldn't bring his lungs to fill. His heart to beat.

"You." A shadow loomed above him. Kilronan's empty stare, a frightening reminder of how far the earl had gone to try and defeat him.

Would he take the final step? Would he succumb to the *Unseelie* magics to finally gain his revenge?

Daigh closed his eyes and waited for the answer.

"Where is he? Where's St. John?" A sharp kick to the ribs that shocked the lightning burn along Daigh's bones. Into his blood. His heart fluttered then settled into a steady beat. His chest rose and fell. "Where's the *Amhas-draoi*? I've some questions for him."

Daigh opened his eyes. Dropped his gaze to the spent pistol gripped in Kilronan's hand. "This grows to be a habit with you, my lord."

"One I'm happy to continue." He pulled a second pistol from his coat. "Shall I indulge again?"

"Not if you want to learn what you came for." He touched his side. Sticky with blood, but healed. As always. He climbed slowly to his feet. Straightened against the afterflashes of pain. All under the watchful, angry eyes of Sabrina's brother. "St. John is gone. Otherwise he'd be dead by my hand."

That obviously wasn't what Kilronan had expected. His brows contracted on a scowl. "Leave none behind to lead us to your master?"

"My enmity is my own, not Máelodor's."

Kilronan cursed, stalking the room with angry, crippled strides.

"Be warned," Daigh said. "Máelodor hunts Brendan Douglas."

"For what reason?"

"For the stone. The Sh'vad Tual. Douglas hid it. Máelodor seeks it. The last piece in his quest to resurrect Arthur. The Great One will break your brother, and Douglas will give up the stone's hiding place. He will have no other choice. Then, if he's lucky, he will be allowed to die." He clenched a jaw over the pummeling of recovered memory. The torture. The brutality. Never ending no matter how much he screamed. "If he's very lucky."

Kilronan's gaze narrowed with suspicion. "Why tell me this?"

Daigh spread his arms in a surrender gesture. "My own reasons." He allowed himself a wry twist of his lips at Kilronan's snort of disbelief. "Believe me or no. It matters not."

Kilronan's voice came low and caustic. "The *Amhas-draoi* think Máelodor is fiction. My attempt to distract them from Brendan's plotting."

"Máelodor has done well in concealing himself. Throwing Scathach's army off his scent. If Douglas dies, the *Amhas-draoi* will believe the threat is over. None will question how he died. Nor what information he surrendered before he was killed."

The two remained locked and unmoving. Neither one prepared to attack or give way. Cold frosted their breath. Rain beat against the windows. Shadows moved across the floor.

Kilronan spoke first. "You tried to murder me. You did kill my cousin."

A man's hatred. A woman's pleading.

Jack O'Gara didn't deserve to die the way he did. He shouldn't have been trying to play hero.

Daigh's hands shook as blood roared in his ears. Drowned out the evidence of his crimes. "I was not free to resist. But that is little comfort against your loss."

"And you and Sabrina . . ." Kilronan's words caught in his throat with a strangled oath. "For that alone, I should—" His hand jumped on the trigger, his whole body crackling with violent energy.

"If it eases your pain." Daigh closed his eyes in expectation of yet another display of Kilronan's hatred. Conjured again the image of Sabrina standing welcoming and warm upon the shore. Instead he saw her lost in pleasure, her face tilted up to his, the silky feel of her skin, the sweet of her lips, the beauty of their joining. The exquisite pain that followed ripped through him as sharply as the earlier pistol shot.

"I don't care how Sabrina defends you, I don't trust you or your motives."

Sabrina defended him? What was wrong with her? He'd worked to earn her hatred. Why wasn't she behaving as she should? Damned infuriating, pig-stubborn, brave-hearted, gallant woman.

"What the hell are you grinning at?"

Daigh opened his eyes on Kilronan's expression of frustrated temper. "Paradise denied."

"You're mad. I'd kill you if I could," Kilronan ground out through clenched teeth.

"And since you cannot?"

"Stay away from my family, Lazarus. Far, far away." Kilronan's gaze flickered and went black, the *Unseelie* within so close to the surface, the man seemed to almost shift with a gruesome light. "I'll do whatever I must to protect them."

Daigh lifted a solemn and stony face to his adversary. "As you wish, my lord."

"And if you find St. John before I do?"

"Aye?"

"Kill the miserable bastard for me."

Daigh's mouth curved in a vicious smile. "In that, we agree."

The mail coach swayed and rocked like a boat on the sea. Windows tightly closed, and the four people sharing the compartment buried under an abundance of traveling rugs, mufflers, heavy coats, cloaks, and blankets, but still the icy draft swept through every crack, making teeth clatter and fingers ache.

Sabrina managed to read over half the novel she'd brought and the two magazines full of optimistic spring fashions, but now she regarded her fellow travelers from beneath lowered lids so as not to seem inquisitive.

A gentleman—perhaps in his mid-fifties—with the leathered face of a man who has spent a great deal of time out of doors in all kinds of weather, smiled paternally back at her.

A rake-thin woman in dowdy gown and a bonnet wreathed in black ribbon eyed Sabrina and the others with suspicion and pushed herself deeper into the corner, jamming her valise between herself and the fourth occupant of the coach—the only one of the passengers who'd remained aboard since their departure from Sackville Street two days ago.

He'd slept most of the time, hat pulled low, collar high, arms crossed over his chest, legs stretched in front of him. Awake, he remained eerily silent, only the thin gleam of his eyes visible from beneath the brim of his hat.

Sabrina had spoken to him once during an embarrassing and frightening encounter in Rathcormuck when a drunken passenger had lurched his way next to her, his breath sour in her face, his hand groping for her breasts. At that instant, the stranger had uncurled from his seat, gripped the drunk's wrist, and spoken in a low whisper that seemed to shiver the already frigid air.

The lecherous drunk never moved again and disembarked at the next stop as if the wraiths of hell were after him.

"Thank you, sir," she said shyly.

He snorted. "Dangerously foolish traveling alone. Does your family know what you're about?"

So much for being polite. She stiffened in outrage. "My family is none of your concern. And I'm more than capable of taking care of myself."

He snorted again. Shook his head. Mumbled something unintelligible but obviously disparaging.

And that was the last time she conversed with the rude man. She only wished he'd leave her to travel on alone. Instead, at every stage there he was. Stretched out and sleeping across from her.

Taking a handkerchief from her reticule, she rubbed the window pane and stared out into the sleet, her mind racing forward to the end of this long trip.

For the first time, it seemed as empty and depressing as the unbroken landscape outside the coach's windows.

The *bandraoi* welcomed her back. Hustled her through the gates past huddled families and old men and women with hollowed, sunken faces who took up space in workshops and barns. Camped under hastily erected tarpaulins, their cook fires smoldering and sputtering in the damp.

Coughing. Muttering. Babies crying. Restless, impatient sounds.

"Who are these people?" Sabrina asked. "Where have they come from?"

Sister Ainnir barely glanced at the cluster of humanity as she hobbled past them. "They're *Other* seeking sanctuary. Fleeing rumors of *Duinedon* persecution."

"But the elders? The children? They're harmless."

The priestess waved away Sabrina's question with a disgusted wave of her hand. "Tell that to the *Duinedon*. They see those bearing the blood of the *Fey* as the devil's brood. Even a babe in arms could grow to threaten their precious mortal world."

Sabrina clutched her valise, relieved when she left the tension-filled yard to climb the stairs to her bedchamber. But the images of frightened faces remained with her even in the quiet comfort of her room.

Had her father and the group of Nine been inspired by such scenes? Had they been wrong to want a world where being labeled *Other* didn't mean harassment and discrimination? Their methods had crossed a line, but when failure could mean death, perhaps that line became less clear? The border between warranted action and malicious cruelty blurred?

She sank onto her bed, head pounding, mouth dry. The nervous energy holding her rigid through days of travel draining out of her in one gush of relief. She gazed around her. The same duck-shaped crack, the same lopsided corner cabinet. Even Teresa's much loved and much read copy of *The Children of the Abbey.*

It was as if she'd merely stepped out for a few hours rather than a few weeks.

Sleep beckoned, but habit had her unpacking her bag, shaking out her gowns, the bright colors and sheer fabrics garish against the austerity of the chamber's unadorned walls and bare floors.

A paper lay folded at the bottom of her valise.

She drew it out. Read the few words written there.

> Tomorrow. Dusk. Outside the gates.
>
> P.S. If you ever do something like that again, I shall wring your neck.
>
> B.

Crumpled it in a shaking hand.

Brendan. Here. Alive and scolding.

For the first time since the horrible, terrible morning when she'd turned her back upon Daigh, she laughed.

twenty-one

"Come in, Sabrina." Ard-siúr welcomed her into the office with a wave of her hand and a rueful smile. "This is an unexpected return. Have a seat." She shoved the cat off its perch upon the closest chair. "We have much to discuss."

Despite the smile and the soothing calmness of Ard-siúr's words, Sabrina quaked with trepidation. Would Ard-siúr send her back to Aidan? Would she take this show of blatant disobedience as further proof of Sabrina's unfitness to become a full *bandraoi* priestess? Would she ask questions Sabrina couldn't answer without betraying her naive stupidity? Would the dull ache squeezing her chest ever go away?

Ard-siúr passed around her desk. Sat down, steepling her fingers beneath her chin as she let her piercing gaze rest upon Sabrina.

She felt the usual sense of being peeled away layer by layer until no secret remained. She played with a thread upon her apron. Ran her finger along a pocket seam. Shifted on the uncomfortable chair. Let her gaze roam the room. Anything to keep from meeting that steady, all-seeing gaze.

All traces of the break-in were gone. The office remained the same cozy chamber of thick rugs, well-polished furniture, brightly woven wall hangings, and cheery comfort.

Her eyes drifted over images of stags in flight, a scene where striped-sailed ships shared the waves with fish-tailed maidens and selkies basked upon rocks beside their discarded sealskins, and an ornate and stylized rendering of flowers drifting in odd curls and swoops, yellow, green, blue, and crimson. Every petal and every stem accented with the same black thread.

Only one obvious gap remained in the otherwise cluttered wall where Ard-siúr had yet to hang something new.

"I was surprised when they told me you'd arrived alone." Ard-siúr's brows rose into her hairline. "I had assumed you would remain in Dublin at least until early summer. Did something happen to cut your visit short?"

Her expression told her she already knew every transgression and only waited for Sabrina to confess.

"I chose to return ahead of schedule." Heat rose to her cheeks, but when she spoke her voice was steady. "You advised me to test my wings before I made the final commitment to the *bandraoi*. I have. This is where I belong. The order is my home, and you are my family."

"Fine sentiments. But were you in such a hurry to let us know this epiphany that you could not wait for a suitable escort? Nor even Jane?"

She winced under a twinge of guilt. Had her flight become known? Had she left poor Jane to suffer her brother's not-unexpected anger?

"I'm sorry, Ard-siúr. Truly. But I had to come back. I couldn't stay. Not after . . ." It was those eyes. They made you want to confess. But it was too raw. Too painful yet to speak of. "I had to come back."

"Did something happen in Dublin, child?"

Sabrina waved off her question with an agitated shake of her head. "No. Nothing. I'm simply ready to go through the final rituals. Please, let me join you. Don't make me leave again."

Ard-siúr gave another of her inscrutable smiles. "Your devotion to us is admirable. As is your self-reliance. Not many young women would attempt such a perilous journey alone."

Was she complimenting her or scolding her? Difficult to tell.

"You must truly have longed to be here."

"I did."

"Or was your desire based more upon your longing to not be there?"

Sabrina faced down Ard-siúr with what she hoped was inscrutability.

"Child, you have great gifts. Your healing abilities are inexperienced but powerful. Sister Ainnir has relied upon you, perhaps more than she should have. And the other *bandraoi* have come to view you as one of them, despite your unpledged status. We have seen you blossom from the shy, unsure girl who shrank from her own shadow to a beautiful and accomplished young woman. You will always have a home here among us should you need it."

Sabrina sensed a big "but" coming.

"But I am still unconvinced that you could be satisfied with life among us."

"Ard-siúr, if you would listen—"

She was cut off with a lifting of one imperious hand. "Let me amend that. I should have said content. You would be all that was proper. None would fault your dedication. But would you fulfill your duties with a heart full of gladness in the rightness of your devotion, or would you grow restless and discontented? The gods would know. They see even more than I do. And what I see is clear as the ghosts in your gaze."

Sabrina dropped her head. There would be no timeless, ancient ritual to calm the tempests in her heart. No safe harbor where she fit in. No place where she belonged. She was truly alone.

"Will you send for my brother?" As if he wasn't furious enough with her.

"I will notify him of your safe arrival. And I will make it clear to him my feelings on the matter. But as I said, you are free to remain with us for now. We are a sanctuary, Sabrina. Not just for you, but for all who need us."

"Thank you, Ard-siúr." Sabrina trembled despite the warmth of the room.

"We shall see soon enough." She rose, nodding to someone who must have just entered the room.

A shadow slanted across Sabrina's shoulder.

"Dyma'r joc gwaethaf erioed." The deep lilting voice rumbled through her. Her throat squeezed shut as a rush of heat swamped her frozen limbs. "Devil take it!"

She turned to face him. Body heavy. Muscles alert and quivering. Heart pumping madly.

He watched her from eyes black as night, features carved in savage angles and stern lines.

Daigh. Perfect. Sinful. Breathtaking. Deadly.

And she, as head over heels as ever.

A fire purred in the stove, the flicker of lamplight and the scents of orange peel and dried herbs creating a calm oasis.

Or what would have been a calm oasis if Sabrina weren't stalking the room like a madwoman. He'd be doing the same if she hadn't beaten him to the floor. Ard-siúr had set him up. And like the simplest of fools, he'd walked right into her trap.

His last sight of Sabrina had been in a gown of palest green, hair a dark treacle spill of silk, lips bruised with his kisses, skin flushed pearl and pink. Yet here in the *bandraoi*'s drab garb, hair hidden beneath a kerchief, and features twisted with frustration and shock, she was unspeakably more beautiful.

"I left you safe in Dublin," he growled.

She rounded on him, fire in her gaze. "What are you doing here, Daigh? How could you follow me after . . ." She returned to her frantic pacing. "After everything."

"I didn't follow. I came two days ago."

He leaned against the desk, arms folded over his chest. It kept him from doing what he wanted, which was smashing the furniture to splinters. He'd meant to put Sabrina out of his life, if not out of his head. Yet she was here, only feet away, where every curve and shift of her body and every flash of emotion in her face ripped new scars across his heart. Tempted him with a lifetime of memories—the real and the glimpsed might-have-beens that plagued them both. "Your brother will see my hand in this."

"I can handle Aidan."

"Not the *Unseelie* that lives within him."

She shoved her hands deep into apron pockets. Turned away from him in a deliberate rebuff. "What are you doing here?"

"I came for the tapestry."

She sucked in her breath on a silent oath, eyes wide and frightened. "But it's been stolen already."

The corner of his lip curved in a cool smile. "No. A tapestry was taken. But not the one Máelodor seeks."

"What's so important about a tapestry that—" Her brows contracted. "A map. A stone," she mused. "Máelodor seeks a map and a stone." Her gaze lifted to his. "The tapestry is the map, isn't it? Somehow it shows the way to Arthur's tomb."

"It does. Máelodor must come for it. And I'll face him when he does."

"You can't."

"I must end this, Sabrina." Now that he'd begun, the words came easier. "I can't be scraped and pulled until the only parts of me left are faded and ragged as a fallen standard. The presence is always within me. Fighting for dominion. If I don't find a way to die, it will take me over body and soul. The *Ambas-draoi* give me no help. I choose the only path left."

Her eyes flickered and went dark, but gave nothing away. "Do you really think Máelodor would send you back to the grave?"

"Not if given a choice." His voice hardened. "I'll take that choice from him."

"You'd face death so cavalierly?"

"I've suffered it once. It holds no surprise. And I will die gladly rather than remain a slave."

"You're not his slave. Máelodor doesn't own your soul."

"He did once. And I feel him in my head still. He seeks to reclaim me. I'll not allow it."

She gave a sharp shake of her head. "I thought I'd never see you again."

"When this is over, you won't."

"What if that's not what I want?" Now tears shone in her eyes. Glimmered in the low flickering light. Sparkled like diamonds.

He gave her a solemn smile. Opened his hands in a gesture of resignation, revealing the scars upon his palms. "Look upon me, Sabrina," he said. "It's what you should want."

"I have thought over all you've told me, Mr. MacLir, including the warnings about the tapestry's safety."

"Then why is the cursed thing still there?"

Ard-siúr glanced where Daigh gestured. The hanging floated in the rising heat from the stove. A casual observer would see nothing but the beauty and the artistry of the blooms. But for the one who unraveled the secret hidden within the colorful array of stylized flowers, the path to Arthur's tomb was written plain as the black thread used to spell it out.

"Perhaps to tempt you?"

He flashed a startled, angry look at the old woman. "What game is this?"

She answered him with a bland, unreadable smile. "I am interested to see what breed of man Máelodor has riven from a few ancient bones and magic best left to the demon world. Does the darkness of the *Unseelie* taint the life it recreates? How much of the man you were still remains?"

Daigh longed to howl his frustration. Arms braced against the desk, he leaned menacingly forward, frightening the cat, which hissed and darted beneath Ard-siúr's chair. "You've only to ask Sabrina to know the answer."

"Her answers might well be worth hearing. Perhaps I shall."

Daigh flushed, unable to meet Ard-siúr's pointed glare. "I never meant to see her again."

She scooped the cat into her lap, where it settled beneath her steady strokes. Glared at Daigh from slitted yellow eyes. "But you have. So what will you do now?"

He hunched his shoulders, his hands loose at his sides. "Hope is not for the undead."

"The gods bestow hope to all," she scolded. "It is for us to hold fast. Refuse its escape. And use it to shape all we do."

"Spoken like a true *bandraoi* priestess."

She nodded her acceptance of his sarcasm as if he'd paid her the highest compliment. "You need not concern yourself about the tapestry. We shall see to its safety."

"Máelodor is determined to have it. He won't give up."

"As Ard-siúr, I am not completely without resources, Daigh."

"You've never spoken my name before."

She continued stroking the cat, its purring loud against the taut silence. Finally she tilted her head, speared him with a look that drilled straight to his core. "And is Daigh your name? Or does it remain Lazarus? You must choose."

"I returned to warn you, didn't I?" he snarled.

She sat back. "Then you have your answer. And your hope."

"Mother? Is that you?"

"Hush now. Try and go to sleep."

"I can't. I'm too excited about my birthday. Paul said he'd be home, Mother. He promised."

Sabrina pulled the covers back up over Sister Clea. Offered her a sip of water.

She'd waited for Brendan as instructed. Hours had passed as she watched the clouds pushing east across the sky until even the most fractious child had fallen silent and the earth cooled and creaked in the early hours before dawn.

Only then had she retreated here to the dimly lit hospital ward. The whisper of sleep among the sick and elderly priestesses. The rain pattering against the windows. Once again, she was struck by the odd sensation of time folding back upon itself so that the past weeks were erased as if they'd never been. Leaving her secure in the knowledge that no matter what occurred beyond these walls, this place, these women, this life would remain.

She'd chafed at the unfaltering routine and the stifling bonds of tradition. Had looked at the horizon and questioned what lay beyond the boundary between earth and sky. And had come away heartsick and frightened at what she'd found. Brendan. Aidan and his wife. Máelodor. St. John.

Daigh.

Too many questions. Too many dangers. Too many ways to be wounded body and soul. If only she could convince Ard-siúr of her devotion. Her need for a life among the steady tread of ancient traditions and out of the rushing current of life outside. She sank upon a chair, arms pressed to her stomach as the gnawing ache of her own stupidity spread from her gut to her chest.

Sister Clea's voice broke the stillness. "Paul has never broken a promise before. He'll come. I know he will."

Overwrought, Sabrina lashed out. "He's not coming. Do you hear? He's not. I don't care what he promised. They were lies. Like everything he ever told you. He's toying with you. Making you think that it can be all right again. But it can't. It can never be what it was. Not even here. Not even where it should be."

Sister Clea's eyes rounded in startled surprise, her mouth pursing and opening, passing the hem of the blanket back and forth in her hands. "Paul doesn't lie, Sabrina."

She started up. Sister Clea had never called her by her name.

The old woman's eyes shone with foggy tears, but her gaze raked Sabrina with a sharpness to draw blood. "And neither does Brendan Douglas. He'll come. He'll be with you soon."

What did the *bandraoi* see? What precognition had swum up through the calcified walls of her mind to glimmer upon the surface for one sparkling moment? Sabrina couldn't ask. Would never know. The clarity was gone. Vanished.

"It's my birthday soon," Sister Clea mumbled. "And my brother will be home."

Daigh looked up at the tall, slender stone, its face glimmering with quartz where moss had yet to take over. The air around it blurred and danced, throwing shadows that had nothing to do with the moonlight moving among the surrounding trees. As he drew closer, the temperature dropped, leaving him chilled. Only his purpose for coming raised a sweat between his shoulders to trickle down his back.

The true *Fey* could grant him death.

Helena Roseingrave had given him the idea, just as it had been her hatred that had torn loose the last bindings upon his memory. The years since his summoning as mirror-bright and steeped in blood as his sword. Máelodor's calculated torment. Inflicted and withdrawn without warning. Long weeks where he received no mercy for his pleading and where his screams begot only more painful treatment. Other times when his every need had been sated and he became a feted prince among men. The Great One's prize and greatest treasure. His sword hand. His strength. His killer.

Would Arthur suffer the same fate? Or would Máelodor's desire to win the hearts and minds of the race of *Other* with his resurrected warlord and king outstrip his darker desire to cause torment? Would the legendary High King fight his slavish bondage to Máelodor as Daigh had tried and failed to do for so long, or would he rejoice at the chance to reclaim his ancient reign? Begin his domination with the toppling of England's mad monarch and his fat princeling son? Would he venture beyond the isles as his army of *Other* grew more confident and more drunk upon their magic until the *Duinedon* world trembled at the unfettered mage energy and even the true *Fey* thought themselves lucky to be safe within their hillside barrows?

Daigh would use every skill he possessed to secure the Rywlkoth Tapestry away from St. John and Máelodor. But he couldn't trust to those same skills to achieve his true and final aim. He would never be allowed to return to the grave. For that release, he would need the help of those more powerful than even Máelodor.

Gritting his teeth, he placed his hand flat upon the stone. The slam of mage energy exploded up his arm. Knocked him back into the grass to stare up into the curl and sparkle of light as it burst like shrapnel from the rock face. He shuddered as jolt after jolt passed through him. It charred his nerves until Máelodor's *Unseelie* magic renewed his body. Stopped his heart for long seconds before the poisonous presence within him revived its beat.

The *Fey* knew him for what he was. They would not suffer his presence. Nor heed his call. Not without a fight.

Refusing to be denied, Daigh crawled to the stone. Placed not one but both hands upon it. Closed his eyes to invoke any and all prayers he thought might summon one of them. And again was tossed backward into a tree, his ribs snapping at the force, only to knit themselves together with a pain barely noticeable against the mage energy flowing wild and seeking around him.

He lay among the dead leaves and broken branches for what seemed minutes then hours then days. Begging the *Fey* to answer his call.

He'd grown good at begging. Grown used to being denied.

It still hurt.

twenty-two

"This way. Hurry. Please."

The child dragged Sabrina toward a workshop used by an itinerant smithy. A dusty, cobweb-infested building with enough nooks and crannies to entice the most rabid of hiders and seekers.

Inside, the gloom fell like a blanket over her head. But the child pulled her blindly deeper into the musty space where only a lurching jump sideways kept her from barking her shins on the huge, rusty anvil in the middle of the room.

"She cut herself. There's blood." The child's fear trembled her voice. Her hand clutched Sabrina's.

Threading their way between a rickety ladder and a stack of crates, they entered the smith's storeroom. Tools hung from pegs upon the wall or lay covered in a fuzzy layer of dust on shelves and counters. In one corner leaned a broken shovel, a scythe with a bent blade, two rakes with missing tines, and a sagging burlap sack. Muffled weeping and loud snuffling came from a corner near the smashed remains of a barrel. One skinny, stockinged leg sticking out at an awkward angle.

Sabrina knelt, plucking aside the splintered staves to discover a scrawny, bedraggled, tear-stained young girl. The gash on her forehead bled all over her pinafore, but it was her ankle that would require Sabrina's aid. Painfully swollen already and bent in what had to be an uncomfortable position. "What on earth did you do to yourself?"

She pulled a handkerchief from her pocket. Dabbed at the cut. Like most head wounds, more blood than harm.

"I was tired of being caught first. I tried hiding up there." The child pointed to a narrow ledge some ten feet above them. Wide enough to accommodate her skinny body, but inconspicuous in the dim space.

"Here. Press this against your forehead while I examine your ankle."

The child sniffed. No more than seven or eight, she gazed up at Sabrina with worshipful, pain-filled eyes.

"And?" Sabrina probed the ankle with gentle fingers.

The girl flinched but didn't cry out. "I used the barrel to climb up, but it broke, and I fell."

"That ankle will have to be set. Here, can you . . ." Sabrina tried levering the girl up, but she moaned, new tears streaking her bloody face.

The floor creaked as someone entered behind them. "Let me help."

Of course. It had to be Daigh. Just his voice sent a buzzing skitter up her spine. The room shrinking and shifting until his presence took up every square inch. She hoped the embarrassing flush of awareness didn't show on her face. Angry at him for her own silly reaction. "Is this your idea of a game?" she hissed. "Stop following me."

"I didn't follow." He drew her eye to the wood splitter he carried before leaning it against the wall.

Stepping closer, he scooped the child into his arms. For a moment, the obsidian gaze brightened. A rough-edged smile tipped a corner of his mouth. "What's this? No tears now. Be a brave lass."

The child hiccoughed and scrubbed at her eyes with the back of one hand, though whether it was due to Daigh's words or stunned awe at the grim-faced giant carrying her, Sabrina couldn't tell.

"What do you think you're doing?" she charged.

"Helping, or will you carry her yourself?" He made as if to hand her the child.

She stepped back. "She's too heavy. I'd hurt her ankle if I tried."

"Then out of my way so I can."

He didn't wait for her answer. Simply ducked his head beneath the doorway, leaving Sabrina hurrying after him, fuming and grateful and furious and excited.

In the hospital ward, he laid his burden upon a cot. Stood back with a reassuring nod.

"What's this? New trouble?" Sister Ainnir approached in a whirl of gray, glancing between Daigh and Sabrina, lips pressed together, eyes gleaming in her wrinkled face. Snorting, she knelt to examine the little girl's ankle and the gash on her head. "These people keep me running from dawn to dusk with their complaints and their troubles. Half the time they don't even heed my advice. I've not seen my bed for the space of ten minutes together since they began arriving. I'm too old for this."

"Let me." Sabrina tried taking the roll of bandages from the priestess's hand.

Sister Ainnir snatched them back with a sharp look. "It's no longer your place." Sabrina blinked stupidly as the woman softened her tone. "Ard-siúr's orders. You're to be treated as a guest until your brother arrives to claim you." She put a gentle hand on Sabrina's shoulders. "I'd have you back in a wink if I could. You know that."

"But—"

She shooed Sabrina along as if she were no older than the child before them. "Run along, my lady. I'll fix the moppet up and send her back to her parents."

A guest? No longer allowed to heal? To help? Aidan claiming her? What was she? A stray puppy?

The words piled on her chest like stone after stone. Making her imminent exile real. She would have to leave. And this time, she knew there would be no returning. She would be taken to Belfoyle and there she would remain until Aidan chose to loosen his restraints upon her. After her escape from Dublin, he'd probably lock her in and throw away the key. She couldn't breathe. Couldn't think. The walls closed in around her.

Warm hands settled on her shoulders. A voice droned in her ear. And she found herself propelled out of the scrubbed infirmary into the clear bleached light of day. A cool wind chilled her face. Snapped her from the downward spiral of her panic. She drew in a quick gasping breath, salty tears sliding into the corners of her mouth. "Oh gods, what have I done?"

Daigh's eyes burned through her, sending a flare of familiar heat low in her belly. "You sought to save a man from drowning. You'd no idea he'd pull you down with him."

Sabrina staggered into the dormitory passage. Toward the stairway to her bedchamber. If only escape could be found in a locked room and dreams. But it couldn't, and so no surprise met the sliding crystalline fog, the lurching dizziness as she tumbled into Daigh's past. The thinning veil of mist revealing a smoke-filled hall full of confused voices. Men and women moved like wraiths, their eyes weary, their bodies crouched and distressed.

Daigh prowled just beyond the firelight. She knew his stance, the cock of his head, the quiet intensity behind his every gesture. He greeted a crew of rough-looking men who'd only just arrived. Mud-spattered. Breathing hard. Daigh looked her way, the flames' flicker dancing across his eyes. His gaze sharpened on her face, his love winding its way through her, stronger even than his nervousness or the gravity she sensed hung around him like a heavy cloak.

The fog closed in, the scene fading back into the gray swirl of cloud, talons sinking into her shoulder wrenching a startled cry from her lips.

"Gotcha, girl."

Sabrina jerked her head up and into the face of Sister Brigh, more shriveled and dried up than usual. "If you think to scold me for shirking my duties, you're too late. I've no duties and you've no authority," she snarled, taking out her anger and confusion on the old woman.

"But I've the sight in my eyes and I know what I see. You and that man. He arrives then you arrive. Neat and tidy. And now I see your boldness when you look upon him. And his lust when he meets that look."

"You're eyesight's failing. Mr. MacLir doesn't look at me with anything but scorn."

She tried wrenching away, but the old priestess's fingers

bit deep into Sabrina's flesh. "You're a fool, girl. He watches you. Always with that empty, black stare. The mage energy swirling round him like a storm cloud. I know what he is. I hear things. Notice things. You should be careful, girl."

"Careful of what?"

Sister Brigh's eyes darted fearfully to the door as she wrung her bony, grasping hands. "He's dead risen. What they speak of as a *Domnuathi.* Evil gave him life. Evil follows him. I see the beast upon his back. The Morrigan's ravens flying close at his heels. No good can come of it."

"Daigh wouldn't harm us. We saved him."

"He'll do as his master bids with as little remorse as grinding a bug beneath his heel." A cruel smile creased Sister Brigh's face. "You fear it's true even as you defend him. I can see it on your heart. He's hurt you already."

Sabrina slammed closed her mind from Sister Brigh's prying, but the priestess had decades of training at infiltrating even the most shuttered thoughts.

"I protect what's mine, girl. This order. My sisters. MacLir must go. If he leaves, the evil and the danger go with him."

"If he leaves, the evil will take him over, and we'll be worse off than we are now."

"The sisters of High *Danu* survived the ages by keeping our heads down and our magic quiet. I'll not have that destroyed. Not by you, Ard-siúr, or him."

Sabrina finally tore herself free from Sister Brigh's vitriol. The dormitory no longer a refuge, she stumbled back into the yard. Daigh hadn't moved from the spot where she'd left him. His eyes lifted to hers, and that same bond of unshakeable love passed between them as in the hazy gloom of a Welshman's hall.

Clouds passed over the sun, throwing his face into shadow. The connection severed.

Daigh turned away.

The men bowed aside and the women displayed shy smiles as Sabrina moved among the refugees. Asking after children or aged parents. Answering questions about a fever here. A rash there. Ard-siúr may have refused her the order's resources, but her skills were hers alone and couldn't be taken away. These she leant willingly along with advice and reassurance.

According to a frantic note from Jane, it would be only a matter of days before Aidan arrived and even these small duties would be forevermore denied her. Poor Jane. Sabrina owed her. It sounded by the tone of ill-usage in the scribbled missive that Aidan had not been exactly pleasant since Ard-siúr's letter had arrived. She would make it up to her. She would grovel as only a best friend could.

"Heard they burned three farms over by Ballenacriagh."

"Is it true the government's begun registering *Other*?"

"Will the *Duinedon* attack us here?"

"They say barracks are being reinforced with regiments home from the wars."

"They treat us as if we were less than human."

"I'll fight rather than let the *Duinedon* round us up like sheep."

"That goes for me as well. Let them come, I say. We're more than a match for the *Duinedon*."

Rumors, like illness, thrived in cramped conditions, and long hours passed as she refuted false reports and calmed troubled minds.

"Gossip is a many-headed hydra. Attack one story and three more grow in its place."

She wasn't surprised to find Daigh watching her from the open barn door. His haunted grave-black eyes, the severe magnificence of his angled features, the herculean strength in his crossed arms and the broad curve of his shoulders. Her resident butterflies took flight once more, beating against her insides until she quivered with excitement.

He motioned toward the cook fires and makeshift tents. "Máelodor is skillful at fertilizing already rich soil. Look at them. Resentful. Afraid. Angry."

"Is it any wonder? We're taught from the cradle to hide what we are from those who don't understand and would label us monsters."

His lips curved in the merest hint of irony. "Yes," he answered softly before nodding once more toward the gathering. "But listen closely. The agitation. The defiance. Us versus them. These are the seeds of revolution."

She glanced over her shoulder, seeing what Daigh saw. The pinched, sour faces, the clenched jaws, the growing impatience. Shuddering, she pulled her shawl close around her. "Is Máelodor powerful enough to manipulate an entire race?"

"Many are ready to rise up. Discontented. Restless. All they wait for is a leader to unite them. The last High King. Máelodor uses it to his advantage."

"But Arthur was a great hero. A champion. He would never—"

"He'll have no choice, Sabrina. As one of the *Domnuathi,* he'll be helpless against Máelodor's powers. A tool to be used by the Great One."

His words and his emotions spilled hot and laced with fury. They battered her mind, dagger-edged and desperate.

He raged at fate. At the heavens. At the gods themselves for deserting him. Leaving him to face Máelodor's evil alone.

She'd watched him ride off once to a death she knew he'd not escape. The vision of that parting and the grief that followed haunted her still. Could she do it again? Could she let him walk away? Without once asking why?

"You broke free. He doesn't control you anymore."

"He lives inside me, Sabrina. Always searching for a way to control me again. Until one of us is dead, that threat remains." Ducking his head, he retreated back through the door.

She should turn now, walk away, and never look back. She'd known from the first that Daigh MacLir brought trouble in his wake. That to fall beneath the spell of that muscled body and those fathomless eyes would spell disaster. She'd known and not cared.

Not then.

Not now.

She followed him into the gloom of the low-ceilinged barn. Daigh brushed down a heavy-boned mare, murmuring to it in soft nonsensical words. *"Paid barnu pob dyn ar weithredoedd un."*

"What are you saying to her?"

He ran his hand carefully over a bare patch on the mare's flank. "See these marks on her side? She's been used cruelly. I'm telling her not to judge all men by the actions of one."

The mare's ears flicked back as she shifted ominously, one leg poised. Daigh merely murmured again, his voice low pitched, more words in a rolling, lilting growl. *"Rwyt ti'n brydferth. 'Dwi'n gwneud yr hyn sydd angen i amddiffyn ti."*

Sabrina leaned against the partition. "Now what are you telling her?"

Daigh smiled. "That she's a beauty of a lass. And I mean her no harm. I only do what I must to keep her well."

Delicious heat lapped against her insides as Daigh gentled the mare with hands and voice. The horse lowered its head, breathing deeply, the large brown eyes half closed, sides twitching at every pass of Daigh's brush.

"Look at her," she said. "She trusts you. Believes you." Their eyes met, Sabrina willing him to see her heart.

A rare and sudden smile lit his face, startling her with its brilliance. Sending her heart leaping into her throat. "How long can we play this game of words?" he teased.

Reckless excitement swept her along just as it had in Dublin when the rugged lilt of his voice, the scent of his skin, the forever depth in his gaze had drawn her on when sanity told her she was mad. "How long do you have?"

"I was closer to Brendan than any of my family. Not that I didn't love my parents, but Mother's love was all for Father. No one else could intrude into that bubble. And as for Father, Aidan was his heir. Brendan his favorite. I, a mere daughter. Not much use. Not much trouble." She twirled a stalk of timothy grass between her fingers. "Not until I could be used as barter."

In heavy weather, the barn loft leaked both wind and water, but tonight only moonshine spread across the floor. A few weak stars glimpsed through broken shingles. What was it about the musty sweetness of hay and the mutter and shift of animals that made confidences possible? Or was it the company? Sabrina sat on the one and only stool. Daigh beside her upon an upturned bucket.

They'd resided thus for hours. Daigh pulling stories from her one after another like ribbons from a carnival magician's sleeve. Never tiring of tales from her years with the *bandraoi,* but also teasing free recollections of the great house by the sea, of tagging after her brothers, whining to be included in their games, her parents' distant affection. All memories she locked away when she departed her home for what she assumed would be the last time. They spilled from her in a cleansing flow, Daigh content to listen. An understanding ear. A strong shoulder to lean on. Something she hadn't had in uncounted years.

She sought to do the same for him, but he dodged her interrogations. Answered questions with questions until she surrendered. He'd not speak of his years as Máelodor's slave. And the dim and hazy memories of his previous life he hoarded like gold, unwilling to spend them on her when he needed all to feed the demon within him.

"Does Lord Kilronan share your father's view? Will he find you a husband untroubled by your loss of maidenhead? An earl's daughter would make many turn a blind eye."

Sabrina speared Daigh with a glare though he remained focused upon the floor and did not see the agitation in her gaze. "I don't think so. His wife surely might intervene if he tried." She knew she spoke truth. Cat would be on Sabrina's side, and no matter what Aidan's feelings, the new Lady Kilronan was a powerful ally. "They may grump and despair of me, but I'm safe enough from old lechers and young fortune hunters."

"You care about your family." He looked over, his face shuttered, his eyes gleaming obsidian. "It's in your voice. The way you speak about them."

"I don't know why I should. They never cared about me."

"How can you say so? Lord Kilronan seemed a protective brother when I met him last."

"Protective doesn't equal loving." She tossed away the stem.

"Is that why you chose to hide away here?"

She didn't grow angry. Didn't defend. Simply shrugged deeper into her cloak. "I'm not hiding anymore."

His mouth twisted in a grim half smile. "Nor should you. You're a brave woman, Sabrina. If you weren't, you would have run the first time you laid eyes on me."

"I did."

He gave a gruff laugh. "You should have kept running."

"I couldn't. What I saw—what I felt—made me stay."

"You can still leave. It might be better. The *bandraoi* will be wondering where you are."

"Ard-siúr refuses my entry into the order. They no longer govern what I do or who I do it with."

She leaned back, staring up through the cracks in the shingles as silence fell between them. If only this could last forever. Yet time rushed forward, carrying them onward toward treacherous shoals. She sensed it in Daigh's slow drawing away from her. The heavy line of his brow, the hardness entering his gaze. Already the pleasure of these hours slipped away from them. She would capture what she could before they vanished forever.

As if sensing her mood, Daigh spoke. "There is not much time left. Already Máelodor's power over me grows difficult to resist. I am being drawn back under his control."

Her heart kicked up into her throat. "But Ard-siúr . . . or perhaps the *Fey* themselves. Didn't you say Miss Roseingrave told you they could free you?" Not yet. Please, not yet.

"No. This is beyond your Ard-siúr's skills, and I have tried summoning the *Fey*, but I am not of any world they understand, and so they ignore my calls. This is my battle."

"You said memories break his hold upon your mind."

"For now."

"Then let's build a wall of memory to shut him out."

He arched a brow. "You would—"

"I would do whatever I could for the man I love."

He sucked in a quick breath, his body tensing. "You must not say that."

"My body is my own. I offer it freely. My love also is mine to bestow where I choose, and that I offer only to one I know is worthy of it."

"I can promise nothing."

"I'm not seeking promises."

He leaned toward her, his lips warm and firm against her own. He kissed her, his tongue gliding within, the sweet drugging taste of him in her mouth. The clean masculine smell of him in her nose. His left hand cradled her neck as he pressed closer, probed deeper while his right skimmed her ribs, the curve of her hip.

Stomach swooping, breasts tightening and tingling in anticipation, she reached up to bring him closer. Opening to him, answering the dipping thrust of his tongue with a teasing flick of her own. His soft laugh vibrated along her bones as he pulled her into the cushioning prickle of loose hay upon the loft floor. Lay beside her, elbow crooked, head resting upon his hand, watching her with a weather eye.

"The one good in being deathless, your brother's outrage holds no threat."

"He doesn't understand."

"He understands too well. He knows the savagery lurking within because he experienced it himself."

"What stayed your hand?"

His brows raised on a question.

"I spoke to my sister-in-law. She says you could have killed them, but you didn't. Why not? What held you back?"

He dipped his shoulder in a quick shrug. "The only force that chains the beast inside me every time it tries to surface. You."

"You didn't know me then."

"I can't explain it, Sabrina. It was your face I saw. Your love I remembered."

Heat stole along her limbs with the strange sensation of being borne along a swift-moving current. Tumbled out and under so that she couldn't say where up and down or light and dark were.

Daigh's stare anchored her, his body hard and solid beneath her fingers. His breath and his heart slow and steady.

"You've been given a rare gift," she whispered. "To recapture the life stolen from you. The fate that would have been yours had you not been killed at Pentraeth with Hywel."

"The woman who would have been mine?"

"She still can be."

Taking his face in her hands, she kissed him on the jaw. The chin. Her breasts crushed against his chest, their hearts thundering in unison. With exquisite care, he popped button after button down the front of her gown. Eased her free of petticoats and stays until she lay exposed, her flesh pebbled against the cool air and his feather-touch. His tongue swirled and sucked the sensitive aureoles. Nipped her taut, the tingle knifing straight to her wet and throbbing center.

She squirmed against the rough splay of his palms and the sweet exploration of his lips as he rubbed and kissed his way over her body. Skimmed her stomach. Stroked her hips before caressing her inner thighs, then probing the aching core of her. She melted into him. Bit her lip against a moan, while fumbling him free of his clothes. In the dim light from a setting moon, his skin shone pale as marble, the scars glistening silver white.

She followed the path of the intersecting lines, each mark a story of soulless brutality, until he gently pulled her hands away. Drew them up over her head. Pinned her beneath him with a stare of such greedy hunger she shivered. Slanting his mouth over hers, he kissed her. Long and deep. Leaving no time for second thoughts or regrets or even a stolen breath.

She wantonly twisted and writhed against his imprisonment. Ground against him. Lifted her head to take his tongue deeper into her mouth.

He broke free first. Gasping against her seduction.

He lay between her legs, his midnight gaze burning a path over her, a devil's smile lifting a corner of his mouth.

"*'Dwi'n cofio hwn*. I remember this," he murmured, his tone wistful. "I remember you."

She rocked against him, letting him feel her growing need. The rising power of her yearning.

And with a groan of animal need, he pushed himself inside her. Thrust deep and hard and fast.

She gasped, the excitement building and growing. The power behind their joining crackling the air between them. She lost herself in the glide of supple muscles, the hard sculpted back, the chiseled face. She watched him pleasuring her. Smiled as their rhythm brought them closer. Stars in her eyes. A deep pooling heat building between her legs. Expanding to flow up from her center. Winding her like a watch spring until, with a shuddering, swallowed gasp he kissed quiet, she peaked. Ground against him, refusing to let the glory end. Waves pulsed through her like ripples in a pool. Outward, fainter, but her body quivered with each pass until spent, she dozed.

The heavens spun overhead, shadows lengthening across the floor, Sabrina asleep in his arms.

Daigh dropped his gaze to where her hand rested upon his chest, the web of scars glowing silver in the moonlight. For a moment, he reveled in the sweet ecstasy of simply being alive. Heart beating. Blood pumping. Lungs expanding with every breath he drew.

He'd had this and lost it and gained it again. Perhaps it *was* a gift. The men he'd fought with and died beside—what would they trade for a chance to break free of the underworld, even for a few precious moments? A chance to gaze upon a sky vast with stars. To smell the musky sweet scent of a leaf-strewn wood. To love a woman to climax.

And how hard would they fight to hold on?

How hard would he?

twenty-three

Daigh sat outside the workshop door, the winter sun glinting off the chaff cutter blade propped between his legs. He worked the edge with his whetstone, even though it had long ago reached killing strength. Still, it kept his hands busy in a task as unconscious as breathing.

Sabrina had joined him, despite—or perhaps because of—the disapproving looks from the *bandraoi*. For the last hour they'd sat in comfortable silence, neither one needing to speak, but both deriving solace from the company.

"If you had the chance to return to Wales would you take it?" Sabrina's question caught him off-guard.

He glanced at her, but she wasn't looking his way. Only the curve of her cheek and the tips of her lashes visible as she fiddled with a reaping hook on the bench.

His hand tightened on the stone. "There is naught left of that life."

"Not the people, of course. But the sea would be the

same. And the mountains. The air and the sky. These things don't change. Even over centuries."

"No, they don't, do they? That is a comfort." He took up a rag. Began rubbing a polish into the blade. By the time he was done, the tool would be better suited as a weapon of war.

"Belfoyle won't have changed either. Not the parts that matter. The beaches. The cliffs. They'll be just as they were when I drove away seven years ago."

"You are less unhappy about returning?"

She shrugged in a noncommittal fashion. "Resigned. It can never be what it was."

"And what was it?"

"You know, that special place where nothing bad can happen. That magic is gone forever."

"True. But so is the child you were. And you've family. Kilronan and his new wife will be there."

She pursed her lips, picking at the edge of one finger. "They're like Father and Mother. So wrapped in one another, there's no room for anyone else."

"Perhaps because they came so close to losing one another."

He shook off the smoke and flame memory, though the hellish aftermath of his failure was harder to ignore. He wore it on his skin. A reminder of what waited in his future if he failed a second time.

"But don't you see? There's no room for me in what they share. It's their family. And as long as Brendan's on the run, he's lost to me as well." She sighed. "Just when I think I can leave it behind me . . . when things might be right again . . . Why does the past always ruin the present?"

"The past and our memories have brought us here. Who knows? Perhaps they will save us in the end."

"Sabrina? May I see you in my office?" Ard-siúr stood at the fringe of women who'd collected around the fire for their morning gossip. One or two looked up from their mugs of thick coffee and blackened sausages, but most merely rendered a quick shrug of interest before returning to their own worries.

"Of course." Sabrina smothered her rush of panic in a smoothing of her apron over her knees. Straightened from where she'd been tending to an ugly steam burn from a cook's pot. Followed Ard-siúr out of the blustering December wind and into the cool, dim passage. Up the stairs. Past the ever-cheerful Sister Anne, who waved a hello before faltering under Ard-siúr's severe gaze.

What did she want? What did she know? Sabrina's thoughts whirled like dry leaves.

Once inside, Ard-siúr took up position behind her desk, motioning Sabrina into a chair, her expression solemn.

"Is there something wrong?" Sabrina donned a look of innocent confusion, hoping the flush of heat staining her cheeks didn't give her away.

There followed a long, anxious pause as Ard-siúr seemed to gather her thoughts, come to conclusions lost to Sabrina. Finally, she spoke. Slowly. Deliberatively. "Sister Brigh has come to me with her concerns over Mr. MacLir's continued stay and your continued interest in him."

"It's no longer Sister Brigh's affair. I'm a guest. Not a novice."

Ard-siúr tapped the tips of her fingers together. "But you are also a young lady of good reputation. I would hate to see you throw that away on one such as Daigh MacLir. As, I'm sure, would your brother."

"Kilronan may control my movements, but not my heart."

"And your other brother?"

Sabrina felt through the fabric of her apron to the note folded within. What was Ard-siúr getting at with her roundabout questions and her long, tension-filled silences?

The head of the order lifted a hand toward the window. "Those men and women out there and thousands like them grow more restless. What will be their fate be should a war between *Other* and *Duinedon* come to pass? Even after seven long years, much depends upon Brendan Douglas."

Ard-siúr folded her hands, her features placid and patient, though Sabrina sensed the dismay and the frustration and the anxiety the priestess worked hard to suppress. Or perhaps those weren't Ard-siúr's emotions at all, but her own roaring in her ears, pounding like a drum behind her eyes.

"It's not Brendan's fault," she argued, though her excuse sounded feeble even to herself. For in essence it was more Brendan's fault than anyone's. He'd been one of the mages who'd begun the nightmare of King Arthur's resurrection. His dark magics as much as Máelodor's had fed the murderous plotting.

Ard-siúr opened her hands as if tossing away her interest. "It is not my place to assign innocence or blame. That is the purview of the *Amhas-draoi*."

Who hunted Brendan and would kill him without a second thought.

Daigh had called her courageous. She didn't feel brave, but she'd not see her brother murdered in cold blood.

Sabrina never flinched. Not even against Ard-siúr's most focused stare. "Did you wish to speak to me about Daigh or Brendan?"

"They both concern me for different reasons."

Holding her breath lest she lose her nerve, Sabrina rose confidently from her seat. "Then you should speak to them. Not me."

A few rotted, slimy staves of wood, a length of old mud-caked rope, four bottles still corked and wax-sealed. This was all the cove gathered to its shores today.

Using the tip of his knife, Daigh dug out one bottle's cork. Tasted the contents. Still good. He took another swallow. Stared out at the waves, letting the steady wash of the surf dull the interminable throbbing behind his eyes. Inhaled the pungent, briny air, hoping to break the press of dread centered low in his gut.

Neither brought relief.

Downing the rest of the wine, he tossed the bottle far out into the pewter-black sea before taking the hill path back.

The Great One's control strengthened. Daigh could no longer deny the dark presence forcing its greasy way back into his mind. Little time remained before he would again be Máelodor's puppet and any hope for escape was gone.

Sabrina caught sight of him as he entered the gate. Looking up from winding a length of bandage round a man's hand, her face broke into a smile, pink flushing her cheeks.

He deliberately turned away, shoving the demon-flare of Máelodor's magics as far from the surface as he could. Hoping she wouldn't catch a hint of his increasing loss of control.

"Daigh?"

She'd followed him. Her gentle touch seared him like a

burning brand. He jerked away, but not before the murderous thunder of his thoughts flared wildly in his eyes.

"Where have you been?" she asked, hesitation replacing the smile of before.

"Nowhere that concerns you."

"It's . . . he's . . . it's happening just like you said, isn't it?"

He clenched his jaw against the frenzied, hot stab of pain centered at the base of his skull. Clamping around his brain until he couldn't think, couldn't see beyond Máelodor's vicious anger. "Leave me. Now."

"I can help." She rummaged in the bag slung over her shoulder.

"There is nothing you can do." He caught her wrist, forcing her to meet his accursed gaze. Her horror laid bare in the blue of her eyes.

"Is this scoundrel bothering you, milady?"

Neither one of them had noticed the approach of Sabrina's patient and two of his mates. They eyed Daigh with a mix of trepidation and swagger, an edgy frustration in the flexing of their meaty fists and the squint in their broad farmer's faces.

Sabrina pulled herself together enough to offer the men a faltering shake of her head. "No, it's all right. Really. Thank you."

The leader of the group tipped his wide-brimmed hat, rubbing at a thin white scar on his chin. "That's all right then, milady. But you let Simms know if there's trouble." He glared at Daigh. "Watch yersself, lad. I seen yer kind afore and I've dealt with 'em as I seen fit." He drew a finger across his throat. "It's yer kind brought the *Duinedon* down on us. Actin' as if yer powers make you better."

Daigh released Sabrina's wrist, gauging this new challenge. "It's no act." A red haze burned at the corners of his vision, a crackling awareness lifting the hairs upon his arms and neck. His stare moved slowly over the intruders, the venomous mage energy alive in his eyes.

They fell back with a startled oath, scuttling away like whipped curs, only the leader glancing over his shoulder with a black look of foreboding.

"They were only trying to protect me," Sabrina said.

He shrugged off her hand, pushing his way past her. "I know, Sabrina. So am I."

Drawing her cloak around her, Sabrina scanned the pale ribbon of road. The darkening spread of trees to either side. The sun had sunk until naught but a haze of orange and yellow brightened the western sky, a smearing of thin clouds painted bright red. Long shadows striped the ground and reached up the walls behind her. Mingled with the smoke from the fires within.

A figure topped the rise. Paused for long minutes as if judging whether to proceed.

Impossible to identify from this distance, but definitely male. Tall. Lean. A greatcoat hung open over high boots.

Sabrina leapt to her feet. Waved, hoping to coax him down.

He lifted a hand in answer. But rather than approaching, he disappeared back over the hill.

And though she waited until full dark and the rising of a late moon, he did not come again.

She slipped within the gate, her dark gown a paler black against the night, a hood covering her hair, yet he recognized her. The agile, clever movements, the slenderness of her body. And when she turned toward the stables seeking him out, her face glowed milky in the moon's dim light. Tears glistening upon her cheeks.

He ducked farther into the gloom, and she passed him without pausing.

Whom had she left to meet? Who would draw her from the safety of the order in the middle of the night?

The answer struck.

Brendan Douglas.

His hands closed to fists, the presence uncoiling to glide up from the darkness where Daigh had chained it. He fought back but it had grown sly enough to evade his few defenses. A pitiless, reptilian smile daggered through his brain until he could barely stand, and he clenched his jaw to keep from moaning.

Máelodor read his thoughts. And celebrated success.

Like a fuse burnt to the touch hole, Daigh's time ran out.

The true battle began now.

twenty-four

The child tugged her skirts. Shoved the note into her hand before running back to the gaggle of children playing tag. Sabrina looked around. Was Brendan hidden beneath the disguise of a thin-shanked farmer unloading bags of seed from a tumbrel? The man hunkered over a dice game? The messenger in tall muddy boots and a threadbare jacket idly picking his nose in the library doorway out of the rain?

She unfolded the note carefully as if it might blow up in her face, dread making her heart thump painfully in her chest.

The crossroads. Come immediately.
B.

She'd said it before: Letters never boded well.

They met upon the road, almost as if he'd been waiting for her. Despite his coarse homespun, weathered boots caked with mud, and a rough leather coat that stretched over his broad shoulders and ended at least three inches above his wrist, he strode forward with a confident air. Head up. Jaw tilted at an arrogant angle. A commanding gleam in his gaze, a broken branch clutched carelessly in a loose fist.

"Should you be out here alone?" he asked, whipping at the tall grass of the verge with his branch.

"We're still on the order's lands."

"So were we once before," he answered, falling in beside her. Nothing of the lover in the ominous, hulking anger. Electrifying an already charged atmosphere. His manner pulsed with barely repressed savagery and a thunderous rage.

She swallowed her tears before they'd show upon her cheeks. She'd known this day approached. Still it hurt with a swift, lancing pain.

Crossing a stile, they entered the orchard. Threaded their way through an arched avenue of bare mingled branches, the order's walls glimpsed here and there beyond a fold in the hill.

"He's mad to risk coming here," he snarled. "Does he want to be caught?"

Her stomach shot into her throat, throwing him a horrified look.

"Aye, Sabrina. I know who it is you steal away to meet." He hunched deeper into his coat. "As does Máelodor."

"No!" She tripped over a root. "You didn't—"

Daigh caught her, muscles rigid, face harsh with anguish. "He draws me back, his power far greater than mine."

"But the memories."

"They're not enough to fight his presence inside me."

The orchard row ended at a tall, overgrown hedge. A narrow slatted gate led to the lane and crossroad beyond.

She paused, a hand upon the latch. "What will you do if Brendan comes?"

"Warn him. It's all I can do."

A snap of a twig, the scuttle of a fox, followed immediately by a sudden rush of beating wings and the croaking scrape of hundreds of crows as they rose into the air. Sabrina's heart thundered, but beside her Daigh went completely still, eyes narrowed, his branch leveled for battle.

Animal rage poured off him in sour waves, a brimstone stench that churned her stomach. It pounded against her and over her like a great wave. Crushing her beneath the weight of it. No barriers she could erect strong enough to keep him out. The link between them unbreakable and unstoppable.

Mage energy fractured the air. A wall of flame leaping between them. A blast of deadly, ground-shaking battle magic.

She dropped her bag, clamping hands to her head as if she might hold it steady on her shoulders, her vision overwhelmed by a pair of baleful, snaky eyes. Pupils constricted to narrow slits. The yellow-red light of its iris streaked with fire.

She lurched and cried out, falling on her knees in the dust. Daigh, hunched and shaking across the road, his branch abandoned beside him.

A pair of shining boots stepped into the corner of her eye. She looked up into the frozen blue stare of Gervase St. John.

"I see you received your brother's note, little sparrow." The words slicked along her nerves like slime. Viscous and oily. He glanced over at Daigh's shuddering figure. A long pause followed that she felt as a quiver of wild anticipation. "And you've brought a friend."

Confused and shaking with sickness, Daigh opened eyes sticky with crust. Cold rain needled his face, and his clothing clung wet and chilly to his skin, making the trembling worse.

Above him, clouds rolled thick and unbroken, creating a false twilight. He sat up, rubbing at the base of his neck. Scanned the trees. The sky to the west where a dim glow marked the sun's descent.

He'd been mistaken.

It was almost full dark. Hours lost.

Sabrina could be anywhere.

"No matter how often I see you, I'm still amazed." St. John stepped from between the trees, his golden head darkened with rain, his greatcoat mud-spattered and damp. "That spell would have killed any normal human, and yet you . . ." He waved a careless hand in Daigh's direction.

Rigid with fury and gut-churning nausea, Daigh's hand fell to his waist.

"Looking for this?" St. John pulled forth a dagger. "I took the liberty of securing it along with the pistols you carried. Seemed wisest to conduct our conversation sans weapons."

Every killer instinct screamed at Daigh to lunge for the man's throat. Rip into him with his bare hands if need be. But the *Amhas-draoi* had Sabrina. Until Daigh knew where she was being held, he'd chain his murderous rage. Let St. John have his gloat.

He shoved the weapon back into his belt. "I see you've finally learned to appreciate my more persuasive techniques."

"Where is she?" Daigh snarled.

"Douglas's sister? She's safe enough. She's enjoying a brief reunion with her brother. Tearful. Emotional. Warms my heart."

"You've no heart."

St. John's face fell into clownish lines, his hand to his chest. "Perhaps I had one once, and it was lost. Or stolen? Perhaps I was born without one at all? Who can say?"

Daigh's fingers curled into his palms, the nails biting into his flesh until blood appeared. Mixed with the rain. "Let her go. She's not any part of this. This fight is between you, me, and Máelodor."

"She may not have started as part of my plans. A dull, tedious young woman like so many females. But she's become such a large part, hasn't she? You know, when you and I last spoke, I was sure she would be the bait to lure her brother in. And then it turned out to be the other way around. Funny how it all worked out, isn't it?"

St. John propped one booted foot on a fallen log. His expression virtuous as any priest's. His innards rotten to the core.

"What do you want?" Daigh asked.

St. John speared Daigh with a frozen stare. "Isn't it obvious? I want the Rywlkoth Tapestry. You were sent for it. But I shall claim it. I had thought to use Lady Sabrina, but why send her when I have you?"

Daigh's breath clogged his throat. His mind churning. "The *bandraoi* will never let it leave their protection."

St. John's smile vanished. "The *bandraoi* will have no choice. Not against a *Domnuathi*. You'll retrieve it and bring it to me here."

"Not until I've seen Sabrina and know she's safe."

"And you don't see Sabrina until I have the tapestry, so"—he spread his hands—"we're at an impasse."

"Damn you," Daigh ground out through clenched teeth. His skin felt like ice, and every second out here added to the miserable trembling he fought to contain.

The man shrugged. "Very well. The suggestion was made. I'll be sure to let your little sparrow know who's responsible for her agony. She shall curse your name with her last breath." He laughed. "Oh wait, I forgot. You're already cursed." He turned to go.

Daigh threw himself to his feet. "You touch her, and I'll—"

St. John swung around, his eyes fever bright, his voice dropped to a near whisper. "You'll what, Lazarus? What would you do in exchange for her life? How far would you go?"

Daigh halted, blood roaring in his ears. A fire eating away at his belly. He should have known he couldn't hide from St. John. The man saw everything with those guileless charmer's eyes.

"You can't say I didn't give you the opportunity to redeem yourself. Show the Great One you've not failed him—again. He's quite annoyed, you know. Wonders if you've forgotten your last reprimand."

Daigh hadn't. That memory had been carved into him along with the scars. Máelodor would enjoy breaking him. Punishment would be endless and unbearable. It would make him pray and weep and beg for death. And there would be no mercy. No rescue.

He was on his own. As he had always been.

"I'll bring you the tapestry." He drew himself up. Met St. John's smug condescension with a withering glare of his own. The whoreson knew he'd won. He almost preened.

"I knew you'd come around to my way of thinking,

Lazarus." He reached out a hand. His fingers barely brushing Daigh's cheek. But even that slight contact was enough to curdle his blood and make sweat break over him.

Daigh shuddered and looked away. Afraid and hating his fear almost as much as he hated St. John.

She woke to blindness. Suffocation. And bound hands.

The bag over her face muffled sound and the coarse rasp of the weave itched. She turned herself inside out trying to dislodge it, giving up only when the heavy heat of her breathing grew unbearable and her wrists had been rubbed raw. She rested her head against the floor, curling her body into a tight ball, trying not to cry. But her throat hurt, and her stomach cramped; and scalding tears dripped salty into the corners of her mouth.

Keep calm, Sabrina. Don't panic. Don't panic.

Daigh isn't dead. Can't be dead. He can't die. He's out there. Alive. And he would save her. She just needed to stay calm and wait.

But calm was impossible. Her heart thundered, and dread pressed down on her until she thought she might die if she weren't freed soon.

Think of something else. Anything else.

She rolled to her knees, crawling as well as she could in her skirts. Seeking to assess her prison. Weak light filtered through the sack. And a breeze. There must be a window. High up. Too small for anyone to enter or exit. Sliding one foot out in front of her. Then another in a slow shuffle, she paced off the perimeter. Barked her shin. Felt around, discovering the lumpy shape of a bedstead, a thin, crinkly straw mattress. Sank down upon it, resting and nursing her sore leg.

She must have dozed. She woke to a head-pounding battering of rage and fear and despair and defiance. It struck her awake with the force of a blow. Scoured her brain with a raw, frenzied power.

"Daigh!" she shouted, shouldering herself to a sitting position. Peering through the cloth as if she held sight. But all was darkness. Not even the light from earlier. "Daigh! I'm here!"

"Damn it all to hell." The voice came weak and raspy, but still recognizable.

Despite the circumstances, her heart beat faster, and a crazy mix of joy and anger bubbled through her. "Brendan?"

There followed a rustle, a bitten-back moan, and a tired shuffling crawl. "Hold still, and I'll try to get this sack off you."

Long, anxious moments and much cursing later, the bag was torn from her head. Sweet air. She gulped in great lungfuls, savoring the coolness on her face. Squinting even against the blue-black dark of night.

Her eyes slowly adjusted, revealing a face. Familiar and yet not. The man kneeling in front of her bore a rugged breadth of shoulder and a muscled frame, though he held himself gingerly as if he were in pain, and he cradled one hand close against his body. His shirt clung damp and filthy to his chest, and even in the blanketing shadows, his face bore a mottled collage of bruising, a lip split and puffy, one eye swollen shut. But the unblemished eye held a familiar gold gleam, and his smile—split lip and all—bore the lop-sided charm she remembered.

Had her hands been free, she would have flung herself at him. Though whether to hug him in welcome or beat him senseless, she wasn't certain.

He'd left her. Run away when she needed him most. Let her think he was dead. And now he was here. She could make up for that last awful parting. Tell him what he meant to her. How much she truly loved him. Or perhaps she should just give him a good fist to the jaw for bringing hell down on her head.

"You," she said, her voice shaky with anger, joy, and fear.

"Try to curb your enthusiasm," he answered dryly.

And just like that, seven years shrank to nothing. Tears spilled over. Ran like rivers down her face. "Oh gods, Daigh said . . . and the notes . . . and then . . . but I tried not to believe. I didn't want to be disappointed. But you're here. It really is you." Horrible, wretched weeping shook her, making her nose run and her throat ache.

"That's more like the response I'd hoped for," Brendan teased.

She snuffled. "You've changed."

"Seven years spent looking over one's shoulder can do that to a fellow," he answered through chattering teeth.

"You're soaked."

"Compliments of a few buckets of water from St. John's flunkies." He bent to examine her wrists. "I can try to undo those knots, but it may take a while. St. John's hurt my right hand. I think it's broken."

She turned her back to him as he began working at the knots, an awkward silence falling between them.

What should she say? What did one say to a brother who, until a few short weeks ago, was assumed long dead? Where had he been? How had he lived? Why had he come back now?

Questions banged around inside her mouth, yet she remained speechless unable to form any of her thoughts into words. Instead she resorted to, "You didn't write that last note, did you?"

"Actually, I did. St. John's arguments became overwhelmingly compelling. And extremely painful. It was only after I had done it that he stomped on my fingers for fun." His breath came labored as he picked with frustrating slowness at the knots.

"But why does he want me? What use could I possibly be to him?"

"The sisters wouldn't question your movements while you lurked about looking for the Rywlkoth Tapestry."

"It really is hidden there?"

"It won't be for long if St. John has his way. He's got orders to retrieve it. Using any means necessary. You, my darling sister, are those means."

"But I don't even know what it looks like. How—"

"Shh," Brendan cut her off. Dropped his voice to a whisper. "Don't tell St. John that. Let him think you know what and where it is. Get him to let you go back for it. And don't return."

"St. John will kill you."

"I'm safe from St. John. He may beat me black and blue, but he's got strict orders to keep me alive. When you get back, go to your Ard-siúr. She can send for the *Amhas-draoi.* They'll know how to handle St. John."

"But the *Amhas-draoi* . . . they want to kill you."

"They'll have to get to the back of the line." She opened her mouth to protest. "Sabrina, I'd rather face a quick execution at the hands of the *Amhas-draoi* than a drawn-out death at the hands of Máelodor. He and I have a long history. None of it on friendly terms." A long pause, a wrench of her arms, and, "There."

The ropes came away. She faced him, rolling her aching shoulders, rubbing her wrists. "I can't leave you."

His face stiffened into a harsh mask. Not at all Brendan-like. This was a man she didn't know. A stranger. "You'll do as your told. Do you understand? This is bigger than me. Besides, my life was forfeit years ago. Whatever St. John uses to frighten you, don't heed him. Just get the hell out of here when you have the chance."

Daigh paused in front of the tapestry for only a moment before tearing the cloth from its nails. Shoving it into his coat pocket and retracing his steps.

Sister Anne remained where he'd left her. Slumped unconscious across her desk. By the time she woke with a knot and a headache, he'd be long departed.

So much for Ard-siúr's resources.

In the outer courtyard, Sabrina's would-be protector paused in tending his cook fire long enough to challenge him, but Daigh never slowed. Instead his steps turned toward the workshops and the traveling smithy's abandoned forge. Plucking up a sharpened billhook, he shoved it into his belt.

"What's yer business here this time of night?" The man filled the doorway, his eyes narrowed, his glowering features pricked with suspicion.

"My business is my own."

"Not if yer skulking about where ya shouldn't."

Daigh felt Máelodor now like a second consciousness. Watching with voyeuristic glee. Filling his mind with hate and violence. "Let me pass."

"Mayhap I'll be hollering for me mates instead. Teach ya some manners. I seen the way you look at that young girl. Not decent. Not respectable. Pat! Jasper! We got that scoundrel cornered."

His mates shoved their way into the closed space of the tool crib. The three of them together stoked high on gin and frustration. Daigh, a tidy outlet for their drunken rage.

He refused the black powers surging through his veins. The ruthless fury that sought blood and killing and death. Máelodor might claim him in the end, but Daigh would not make it easy.

Instead, he used the strength born of tilt-yard training and the cunning honed through countless border raids to level the first man with a quick fist to the jaw, his companions with a flurry of punches that left one doubled over in a retching heap, the other spitting blood and teeth.

Stepping over them, he slipped back into the night. Disappeared through the gate, the weight of Ard-siúr's disappointed gaze boring into his back.

He turned back, shouting into the night. Knowing she would hear. "Your bones were wrong, old woman! There is no hope for the damned! And I have betrayed you all!"

twenty-five

Máelodor had always wished for the power of flight. To soar above the clouds. Look down upon the ants as they toiled and slaved in the fields and towns. To be one with the heavens. As powerful as the *Fey* themselves.

The nights he dreamt of climbing the skies, he always woke refreshed, without the grate of brittle bones or the ghost-pain in a leg that was no longer there. But these nights were few. His dreams now were taken up with darker forces and more sinister fantasies than the innocence of flying.

The traveling coach lurched, dropping heavily into a rut. Bouncing free. He grit his teeth against the constant jostling and swaying. Every pothole only served to remind him of his waning strength. Of the sacrifices he'd endured to summon a *Domnuathi* and bind him to the cause. Of the enormous drain on his powers to seek out his wayward creature.

He would need to expend more power to crush the

Domnuathi's stubborn will. How Lazarus had managed to break free of his bondage, Máelodor couldn't guess. But it would not happen again. He would see to that.

Still and all, he could not be dissatisfied. Willingly or not, Lazarus had revealed the truth. Brendan Douglas was at Glenlorgan. The hunt was nearing its conclusion.

It would be mere miles until he could look upon the treacherous face of the man who'd betrayed the Nine, including his own father, to save his pathetic skin.

Skin, Máelodor planned on flaying inch by excruciating inch. He trembled in anticipation.

Rapping against the carriage roof, he urged his coachman to increase the pace.

To hell with his bones, he had a reunion to attend.

Sabrina had done what she could for Brendan's hand, though the bones had been crushed almost beyond even her repairs. She'd cleaned his lip. The deep gash across his ribs. His torso carried the same mottled bruising as his face as if St. John had taken to him with a club.

"Fists only," Brendan explained, wincing at every pass of her dampened cloth. "But there may have been a few pieces of furniture, and at one point a spur caught me. That's the mess across my ribs there."

As the hours dragged, Brendan's face paled to a sickly gray, color high upon his cheeks. And his grip on lucidity loosened despite her attempts at reducing the rampaging fever. He drifted in and out, sometimes muttering incomprehensible gibberish, sometimes frighteningly quiet, barely a breath steaming the chilly air. She'd beaten upon the door, hollering for help to come. Bring a blanket or even a candle to break the unceasing gloom.

The first time she'd received only a curse and a shout for silence in response.

The second time, the door cracked open to reveal a sinister bearded man who pushed a plate of food through the door at her along with a jug of sour ale.

Brendan roused himself to poke at the burnt fish. Tear off a hunk of the bread. "There's at least two blokes besides him. Twice as disreputable and three times as quick with their fists."

"But surely your powers . . . I mean you were always so . . ."

He gave a gruff snort. "Magic can't stop a bullet or turn a blade. And St. John's powers as an *Amhas-draoi* are far greater than mine. The first time I tried to escape . . ." He wrapped his hands around his knees, his face bleak. "Let's say, it ended badly. The second time . . ." He clenched his jaw and looked away. "The hand was the least of it. Between St. John's mage energy and his bully-boys' brute force, I'm stymied. Besides, I can't leave you, and I'm too weak to protect both of us. I'm afraid if you were looking for me to play hero, I'm singularly unequipped."

His impudent tone didn't hide his mounting fear. She felt it as an added press upon her own sagging spirits. It wouldn't take much to peel away his remaining bravado. And the waiting only made it that much worse. Every sound made them jump. Every shout caused them to steel themselves for St. John's arrival. But he did not come.

Even panic loses its edge over time. The body slowly adjusts to the dry mouth, the closed throat, and the sweaty palms. Fear becomes normal.

By the time the sun dragged itself into a gray, misty sky, Sabrina had reached that stage, immune to the knots in her chest and the flip-flop of a stomach long since emptied of its last meal.

She'd offered Brendan the pallet. He slept. Finally. But it was a short-lived rest, soon broken by disjointed muttering. "Lissa . . . the stone . . . Jack!" He woke with a jerk. Scrubbed a hand over his face as he sought to pull himself from his fever dreams. "Have I been asleep long?"

Sabrina had taken to drawing patterns in the dirt with a piece of stick. "A few hours."

"Any sign of St. John?"

"No. No one."

Sighing, he slung his legs over the side of the bed, raking a hand through his wild hair. "Thank the gods. Not up to seeing him again right now. And Máelodor . . . well, least said about that . . ." He peered at her from his one good eye. "Have you slept at all?"

"Not much. No."

"Here. If you squash up next to me, we can combine our heat."

He pulled her up onto the pallet beside him, curling her into his shoulder. "There now, better?"

"Much." She tried not to worry over the amount of heat he generated alone. "Brendan?"

"Hm?"

"Why did you do it?"

A long silence. Long enough she wanted to cut out her tongue. Why had she asked that? What did it matter now? Didn't they have enough troubles without dredging up more?

"Which 'it' do you refer to?"

She couldn't back away now. She'd asked. She'd get an answer. Even if it wasn't an answer she wanted to hear.

Because though it seemed like ancient history, the actions of those long ago days still rippled outward in ever-widening, every-strengthening circles.

"All the things they accuse you of."

Another long silence stretching thin as spring ice. "My notoriety has grown for every year they couldn't catch me. I'd not be surprised if I were being held responsible for blighted crops, solar eclipses, and plagues of locusts."

"That's not answering me."

He sighed. "I was a different person back then."

"What changed your mind?"

His body stiffened, his arm sliding away to leave her chilled with more than cold. "Perhaps someday I'll tell you."

She drew her knees up to her chest, resting her head upon them. Rain pattered against the roof. Dripped with tortured regularity upon the floor. "Why did you come back?" She hated the quaver in her voice.

Brendan's answer came thick as if he were once again close to a slide into unconsciousness. "Heard Father's diary had been found." He drew in a shivering breath. "Hoped to beat him . . . didn't work out . . ."

"Who's Lissa?"

"No one anymore. Go . . . sleep."

She didn't want to. Couldn't.

But did.

A short, grimy man let St. John and Daigh into the cottage. Another filled them in on the prisoners.

"Barely et, sir, though I gave them what you left. Heard them in there talking, but couldn't make heads nor tails of what they said through the door. Gentleman's not tried nothin' for a while, though we been watchin' for it. He's poorly. Mebbe that's what's keeping him quiet."

"Bring them out."

"Aye, sir."

The men disappeared up a narrow stair, their boot heels echoing on the floorboards above Daigh's head. Raised voices followed by a dull thud of fists striking flesh. A woman's scream.

Daigh strained against the black rage. The presence so close to the surface, the gleam of the serpent's eye filled his vision. The glistening, black scales slid just below his skin. Every second his humanity unwound like wool from a skein.

"Here they are, sir."

St. John motioned the couple forward into the room.

Sabrina started in her captor's arms. "Daigh!" Was yanked back fiercely.

Beside her, held upright only by the men supporting him on either side, slumped Brendan Douglas. He cocked a head up, one golden eye studying him from beneath a shaggy head of hair. "So, Máelodor managed it after all. A *Domnuathi*."

Daigh stiffened, addressing St. John. "You agreed. The tapestry for their release."

"No," St. John countered. "I agreed the tapestry and I'd not carve your lover into bite-size pieces. Did you know the sea lies a mile southeast of here? My associates, when they're not engaged by me, own a fishing boat. According to them, a body weighted and dumped just yards offshore will never be found."

"You lied." Tugging the billhook from his belt, Daigh surged forward, only to be brought up short by Sabrina's captor pressing a cocked pistol to her temple.

"Careful," St. John admonished, holding a hand out for the makeshift weapon. "You wouldn't want to be responsible for a stray shot, would you?"

"Bastard," Douglas rasped. But a brutal punch left him hanging useless between his captors.

"What of Sabrina's brother?" Daigh asked, slapping the billhook into St. John's open palm.

St. John shrugged. "He's not part of our bargain."

"She's no more use to you. Let her go." Daigh tried to keep the pleading from his voice, but by the smug curl of St. John's lip, the man knew full well to what extent Daigh would go to secure Sabrina's release.

"And why should I?" He studied Daigh with renewed interest.

Palms damp, skin crawling, his stomach churned as he stared the man down. "Because I asked."

St. John opened his mouth as if to reject his request, his expression slowly changing as if he read something in Daigh's eyes that pleased him. He motioned toward a dimly lit back passage.

Without once looking at Sabrina or her brother, Daigh followed St. John out.

They had been returned to their prison, Brendan dumped unceremoniously upon the bed, and given a rough boot to the ribs to keep him quiet. She, shoved inside with a leer and a filthy remark that left her face flaming. When the door finally slammed behind them, the turn of the key came like a turn of a knife in Sabrina's breast.

She slid down a wall to huddle upon the floor, arms wrapped about her drawn-up knees.

"Damn it. Seven years hidden, and just like that—"

A bout of coughing interrupted Brendan's tirade. He lay back on the bed, an arm shielding his face as he sought to recover.

"Daigh didn't do it because he wanted to. He did it to save me." She pressed a hand to the dull lump just under her breastbone.

"Why would a soldier of Domnu barter to save you? And why does St. John assume you're lovers?"

Sabrina flashed him a look.

Brendan lowered his arm to cock a quizzical brow in her direction. "Thought I hadn't caught that, didn't you? This isn't the first time St. John has used you as a weapon against the *Domnuathi*."

"It's not?"

"What is there between you and Máelodor's creature?"

She caught herself picking the nail of her right index finger. Whipped it behind her back. "If I tell you something, will you promise not to laugh?"

He grew serious. "Can't say I'm in a jolly mood."

She cocked her head, regarding him steadily. "That's hardly a promise."

He sighed. Tenderly leveraged himself to a sitting position. His bruises stark against the chalky gray of his face. "Have I ever laughed? Even when you came to me with tales of trolls under your bed, did I let out so much as a snicker?"

"No, you didn't." She paused. "But that turned out to be true."

"Needless to say, in this, Sabrina, I'm the same as I ever was."

She gazed on him long and hard. In almost every way, he was so different from the thin, gawky, untidy brother of her childhood. The one whose manner held a guarded reserve, his true emotions carefully hidden beneath a veneer of sarcasm. Except with her. Or so she'd always thought. But his confessions had shaken that faith. Had she really known Brendan at all?

He seemed to understand her dilemma. Hurt dulled his already beaten features, and he hunched his shoulders. "Please, Sabrina. Trust me."

His need ripped through the last of her worries. Aidan had been the brother she idolized. Brendan was the brother she loved.

"I'm part of Daigh's past." He scowled his confusion. "I know it sounds insane, but I'm able to fall into his memories. I see things as he remembers them, but they're memories of me. And him. Together. It's more than a vision, it's as if I'm there. As if I traveled through a portal to the past. As if his memories are a way through time itself."

His eyes grew steadily wider as she spoke. His concentration almost visible in the keenness of his gaze. "You . . . but . . . how . . ." He seemed to ponder her confession, tapping his chin. Mumbling to himself. "Think, Brendan . . . that would mean . . ."

"You don't think I'm mad, do you? Or that Máelodor's spells have infected me with some evil magic?"

He focused back on her with a start as if he'd forgotten she was there. "Mad? Who called you mad?"

"Aidan said—"

Brendan snorted. "You know our brother's opinion of magic. I'm sure it hasn't changed much since I last saw him. No, Sabrina, you're not mad. I've heard of this phenomenon, but it's rare. There are few *Other* who can pass through time. The true *Fey* guard that power fiercely."

"I can't pass through any time. Only his time. His memories. And I don't do it intentionally. It just happens."

Pent-up frustration and fear spewed out of her in a torrent of explanation and conjecture and worry and grief until sobs choked off her words. Brendan was as good as his word. He listened to everything, interrupting only to ask a question here. Obtain a clarification there.

Rain dripped puddles across the floor and their breath fogged the chilly air. Brendan's shaking intensified, fatigue and sickness carving deep lines into his face. But the scholar's light burned intensely in his eyes.

"He uses memory as a way to fight his bondage? Incredible. Nothing like that was recorded in the texts." His finger's tapping sped up. "Could Daigh be pulling you in unintentionally as he fights Máelodor's control?"

"How?"

"You've said just before it occurs, you experience a surge of emotion to the point where your normal empathic gift is flooded. Like a dam releasing a wall of water."

"But how are the two connected?"

"Suppose he's opening the door with the force of his emotions and, without even knowing it, you're falling through."

"How do I stop it from happening?"

His nervous tapping stopped, his expression at once both sympathetic and fearful. "Once Máelodor arrives, I don't expect it will be a problem."

She wiped her cheeks with the back of her hand. Stared up at the rain-streaked window, numbness stealing over her with every moment passed in horrible uncertainty.

He broke the silence first. "You never answered my original question."

She lifted tired, burning eyes to her brother.

"Was St. John speaking truth when he called you MacLir's lover?"

She faced him defiantly. "He was."

He exhaled on a sad sigh, rubbed a hand over his stubbled chin, shaking his head. "Oh, Sabrina."

"Have I shocked you? Are you disgusted that a sister of yours could lay with a man unwed? That no proper gentleman shall want to marry me now that I'm ruined?"

"No, I worry over the sorrow still lying in your future."

"Daigh hopes to provoke Máelodor into killing him." Her words seemed to reverberate in the air like an echo.

Brendan's mouth thinned to a white-rimmed line. "Death would be preferable. But I fear it is an impossible hope."

But did Brendan refer to Daigh's hopes or his own?

twenty-six

The coach drew up in the muddy farmyard of a ramshackle cottage. Chickens scattered. A skinny dog strained at the end of a rope, barking ferociously. Smoke rose in a thin, white trail from a sprouting, sagging thatched roof.

Máelodor emerged from the conveyance as a rangy, bearded man strode from the barn, hollering for silence. Catching sight of the coach, he gave one last swiping kick to the dog before dashing through the rain to the house. Ducking his head inside, shouting the news.

St. John appeared at the door, shrugging into his coat, an obsequious smile of welcome upon his flushed, sweat-glistened face. "Great One, I wasn't expecting you so soon. I would have prepared more suitable arrangements."

Máelodor clutched the stick, excitement warming a body forever cold. "Douglas. He's here. In Glenlorgan. I've seen it for myself."

St. John's smile widened, though it never reached his

eyes. "He's closer than that. He's within. I captured him four days ago."

Could retribution finally be at hand? Máelodor's heart lurched wildly, his skin hot, then cold. His lungs pumped as he wheezed, "Show me."

"There's someone else you may want to see first."

St. John lent Máelodor his arm. Led him through the front door into a sparsely furnished room. A few broken sticks of furniture. A table upon which someone's dinner congealed. A fire burning down to a few red embers in the grate. And a man filling a far doorway, his face black as a storm cloud, carved in graven lines.

Máelodor clutched St. John's arm tightly. "Lazarus."

The man's throat worked, his hands clenched to fists, his whole body quivering with repulsion, rage, and despair.

Máelodor feasted upon these dark emotions. Used them to begin re-creating the subtle connections that would bring the *Domnuathi* to heel.

Lazarus's face went blank, his mind slamming shut against Máelodor's prying. Even now, attempting to defy his master. To become what he could never be. Human. Free.

Máelodor probed deeper, coming up against the same entrenched wall where no mage energy dared cross. Surprised by the strength of this defiance, he retreated. Let Lazarus feel a moment's success. Then with a signal to St. John, who nodded his understanding, he tried one final time.

The tendrils of his mind lashed out, catching hold of the soldier of Domnu. But this time St. John added his strength to Máelodor's. The *Ambas-draoi*'s battle magic caught Lazarus square in the chest, driving the breath from his lungs, singing nerves. He collapsed on a howl of anguish, setting off a renewal of the dog's frenzied barking. His break in concentration momentary, but long enough for Máelodor's needs.

Máelodor burrowed deep, filling the hollows in Lazarus's mind with his coiled awareness. The serpent's presence unshakeable and unending. And when Lazarus looked again upon his master's face, there was nothing left behind the *Domnuathi*'s black gaze but death.

Sabrina felt a jerk upon her mind, fog seeping across her vision. She shouted for Brendan, grabbing his hand as she plunged into the sucking dark.

The air cleared, her eyes adjusting slowly. She lay in a warm bed, Daigh's body pressed against her back, cradling her close. One hand splayed over her belly, his breath soft upon her neck.

"A girl child as strong-willed and feisty as her mother," he murmured, his touch igniting a fire between her thighs. "I'll be back before your time, and we shall welcome her together."

Salty tears slid into her mouth. Stained her pillow. He would not see his child. He would not return.

This was the end.

A great roaring filled her ears, the fog enveloping her like a shroud. The bed, the room, the world dragged ever downward until nothing remained but a void of endless black.

The roaring pressed against her brain. Squeezed her organs. Rattled her bones and shook her blood. She sought to clamp her hands to the sides of her head. Felt the heated grip of Brendan's fingers once more threaded with her own.

She opened her eyes, but the roaring continued. Only now she recognized it for what it was. Screaming. On and on. An endless, anguished howl battering her mind, the fiery unblinking eyes of a serpent stripping all before it, coils wrapping round and round as walls crumbled, ramparts collapsed, retreat impossible.

This was the end.

How long had he been unconscious? Long enough for someone to drag him here. Dump him on the bed to recover, but the rank odors emanating from the thin, soiled sheets made vomit rise into his raw throat. Gagging against the spasms, he forced himself up to shaky feet. Scrubbed a hand over his face as if he might wipe away the shame.

He closed his eyes, knowing he'd sacrificed the last and most precious memory he possessed and still it had not been enough. Sabrina was lost to him. And he had failed her.

He peeled back his sleeve. The brand burned as if a million stinging ants lived beneath his skin. He dug at it until blood welled from the long rakes left by his nails, but the crescent pierced by the broken arrow remained visible. Nothing could erase Máelodor's mark of ownership. Nothing could tear the mage from his mind where his serpent's fangs had now sunk deep enough that only death could shake him loose.

"Douglas remains stubborn." St. John lounged in the doorway, spearing Daigh with a lecherous smile, his gaze sliding over him with greasy enjoyment.

Daigh clenched his teeth and ignored him. What did it matter now? "Douglas will die rather than surrender the location of the stone. His honor demands no less."

"He's a traitor," St. John snapped to attention. "He has no honor."

"From one who knows."

St. John's face went pale, his eyes sharp as cut glass. "My loyalty is to my race. That is the only trust that matters. Arthur's return will bring about a new celebrated chapter in a history gone sour and forgotten."

"Or it shall bring death and destruction and an end to any chance for peace between *Other* and *Duinedon*."

"Enough conversation." St. John tossed the billhook upon the bed. "You may need this yet. Máelodor commands your presence immediately."

Daigh bowed his head. "I am his to order."

"If you don't want more of the same, you'd do well to remember that, my beautiful beast." St. John's smile returned, brighter than before, his lips brushing Daigh's cheek as he passed.

He never even flinched. "It is all I *can* remember. All I have left."

Máelodor gazed upon the tapestry spread out before him, staring at the interwoven flowers with a frightening light in his eyes. "You've done well, St. John. I'm more than convinced you will make a most competent lieutenant for the new king's reign. He shall come to value your support as I do."

St. John gave a brief bow. "I'm honored at the confidence you've placed in me. I vow to serve my new king as I have served you, Great One. With all my being."

Máelodor's lips peeled back from his mouth in a reptilian grimace, his hand fondling the head of his cane. "With the Rywlkoth Tapestry in my possession, there is but one final missing piece. And that too shall be ours soon enough." He hobbled toward the stairs. "Come."

Daigh fell in behind them, his mind alive with an oppressive feeling of impending oblivion. The presence swelled to a crackling roar. Drowned out his questions with certainties of its own. Scoured his mind clean of doubt. Of compassion. And finally—of humanity.

The upper passage lay scattered with refuse, one gaping doorway revealing a chamber filthy with blankets, old food, a bucket catching drips from the leaking roof in a steady stream, the scattered remnants of a dice game. St. John passed it by with barely a glance. Came to the next, jamming a key into the lock. Opening the door with a screech of rusty hinges.

This chamber reeked with vomit and piss. Only the breeze whistling through the badly chinked walls and a cracked window kept the air from growing suffocatingly foul.

Daigh kept his eyes off the woman huddled on the rough straw pallet, though he felt her presence like a knife pressed to his throat. Instead, he focused on Douglas. His bruises had been added to since Daigh's last visit, the marks vivid against the chalky white of his face. An arm rested close against his side, his splinted hand black and purple and curled clawlike into his palm. But his eyes when they fell upon Máelodor narrowed with deadly intensity.

"Back so soon?" he chided from a swollen, bloodied mouth. "I'd have thought you and your pet *Amhas-draoi* might have some new fun planned. Drowning puppies? Beating up grandmothers? The possibilities are endless."

Máelodor's wreckage of a body straightened. Shoulders thrown back, head high. Shedding for a few brief moments, the age and infirmity as he regarded Douglas with a contemptuous sneer. "Always the jokester. That tongue shall get you in trouble if you're not careful."

"I'll risk it."

Máelodor's gaze shifted toward Sabrina. "But shall you risk your sister?"

Brendan blanched.

"That's right. It's all very well to play the hero with your own life, but if she were to suffer for your continued silence?"

"I'll answer for my own crimes. Not her."

"Your father was so proud of you, but surely you knew that. He held you up as proof of *Other* supremacy in general and Douglas superiority to be specific. The *Fey* blood ran hot in you. Powerful."

Brendan's lips pinched tight, his expression hardening.

Máelodor shook his head with mock sorrow. "I can only imagine what his disillusionment was when he realized it was you who betrayed him to his death."

Sabrina uttered a strangled gasp.

"What's this? Your sister doesn't know? Aye, Lady Sabrina, it was your brother and Kilronan's favorite son who betrayed us all to the *Amhas-draoi*. I suspected it but had no proof. And would Kilronan hear my warnings? He accused me of jealousy. Ignored me. And in doing so, sealed his fate. And that of us all."

Brendan focused on Máelodor with enough venom in his gaze to kill. "It was a lost cause then, and it's a lost cause now. The *Duinedon* will fight with every weapon at their disposal."

"Perhaps, but their numbers have been sorely depleted in this century of war. Their soldiers are weary. The people dispirited with their current rulers. They want peace. Prosperity. A new beginning. Arthur can give them that. He can restore the world as it was in the Lost Days."

Brendan's defiance mounted, though he had not once looked to Sabrina. As if afraid of the emotion he might encounter. "Even weakened as you claim, the *Duinedon* are still strong enough to defeat us. We can't hope to succeed against their numbers. You'll have brought the High King back to certain slaughter and ignoble defeat."

"There are those who could be brought to fight on our side. For the price of their freedom."

Daigh hadn't thought it possible for Douglas to go any whiter, but his whole face seemed to collapse, his body crushed by this revelation. "They can't survive in this world. You know that."

"Not in their current form. But if presented with human hosts . . ."

"You're mad. Their fealty will last only as long as their prison walls." He sought St. John's aid. "What he proposes is madness."

St. John lashed out with a boot, sending Douglas sprawling. "A chance I'm willing to take."

Máelodor raised a hand. "Enough. My powers are not so lacking, son of Kilronan. And with your help, I will be greater still."

"It won't work," Douglas muttered.

"Give me the location of the Sh'vad Tual, and we shall see who is right and who is wrong."

"Never."

Máelodor motioned Daigh forward. "Kill her," he ordered. "Douglas needs to see his sister die and know he could have stopped it had he only been more cooperative."

"You kill her and you've lost your only bargaining chip," Douglas brazened. "Besides, I'm no fool. Either way, you'll not leave anyone alive who can raise the warning against you."

"Always so clever, young Douglas," Máelodor sneered. "Then I shall amend my words. I can kill her quickly or I can kill her slowly. That becomes your choice."

Daigh risked his first glance at the woman whose fate hung by a thread. She hunched as far back against the wall as she could, hands clutching her stomach, face eerily expressionless.

For an instant, their eyes locked, hers shiny with tears. But it was he who looked away first, unable to offer her anything but a clean death.

"You're not his slave," she whispered.

Daigh kept his gaze fixed upon the battle of wills between Douglas and Máelodor.

"Don't let him win." Her voice came soft as a last breath.

His blood moved sluggish and frozen in his veins, his mind carrying naught but a soldier of Domnu's cold-blooded indifference. He couldn't speak. Couldn't move. Could only listen to her futile pleading.

"You're not Lazarus. You're Daigh." One final entreaty, this one ending on a sob that would have torn at his heart had he one left. But that, like his memories, had been taken from him, leaving naught but the presence in its place.

"Kill her," Máelodor commanded. "Prove your allegiance."

Hate. Terror. Evil. Violence. Murder. The emotions took physical and horrifying form. A scarlet and golden river of flame and smoke. The open maw of the serpent widening as Daigh teetered on the edge. He scrambled for a hold against the gaping emptiness. Anything to stop his final tumble into hell.

"Do as I say!" Máelodor screamed.

Daigh drew forth the billhook. Stepped forward, his body no longer his to command.

"No!" Brendan lunged between them, mage energy crackling the air. The spell on his tongue bursting forth with the speed and strength of a final stand.

Daigh faltered, his head exploding as it had been cleaved in two. His weapon fell from a hand gone suddenly numb as he dropped to his knees.

"Sabrina! Now!" Douglas shouted. "Stop him. Use the memories. Find him and—"

Douglas's instructions ended in a grunt of pain as St. John backhanded him to the floor. Stood above him, murder in his gaze.

Daigh looked to Sabrina. The blue of her eyes sweeping him under like a cresting wave. Her hair floating about her shoulders as if caught in the flow of an ocean current.

Letting go of his last handhold, he sank deep, letting her carry him away.

She didn't know what she did. How she did it.

Dropping through the fragmented, scattered layers of Daigh's memories, she took up the gossamer threads of his past, winding herself into them. Becoming a piece of that lost life. Entering as if stepping through a doorway.

If Brendan was correct and the veriest scrap of memory was enough to loosen the mage's hold upon Daigh's soul, what would a deluge of memories beget? And would she be strong enough to hold herself in this time and place long enough to create them?

There was no way but to try. Failure meant death.

The air thickened and condensed with rain and cloud. Fog muffled her footsteps, creating ghostly specters of the wooded Welsh glen. But he was just as she knew he would be. Eyes sparkling soft and as gray-green as the fog, untouched by shadows, body bearing none of the jagged edges of his present blighted existence. He reached a hand for her. Wide. Callused. Warm. It enfolded her fingers. Drew her in.

"I know you," he whispered. *"Cariad."*

She smiled, stepping into his embrace.

twenty-seven

Daigh's mind fractured like a fist through a mirror. A million shards. A million crystalline memories. Pristine. Without flaw or fault. And sharp enough to sever the strongest prisoner chains.

Energy flooded limbs suddenly free of the taint of Máelodor's dark magics. The oppressive presence no longer coiled at the base of his brain. He struggled to his knees, shaking his head as if to clear it, but the memories clung like burrs to cloth. Throbbing the very air. Filling him like an empty wineskin with moments and impressions as clear as the scene before him. He knew who he was. What he was. The being known as Lazarus shed like a discarded cloak.

"St. John. Kill her!" Máelodor screamed, spittle flecking his mouth, his eyes wild and unfocused.

Douglas lay bloody and dazed upon the floor, Máelodor's cane pressed to his windpipe, the master mage crouched above him like a vulture.

St. John advanced upon Sabrina, who lay still as death upon the pallet. "What say you, Douglas? Shall we carve a few scars into your pretty sister's face?"

All eyes upon St. John, none noticed Daigh reach for the discarded billhook. Close his hand around it. Roll up and forward in one fluid thrust aimed at St. John's back.

Not until the last possible second. Then Máelodor shouted a warning as St. John swung about, the sharpened tool ripping a long gash through the fabric of his coat. "You!"

His retaliatory spell hit Daigh like a wall of crushing stone.

Darkness closed in as his lungs worked frantically for air, his tongue thickening, his throat closing. No gentle suffocation, but a pressing sense of panic. His struggles availed him nothing. No mage energy answered his summons. He was powerless.

"Play fair." Reaching out with his ruined hand, lips moving in a soundless whisper, Douglas shattered the room with a thunderous tremor of answering magic. Walls bowed, the floor heaved, and dust and thatch drifted in the fetid air.

St. John fell, his spell dissolving while Máelodor stumbled to his knees, his face contorted with pain and an insane fury.

But no sooner had the master mage hit the floor than his body wavered and shifted. Shadows overlapping shadows. More than human, less than snake. Eyes round and red and lidless. Mouth unhinged in a gaping fork-tongued grimace. A great hood spreading above a scaled head while his body lengthened and contorted with the striking speed of a snake.

"He's a Heller!" Douglas gasped.

"Gelweth a sargh dyest. Pádraic eskask." The words slithered ominous and black from Máelodor's mouth. *"Drebeveth besh distruot."*

From the center of the room, an enormous serpent took shape. A rippling, reptilian monster.

Fangs bared, it lunged for its closest prey. Daigh.

The fog smothered her in its damp, cloying folds. The trees and the holding and the path and the weeping left behind. Word had come. The men were dead. Word had come of the death of a prince and the slaughter of his companions.

Keening filled the air. Rose like the thick, black smoke of the cook fires. Sabrina had stayed as long as she dared. But word had come, and there was no more reason to hold fast to this time and this world.

Her life here had been full, the memories precious. But her lover was dead, and she was released to return to her home and her time while he slept the passing centuries in a grave, awaiting the odious spell that would summon him to a new existence among the living.

The fog thinned to silver strands, the enormous, sheltering woods contracting to the dingy walls of a cottage, the prickle of a straw mattress beneath her cheek. Years for her shrinking down to mere minutes for them.

He stood with his back to her. Sword-straight. Shoulders braced for battle.

She reached with her mind, touching the heat and love and strength of a man she'd parted with in tears and pleading long months previous. But nothing else.

She had beaten Máelodor. Saved Daigh.

Word had come. And though she had lost him in one life, she had gained him in another.

The great snake undulated from side to side as if assessing the easiest target. Winded and heart pounding, Daigh backed against the edge of the pallet. Weakness buckled his legs while sweat poured between his shoulder blades. Streamed into his face. He wiped it with the back of a sleeve.

The snake took that moment to strike.

Its tail whipped St. John's legs from under him as it lunged at Douglas, still lying prone upon the floor.

Daigh shoved the man out of the way, taking the fangs deep into his own arm.

With his free hand, he slammed the billhook down and down again until the snake released him. Blood poured green from its wounds, burning Daigh where it spattered his bare flesh.

The snake struck again, but this time St. John used the moment to launch his own attack.

Daigh parried the snake, but was too slow to thwart St. John's thrusting knife, which caught him a raking slash across the collarbone.

The *Ambas-draoi* sought to follow up one success with another, his dagger flashing against the growing darkness, his gaze alive with a diamond's icy fire, full lips parted in a ruthless grimace.

Daigh's stomach tightened with nausea, acid eating its way up his throat, but he evaded St. John's assault by a hairbreadth, though he knew it would only be a matter of time.

"Drebeveth besh distruot," Máelodor's voice rasped low and venomous. *"Ladhesh esh'a peuth. Kummyaa nagonaa byest."*

"He's escaping," Brendan cried.

Daigh dared take his eyes from St. John for long enough to see Máelodor duck out into the passage. He tore after him, but St. John stepped in his path, dagger at the ready.

"He leaves you to die," Daigh uttered from a jaw clenched tight against the pain in his arm. Already his fingers tingled and his vision sparkled with bursts of white light.

St. John drew himself up. "I'm Lancelot. The battle hand of Arthur himself. Máelodor knows my worth."

The curse he unleashed cut into Daigh like hot knives, every breath a new horror. Then just as suddenly, the spell dissolved as the snake struck at St. John. And again.

His focus interrupted, the *Amhas-draoi* bellowed, "Máelodor! Your beast. Call it off!"

Daigh raced for the stairs, but the snake threw its coils beneath his feet. He stumbled, throwing an arm out to catch himself. Something snapped in his wrist, agony shooting to his shoulder until he almost passed out from the pain.

The worn grip of the billhook met his throbbing fingers. "Daigh." A whispered voice. Rejuvenating as a plunge in a snowy mountain-fed stream.

He forced his fingers to close around the handle. Adjusting his grip, he took difficult aim. Waited for an opening though every nerve screamed for vengeance and his arm grew heavier with each passing second.

St. John's golden features bloodied and streaked with gore, his breathing fast, his body quivering, he bellowed curses at Máelodor while dodging the snake's frenzied attacks. Swinging under the snake's guard, he stunned it with a brutal crack to the skull, thrusting up into the snake's throat, blood pouring over his arm in a blistering, green, noxious wave.

It was Daigh's only chance.

Even as St. John screamed his victory, Daigh released the billhook with a whiplike snap. Sent it thudding hilt-deep into the *Ambas-draoi*'s chest.

The man toppled to one side, eyes glazing in death, mouth twisted in a cruel rictus.

Without pausing for breath, Daigh threw himself at the door. Máelodor couldn't be far ahead. He could still catch him. Still retrieve the tapestry.

"Brendan!" Sabrina cried.

Daigh spun around in time to see the snake once more lunging for Douglas, who scrambled to escape. Thrusting himself between predator and prey, Daigh felt the pierce of the snake's fangs in his chest and back like a fiery double punch. As he was pulled from his feet, feeling flowed from his body with his blood.

But this time and this death there was light rather than darkness filling his vision. It spread over him. Burned through him. He knew his name. Knew his life. Heard his comrades' fond welcome.

He was finally going home.

"Dehwelana dhil'a islongh. Pádraic eskask."

Arrayed like *bandraoi* of old in gowns of ceremonial white, gold torques encircling their throats, heavy gold cuffs upon their wrists, the carved lines of their faces frightening in their solemnity, Ard-siúr and Sister Brigh stood in the doorway, voices lifted in challenge.

"Boesesh nesh fellesh." The chant seemed to reverberate in the air like a rumble of summer thunder. *"Dehwelana dhil'a*

islongh. Pádraic eskask." Louder. Stronger. Each syllable storm-edged and hurricane fierce.

The serpent froze, its glittering, maddened gaze focused upon the two women approaching it with slow, even steps. Yet it made no move, as if they'd charmed it into submission.

"Boesesh nesh fellesh!" The words splitting the air with lightning ferocity.

The great snake dropped Daigh to the floor on a shuddering, writhing, hissing scream. Its tail lashing furiously from side to side. Smoke billowing from its mouth, flesh melting from its bones until naught remained but ash drifting upon an oily breeze.

Sabrina wasted not a second, ripping free Daigh's shirt, laying bare long twin gashes slicing through muscle and bone. Blood bubbled with every panting breath, his skin a sickly pale green. "It's not working. He's not . . . why isn't he healing? What's wrong?"

"He's free of Máelodor's taint." Brendan lent the last of his feeble strength to her frantic attempts to keep Daigh from slipping back to *Annwn*'s underworld. "Free of his mage energy. And free of his protections."

"He'll die." Her hands hovered above his chest as she sought to calm the frantic race of her heart. Concentrate upon the surge of the mage energy within her. Shape it to her needs.

"Your powers saved him once," Brendan urged.

Daigh's breathing slowed then stopped, the silence deafening. "I'm not strong enough," Sabrina gasped, weeping. "I'm not—"

"You're more than strong enough," Ard-siúr replied sternly. "More than ready. A true High Danu *bandraoi* forged in fire and blood and magic."

"Do it, girl, or he's dead," came Sister Brigh's scold.

Drawing upon her training and her love, she concentrated on the mage energy. Felt it seep into every cell and nerve. Every corner of her mind and body infused with Brighid's healing fire.

Behind her, voices floated through her consciousness.

". . . do not run . . . confess . . . protect you . . ."

"can't . . . Sabrina thinks . . . she'll hate me . . . flee . . ."

A loud clatter in the passage then a voice from the grave, sardonic as ever. "Brendan . . . look bloody awful . . . passed them outside Glenlorgan . . . no more dallying."

Wouldn't Aunt Delia and the tragic Miss Rollins-Smith be surprised? But Sabrina dared not turn around. Not even to confirm her guess.

The mage energy poured like water from her hands. Filled Daigh with a shimmer of *Fey*-wrought healing. He jerked once, inhaling on a shallow, gurgling breath. The way to *Annwn* closed and barred. Though not forever. Mortality was his once more. He would die. But not today.

A fluttering roll quickened her womb. Not butterflies this time. But something infinitely more precious. Conceived in one life to be brought forth in another.

A girl child. We shall welcome her together.

Daigh's words muttered in the security of Gwynedd's vast forests. She would see to it he held to them.

twenty-eight

Tremors shuddered through him, chattering teeth, making fingers numb and jittery. Even his skull ached as if his brain had rattled itself loose. He tried swallowing, but his throat felt scraped raw, his tongue swollen and useless. He opened his eyes, squinting against a blinding glare. Sending new shocks of pain through his sloshy, scattered mind.

Slowly his sight returned. His surroundings fading into a cell-like room lined with cupboards, a low shelf running the perimeter. A sink with a pump. His pallet jammed into one corner. A cane-backed chair drawn up close.

But this time he remembered.

Everything.

"Back where I started," he croaked, attempting a smile.

"Not quite." Sabrina leaned forward, face aglow, tears sparkling upon her dark lashes. "You are free of Máelodor." Her hand found his. "We are free of Máelodor."

Her lips found his. Her kiss intoxicating as wine. His

body stirring with heat separate from the mountain of blankets heaped upon him.

"The life I remembered," he murmured. "You really were there. It was true because you made it so."

"It was. And it can be again."

Movement caught the corner of his eye. A shadow against the wall. A body in the corridor. Listening. Awaiting his answer.

His smile faded as reality burst the dream like sun through cloud. He eased her away, his heart breaking at the doubt surfacing upon the gem blue of her eyes. "Nay, Sabrina. You have given me my life. But I can offer nothing in repayment of such a debt."

Lines furrowed her brow, tiny creases beside her downturned mouth. "I don't understand."

"It's simple. My crimes against your family remain unanswered. I'm a man without hearth, livelihood, or country. It's best if you simply forget."

Her hand fell to her stomach as if he'd punched her, her gaze hard. "Best? For who? You? Me? My brother?"

He rolled away from her, wincing at the echoes of old pain beneath his tightly wrapped chest. Stared at the wall, hoping she'd leave before he changed his mind and to hell with the honorable thing. He felt her glare like a push against his temples.

Her final words came brittle with confusion and pain. "I told you once that my body and my love were mine to bestow where I chose. I had thought you were worthy. I thought wrong."

He did not reply.

Lady Sabrina Douglas.

Sister and daughter to earls.

Bandraoi priestess.

How could he let her throw herself away on a landless, penniless sword for hire?

He couldn't. And so he lay hunched with tension until the door closed quietly and he was once again alone.

They had gathered in Ard-siúr's office. Sabrina, a reluctant addition. She had not wanted to come this afternoon. Despite her bold words, she had wanted only to curl up in her bed and be gloriously sick. But Sister Brigh had not taken a polite no for an answer.

So instead, Sabrina had donned her baggiest gown, a camouflaging apron, and walked with rounded shoulders, hoping to disguise her condition. She had counted up the cycles. Checked her math. Five and a half months gone. It wouldn't be long before no amount of disguise could conceal the child within her.

Daigh's child.

The gods must be truly laughing at her. She had but to open her mouth and Aidan would repudiate her. Release her from the stranglehold of familial ties. But it was far too late. She'd snared herself in her own conniving and now must pay the price.

Miss Roseingrave parted the curtains, glancing out upon the feathery afternoon clouds. "We searched east and north as far as Cork and Macroom. West to Baltimore, but no sign of him. He could have sailed from any harbor or simply faded into the west country."

"And Máelodor?" Aidan asked, pacing the room in impatient circles.

"We found his abandoned coach on the Kinagh road outside of Ballyneen, but he wasn't aboard and his coachman had been killed. No sign of the Rywlkoth Tapestry either."

"But you finally believe me."

The *Ambas-draoi* seemed reluctant to admit it, but she nodded. "I do, Lord Kilronan. But there will be many among the brotherhood who remain unconvinced of Douglas's innocence and Máelodor's survival. St. John had many years to sow his lies and half-truths. It may take as many years to root out them out."

"Years we don't have. Hell, we don't have bloody months. Not if Máelodor's obtained the tapestry and the diary. He needs only to discover the Sh'vad Tual to summon Arthur and launch his war."

Cat's voice broke into the argument between Aidan and Miss Roseingrave. "Brendan hid it, and Brendan's not talking. Sabrina told you so."

"But if Máelodor catches him again . . ." The sentence trailed away as each of them envisioned Brendan's fate should he find himself once more subject to Máelodor's mercy. Only Sabrina need not delve into her imagination. She'd lived through it. And still woke sobbing from fear.

"Are you sure Brendan didn't tell you anything, Sabrina? Where he might go? Where he'd hidden the stone?" Aidan asked.

Unexpectedly the center of attention, she slumped farther into her seat. "No. Nothing."

"And how did Douglas escape?" Miss Roseingrave prodded. "You say he was ill and wounded. How could a man so gravely injured disappear so completely without assistance of some kind?"

Sabrina lifted her gaze to stare upon the *Ambas-draoi*'s dangerous beauty. Forced herself from glancing toward

Ard-siúr or Sister Brigh, who remained silent as the arguments raged. "I don't know."

Miss Roseingrave returned her gaze unflinching. "Though if you did, I wonder if you'd tell us."

Sabrina's lips curved in a cool, enigmatic smile.

Dropping the curtain back in place, Miss Roseingrave dismissed her with an annoyed toss of her head. "We're getting nowhere. I leave for Skye. Scathach and the leadership must be informed of St. John's treachery and death. We must look to who else among the *Amhas-draoi* Máelodor may have turned."

Aidan frowned. "And Máelodor's *Domnuathi*?"

"Daigh," Cat quickly inserted.

Sabrina's affection for her sister-in-law grew with every new encounter. Cat's staunch defense of Sabrina had done much to blunt Aidan's wrath in the days since their harried arrival at Glenlorgan. And her sympathetic presence had been a calm amid the storm of Sabrina's blighted hopes. Only now and again had she noticed Cat's eyes upon her, a fleeting glimpse of some deeper emotion upon her face. A worry breaking through her usual tranquil calm. But whatever her thoughts, she said nothing, and Sabrina was left to wonder if Cat suspected.

"Were it not for him, Máelodor would never have gotten his hands on the tapestry at all," Miss Roseingrave muttered.

Sabrina stiffened, her jaw clenched in a belligerent jut, her body shaking with outrage. "He did it to save me. And he almost died trying to stop Máelodor from escaping with it. Where were you, Miss Roseingrave?"

The charge brought a flush of angry heat creeping up the woman's throat to stain her cheeks, but she still dismissed Sabrina's strident defense with an offhand shrug. "The man is no longer a threat. And therefore no longer my concern."

Ard-siúr spoke up. "Mr. MacLir may stay at here at Glenlorgan until he is fully recovered. He has not been given an easy road, but he has shown he will travel it with much strength and courage."

"Very well." Miss Roseingrave's mind was already moving beyond them to the challenges ahead. She threw a long traveling cloak about her shoulders as she strode for the door. "Lord Kilronan, I'll send word to Belfoyle once I know more."

Aidan answered with a sharp nod while Cat gave Sabrina a sidelong glance from beneath downswept lashes.

"We too leave shortly, Ard-siúr," Aidan said when the *Ambas-draoi* had departed. "The sooner Sabrina is away from here, the sooner she can put this whole tragedy behind her."

Ard-siúr's answering stare had Aidan shifting uncomfortably, his expression losing a shade of its conviction. Sabrina knew that look all too well, and felt a pang of sympathy for her older brother.

Finally, Ard-siúr blinked, her hand reaching to stroke the cat curled dozing upon her papers. "Lord Kilronan, it is for you to steer the proper course, but sometimes it is best if we release our grip upon the rudder and let the currents guide us. We may find they bring us where we were meant to be from the very first."

The stern bones of his face remained as implacable as marble, but then Cat drew up beside him. Her hand rested lightly upon his arm. Their shared gaze shutting Sabrina out like a slamming door.

He sighed. "Perhaps—"

But Sabrina interrupted, surprising even herself with the words that came. "Thank you for interceding, Ard-siúr, but I want to leave." Her clenched hands whitened, her stomach rolling up into her throat. "It's time for me to go home."

Sabrina hung back after the others had left to see about traveling arrangements. Knocked upon the open door. "Ard-siúr?"

The cat leapt from its place on the desk to shoot for Sabrina's ankles. Twining itself about them. Purring madly as it rolled belly-up at her feet.

"Silly tabby. You'll get stepped on flinging yourself at people like that," Ard-siúr chided fondly. "Come in, child. Come in."

But even as she smiled her welcome, fatigue etched deep crags into her already wrinkled face. Worry trembled her hands, apprehension burning low at the edges of her gaze. It hardly seemed right to saddle her with more questions, but Sabrina must know.

"How did you know where to find us?" she asked.

This seemed to startle Ard-siúr from her deep reserve. Her eyes widened a fraction, her mouth curving in a clever smile. "Sister Brigh followed Mr. MacLir."

"But she hates . . . I mean, she's never liked . . . why?"

"Perhaps Sister Brigh should answer your question. But remember, Sabrina. This has moved beyond personal enmities. The future of *Other* and *Duinedon* lies in the balance."

"I understand that. I'm just surprised Sister Brigh did too."

The coach stood waiting. A groom at the head of the left leader while Cat and Aidan made their final farewells to

Ard-siúr. Catching sight of Sister Brigh hobbling out the gate, Sabrina made her hasty excuses to them all and chased after. She'd had no chance to speak with the *bandraoi* until now, and in fact hadn't even laid eyes on her since the meeting in Ard-siúr's office. As if Sister Brigh was avoiding her.

Beyond the gate, the road lay empty, the overgrowth to the right still rustling from a body's recent passage. Sabrina followed. Down the hill and into the deep, stifling gloom of the heavy wood. Over the rocks of a shallow streambed. Beneath the scraping limbs and raucous stir of chattering birds until Sabrina spied Sister Brigh ahead, a stooped gray figure among the reach of winter trees and the dank smell of muddy leaves.

Here amid the oaks, the musty, sweet air seemed to vibrate with energy and always there moved the shadows of those unseen, their ears pricked and listening, their laughter like wind-tangled leaves. The true *Fey* had long ago claimed this place as their own. The *bandraoi* respected that and came here only when their hearts were sore or their minds afflicted.

Sabrina caught up to the aged priestess with ease. The difficulty came in forming the question plaguing her.

The aged priestess finally broke the oppressive silence. "Did you come here to pester me, or is there something you want, girl?"

"Ard-siúr told me what happened. Why did you do it?" Sabrina asked, knowing Sister Brigh understood. "You were the one who wanted Daigh to leave."

The High *Danu* priestess paused in her ramble, laying a bony hand upon the rough gray bark of an enormous oak as if drawing strength from the ancient, sacred tree. "I told you already. I do what I must to protect the order from any threat." Contempt burned in the deep-set hollows of her face. "That doesn't mean I have to like it."

Daigh tossed back a pint. Ordered another from the doxy threading the tables in search of customers. She shot him a hopeful look, which he ignored. Sent a smile and a wink toward the man shaking the rain from his greatcoat as he entered the dimly lit, smoke-filled tavern. His clothes marked him as either lost or foolhardy. His build and expression guaranteed his safety regardless.

Another rejection and a holler from the barman, and the woman flounced back to the kitchens, leaving the newcomer to scan the crowd as if searching for someone. He stepped out of the shadows, his face revealed in the half-light of the dingy tap.

What the hell was he doing here? Daigh's hand tightened around his pint-pot. His stomach tightened against the ache low in his gut. But he made no move as the man approached. Slid into the seat across with a look upon his face as if he wished he were anywhere but this squalid Dublin tavern.

"The shoe's on the opposite foot, MacLir," he growled. "Now I'm hunting you."

Daigh scowled. Where was the maidservant with his beer? "What do you want, Kilronan?"

His Lordship lit a cheroot from the candle between them. Inhaled, before stubbing the whole onto the tabletop. His golden brown eyes never leaving Daigh's face. "One question only—do you love her?"

Daigh's stomach dropped from under him even as blood roared in his ears. "What the hell—"

"Answer me, MacLir. Do you love Sabrina?"

Daigh's gaze dropped to the empty tankard. How many had he downed hoping to find solace at the bottom? How many nights had he spent beating back the desire that would send him riding hell for leather straight to Belfoyle? Too many. He pushed the beer away. What point was there in hiding the truth? "I do."

Kilronan sat back, though whether he took joy or sorrow from Daigh's answer was unapparent in the tension rising off him.

"If a confession was all you wanted, you have it. Now leave."

"It's not what I want that matters," Kilronan replied. "It's what Sabrina wants. And needs. A father for her child."

Daigh started in his seat, his heart crashing against his ribs.

"She's eight months gone already," Kilronan added, almost as an accusation.

"That can't—" Daigh sucked a breath through his clenched teeth. Counted back.

And understood.

But Sabrina had to have known when he'd sent her away, and still she said nothing of it. Did she really want him, or did the Earl of Kilronan merely want a husband for his sister and an avoidance of scandal when the babe was born?

"Did Sabrina send you?"

A flicker of something passed within the well of Kilronan's gaze, giving Daigh his answer. "She doesn't know. I didn't want to lift her hopes in case I failed." His fingers tapped impatiently upon the table. "I've wasted weeks searching for you. But if we leave tonight and ride fast, we can be at Belfoyle within a few days."

A child changed everything. And nothing. Daigh

remained what he had been when he'd left the *bandraoi.* A man without anything of value to bring to a marriage but his love. Cheap goods, to be sure. "Surely there are men of status who would welcome an alliance with your family," he said, rubbing at a stain upon the table. "Despite the cuckoo in their nest."

Aidan took a moment to answer. Or perhaps it was a moment to control his temper, for when he spoke, his voice rasped hard and bitter. "So you won't come? Not even for your own child?" He pushed himself up with a snort of disgust. "I should have known this was a fool's errand."

Daigh matched anger for anger. "If you tell me you'd welcome my presence as Sabrina's husband, you'd be lying, and we both know it." His heart beat like a galloping horse, his fingers so tight about his tankard it must crumple beneath his grip. "Knowing what I was? What I've done in the name of evil? You'd be right to deny me her hand. Mad to do aught else."

Aidan shook his head, his expression grave. "No, for those crimes, you're right, I could never lay my hatred aside. But for those things you did that saved my family. For those I could easily call you brother."

The sea shone dull and heavy as lead beneath a sky littered with low, gray clouds. They reminded Sabrina of plunging horses as they rolled landward, their edges streaked with flashes of lightning like sparks from their hooves.

Her hike down to the beach had been met with doubt by both Cat and Jane. But then the pair of them had been watching her with varying shades of concern for weeks now. She was almost sorry Ard-siúr had allowed Jane to leave Glenlorgan to attend Sabrina's lying-in. Double the support, but double the worry.

At least she was spared Aidan's hovering, solicitous presence.

His response to her condition had surprised her. She'd feared discovery, afraid of both his anger and his disappointment. But upon her confession, he'd neither raged over her ruin nor threatened to abandon her to her fate, and she'd left the interview dazed and contrite. She'd been wrong about so much. But in one thing, she had sorely misjudged. Aidan's love for her was real. Strong. And unbreakable. He had proved it to her then, and in the months following.

It was only three weeks ago that he'd departed Belfoyle without explanation, though he sent regular letters to Cat, who folded and tucked them away whenever Sabrina entered the room. No doubt it had to do with Brendan and Máelodor and the *Amhas-draoi*. Matters she'd sought to dismiss from her mind even if she couldn't ignore her changing body. That was a constant reminder of what else she'd been wrong about. Whom else she'd misjudged.

Rain flashed upon the waves, speckled the beach, pattered against her hood. It would be a long climb up the cliff path back to Belfoyle. And she wasn't yet ready to return to the house. Even after almost three long months here, surprises still leapt from corners, memories springing fresh with every room she entered. She'd yet to exorcize all her ghosts, nonetheless what she'd once told Daigh held true. Though much had changed in seven years, the sea and the sky and the land remained constant. And that was indeed a comfort.

What began as a light drizzle intensified as if a curtain had been drawn across the sky. Rain sheeted in torrents, scooping channels through the sand and stone on its way back to the ocean. Dimming the long afternoon light to dusk.

Ducking beneath an outcropping of rock, she waited for an easing of the deluge. At least it was a warm April shower and not the icy lash of winter.

The child moved within her womb, its tiny fists and feet rippling across her belly. Running a hand over the bulge of her ungainly abdomen, she whispered. "Shhh, my sweet." Sent her love out upon a soft ribbon of thought. "Mother is here. Mother loves you. It won't be long, my darling. Soon, I shall hold you in my arms."

But what came back to her burst against her mind like the pounding surf.

Joy. Fear. Remorse. Loneliness. Excitement. Uncertainty. Heartbreak.

They staggered her back against the sharp face of the veined granite, breath trapped in her throat, knees weak.

A fog-wrapped figure leapt the last few feet from the path to the beach, boots crunching against the rocks, greatcoat sweeping out behind him, the rugged angles of his face sharper, the hollows deeper. He approached her out of the storm like a spirit from the grave.

Or a man from her past. Both her pasts.

She braced herself against the rock face, using it both to hold her steady and to assure her she didn't dream. But it was as solid and real as he was.

Hair plastered to his head, coat sodden through, he stopped a few feet away. His gaze traveling over her, the black of his eyes as unreadable as ever.

"What are you doing here?" She crossed her hands over her stomach as if she might protect it from that soul-stripping stare.

"I once promised you we'd welcome our child together. I'm back to honor that promise, albeit six hundred years late."

"Aidan brought you, didn't he?" she asked through a mouth gone dry.

"Aye. He found me to tell me of the child."

She struggled to wrap herself in the familiar bitterness and anger of the last months. "So now that you know, you can leave again."

His expression remained inscrutable, though shadows flickered and died in his eyes and his hands fisted closed at his sides. "If that's what you wish, Sabrina, I'll go."

What did she want? Daigh could be hers, but it would be a marriage based on duty, not on love. If he loved her, he would have stayed with her. Wouldn't he? But there was the child to consider. Could Sabrina send Daigh away if it meant consigning the baby to a life of bastardy? Oh, why did life have to be so complicated?

She lifted her gaze skyward as if looking for guidance upon the clouds. But she'd learned the hard way the gods spent little time worrying over the fates of mortals, even those who shared their blood.

"I've nothing to offer you, Sabrina," he said. "No wealth. No lineage. Nothing but the strength in my hands and the depth of my love. But with these we—"

"What did you say?" A queer, fluttering excitement beat against her ribs.

"I am penniless and without family."

"No, no after that. What was that last bit?"

He ducked his head, his lips curving in a sheepish smile. "I've nothing but the strength of my hands and the depth of my love, which is without end. But these I give to you freely. I would have you for my wife, Sabrina." When she opened her mouth, he stopped her. His voice now confident, almost defiant. "Not for the sake of the child, though that alone is a gift without price, but for you. I love you. In that life. In this. And in any that may lie in our future. Will you accept me?"

She nodded, her body at once both heavy with child and light enough she might shoot to the moon. "I will."

"What of your vow to remain unwed and true to your gifts?"

She tipped her chin up to meet his gaze, cheeks flushed, body alive with excitement. "Would you deny me my *Other* birthright? Would you force me to choose between the parts of myself?"

He pulled her close. "If I marry you, Sabrina, I marry all of you." His hands curved around to cradle her against him as he bent to kiss her, his lips cool and soft, his body ferociously warm.

"Then yes and a thousand times yes." She returned his embrace, the strength in his stance an anchor against the ecstasy bearing her away. Tears mingled with the rain sliding down her cheeks.

"I'm back, *cariad*," Daigh whispered. "For you."

Turn the page for a sneak peek at

HEIR OF DANGER

the final book in Alix Rickloff's
thrilling Heirs of Kilronan series

One

Cornwall
April 1816

King Arthur's tomb lay hidden deep within an ancient wood. For centuries uncounted, the sheltering trees grew tall, spread wide, and fell to rot until barely a stone remained to mark its presence.

With a hand clamped upon the shoulder of his attendant, the other upon his stick, Máelodor limped the final yards through the tangled undergrowth to stand before the toppled burial site. The mere effort of walking from the carriage used much of his strength. His shirt clung damp and uncomfortable over his hunched back. The stump of his leg ground against his prosthetic, spots of blood soaking through his breeches. Every rattling breath burned his tired lungs.

"This is it," he wheezed, eyes fixed upon the mossy slabs. "I feel it."

He didn't even bother to confirm his certainty. No need. Once decoded, the Rywlkoth Tapestry had been clear enough. Its clues leading him unerringly to this forgotten Cornish grove.

Excitement licked along his damaged nerves and palsied limbs, casualties of his unyielding ambition. The Nine's goals had been audacious, but Máelodor had known long before Scathach's brotherhood of *Ambas-draoi* descended like a wrath of battle crows that, to succeed, authority must be vested in a single man—a master-mage with the commitment to sacrifice all. To allow no sentimentality to sway him. To use any means necessary to bring about a new age of *Other* dominance.

He was that man.

His continued existence obscured within a web of *Unseelie* concealment, he'd called upon the dark magics to re-create life. Resurrecting an ancient Welsh warrior as one of the *Domnuathi.* A soldier of Domnu in thrall to its master and imbued with all the sinister powers that inspired its rebirth.

That first trial had ended in failure. The creature escaping Máelodor's control.

But he had learned from his mistakes. It would not happen a second time. Once resurrected, the High King would serve the man who restored his life and his crown. Would obey the mage who brought forth a host of *Unseelie* demons to fight for his cause. And would fear his master as all slaves must.

Mage energy danced pale in the green, humid air. Mistaken by any who might stumble into this corner of the wood as dust caught within the filtered sunlight. But Máelodor reveled in its play across his skin before it burrowed deep into his bloodstream. Melded and merged with his own *Fey*-born powers. Growing to a rush of magic so powerful he closed his eyes, his body suffused with exhilaration. The same uncontrolled arousal he usually sought in the bedchamber or the torture chamber.

His hand dug into the man's shoulder until he felt bones give beneath his grip. No cry or flinch at such harsh treatment. He'd chosen Oss as much for his brute strength as his slit tongue. Máelodor's body jumped and spasmed as bliss arced like lightning through him. And it was he who cried out with a groan in orgasm.

Sated, he motioned Oss forward, the two moving at a crawling pace over the uneven ground until he stood at the edge of the toppled granite slab, close enough to lay his hand upon the rock. The mage energy leapt high, buffeting him as it sought to understand this intruder. Moving through him in a questing, studying twining of powers.

Arthur's bones lay only a mere stone's thickness away. Once he possessed the Sh'vad Tual, Máelodor would finally have all he needed to unlock the tomb's defenses. Triumph would be his at last, for who was left to stop him.

The *Ambas-draoi* had long ago assumed his execution. The rogue mage-warrior, St. John, doing much to turn the eyes of Scathach's brotherhood toward another and discredit any rumors of Máelodor's survival.

Brendan Douglas was their quarry. The treacherous dog could only hope they found him before Máelodor did. For once Douglas fell into his clutches, so too would the Sh'vad Tual. One would unlock the tomb. The other would feed Máelodor's unholy desires for months.

It was fascinating how long one could string pain out. An unending plucked wire where a simple tug anywhere could bring excruciating agony yet death remained always just beyond reach. It would be thus for Douglas. The man who had brought the Nine down would suffer for his betrayal before joining his father and the rest in *Annwn*'s deepest abyss.

Máelodor's *Domnuathi* had captured the diary.

Máelodor himself had stolen the Rywlkoth tapestry.

Brendan Douglas would hand over the stone as he begged for his life.

"We're close, Oss. No longer will the race of *Other* live in the shadows, fearing the mortal *Duinedon*. It will be our time again. We shall not so easily let it slip away from us again."

The bearlike attendant nodded, his empty eyes never wavering. His stance wide, his arms hanging apelike at his side.

"Help me back to the carriage. I'm expecting news of Douglas."

In silence, the pair—aged cripple and mute albino—stumbled through the tangle of brush, leaving the tomb behind.

But before the stones merged within the wood's defenses, Máelodor turned back. Whispered the words that would unlock the door. "*Mebyoa Uther hath Ygraine. Studhyesk esh Merlinus. Flogsk esh na est Erelth. Pila-vyghterneask. Klywea mest hath igosk agesha daresha.*"

Trees shook as birds rose in a chattering black cloud. The sun dimmed, throwing the grove into sudden darkness. A faint chiming caught on a plucking rush of wind. And refusal blossomed like a bloodstain in Máelodor's chest. The answer came back to him—

No.

Dun Eyre
County Clare, Ireland

"Stand still, Elisabeth. The woman can't do her work with you spinning about like a top."

Elisabeth subsided under Aunt Fitz's scolding. Inhaled a martyr's breath, trying to ignore the burning muscles in her arms and the tingly numbness moving up from her fingertips. It was all very well for her aunt. She wasn't forced to stand with her arms spread wide, pins poking her in the small of her back, the feeling draining from her appendages. She rolled her neck, hoping at least to ease the tension banding her shoulders.

"Stop fidgeting. You know, if you didn't keep nibbling between meals, Miss Havisham wouldn't have to adjust the gown."

The modiste glanced up. "*Mm. Phnnmp. Mnshph,*" she mumbled around a mouthful of pins.

"And that's very kind of you, I'm sure. But I'd rather Miss Fitzgerald refrain from extra desserts and late-night tea and biscuits."

Elisabeth glared at her aunt's reflection in the cheval mirror. It was a familiar argument between them. Aunt Fitz—her own figure rail-thin—had always viewed her niece's voluptuous Renaissance body with displeasure. Or perhaps with jealousy. Either way, visits by the modiste always ended in short tempers and long silences. And an overwhelming urge in Elisabeth to eat something toothachingly sweet just out of spite.

She risked smoothing a hand over the swell of one hip, the slide of the pale silk cool against her palm. "Perhaps you could simply throw a sack over me and save all this bother."

"Don't be pert, dear," came her aunt's response as she sank into an armchair by the fire with a tired rub to her temples.

Miss Havisham stood with an accommodating smile. "There now, Miss Fitzgerald. You can take it off."

With the assistance of her maid and the modiste, Elisabeth wiggled out of the gown.

"I'll have the alterations completed by tomorrow. Oh, it shall be absolutely stunning. You'll be a vision. Mr. Shaw will think he's marrying an angel."

Elisabeth stared hard into the mirror, doubting even the expensive and exclusive Dublin modiste could affect that kind of transformation. But it was pleasant to envision appreciation lighting Gordon's eyes upon seeing her in the creamy lace and silk confection.

Miss Havisham chattered on as she packed up her bags. "It must be so exciting. Having all your relations gathered together. The anticipation of starting a new life with such a respected and very handsome young man."

"It was exciting the first time," Aunt Fitz groused. "This time, it's simply tedious."

Elisabeth blushed, color staining her neck and cheeks. Eyes may act as windows to the soul for others, but in her case, all thoughts and feelings appeared pink and splotchy upon her face. Not a pretty picture when combined with her red hair. "You didn't have to make such a to-do over the wedding. In fact, I'd have been happier had you not."

Her aunt's lips quirked in a sympathetic grimace. "I know, child, but Aunt Pheeney would never have forgiven us. You know how she loves a spectacle. Let's just hope *this* wedding comes off without a hitch. I don't have the strength for a third. And neither you nor I are getting any younger. You'll be twenty-six this summer. Most of your friends wed long ago, their nurseries full."

Elisabeth stood still while her maid secured the tapes of her morning gown. "Thank you for reminding me of my approaching decrepitude."

"I'm only saying that once a woman reaches a certain age, it becomes more difficult to entice the—"

"I know what you're saying, Aunt Fitz. And you're right. It's just taken me this long to find a suitable man. Someone I could respect enough to build a life together. Gordon Shaw is that man."

"I hope so, or we've gone to a lot of bother for nothing—again," Aunt Fitz mumbled before plastering on a cheery smile at the sight of Elisabeth's tart frown. "No, you're right, Lissa. He's a fine man and a suitable husband."

Lissa. Why had her aunt used that silly childhood pet name? Did she mean to confound her just when she most needed confidence? Or was it a slip of the tongue after an interminable day of wedding arrangements?

Only one other person had ever dared call her Lissa past her tenth birthday. One infuriating, exasperating, unconscionable, miserable horse's arse.

The dis-Honorable Brendan Douglas.

Music reached her. Even in her bedchamber, so far from the light and color and laughter of the drawing room downstairs, strains of Mozart floated 'round her like a ghost. The second movement of his piano concerto no. 27, of all things. She'd once thought it her favorite piece. But that had been many years ago. Now, just hearing the familiar chords set her teeth on edge.

First Aunt Fitz's use of that ridiculous pet name and now this. Memories hung heavier in the air tonight than they had in many a year. Like a fog, clinging to the back of her throat. Squeezing the air from her lungs. Though that might be her stays. Hard to tell.

She placed a drop of scent behind each ear. At the base of her throat. Repinned a straggling piece of hair. Silly things. Inconsequential things. But they kept her safely in her chair while that horrible, incessant tune played belowstairs.

As a final gesture, she lifted a hand to the necklace Gordon had presented her at dinner. Amid a chorus of *ooohs* and *aahhhs* from female relations and the menfolk ribbing him mercilessly about his besotted state, Gordon had fastened the opulent and conspicuously expensive string of sapphires about her throat. She leaned back into his hands, but he retreated with a singularly unloverlike pat on her shoulder.

The necklace was stunning. Spectacular. A work of art. And completely not to her taste.

She reached behind, undoing the clasp. Laying the gaudy choker carefully back in its box. The music swelled as she searched her jewelry case. Lifted out another pendant to wear in its place. A plain gold chain. A simple setting. And a stone more breathtakingly dramatic than any she'd ever seen.

Large as a baby's fist and still chipped and rough as if it had only just been mined, the milky translucent crystal was slashed with veins of silver, gold, rosy pearl, and jet black. Depending upon the light, it could shimmer with flame-like incandescence or smolder like banked coals. Tonight, it glimmered in the curve of her breasts. The subtleties of its colors accentuating the honey tones of her skin, pulling glints of gold into her brown eyes.

Would Gordon understand, or would he glimpse her neck and see only her refusal to wear his costly gift? Best to wear the sapphires tonight.

She started fumbling at the catch when the door burst open on the girlish round features of Aunt Pheeney.

"Are you still lolling about up here? My dear, everyone is beginning to think you've gotten cold feet. Even Gordon is concerned. You know what they say about time and tide . . ."

"I'll just be a moment."

Aunt Pheeney would not be put off any longer. She dragged Elisabeth from her chair. "No more hiding away up here. This is meant to be a celebration. Not a wake."

"I know, I only need to—"

"No more delays, young lady." Aunt Pheeney had already bullied her halfway to the door. "Come downstairs now." Her usually cheerful features rearranged themselves into what for her passed as stern lines. "That's an order."

"Yes, ma'am." Elisabeth allowed herself to be led out, Gordon's sapphires abandoned upon her dressing table.

As they descended the stairs, the music rearranged itself into a proper country dance. Men led their partners onto the drawing room floor, the furniture removed for the evening, doors flung wide to create one enormous, glittering, laughter-filled expanse.

Elisabeth cast her eyes over the sea of guests. Most of them family, though neighbors and friends, some from as far away as London, had come to be a part of the wedding festivities. The marriage of the Fitzgerald heiress had been a long time coming. Everyone wanted to be there to witness it. Or, a more cynical voice nagged at her, say they were present when Elisabeth Fitzgerald was jilted a second time.

Aunt Fitz and Lord Taverner chatted in one corner. Elisabeth's guardian no doubt discussing marriage settlements and jointures and land trusteeships. Aunt Fitz nodding thoughtfully, though she bore a hawkish scowl.

Cousin Rolf, dashing in his scarlet regimentals, and beautiful Cousin Francis, in white and gold, whirled their way through the set while Cousin Fanny and Sir James grazed from the passing platters.

Uncle McCafferty deep in conversation with a gentleman she didn't recognize. Obviously one of the London crowd invited by soft-hearted Aunt Pheeney, who felt anyone she so much as passed three words with merited an invitation.

Gordon and his half-brother, Marcus, stood amid a group of sober-clad companions. Gordon's handsome features and athletic physique, as usual, drawing the eye of every woman in the room. She squared her shoulders. Plastered a smile upon her face. In a fortnight, this absurd spectacle would be over. She would be wed.

"Come along, Elisabeth. They're all waiting on you," Aunt Pheeney coaxed. "Behold the bride cometh."

"I think that's bridegroom, Aunt Pheeney."

"Tish tush, close enough."

The music ended. But only for a moment before the scrape of violins began again. Different couples. Same pairings and partings to the steps of the dance.

She held back, slightly breathless, a strange tightening in her stomach. "Let me just collect myself for a moment and I'll be in." At her aunt's skeptical look, she added, "I promise," and kissed her soft, dry cheek.

Her aunt patted her hand. "Very well, child. But a moment only."

Elisabeth watched the scene below her as if she were a little girl sneaking down from the night nursery to catch a glimpse of her mother and father among the florid, laughing faces.

Even long after their deaths abroad when Aunt Fitz and Aunt Pheeney had been the ones hosting the lavish balls and jolly house parties, Elisabeth's gaze had always wandered over the tableaux below her as if she might spot her mother's titian hair or her father's broad back amid the throng.

Taking a deep breath, she stepped from the comfortable shadows of the hall into the blaze of a thousand candles. Immediately, Gordon lifted a quizzing glass to his eye, studying her for a long moment before he lowered it, a question glinting in his eyes.

She tried smiling an apology, but he'd already turned back to the men in response to a chummy slap on the back that left them all guffawing in good humor.

But another's gaze had yet to look away. The stranger with Barnaby. The weight of his stare sent heat rising into her cheeks until she realized it wasn't her face he was fixated upon, but her chest. Hardly the first man to be so bold, though it unnerved her just the same. Let him ogle his fill, then. What did she care? She lifted her chin to return his steady regard with her own.

He stood well above Barnaby, perhaps even of a height with Gordon. But whereas her betrothed possessed a wrestler's build, this man's lean muscularity spoke of agility and nuance. A swordsman. Not a pugilist.

His gaze narrowed as he bent to sip at his wine. Tossing

Barnaby a word while keeping her under watch. There was something familiar about him. The way he stood, perhaps. Or the slash of his dark brows. His eyes finally moved from her breasts to her face, a rakish invitation playing at the edges of his mouth. Warmth became a flood of scalding heat. No, she certainly did not know such a forward, insinuating gentleman.

And with a regal twitch of her skirts, she entered the fray.

The hours passed in a haze of conversation and music. She barely sat out a single dance. Traded from partner to partner as each man sought to compliment her beauty and impart his good wishes. Gordon spoke for her first, of course. Led her to the floor, his hand gripping hers as if she might try to escape. He made only one comment upon her choice of adornment. "I'm sorry you didn't like my gift. If you'd prefer, we can choose something more to your liking."

Guilt dropped into the pit of her stomach, and she smiled more brightly than she otherwise would have done. "I wouldn't trade it for anything in the world." He arched a brow, which made her words spill faster. "But it didn't go with my gown, you see. Tomorrow evening. I promise. I have a new gown it will suit perfectly." She went so far as to bat him playfully on the arm with her fan.

Gordon offered a pained smile. "Wear your little bauble, Elisabeth. Among this company, it's quite beautiful enough."

"What do you mean by that?"

"No need to fly into the boughs, my darling. I only meant that I find you faultless in anything you decide to wear."

Her prickles smoothed, she gazed up at him in clear invitation. They could slip away for a moment or two. There were alcoves aplenty. And it wasn't as if they weren't going to be wed in a few days.

Unfortunately, Gordon stepped back at the same instant she leaned forward, almost unbalancing her. He cleared his throat, a decidedly proper expression on his face. "Careful, Elisabeth. Your great-aunt Charity is casting dagger glances our way."

She straightened, smoothing her skirts. Tossed a demure smile over the crowd, all as if she meant to almost topple feet over head. "Oh, pooh for Great-Aunt Charity. Glass houses and all that rot. If half the stories about her are true—"

"Still, my dear. It wouldn't do to antagonize her unnecessarily. I don't want her thinking I'm a scoundrel."

"What if I like scoundrels?"

"You're such a tease, my dear." He acknowledged an impatient summons from his brother with a wave. "Marcus is after me to make a fourth, dear heart. Will you be all right on your own?" He smiled. "Silly question. Of course you will. You're a natural at this sort of social small talk. And besides, it's family. Not a bunch of strangers, eh?" He chucked her chin as he might a child's before leaving without a backward glance.

She took advantage of the respite to snatch a savory and a glass of ratafia from a passing tray. Nibbled as she watched the crowd of parrot-bright ladies and dashing gentleman. They laughed, danced, drank, and in one or two instances sang. Boisterous. At times rowdy. But always good-natured.

Among this company . . . what had Gordon been

implying? And why did she feel she'd been chastised like a child? She shook off her questions with a sigh and a sharp flick of her fan.

"Abandoned at your own festivities?" came a voice from behind her, thick and dark as treacle. Definitely not Great-Aunt Charity, who possessed a parade ground bellow.

No, Elisabeth knew that voice. That impudent tone.

She swung around to come up against an unyielding chest. Her glass of wine sloshed onto his coat, staining his shirt front dark red. He stepped back with a quick oath. And the moment burst like a bubble. The man from earlier. A stranger. Not him. Not at all. What was wrong with her that she jumped at shadows?

"Forgive me." She blotted at him with her napkin.

"Here, allow me." He eased it from her hand as she belatedly realized the unintended intimacy of her actions.

"I . . . oh, dear . . . you don't think . . . oh, dear," she babbled.

He dabbed at the spot before crushing the napkin and shoving it into his pocket. "No matter. At least it's not blood this time."

What on earth did he mean by that?

He lifted his head, his veiled gaze finally meeting hers dead-on. Eyes burning golden yellow as suns, the irises ringed in darkest black.

She crushed a hand to her mouth to stifle the sound choking up through her belly.

His lips twitched with suppressed amusement. As if this were in any way funny. Earth-shattering more like. "Hello, Lissa."